Nationwide Praise for MVFOL

HEAD

D0462451

"Inspired . . . Yamanaka . . . . in landscape, [but] it is the rau . . . . acters that . . . .

"[An] incisive look at Japanese-American girlhood in working class Hawaii . . . Simultaneously wistful and tough—like its hero, Toni Yagyuu . . . *Heads by Harry* nearly explodes with heart."
—*Chicago Tribune*

"One doesn't often get to read about growing up in Hawaii, much less pig hunting and taxidermy, which makes this funny novel a rich crash course in all those art forms."
—*Los Angeles Times*

"Yamanaka infuses her characters' pidgin English, their coarse dialogue and their sometimes brutal behavior with gut-level poetry and fresh vernacular. With this stirring novel, the potency and honesty of Yamanaka's view of Hawaiian life achieves the haunting force of myth."
—*Publishers Weekly* (★Starred Review★)

"Wait two hours after eating before sitting down with this raw, beautifully crafted story of roughnecks who will really get under your skin."
—*Washington Post*

"Yamanaka's voice is a welcome breeze . . . *Heads by Harry* is Yamanaka at the peak of her vibrant, soul-baring yet self-mocking style."
—*TimeOut New York*

"Yamanaka's novels possess a unique and riotous energy as they conjure Hawaii's spiky cultural brew . . . [*Heads by Harry*] is unparalleled in its fresh, funky language, honest and earthy characters, and mesmerizing predicaments."
—*Booklist* (★Starred Review★)

"High-energy fiction from a talented writer . . . hilariously rendered."
—*Kirkus Reviews*

Other books by
Lois-Ann Yamanaka

BLU'S HANGING
WILD MEAT AND THE BULLY BURGERS
SATURDAY NIGHT AT THE PAHALA THEATRE

For Young Adults

NAME ME NOBODY

Avon Books are available at special quantity discounts for bulk purchases for sales promotions, premiums, fund raising or educational use. Special books, or book excerpts, can also be created to fit specific needs.

For information, please call or write:
Special Markets Department, HarperCollins Publishers, Inc., 10 East 53rd Street, New York, NY 10022-5299. Telephone: (212) 207-7528. Fax: (212) 207-7222.

HEADS by HARRY

a novel

Lois-Ann Yamanaka

AN AVON BOOK

This is a work of fiction. Names, characters, places, and incidents either are the product of the author's imagination or are used fictitiously. Any resemblance to actual events, locales, organizations, or persons, living or dead, is entirely coincidental and beyond the intent of either the author or the publisher.

AVON BOOKS, INC.
An Imprint of HarperCollins*Publishers*
10 East 53rd Street
New York, New York 10022-5299

Copyright © 1999 by Lois-Ann Yamanaka
Cover illustration by Barbara Lambase
Inside back cover author photo by Marion Ettlinger
Interior design by Abby Kagan
Published by arrangement with Farrar, Straus & Giroux, Inc.
ISBN: 0-380-73316-1
www.harpercollins.com

All rights reserved, which includes the right to reproduce this book or portions thereof in any form whatsoever except as provided by the U.S. Copyright Law. For information address Farrar, Straus and Giroux, 19 Union Square West, New York, New York 10003.

The Farrar, Straus and Giroux edition contains the following Library of Congress Cataloging in Publication Data:

Yamanaka, Lois-Ann, 1961–
    Heads by Harry / Lois-Ann Yamanaka
        p.   cm.
    1. Japanese Americans—Hawaii—Hilo—Fiction.   I. Title.
PS3575.A434H4   1999
813'.54—dc21   98-39499

First Bard Printing: March 2000

BARD TRADEMARK REG. U.S. PAT. OFF AND IN OTHER COUNTRIES, MARCA REGISTRADA, HECHO EN U S.A.

Printed in the U.S.A.

OPM 10 9 8 7 6 5 4 3 2 1

If you purchased this book without a cover, you should be aware that this book is stolen property. It was reported as "unsold and destroyed" to the publisher, and neither the author nor the publisher has received any payment for this "stripped book."

For Harry T. Yamanaka, Daddy, Artist, and
Friend, and Katsumi Narikiyo, Grandpa, Deer
Man, and Humorist

For John Torao Sebastian, Charles Heima, and
Samantha Rei, who chose us all in this life

HEADS by HARRY

One

A roseate sky envelops Mauna Keʻa on the Big Island of Hawaiʻi, youngest in the chain of Hawaiian Islands, and the only home I have known.

Through the Saddle Road to Waikiʻi, we take the lonely drive between two mountains, sleeping volcanoes, the tallest mountains in the world from the sea floor up:

Mauna Loa, purple dome sister.

Mauna Keʻa, regal white brother.

And the Saddle Road between them is an undulating stretch of broken asphalt.

We wait downwind from the blue pheasants sated in a morning drizzle. This is the day that my father lets me shoot first, the Japanese blue pheasant, my first trophy—wings spread, cobalt-iridescent feathers, and vermilion glass eyes. My pheasant poised to fly from an ʻōhiʻa branch.

When I was sixteen, my father gave my older brother, Sheldon, and me Labrador retrievers, two black babies with yellow eyes and breath that smelled like tuna fish and yeast. The breeder, a hunter from Keaukaha, threw the puppies into the brackish ponds at Leleiwi.

"Pure water dogs," my father said as he moved his hand over the glossy sheen of fur.

On every other hunting trip, Sheldon got to shoot first. He always missed. My father would swear loudly, "Goddammit you, Sheldon, I hate wing shooting." He'd take a single shot sending a bird whirlwinding midair.

He told the family as we ate our breakfast that morning at Waiki'i, "Them other hunters watch too much TV, especially *American Sportsman*. Who the hell like the dog flush the damn bird?"

My father preferred sneaking up on his game, then taking good aim. Shooting a stationary target allowed him to choose the point of bullet entry.

"Now *that's* sporting to me," he said. "But shit, every time I let Sheldon shoot first, damn kid miss and I force to snag the bird up in flight. Not Toni."

Mommy nudged him hard, so my father dropped it. Sheldon didn't care. I saw it in his sassy face. All those other times we hunted with our father, my brother was shooting junk on purpose, so he wouldn't have to come on any more hunting trips as he flushed the birds with his falsetto voice and ballerina arms. He wanted to stay home and make sushi with our little sister, Bunny.

But this morning, like every other time my father could've uttered *words* immersed in his singular affection for *me*, he looked at me and smiled instead. Then he changed the subject.

"Where the egg rolls you made, Bunny?" Food conversations in Japanese families put us all at ease. If we were all eating, then we were not talking. "Mary Alice, you like shoot today? Pass me another musubi. What about you, Bunny? Where the fried wing dings? So who's hunting with me?"

My mother and sister opted for waiting in the truck. It was too cold. The dogs were smelly and wet. The brambles scratched their delicate arms. "We'll keep the truck warm.

Good luck, goodbye, goodbye," Mommy said, waving us off with a half-eaten wing ding.

I see, through my father's eyes, the Saddle Road, Mauna Ke'a sloping in shades of maize, olive, and lavender. I see a white rim of clouds at the level of condensation encircling the summit of the mountain.

I follow his eyes to the summit, where on this island of rain forest, desert, tide, and vale, I once touched snow with my bare hands and traveled above the stratum of white clouds with my father.

I see, on this day, grassland intensifying the space in front of us, so that everywhere I look is distorted by heat waves, except for the sky, which is milky blue by seven in the morning.

I walk beside my father, who points out to me the groves of māmane growing in the gullies of Waiki'i. He looks for the palila honeycreepers, indigenous but nearly extinct, tiny yellow birds with beaks like finches that feed on the blossoms of the māmane.

My father passes to me a seed pod from the māmane tree. He shrugs his shoulders and sighs sadly. "Too many mouflon sheep eating the trees," he tells me. We walk on through the kikuya, thick shrublike grasses, and into the openness of the fields.

"Toni, you shoot first," my father says. I look at him and he nods deeply. "Give her the gun, Sheldon." My brother quickly turns toward me.

"Be my super-cali-fraga-listic guest, honey," he says as he holds the barrel with the tips of his fingers and swings the butt at me. I hold the old .410 that I shared on so many trips with my brother. The gun I practiced on with my father at the Police Academy range.

"Walk into the wind, muffle your step, and the wind bring the bird scent to Sonny and Chiba." I hear the tiny bell I attached to Chiba's collar stop. And I stop. My dog never flushed the game. I taught her not to so that my father would never call me American Sportsman wannabe wing shooter, one-shot. A light drizzle lapses in the upland wind. "Better for you. Drown your scent," he whispers in my ear.

Sheldon drags his ass and yanks at the kikuya grass as he follows our trail. He's stomp-stomping and singing, "A hundred mirrion meee-ra-culls, are happening ebbry-day," and then the pheasant, a Japanese blue, flushes, two, three of them. I raise my gun, *I am shooting first*, and I fire once.

This moment lasts like a picture.

I see the tunneled falling of a blue bird through the lucid expanse of sky.

Sheldon rolls his eyes.

My father lowers his gun.

Chiba crosscuts through the kikuya grass for the bird.

The smell of pheasant blood stains my hands for hours, unwashable.

No words, all my life he offered no words.

My father gives me a firm pat on the shoulder.

There were wild thimbleberries in the Laupāhoehoe Forest Reserve. I would bake a thimbleberry pie for my father. Or I'd make for him a thimbleberry jam by sprinkling packets of pectin into the slow pop of red boiled jell after adding the C & H, cup after cup.

I went with my father and his hunting friend, Cardoza, to gather the berries.

I had seen fieldworkers picking strawberries on *National Geographic*. I saw cherries that grew on trees.

I wanted to be the girl who picked berries for her father, the girl he lifted into the Big Island sky in the 8-millimeter film starring me.

And in this film, I see my father looking at me with his face full of calm affection, his gestures, his nod, in the crackling of celluloid through an old projector, and the flickering light.

My father and I follow Cardoza into the reserve. He turns to remind me to bring the Ziploc for the thimbleberries. We walk down the dark trail and into the forest.

There is a soft grunting noise.

Shhh, no noise.

Be cautious with each step, he motions to me.

Shhh, don't snap the twigs or rustle the leaves.

My father points to a hollowed area under a kukui tree. Cardoza nods, still filming all the while. I cannot see. The whole underside is hidden by vast overgrowths of wild thimbleberries. My father readies his gun, and I creep closer. I reach for the wild berries, straining to look over a log and under the next to see the backside of a huge black sow. I hear the suckling.

My father shoots the sow near her head without warning. He wants her for smoked meat. The piglets scatter at first, so young and unafraid, they scramble around me.

"Gather them up, quick," he says, pulling burlap bags from his pack. The sow, still breathing, gurgles and foams as I run after the piglets. "Put them in the burlap bag, hurry up, Toni, run, quick, run." I manage to catch four of them, kicking and crying, and I shove them in the burlap bags.

Cardoza begins skinning the sow after a couple of stabs in her throat to stop her noise. But her sounds don't stop until he skins a portion of her hide off the flesh.

I take the fourth and smallest piglet out of the bag before my father secures the other three to his waist with rope. He lets me carry her out of the forest. When I put my knuckle to her mouth, she suckles it. Her mouth smells like a puppy's, tuna fish and yeast.

I was a girl who wanted to pick berries for her father.
He shot a sow and smoked her meat.
I got a piglet.
I named her Fern.
Neither of us bothered to pick the berries.

He let me keep Fern in the apartment above our taxidermy shop, Heads by Harry. It was summer and my piglet followed me downstairs like a dog, except smarter. I had her paper-trained in no time. I bathed her in the tub with Suave strawberry shampoo.

I named her after Fern Arable in *Charlotte's Web*. I was Charlotte. Sheldon was Templeton. Bunny was off reading Dr. Seuss's *There's a Wocket in My Pocket*. I liked the name Fern. The name reminded me of the Laupāhoehoe Forest Reserve full of hāpuʻu where I found the piglet I fed with an EvenFlo bottle.

But there is never a happy ending in stories with a child and a wild animal. E. B. White knew.

When Fern got too big to live in the apartment above the shop and feeding her two man-size meals a day became too costly, everyone had an opinion outside of Heads by Harry.

"Smoke that damn wāhine buta," Niso-san said to my father. "Too much-i eat-u buta kaukau. Too much-i oinku, oinku, oinku. Pee-yeu, and ku-sai, nei, the un-ko and shi-shi."

"No, the meat too tender. No smoke um. Go kālua the pig. She so fat, the whole thing be one rump roast," Mr. Lionel Santos said. "Kālua in the imu. I help dig the pit. Me and my boys."

"Let's huli huli the pig with lots of rock salt," Uncle Herb said, smacking his lips. "No, Mildred? It's too much humbug to dig the imu. We'll buy the liquid smoke and let's make some laulau."

"Well, Toni ma dear," my father said to me, "I thinking about you."

I was such a little girl. And he gave this so little thought.

That weekend, we return to the Laupāhoehoe Forest Reserve. My father finds the kukui tree surrounded by the thicket of wild thimbleberries and takes Fern off of her leash. She won't run. She sits there at first and then roots her snout in the soft mulch near the base of a thimbleberry bush. I pull a handful of berries off of the thorny branches and open my palm to her soft grunting snout.

"What the hell you doing, Toni? We trying to make your goddamn pig go born free and you feeding her from your hand. How she going fend for herself?" My father sits down on a fallen log as Fern nuzzles up to him, lifting his arm with her heavy snout to pet her head. He puts Fern's head in a gentle choke hold and knuckles the top of it.

"I can give her to the Portagee by Uncle's house."

"He probably eat her, Daddy. I not stupid, you know."

"Well, you the damn fool been treating her like your pet dog."

"We just keep her already, Daddy."

"Where? In our goddamn apartment in downtown Hilo? You nuts, little girl."

"What we going do, Daddy?"

"I don't know what the hell to do about this goddamn pig," my father says, exasperated. "See what you did, you damn kid. No talk to me for little while. Let me think."

I wander off with my pig and pick wild thimbleberries for her. Most she eats, but a Baggie-ful I take home.

Later on, my brother made jam.

We did a Fern Arable and gave the pig to Uncle Herb, who at that time lived on his in-laws' sugarcane land out in Pepeʻekeo. And as happy endings go, she lived a fine life of leftover slops from the Saloon Pilot cracker cans my uncle gathered up each afternoon from the neighbors, who gladly contributed because the pig was smart.

Bark. Sit. Shake hands. Bang! She'd roll over and feign death. Mrs. Freitas always gave the burnt bottom from a pot of Portuguese bean soup if her grandchildren could pet the pig. Efrem Garcia threw in butbut and mochi rice while his children, nieces, and nephews clapped at the tricks. Sheldon, Bunny, and I visited every weekend with a bucket of slops and cold Nāʻālehu milk.

We visited Fern every weekend, up until the night Melvin Spencer's pig dogs got loose and killed Fern right in her pen, right next to her pig house.

I begged my father to bring her back home.

"What for? What I going do with that fat dead pig at the shop? You tell me, Toni."

"Somebody might eat her, Daddy."

"I heard Uncle Herb telling Mr. Spencer he could kālua the pig," Sheldon told my father as he draped his arm over my shoulders.

Bunny cried for days. Sheldon pounded a cross out of hi-bachi wood scraps from the alley out back.

I was a little girl immobilized by inexpressible grief.

The day my father sits me on the stool next to his shop table I know what will happen. "Everything coming off," he says, making the first incision, "the ears, eyelid, and the lips. And then we take off the excess meat from the skin. Here, hold your pig straight for me. I show you where those damn dogs been bite Fern."

Her belly is ripped, neck covered with massive dog bites, and one ear nearly torn off. He points with the tip of his knife to the internal bleeding and massive bruising.

"She never even fight back," he whispers to me.

I say nothing but rest my head on his shoulder.

"Okay," he says, taking a deep breath and pulling himself together, "you watch Daddy be real careful around the eyes. I no like you blame the Portagee man. This was a freak accident of nature."

I watch my father's knife bite into the delicate flesh. The skin tightens near the skull, so he removes it with short flicks of his blade. "Hold the ear for me," he says. He doesn't want to lose it. He helps me sew it back on later.

And when the skinning is done, my father says softly, "Say your final words to your pig. Daddy going in the back get the preservatives ready. In two, three months, she be yours again. I let you hang her up in your bedroom. Right above your bed."

"Bye, Fern."

"Get in there, Sheldon," my father says, giving him a shove. "Say bye to Toni's pig. Go get Bunny and bring the cross you made. And no touch nothing."

Bunny places the cross over the cape of bristly skinned hide.

"Some pig," Bunny says.

"Terrific," Sheldon says.

"Radiant." I place both hands on her empty face.

My father lets me mold the plaster of Paris around the maggot-eaten skull. I push the molding clay into the eye sockets and choose the color of the glass eyes. My fingers shape the browridge smooth. I sew down the back of the cape and brush Fern's bristles.

"Leave her mouth shut."

"Why?"

"She ain't a wild boar."

"Good," my father says. "Save the Parowax for some other boar mount."

"Tilt her head."

"You tilt it, Toni," he tells me, "like she asking for papaya. You know her best."

I lift the snout up like Fern's being sassy. She acted this way when she wanted me to pet her head.

"No emotion when you mount," my father says. "That's the number one rule of taxidermy. You have to distance yourself from your subject, okay, Toni ma dear?"

Weeks later, my father building to the proud moment, the whole family comes into the bedroom as he pounds a nail into the wall and hangs Fern above my bed, head to head.

And then I saw it again. But it was brief and in real time, no 8-millimeter film to record that look of calm affection in his gestures and his nod.

He never looked at me that way again.

And I never made him a thimbleberry pie.

• • •

Around this time, Sheldon named our father Harry O., for the TV show starring David Janssen. Harry O. is the name everybody calls my father to this day.

"What you guys think?" Sheldon asked that infamous night, a night full of termites swirling their lunatic wings around the TV, the only light on in the living room. "Don't you think this *Who Is Who* is perfect? Daddy look exactly like David Janssen even if he Japanee and David Janssen haole."

And Daddy smiled a smile that said he liked looking like David Janssen better than looking like Mako or Pat Morita. "It's the receding hairline," Mommy said, pulling a termite wing and worming insect body from Bunny's hair. "But our Harry O. has to do the comb-over-the-bolohead pretty soon."

It was the nickname that stuck forever.

I prayed it never happened to me.

And who knows why, nobody ever did it to Sheldon; he did it himself. He wanted to be called Shelly for Shelley Fabares, who was the cutest teenager on *The Donna Reed Show*. And Shelly for Shelley Hack, who he felt was the best swimsuit model in the Simplicity pattern book.

I said, "Yeah, right, Shelly," hoping it would stick forever.

It was also around the time of his naming that Harry O. started letting Sheldon and me shoot while bird hunting with Mr. Santos and his boys, Butchie, Wyatt, and Maverick. Some macho role modeling might help his son, Shelly. I went along as Harry O.'s *real* hunting buddy, even if I had to share the old .410 with my brother.

Bunny stayed home with Mommy. " 'Cause she the feminine one, girly-girl inside and out," Harry O. always said. "She might be the first Cherry Blossom Queen from Hilo, what you think, Mary Alice?" And Mommy always smiled that cherry-blossom-in-spring Yanai City smile.

And Harry O. never cared if Sheldon wore Bunny's eighth-grade banquet dress with his feet squeezed into my Famolare high heels for a laugh in our living room. But as soon as he was out in the public eye, my brother's tunta ways gave my father ulcers.

"And you, Toni, you listen and listen good," Harry O. said to me while loading the guns on the rack. "If you call your brother Shelly in front the Santos boys, I going slap you silly. I don't know where he get all those crazy ideas in his head. I should disconnect the damn cable TV." My father always blamed what we saw on TV for our aberrant behaviors.

On this hunting trip, Sheldon and I sat in the bed of the truck with Butchie, who was always pretty nice to us but way older; Wyatt, who hated my brother passionately and burped and farted a lot in his direction; and Maverick, who was the same age as Sheldon.

"Where Harry O. taking us, Butchie?" Maverick asked his big brother, the wind cutting his long hair, surfer-streaked with golden strands, unlike Sheldon's Sun-In'ed and lemon-juice-burned hair with split ends that he said added volume. Maverick wore his hair in a long, layered shag, and had a way of moving the wispy strands away from his full lips that inspired both Sheldon and me.

"Mauna Keʻa Unit A," Butchie answered. He was more squat and compact than Maverick and had a full sheepskin growth of hair on his chest. "Harry O. said get plenty turkey up there. He smoking the turkey meat for Herline's grad party."

Wyatt lit a cigarette and ashes whipped in the direction of Sheldon's face. I brushed a burning ash from my shoulder. But he did it until he flicked the butt away. He was the tallest and bulkiest of the brothers with large hands, dirty finger-nails, and a permanent five o'clock shadow.

"You guys making big party for Herline? We invited?" Sheldon flirted and acted cute for the Santos brothers all the time, flipping his burned-out hair and turning the so-called ravishing side of his face toward Maverick. But nobody answered. And for the flirting, Wyatt got mad. All the way up the purple slopes of the mountain, Butchie, Wyatt, and Maverick talked among themselves with lots of fucks and shits and asses, Sheldon craning to hear the good parts.

Once up near Mauna Ke'a Unit A, Harry O. finally found a spot to park the truck. Everybody unloaded their gear. "Okay, me and my two kids go this way. Butchie and Wyatt that way." Wyatt scowl-smiled, pleased to be separated from Sheldon and me. "Maverick, you go with your daddy up that way." Harry O. was the boss of the bird-hunting trip because he was the taxidermist and the meat smoker. "Mr. Ute told me the turkeys was all by the big clearing, Lionel."

"I know where that is. We go, Maverick," said Mr. Santos with a macho head jerk toward the 'ōhi'a grove. "Wyatt, no shoot wild, you hear me, boy? And walk with the safety on." Wyatt nodded his head slowly and sarcastically as he walked away.

When the Santos men stalked off, Harry O. pushed the gun on Sheldon. "Son, you the shooter. Toni ain't shooting, and me, I waiting till you take three, four shots. Today, Lionel and his boys going see that *you* can be the one bag us some turkey."

I looked at Harry O. "Yeah, right."

My father looked at me with utter desire for his boy to be a boy. And he wanted me to believe this too. He slapped Sheldon hard on the back, sending my brother tripping into a patch of wild orchids on the side of the trail.

"And you, little girl, you watch the two Yagyuu hunters in action. Maybe I let you shoot today too, after Sheldon blast a couple of turkeys up the ass." My father was confident. Confident in his beliefs about the possibility of change and good male role modeling. We walked through the 'ōhi'a trees. "No be stomping like a goddamn herd of elephants," Harry O. whispered.

I heard the turkeys clucking in the distance. "Females," Harry O. told us. "They regrouping." We walked toward the clearing full of pili grass and wild fern. Harry O. moved the faya brush out of his face. The clucking went on, low, low, the sound coming from a clump of bushes near a tree.

Harry O. pushed Sheldon's back to lead us. Ten yards away from the clucking, I saw Sheldon move with his shotgun off safety. Then Sheldon screamed high and shrill to flush the turkeys like an American Sportsman he saw on TV but looking more like the prima ballerina he practiced to be in our bedroom. My brother waved his skinny arms and screamed in an operatic falsetto to flush the turkeys. He raised his gun.

"No, Sheldon! No! Too hard to shoot. Shut up! What the hell you doing?" Harry O. yelled.

Up vaulted Wyatt and Butchie, Wyatt clutching a turkey call box. Harry O. grabbed the gun from Sheldon and shoved it at me.

"The safety off?!" He removed his orange hunting hat and whacked Sheldon over the head. "You goddamn stupid kid." Sweat beaded on Harry O.'s brows. And after a moment of relief, he yelled at my brother, "You could've kill somebody. You sit here. Sit down! Dumb jackass. We pick you up on our way back." He gave Sheldon two more hat slaps. "C'mon, Toni. You okay, Wyatt?"

And Wyatt sneered in our direction, with an expression that said, "It was nothing. I'm not afraid of faggots with guns. And that .410 is such a small-ass gun anyway." In his momentary sneer and wave of his huge arm, he was laughing.

I walked out of the clearing with Harry O. and turned to look at Sheldon. Through the faya that extended arms of green clutter between us, he stared straight back at me, not a tear in his glassy eyes.

Harry O. had no business sense. If it was up to him, he'd have an open Igloo, musubi, and smoked meat in a frying pan all day for anyone who dropped by. As it was, he brewed pot after pot of coffee for the morning old futs who sometimes came *every* morning with hot malasadas from Robert's Bakery and came back *every* afternoon for the smoked meat and beer, "talk story," and "chew the damn fat," as Harry O. would say.

"Hey there, Toni ma dear," Harry O. said to me as I made space on the old card table for a pan of smoked meat. It made me feel good to be the only Ma Dear in the family, even if he said it in later years only when he was a little drunk.

Mr. Lionel Santos sat with Harry O. through the happy hour or until Mrs. Mei Ling yelled from the Mamo Theatre across the street, "Get your fuzzy ass over here, Lionel, and open the stinken ticket booth for the six-thirty show. I busting my ass getting all the hot dogs in the machine. My father turning in his grave seeing his daughter doing all the fricken work in this damn theater."

Butchie ate a handful of sunflower seeds outside of the shop. Wyatt squatted against the wall and spat when I looked at him. Mr. Ute, an old man that Harry O. took hunting, sat old-man style, legs spread, on a low stool. Uncle Herbert was there too and Niso-san, who owned Niso Camera Shop next to our shop.

Finally, Mrs. Mei Ling came stomping across the street. "Where you stay, Mary Alice?" she yelled into the shop.

"Yeah, what, Mei Ling? I frying chorizos."

"Our stupid husbands getting all drunk again. And Lionel, he miscount money, he let kids who look eighteen go in for twelve-and-under price, acting dumb and singing 'Cherry Pink and Apple Blossom White' in the booth at the top of his lungs. Shit, these two-bit big-game hunters."

Butchie told Wyatt to get a Pearl Light for their mother, who seriously needed to cool her jets. Both Maverick and Wyatt always listened to Butchie. Even if he was the smallest, he could kick their ass.

"Come here, my babe. My little Chinee babe," Mr. Santos said, pulling his wife close to him. She sat on his lap and pouted but contented herself with all of the attention.

"Yeah, the little Pa-ke big baby with the Portagee mouth." Harry O. chuckled at his own joke.

"I heard that. You watch your lip before I tell Mary Alice about that old fut Ethel Mizuguchi visiting you for lunch. I was watching you and that sassy wāhine laughing and eating bento."

"That shinabetoru obasan with blue hair? Please. Ethel came *one time* to see if I had feathers for her senior citizens lei-making class. That's all, and she just so happen to bring lunch. What the crime in that, gunfunnit?"

I left to get the stools Harry O. had just made from the mango stumps Mr. Ute brought down to the shop. Harry O. always said we'd all get piles sitting on the cement.

All of a sudden, Bunny came running down Mamo Street, her shoe box of makeup products clacking. Bunny was crying, her clothes and bags a tangled mess. Sheldon wasn't with her.

"Mary Alice!" Harry O. yelled into the shop. "Come get your daughter."

Mommy barreled out the door. "What's the matter, Bernice?" Mommy wiped her hands on a dishtowel tucked into her shorts. She took the shoe box and clothes from Bunny. "Where your brother? I thought you met him after school?"

Bunny wiped her face with both hands. "We was with all of Sheldon's girlfriends after the variety show. Sheldon and me was about to walk home. And then you know David Asato and the other small Japanee guy, PePe, right, Toni?"

"Yeah, so what?"

"They came by us and started making trouble with Sheldon 'cause of his dress—" Bunny paused and turned fast toward Harry O.

"What dress?" Harry O. clenched his fists.

"For his act in the variety show. Never mind, that's not the important part."

"What goddamn dress? I thought Toni was his partner?" Harry O. looked at me for confirmation. He smiled meekly at the old-timers and the Santos brothers.

"They started to call Sheldon fag and pussy and Nancy Kwan. And none of his stupid girlfriends backed him up. So I asked Sheldon, 'They always say this shit to you?' And he tell me, 'Yeah, every day.' How come you never do nothing, Toni?"

I shrugged my shoulders.

"So where Sheldon?" Mommy asked.

"Wait, that's not the end. So then I stepped up to David and told him, 'No mess with my brother, you asshole.' And he said, 'Why, what you going do, cunt?'"

Aunty Mei Ling and Mommy gasped at the word.

"Then he shoved his tennis racquet in my chest. So Sheldon rushed him. PePe and David started pounding Sheldon and nobody was around to stop them. All his jackass girlfriends was just standing there like lumps on a log. Then Sheldon got up and tried to run. But by the time I got to the street, I never see which way he went."

"Goddammit, what dress?! Toni, you wore Bunny's dress?

Hah? What? Or was Sheldon the one wearing the dress? What the hell's going on? My son better not be wearing no dress."

"Never mind the dress, Harry." It was Aunty Mei Ling. "Mary Alice, that's Kenneth Asato's boy. You know Kenneth —the one who think he kingpin at Hilo Lanes? The Rainbow vacuum cleaner salesman? Handing out those cheap-ass pens like they made of gold."

Aunty Mei Ling turned toward Maverick. "You listen to me, son. We been friends with the Yagyuus for God knows how long. We not going sit here and let those little punks do this shit to Bunny and Sheldon. On Monday, you and Wyatt straighten this out, you hear me?"

Nobody said a word. I turned toward the back steps and saw Sheldon's shadow move up toward the apartment.

"You hear your mother, boy?" Mr. Santos stood up and stared until Maverick nodded a quick yes. Then Mr. Santos crossed the street and waved goodbye as he stepped into the ticket booth. The fluorescent light flickered on.

Butchie got up next and put his arm around my sister. "You all right, Buns?" He was brotherly in his affection toward us. "Let me know if I can do anything, Aunty. I kick their ass myself, but better Maverick and Wyatt 'cause they juveniles. They get couple slaps on the hand when the cops come." He put on his red usher vest.

"You hear me, son?" Mrs. Mei Ling said to Wyatt as he got up to follow Butchie. He looked at me, staring with his black eyes. He said nothing but cracked his knuckles and stretched all six foot four of himself by hanging on to the doorframe of the shop. He nodded his slow and sarcastic, smirky-lipped yes.

Niso-san went back to his camera shop and Mr. Ute walked toward KTA.

"Stay for dinner, Herb," Harry O. told his big brother.

"Yeah, let me call Mildred."

"Go use the phone in the shop." Harry O. stood to get the phone for Uncle Herb. "No need end our happy hour over Sheldon."

"We cannot let anybody hurt Sheldon," Aunty said softly. "He get his ways, Lord Almighty, he get plenty of his own ways, but underneath all that, he get good heart. And he Aunty Mary Alice's boy." Aunty Mei Ling put her arm around Mommy, who rested her head on her shoulder. Bunny, as if on cue, began to sob. They applied their female help-me pressure on Maverick.

I stepped off of the sidewalk and looked up toward our bedroom window. The gauzy curtains moved in and out. I saw my brother leaning on his arms, the curtains clinging on to the contours of his broken, sad face.

That next Monday, as I watched Maverick take the long walk across campus, his face looked like the saddest time of day for me. It was the early evening, the lights still off in dark windows, the blue-gray flickering of a TV, and the mottled pastels in Hilo skies. It was the time of day when I felt weak and empty. For a moment, I saw that in Maverick's face.

Wyatt was behind him. I hid as Sheldon bounded to his feet. All of Sheldon's girlfriends clutched their books and stared in communal awe. "Which fuckheads hassling you, Toni?" Maverick asked.

"Him, over there, Maverick," Sheldon screamed. "There— David Asato, the one with the knitted vest." David Asato and PePe Akasaka turned around.

"Not, wasn't us. We didn't do anything," PePe squeaked.

"You fuckin' shut up," Wyatt said as he shoved PePe's back

into one of the tables. "My brother wasn't talking to you, asshole."

"Was . . . wasn't us. What we did? He's lying," stammered David Asato, rich tennis punk in OP shirt.

"Was. Was you two guys, PePe and David," Sheldon said with teary vibrato in his voice. This time it was for real.

"Toni?" At that moment, I knew Maverick wanted to defend me, not my brother. But this was not for my sake. It was for his own macho high school image. Yet his words to me came out softly.

"Who, Toni?" Wyatt yelled in my face as he yanked Sheldon's skinny arm to get him out of the way. I nodded toward the two tennis geeks.

Wyatt shoved David from behind. Sheldon jumped and clapped. Maverick put his arm out on Wyatt's chest to hold him back. "You ever fuck with Toni and Sheldon again, asshole, and I coming back to broke your fuckin' ass, you hear me, punk?" Maverick gave David Asato a hard, demeaning crack to the side of his head. "And you, you asshole," Maverick said as he pointed to PePe Akasaka, who had backed up right into Wyatt's body. "See my brother Wyatt? He eat Japs like you for fun. Now get the fuck out of here."

But Wyatt grabbed PePe by the throat and side-cracked his face. David Asato ran down the sidewalk with his racquets and bag as the vice-principal and campus security dragged Maverick and Wyatt to the office. Sheldon pirouetted, sticking out his tongue and wagging his ass at the rest of the tennis player boys. I looked at Sheldon and knew that we felt the same about Maverick Santos.

Maverick Santos, who was going with varsity cheerleader Lynette Vasconcellos; Maverick Santos, whom years later Sheldon, whenever he talked about this, equated with Richard Gere in *An Officer and a Gentleman*, and I guess he was Debra

Winger; Maverick Santos, who always watched me with a sidewards glance.

It was Maverick Santos whose graduation picture found a place on our bedroom wall, next to an airbrushed poster Sheldon screened in art class that said "S Loves M," surrounded by hearts, trellised vines, and flowing pink ribbons.

My father gave me an eye for wood: driftwood on the southern shoreline of the Big Island, awash with fishing-boat debris all the way from the Japan Sea. Bagasse spewn out of huge sugar-mill flues on the windward coast of the island cushioning balls of blue and green blown glass, decades old, from fishing boats—balls of crystal, all sizes, bobbing their perilous way to the crashing shores.

And I gathered for him arms of naupaka wood from Ka'alu'alu near South Point. In the pasturelands outside of Pāhala, a sugar plantation town near the southernmost tip of the United States, I walked with my father to the broken windmill over graying 'ōhi'a fence posts to find driftwood for natural bird mounts in Heads by Harry.

When I was a very little girl, I ran ahead of him along the breaking tide. The broken glass, sanded and smooth, jeweled the shoreline like citrine, emerald, and blue topaz.

When I was a very little girl, I ran ahead of him through the staghorn and wild orchid. He filled my canvas pack with wood. My father pulled kiawe thorns from my slippers.

He mounted for me the kōlea on a floater from a tuna boat in the Japan Sea. This golden plover perched on his stretch of place, year after year, returning messenger of the gods of Hawaiian legend. I carried a floater home laced with a torn fishing net. He poised the bird agitated and alert.

He mounted for me the 'auku'u, stern on stone and wood, fish and frog in his beholding yellow eyes, white wedding plumes. This was my black-crowned night heron from Kīpū, Kaua'i, oldest of the inhabited Hawaiian Islands.

My father gave me the eye for driftwood, for beauty in gnarled arms, the twist and trellis of fine lines, to see splendor in the awry, to look, always look, and to listen.

The summer I turned sixteen, Harry O. took me to look for driftwood to fill the wooden locker box in the back alley, which was rank with the smell of old wood and mildew, the damp of the asphalt, and the sharp-sweet of Varathane.

My father would lift the barbed wire along the roadside of Kapāpala Ranch for me, walking past fresh piles of shit that Harry O. identified as pig, cow, horse, goat, wild dog, and then estimated the approximate date and time of excretion. He dispensed important survival information to me, hunter that he was.

And then he'd toss the dried cow pies like Frisbees at me until I yelled at him to knock it off; this was the last time I was ever coming to get wood; I got better things to do than hang around with an old fut like him, a hideous, hideous lie. I wanted nothing more than to hang out with him.

My father and I went on many expeditions where he'd create lots of common-sense situations for me. What if you got lost in the forest? What would you do? What if you heard a pack of wild dogs? How do you mark your trees and rocks?

We collected burlap bags full of driftwood, bringing the coiling gray 'ōhi'a back to the shop for a good coconut brushing and two coats of varnish.

There was little money in this for me but a lunch of gravy burger and a boiled egg at Hirano Store in Glenwood, Harry

O.'s treat, and his promise to me one rainy afternoon, a slanted rain through volcanic fog.

"I teach you how to drive this Scout," he said. "You should learn how to drive standard. What if you in one emergency situation, and the only car around is standard? Then all pau. Your fault. Death is a tough burden to bear, little girl."

I wouldn't even argue with him, not if I was going to finally learn to drive, even before Sheldon. It was always a big deal for me to do anything before my brother. And learning to drive first—I nearly sang my own chorus of "A hundred mirrion mee-ra-culls," even if our family owned the only lavender International Scout I had seen in my entire life.

Harry O.'s Scout used to be a fire engine red, which was bad enough before Sheldon told Harry O. to take the Scout to Hawai'i Community College, where the auto body students did car paint jobs for almost free.

And Harry O., checking into Sheldon's suggestion, was so pleased to find his son correct for once on a macho subject like auto repair and maintenance that he asked Sheldon to choose the new color for the Scout.

The two Yagyuu men drove down to HCC. Sheldon studied all the paint charts and then picked out "Metallic and Maroon." He bragged, "Bad ass, Bunny. Wait till you see Harry O.'s new, I mean new, put some rims on that ass-spanking, brand-new Scout."

And I guess it was metallic and maroon. When the auto body students blended the paints, they must've swirled it a little too silvery. Our Scout was metallic lavender. And Harry O. blamed Sheldon, punishing him by not allowing him to learn how to drive, even when Sheldon begged and pleaded that he was one of the few seniors without a driver's license.

"Tough shit, Shelly," I told him that afternoon of my first lesson. I climbed into the passenger side of the Scout.

"You shut your mouth, Toni," Harry O. said to me. We headed toward Hilo High School. He would make me drive around and around the parking lot until I managed to get smoothly out of first gear.

"This Scout don't have synchro mesh, so you have to come to a complete stop before you put it in first gear," he said. "or the gears grind, you hear me, Toni?"

I heard. But I didn't understand. This was my first lesson. Synchro mesh? What the fuck was that?

And then I got behind the wheel for a long session of herky-jerky, herky-jerky, grind the gears, burn rubber, squeak and yank, three heads jarring back and forth, Harry O. yelling, "Clutch, Toni, clutch," Sheldon screaming and snorting in the back seat, Harry O. yelling at my brother, "Knock off the pig sounds," and the high school football team practicing that summer day on the field, laughing and pointing at the jerking lavender metallic Scout.

Maverick and Wyatt Santos jogged over in their gray cut shirts, athletic shorts, and helmets pushed up on their heads. They leaned on the fence where the Scout came to a yanking halt. Harry O. fumed. Sheldon opened his side window so that Maverick, his most recent real love of his life, could see his floozy self.

"What, Harry O.?" Maverick said to my father. "Came to catch whiplash? Only joking, Toni."

"Let me practice next, Harry O.," said Wyatt, who looked at me and then spat in the fence, leaving a phlegm globule hanging and swaying a spit strand in the wind.

"Fuckin' pig," I said to him.

"Watch your mouth," my father snapped.

"Why he always spit after he look at me?"

"No mind her," Sheldon chimed in. "She making ass and she

covering up her shame with her filthy mouth, right, Tone?"

"You shut up, too," Harry O. said. "What you was saying, Wyatt?"

He spat again. "My father refuse to let me get my license after I flunk last year. What he said, Maverick?"

"He said something like you was a damn sonofabitchin' undeserving, fricken lolo-ass, bonehead, good-for-nothing bum. Something like that."

"Yeah, something like that," Wyatt replied as he lifted the helmet off his head and threw it to the ground.

"And remember," Maverick went on, "Daddy said if you like go prom, Wyatt, you can catch the Hele-On bus," Maverick said, laughing.

"That sound like Lionel," Harry O. said.

"The bum on the bus. Don't forget to wave your arms at the bus stop or the driver not stopping for you and your pig date," I muttered under my breath.

"I heard that, Toni," Wyatt snarled. "Fuck you, bitch."

"You heard that, Harry O.?" I said, ready to climb out the window and yank out a clump of Wyatt's sun-damaged long hair.

"You deserve it," he said. "Shut your mouth when the men talking."

"So let my brother practice, Harry O., so we burn out one transmission instead of two," Maverick said.

"And whop my father's jaws, 'cause I no like go prom," Wyatt said as he kicked the fence to get sand off of his shoe. "And I already know how for drive standard."

"Funny, funny, you comedians," Harry O. joked. "Toni, concentrate on what you doing instead of listening to us. You making shame for the family." I knew Harry O. only half meant it, always trying to out-macho the next guy.

Then Maverick side-hopped over the fence and walked to my side of the Scout. "I teach you, Toni, and I never yell even if we catch whiplash." Even his sweat smelled sweet. I watched the way his lips curled over his teeth whenever he talked and it made me moist.

"Teach me, Maverick," a moister Sheldon squeaked as he leaned in between my face and the open window, those ballerina arms flapping.

"Pass," said Wyatt, spitting high into the air and running back toward their football practice. "C'mon, Maverick, before Coach DeRoy make us crab-walk." I watched Maverick's glossy, brick-laden abs turn from us as if in slow motion and Wyatt's solid mass run into the hot afternoon, into the heat waves, sinuous and thick.

I herky-jerked us a few more times around the parking lot until Harry O., so fed up at my uncoordination, got back into the driver's seat and headed home. "You let me know when you *think* you can handle this, Toni," he told me as he backed the Scout into our garage.

"Why can't I learn on Mommy's automatic like all my other friends?"

Sheldon giggled perversely in the back seat. "Friends? What friends?"

" 'Cause you ain't like your other friends. You one Yagyuu, just like me, and don't you ever forget it." He walked into the back door of the shop.

I spent the next three hours reversing out of the garage and then first-gearing it back in until my feet understood the timing, the high catch of the clutch, the gears grumbling into first. And Harry O., finally calling me in to dinner, never said a word.

The next morning, we drove on steep hills by the Lyman House Museum, Harry O. and I. "Not bad," was what he said as I gassed it, lifted the clutch slowly, the smell of the ethyl, a nauseating high. I glanced at my father and moved us forward up Haili Street, never once rolling backwards.

My father would let me drive him to gather driftwood thereafter, but never once rested his eyes to sleep. When the radio went dead outside of Volcano, he'd tell me about beauty, the formation of distinct geographic features on the slopes of Mauna Loa, see splendor, and look, always look. My father who pulled thorns from my slippers. My father who told me to shut my mouth when the boys talked.

Daddy, you listen and watch.

"Listen," he said, "reverse in. You never know when you might need to make a fast escape."

But to escape, I always had to be the driver.

The summer before Sheldon's senior year, he decided, along with Bunny, to take sewing lessons from Mrs. Otsuji, who taught drafting, not just sewing from Simplicity or Butterick patterns, but drafting and designing in the basement of her house up in Kaūmana.

Mabel Otsuji's School of Fashion Design was listed in the Big Island Yellow Pages *and* advertised on COMTEC cable. Anybody who was anybody, a Keywanette or cheerleader, a homecoming queen or Winter Ball attendant, took sewing from Mrs. Otsuji and not Mrs. Maruyama in the side storeroom of the Singer store.

As much as Sheldon irked the piss out of me, I never brought his fashion-filled intentions to my father's attention —not for Sheldon's sake but for my father's sake.

Harry O. openly wished for a rugged bush of hair on Shel-

don's chest, a thick Okinawan mustache, a cigarette-smok-
ing, gun-toting, NFL-loving, tobacco-spitting, ass-cleavage-
mooning, macho duck for a vocationally trained, yet college-
of-business-administration-graduate of a son.

He got, instead, a Qiana-fabric-fingering, thimble-collect-
ing, *Vogue-* not Simplicity-pattern-loving clothing designer of
a son. My brother would never tell Harry O. his dreams.

But neither did I.

Bunny got her dreams in cash, sewing money out of our
father, hundreds easy. Her Cherry Blossom aspirations made
it possible. She'd say, "I can put sewing *and* drafting as two
of my favorite pastimes on the Cherry Blossom application."
Harry O. nodded and handed over the wad of money for the
lessons directly from his cash register.

Her dreams materialized in cash.

"Can I have some money for fabric too, Daddy?" she said
with her sweet cherry blossoms in spring smile. "I buy from
the *remnants* table at Helen's Fabrics or Hata's, please." Hu-
mility was a virtue in this wonderfully self-sacrificing youngest child, enough yosha to bring herself to *buy remnants.* "And
notions, rickrack, and pinking shears too?" My sister always
went for the kill.

I'd hear the ring of the cash register again, the lifting of
the rusty money-holding hinges, and Harry O.'s candied
words, "You one good girl, Bunny. Always industrious and
trying to save a dollar by making your own clothes. Maybe
one day you teach Toni too?"

I cringed. I was in the shop that day like every other day
the summer I spent helping him out. I continued sweeping
the white dusty floor, then aggressively wire-brushed the
pieces of driftwood on the shop table. Bunny smiled my way
and nodded. Harry O. continued, " 'Cause Toni don't know
how to dress nice. And when she do buy clothes, look like

she went shopping at the Hilo Army Surplus store. Here," he said, handing Bunny another ten, "make Toni one nice dress for Daddy, okay?"

Bunny was a home-sewn clothes horse.

I never saw the dress she was supposed to make for me.

And Sheldon, who hid his apprenticeship in Mabel Otsuji's sewing classes, resorted to collecting rebates from candy wrappers, which landed him a ton of dollars from nights of hanging around Butchie Santos as he emptied the trash from the theater crowd. Night after night, matinee after matinee, Sheldon wiped down Mars, Rocky Road, and M&M wrappers.

My brother always knew how to make a fast buck. When we were very little, Sheldon enlisted Bunny and me to scrub the mossy sidewalk outside of Heads by Harry and Niso Camera Shop with Ajax. Then we scrubbed the lobby of the Mamo Theatre.

For a whopping five dollars, we'd sweep up downy feathers, Borax, excelsior, and scraps of raw sheep wool off the floor of the shop. He'd tell me how to arrange the rolls of toilet paper and duct tape. Bunny organized the bottles of Red Passion Cutex for pheasant faces. I stacked the slabs of Parowax Harry O. used for finishing the menacing boar tongues.

He found for us odd jobs all the time, so he justified a 50-25-25 split. He was a master of manipulation. If I brought it to Mommy's attention, I would be accused of being hell-bent on retaliating against my brother, reading too deeply into his motives, a real black heart I was, and evil to even think such things of family, of blood.

I drove Bunny and Sheldon everywhere in a dull gray secondhand Plymouth Arrow that Harry O. got for $700 and two free sheep head mounts from Niso-san's nephew Roy in Pāpa'ikou. I took Mommy to acey-deucey night at Aunty Mildred's and Sheldon to his Future Homemakers of America summer officers' meetings. He was the secretary.

I dropped Bunny and Sheldon off at Mabel Otsuji's School of Fashion Design, and when I picked them up, they had armloads of fabric and rolls of drafting paper, a huge sewing chest, and were full of the gossip-of-the-popular that I was not a part of in any way.

Their talk went like this: "So you know what Lynden told me?" Sheldon says to Bunny. And then they whisper.

"Not. No lie, Sheldon!" Bunny replies. "But she said that Lisa Hanabusa and Sandi Abe wanted to nominate me for the Keywanettes."

"Don't be a Keywanette," Sheldon says. "Be a Sweetheart for the Key Club. They only ask two sophomore girls every year. That's more prestigious."

"I cannot be both Keywanettes *and* Sweetheart?"

"I never saw that happen yet," Sheldon muses. "I can ask Lynden."

"Shoots, Sheldon. That's why you my best brother."

I feel their glare at me as Sheldon continues, "Unlike our sister over there behind the wheel whose biggest deal so far in high school—don't get me wrong now, community service is big on the college apps—is joining the Sierra Club to clean rotting bagasse off the beach at Bayfront *while* Maverick and Wyatt get Canoe Club practice, mind you. And getting her license so she can drive *us* around."

"Fuck off, Shelly," I tell him, "before you walk home with your sewing basket."

"Nah, just kidding. Ho, cannot take a joke?" he whines. "Yeah, she try make me walk," he whispers to Bunny. "I bust up this car big time, honey."

"Go for it, dummy, the damn car already bust up."

"She just jealous, Bunny, 'cause you *pops* and she not."

And the air goes still. I let it go still to make him *feel* like he's won. Day after summer day, weeks, months, years after, Sheldon always won.

I continued to help Harry O. in the shop, never getting paid, went to Sonny Chiba movies at the Mamo Theatre with my father, drove Sheldon and Bunny around like the king and queen of Hilo, and by the time the summer ended, Sheldon and Bunny had drafted and sewn enough clothes to last them two months in school without repeating a single outfit, the way they had planned all along, so they both could be voted Best Dressed in the Hoss Elections, a feat never before accomplished by two family members in different grades at Hilo High School. They kicked fashion ass.

The day before school started, Bunny and Sheldon were in the middle of deciding what kind of fashion statement they wanted to make on their first day back. Harry O. mounted for me a Japanese blue iridescent pheasant.

I watched him intently as the bird's sepia wings spread and amber beak opened. He painted Red Passion Cutex on the face, and posed it on an 'ōhi'a log I varnished myself.

He worked every blue feather in place, lifting the feather horns on its head with tweezers, wing wires and feet wires trimmed, and with an artist's soft brush swept the specks of Borax off the bluest body. And then he passed it to me. This trophy, I put in the picture window of Heads by Harry.

T w o

My mother, Mary Alice, we have to call *Mommy*.

Not *Ma*, which is too low-class.

Not *Mom*, which is too haolified.

Not *Mother*, which is too pretentious.

But Mommy, which she demanded from the time we were born.

My mommy had put together, once again, the most festive New Year's block party on Mamo Street.

Sheldon's senior year, my junior year, and Bunny's sophomore year, all of us were there. Lionel and Mei Ling Santos, Butchie, Wyatt, Maverick, Herline, her boyfriend and baby girl, Chastity, Niso-san, Mr. Ute, Uncle Herb and Aunty Mildred, cousins Joy and Pearl, hookers Paula and Franjelica, even a plate for Frankie Bobo, the one homeless man in Hilo.

The men and boys always sat outside the shop in the sheer cool of these December nights with the Igloos and enough fireworks to ward off evil spirits in this world and the next. Every year, Mr. Santos and Uncle Herb hung 10,000 Duck Brand firecrackers from a bamboo pole outside of Heads by Harry, 10,000 outside of Niso Camera Shop, and 10,000 outside of the Mamo Theatre. This enabled 30,000 wishes at 12 a.m. to slip in and out from the thick cirrus of gunpowder smoke and the deafening crackle of the explosives.

The women and girls plus Sheldon always congregated in the downstairs kitchen and dining area. Aunty Mildred had been sipping on Asti Spumanti all night, leaning her thick arms on the Formica table, staining the rim of her champagne glass red, her false eyelashes peeling off on an otherwise impeccable Shiseido face.

And as at every other New Year's party, her lips got loose and pissed off Mommy for weeks into the coming year. This year, it was the compare Joy-with-Bunny talk that did it. We were cousins whose deep mother-embedded competitions made cause for spitting on each other's graves.

"So anyway, Mary Alice, like I was saying, Joysie's been so busy with her piano and ballet, plus being sophomore class vice president, it has to take its toll someplace, but lo and behold, she made a 3.8. She's disappointed for her B in PE, but I told her, 'Never mind, Joysie, I'll have a conference with Mr. Takamine, and make him stop playing God with his grades.' What do you think, Mary Alice? You and I know lots of teachers who like to make their top students have a flaw in their GPA, am I not right?"

Mommy steamed. "I cannot stand parents who come into my class and demand better grades for their kids. You never had a parent like that, Mildred? I had plenty and they pissed me off with their holier-than-thou talk about their rotten, spoiled, full-of-attitude, lazy-ass kids." Mommy said nothing else and continued to peel the crispy skin off her pūpū turkey tails. She sucked the oil off of her fingers with a loud smack.

Every time that Mommy nearly strangled her sister-in-law, she'd complain to me that Aunty Mildred was too high and mighty: Aunty Mildred thought she shit ice cream and farted rose petals; Aunty Mildred was the crummiest teacher she ever met, the kind of teacher who passed out worksheet after worksheet; her students learned nothing. But there was Aunty Mildred shopping for her next week's wardrobe in Fashion House like her job was a social event.

"And acting like she no talk pidgin," Mommy would go on. "She grew up on the goddamn Hakalau plantation. What she trying to hide? And her family was the piggery owners, damn princess of the buta kaukau."

That New Year's Eve, the feud continued. "Mary Alice, are you listening to me?"

"What, Mildred?"

"How's Bernice doing at Hilo High?" she sniped. "You know, I'm so glad they opened Waiākea High School, because, frankly speaking, all the college-bound, upper-class kids come from our side of town," Aunty Mildred whispered to Mei Ling Santos.

And that was when Mommy unleashed. "You know, I not the type to brag, and I didn't want to say nothing, but since you asked, Mildred, Bunny made the JV cheerleading squad. She's sophomore class rep, Keywanettes, and Sweetheart for the Key Club. What else, Sheldon?"

"She made the prom court."

"Yeah, she's in the prom court."

"And 4.0," I said softly.

Aunty Mildred fell silent. "Pour me some Asti, Mei Ling."

"Well, *you asked*," Mommy added.

"I certainly did. Their academic standards are lower at Hilo High," Aunty Mildred muttered. "What about *Toni*?"

"What *about* Toni?" Mommy replied. But faster than Aunty could think in her tipsy state: "What about Pearl? Still doing the books down at the Hukilau Hotel? When is she supposed to finish her degree at the community college? She still trying to pass the CPA exam? Oh no, you cannot take the CPA exam till you get a four-year college degree, stupid me. This would be what, her fourth year in that dinky two-year college?"

"Well, you know how hard it is with an infant. Pearl's so busy with Nathan that I told her to forget her degree for a while and be a good mother."

"Hāpai, knocked up, shacking up, then bam—a shotgun wife." Mommy stood up and laughed while taking out another tray of hot turkey tails from the oven. "Maybe the men folks like some more pūpū," she said as she dumped the sizzling asses onto a nice Chinese plate. "Close your mouth, Mildred. Catching flies is so unbecoming."

Mrs. Mei Ling went after Mommy. The slip-on, sexy stilettos she wore even with shorts clicked on the concrete. I followed them out, Sheldon not too far behind me. "Every year, the same damn song," she whispered in Mommy's ear.

"I just have to broke her face," Mommy said out loud, "she always get drunk and then talk shit about the kids. It's a wonder Joy and Bunny like each other so much the way Mildred compare them from the time they was born."

We all cut through the shop. "Sheldon, bring some small stools out front for us," Mommy told him, and Sheldon, smart enough not to grumble or defy any request Mommy made of him from now until she wasn't mad at Aunty Mildred anymore, quickly turned around and carried five small stools to the front of Heads by Harry.

"Who you taking to the prom, Sheldon?" Mrs. Mei Ling asked as he set down a stool for her.

"Sharon Yoshioka, friends only. She the VP for the Future Homemakers of America. She said if I take her, she choose me as one of the delegates to Honolulu for the state FHA convention." My brother always had ulterior motives. "Why, who Maverick going with, Aunty? Why he no take Toni? This haole guy asked her, but he dorky." Sheldon stopped suddenly, staring at me with that wimp-ass smile of his.

"I not going," I quickly said.

"Maverick, who you taking prom?" Mrs. Mei Ling asked loudly. For a moment, all faces turned in our direction before returning to conversations about pig hunting and mouflon season.

"What, Ma?"

"Come here," she yelled as Maverick and Wyatt made their way to where we were sitting. "What you think, Mary Alice? Our two kids should go prom? Maverick, who you taking prom? Why no take Toni?"

I hated being forced on Maverick. My brother grinned widely, knowing I was in some perverse spotlight that he manufactured but secretly wanted for himself. Bunny looked on and nudged Joy. Mommy held her breath, that maybe yes, I had a chance to go to a semiformal high school event with somebody handsomely pretty if only for the prom picture as proof for the future grandchildren.

"So what, Maverick, why no take Toni to the prom?" Mrs. Mei Ling went on.

"I taking Lynette Vasconcellos, Ma. I told you."

"Oh."

"What about Wyatt?" Maverick said. "He ain't asked no-body yet."

Wyatt turned to the sound of his name. "What? Who? Toni?" He looked at me and I looked back, daring him to spit. "Nah, fuck that. I ain't dressing up and making good manners." He hooked his fingers behind his head and stretched, his biceps bulging.

I thought, holy shit, who in their right mind would dream *this*? When Sheldon and I played Mystery Date, it was *never* my dream to go with the guy behind door number 5, the one

with the burnt-out long hair, the one who burped and farted
indiscriminately even in elevators, the one who wore a zipped
hooded jacket as a shirt and ripped Levi's with no underwear
to school. He flunked high school, brimmed with anger, and
dreamed to be a janitor in the theater his family owned.

"Pass," he said. "I ain't going prom this year, not last year,
not any year. Proms for fags except Maverick. Lynette forcing
him to go. I meeting Maverick them down Isles after they
all pau fagging out."

I felt my breath extracted out of me.

Faces turned inward into my body.

Glass eyes.

My own melting.

I have since learned that sitting helps.

Or leaving.

Or flunking out.

Or quitting.

Then they all expect nothing from you.

"Me and you can wait at Isles, Toni," Wyatt said, looking
right through me with dark eyes and raising one eyebrow,
"or you like look stupid and go with that haole?"

"Fuck you, Wyatt," I said at last.

"Why, what I said? I no like go prom, but no mean we
cannot party while all them other fucks acting stupid," Wyatt
whispered to me. He lit a cigarette and put his sunglasses on
as he leaned against the wall.

"No smoke in front of Ma, stupid," Maverick said, shoving
his brother.

"No call me *stupid,* asshole," Wyatt said, shoving his
brother in the chest but still flicking the cigarette onto the
wet street.

"Hell freeze over before I go anyplace or do anything with
you, Wyatt," I said to him, Sheldon giggling on the side of

me. "And who the fuck wears sunglasses at night, hah? Only stonies and stupid pigs like you."

"Knock it off, Toni," Mommy said to me through gritted teeth.

"Go with the haole. You match. Weird with weird. How come Toni no more boyfriends, hah? I wonder why." He scratched his head and made a bonehead face. "Loo-zer, that's why," Wyatt said, pushing his way past all of us to sit curbside with Mr. Ute's druggie nephew Roy.

"Eh, Wyatt, don't you dare talk like that to my sister." It was Sheldon.

"And you, you fuckin' . . . give no thanks to me and Maverick, shithead. What you think we looked like in front of all the boiz? Defending you . . . you . . . I sick of hearing you talk," Wyatt said, standing up now and charging toward Sheldon.

"Daddy, Daddy!" Mrs. Mei Ling screamed. "Lionel, get your fuzzy ass over here. Lionel, come talk to your rotten son." Her words trailed off as she got up and stormed over to get Mr. Santos.

I felt someone's hands on my shoulders. I thought it was Mommy ready to yank me into the next world. It was Butchie. "I take you, Toni. I old enough to be your uncle, but I no care. Me and Maverick can rent the limo."

I didn't care, I really didn't care. Why was it such a big deal in this town? "Okay, Butchie," I told him. I felt gray waves in my body all the way to my feet.

So it was Butchie Santos and me. My Mystery Date was the weight-lifting, buffed but short, hairy-chested theater usher, sometimes janitor, and ticket ripper old enough to be my uncle, a kind and gentle uncle. I didn't care. I really didn't.

The night of the prom, Butchie held out his hand for me.

I stepped toward him and fell off the side of my heels. I slid into the back seat of the limo. Maverick smelled like Aramis, a slight flush in his cheeks, his golden hair slicked back. I almost fainted from my own moisture.

"Go up Lynette's house," he said to Wyatt. "Up Kaūmana." Wyatt turned and saluted from behind the steering wheel.

"I thought he didn't have his license," I told Maverick.

"Our Uncle Marshall own the limo company. He trust Wyatt more than his own wife. You look okay, Toni," he said like he meant it. "I never know you had cleavage."

"Yeah, nice," added Butchie, whose tux was too long for his arms.

"You no feel stupid, brah, going to this shitless high school prom?" Wyatt asked Butchie. Wyatt had no shirt on with a red bow tie around his neck. A gold chain with a boar's tusk hung between his brown pecs. He had his hair tied in a ponytail and a puakenikeni blossom behind each ear. "You so old."

I began to feel glassy and see-through again.

"What the fuck? Friends, right, Toni? Not like we getting married. That's how all you punks act in Hilo. You go out one, two times with one chick, and you guys all married. Get a grip, stupid childrens."

They never talked back to Butchie. What he said held a final-word kind of power. He was always a tough motherfucker who could kick anybody's ass twice his size. He chipped his front tooth in a big brawl and had scars on his nose and chin.

Wyatt pulled into Lynette Vasconcellos's driveway. Lynette came out of the house in a maroon gown, so tight that she waddled, and squeezed her Lynda Carter Wonder Woman hips, big-ass boobs, then gorgeous face next to Maverick.

"So whassup, boiz? Let's par-tay. Hi, Antoinette," she added while pulling out a pint of Southern Comfort from her white patent-leather clutch. She squirted herself with Scoundrel. "Who that driving? That's you, Wyatt? Stop at Irene's Liquors for Spanada and Boone's Farm Strawberry Hill. Oh, maybe we should get some Bacardis, 'cause can fit in mines and Antoinette's bag. Last year prom, my cousin Angela took in three pints Kamchatkas, how you like that? This your big brother, Maverick? Eh, you work down the theater, hah? I seen you the time we went *Saturday Night Fever*, yeah, Mavs babe?"

Into the night, Lynette's mouth kept revving on. "And then I told Maverick, Toni, if I get hāpai, pau for us 'cause my father going kick my ass. That's why I brought rubbers in my bag, and I hate being so open, but I we close, right?"

I wanted to say no, but Lynette continued. "I not on the Pill, 'cause I heard make you bloated and gain twenty pounds, but how we going screw tonight if Wyatt driving and we came with *you* and Butchie? How come you never eat your prime rib? What, was too raw? Shit, I said 'well done' and mines had blood inside. Me and my mother, we cannot eat meat that get even the smallest little blood. My father and brother, eh, rare all the way. Let's dance, Mavs. This the theme song, 'You My Everything,' and you know how I feel, right? You are my everything, babes."

Butchie sighed deeply and shook his head. "She must be *very, very* good," he said to Maverick, who laughed. "Go dance with Toni and I dance with Lynette. Look like your ears need one rest."

Lynette stumbled as Butchie led her onto the dance floor of the Crown Room. She leaned her body into his.

Maverick said little, his face bent down toward mine. "There Sheldon," he said at last, sweet rum breath. "He waving at us."

"He wants to dance with you," I said to Maverick.

"Pass."

"You his hero," I told him.

"I know, fuck," he said. And after a while, "What about you?" He passed his hands over the small of my back and my fingers brushed his neck.

"What about me?" I asked.

"Never mind."

"Mavs," Lynette breathed into our space, "dance with me." She spun herself around, knocking two centerpieces off of tables.

"We better go, brah, before the teachers come around," Butchie said to Maverick as the two of them held Lynette up. They walked her out the side door. Wyatt was smoking a joint in the limo.

"What, pau the prom?"

"No," Maverick said. "But Lynette pau."

"I pau what, Mavs? Pau the prom? Where we going? We going Isles for drink? Where the cooler? Eh, I smell dope. I like one hit. Take a hit, take a hit, blow your fuckin' mind," Lynette sang as we pulled out of the hotel parking lot. Those were her last words before she passed out on the floor of the limo.

Butchie, Maverick, Wyatt, and I sat on the edge of the pier at Isles, sharing a bottle of Spanada, the waves wrapping around the bulbous lava rocks covered with sea grass.

Maverick leaned into me. "You can see Mauna Keʻa from Isles on a clear night like this," I said to him. I took off my nylons and Wyatt grabbed them from me to wear like a lei around his neck.

"The Hāmākua coastline and the lights up Kaūmana," Butchie said. "Try look, you guys, there the sugar mill."

"Eh, check out that canoe sliding in the bay," Wyatt said.

"Where?" I asked.

"Coming in," Wyatt said. "You cannot see the canoe?" He looked at me.

Nobody else saw it.

"What about you, Toni?" Maverick asked again.

"What about me?" I told him.

"Who your hero?"

"I don't know. I got none."

"What the fuck you guys talking about?" mumbled Wyatt, who shoved me hard to take the bottle of Spanada. "You talking bubbles. Like talk bubbles? Go talk with Maverick's date." The four of us laughed.

Bugs swirled around the orange streetlights. A fish flicked its silver body in the water. I could smell the sweet ferment of cane.

Sheldon cut out the last couple of months before graduation almost every day. He worked at Helen's Fabrics and collected vintage aloha prints and old kimono prints that Helen had mothballed in the back storeroom for about three decades. Week by week, he grew on Helen, then Helen, the proverbial nice Japanese elder lady, passed over her vintage fabrics to my brother.

"I almost like Helen's son, so it doesn't matter if I inherit all these fabrics," he said. "I bring her homemade chichi dango and party mix. And I never act cocky to her like some of the other yardage cutters, damn obasans with a bad attitude."

He worked and smoked dope with the rowdier of the Future Homemakers of America crowd, which amounted to sharing half a joint a day among three of them, Sharon Yo-shioka, Charlotte Gomes, and Sheldon. They acted stoned and silly, catching the munchies as an excuse to have lunch at Jimmy's or Cafe 100 every day, Sheldon's treat.

And after he got his letter of acceptance from the University of Hawai'i, he really didn't give a shit about school. His college counselor at Hilo High called Mrs. Mary Alice Yag-yuu, not knowing it was actually me he was talking to.

Sheldon knew he'd be gone soon and if he cut school, nothing would change. "I still marching with my class at graduation," he said to me, "then I kissing this sorry town aloha nui loa."

One weekend in May, Harry O. and Mr. Santos took Maverick and me pig hunting up in the Laupāhoehoe Forest Reserve, the same place I had found Fern. The morning air was crisp, Mauna Ke'a was glazed in white snow. Harry O. armed all of us to shoot pig for smoked-meat pūpū for the 1,000 guests at Maverick and Sheldon's graduation party. I tucked a Ziploc bag into my pack for thimbleberries.

"That Wyatt," Mr. Santos said while dumping some Diamond Head sodas in his cooler, "he might not graduate again, shit. I told that kid, 'Brah, you no graduate *this* year, then no shame me and this family by going back to Hilo High next year. Just drop out and fade into the walls someplace far away from my sight.' I kicking his sorry ass out of my house if he no graduate, I tell you."

"Where the boy today?" Harry O. asked.

"Damn kid, I making him paint the theater bathrooms with Butchie. And Butchie all pissed off to the max 'cause he wanted to come hunting. But if he no supervise Wyatt, the boy go surf down Honoli'i. That's the kind boy I get, damn punk, cannot trust him two feet out of my sight. And drunk, drunk, drunk all the time. I think the boy on drugs."

"Never mind," Harry O. said. "The four of us going catch plenty meat for the graduation party."

Mr. Santos nodded, a look of disgust on his face. "Where Sheldon? This his damn party."

Harry O. mumbled something to the effect of sushi and not being fooled about those damn dresses. "Sheldon working at Helen's," he said. "She treat him just like her own son. I guess somebody should. You think you disgusted with *your* boy," he said to Mr. Santos, "at least your boy act like one boy. I trade you any day."

Mr. Santos shrugged his shoulders, then nodded in agreement.

Maverick loaded the guns and the coolers in the back of the truck. His papered bull, Smut Dawg, kept us company for the long ride out to Laupāhoehoe. Harry O. begrudgingly allowed Maverick to bring the dog even if it was illegal to bring one into the reserve. And lucky that he brought the dog, because it served as a conversation piece way past Nīnole.

"He ain't that smart," Maverick told me while holding back his long hair with one hand, "but he can grab. He kind of fearless, but stupid, you know what I mean?"

"These bulls cannot track too good," I told Maverick. "Better to breed them with some kind terrier mix, what you think? This one get papers?"

"Yeah, but bulls, they hang on and they no hesitate." Maverick looked at me struggling with my own hair whipping in the wind. "Braid my hair for me, Toni," he said, scooting between my legs and passing me a rubber band from his pack.

"Me and my dog, we been through some shit, no, Smut Dawg, you dummy?" Maverick said to his dog, whose tongue was hanging and slapping out of the side of his mouth.

"Man, but I seen some dogs get sliced up," I said as I ran my fingers through his soft hair and felt the warmth of his body press into my inner thighs.

"You still take your dogs bird hunting?" he asked, stopping to contemplate the ease of our conversation. He looked at me briefly, then quickly turned toward the mountain that never moved even as we whisked down the wet highway. "Come," he said, patting the space between his legs, "I braid your hair."

We continued talking. "Harry O. said when Sheldon go college, I can have his dog. But the dog all confused, 'cause Sheldon changed the dog's name to Suzie Wong. In the field, I yelling, 'Sonny, Sonny, Suzie, Suzie,' and I never know what name the dog might answer to. He acting all stupid, and we yelling all loud, so he flush the birds."

Maverick and me laughed hard. "I don't know what I going do after I grad," he said after a long time of uncomfortable silence. He flung the braided rope of hair so that it rested on my breast. "At least Sheldon, he fucked up big time at the end of this year, but at least he going someplace, know what I mean?"

I didn't know how to save him, like he had saved me and my brother that day at school. I wanted to tell him about college applications and room and board like I knew it all, when at the time, I didn't—like college was the answer for everyone biding a few years, eighteen-year-olds wasting money and not ready for life. Like Aunty Mildred always said, we all should be forced to work for five years after high school.

"So what you going do?" I asked him. I watched his lips curl over his perfect teeth as he formed his next sentence.

"I don't know, but my father said do something, shit, auto body, carpentry, he tell me. I wanted to be one of the bird specialists up at the national park, but I don't know how . . . I mean, every year I was only taking metals and auto shop in school 'cause of my counselor. He said my scores not so high. I never even know what scores he was talking about. So he tell me I on the vocational track. I should've been taking biology, but fuck . . ."

Maverick and regrets—I choose to remember him this day surrounded by ʻōhiʻa lehua and hāpuʻu fern taller than all of us in the Laupāhoehoe Forest Reserve with Smut Dawg at his side on the trail. Sunlight fell through the canopy of banana poka, the sweet smell of the yellow fruit that Harry O. gathered later for Bunny to make poka jam and pie. And thimbleberries for a pie I could make for my father.

We heard the barking of someone else's dog, and Maverick's bull took off down the trail. Mr. Santos and Harry O. disappeared into the fern grove. Maverick stopped for me until we heard the sounds of a large boar and he too ran to catch up. But when we got further into the thicket, there were no other hunters, and no other dogs, just the huge boar and the pit bull in a muscled frenzy of guttural snarling and grotesque grunting.

Mr. Santos looked to take aim and Harry O. yelled, "No, Lionel, the kids! Move, Toni! You in the way, Maverick! Maverick, stop!" I pushed him away and he shoved me back, sending me into the muck of a sty. And then I saw Harry O. take a single shot at the boar's head, its mass of bristles quivering. The boar lay on its side with Maverick's bull under it.

"Daddy, my dog," Maverick strained to say as the two of

them ran for the bull. "See, Daddy, we should've brought the other dogs."

"We wasn't even suppose to bring this one," Harry O. said.

Smut Dawg had grabbed the boar's soft belly, holding it down, waiting for Maverick. "You fucka, you fucka, you fucka," Maverick yelled over and over as he stabbed the boar with his hunting knife, the sound of an animal dying and whining, the thick gurgle of last air and blood.

"My dog, Daddy," Maverick said again.

"Where he cut, son?" Mr. Santos asked. "Turn him slow." And when he did, "His stomach," he managed to say.

I gagged, and Harry O. moved me aside. "Sit down, Toni." I was covered with mud. "Maverick, his guts all hanging out."

"I ain't blind."

"No talk like that to Harry O., goddamn you, boy," Mr. Santos said.

"Never mind," my father said. "He all nuts over this dog."

Maverick took off his T-shirt and I nearly fainted at the sweat beading on his broad chest, its golden coffee color, and all of the blood on him. He undid the braid on his hair and it fell to his shoulders. Maverick gently pushed the dog's guts in place as the dog cried. He wrapped his shirt like a tourniquet around his midquarters.

"Better you put him out of his misery, son," Mr. Santos said.

"I ain't leaving him here." Then Maverick looked at me. It was that face, the face of evening.

Maverick lifted his bleeding dog on his bare shoulders, its head dangling and eyes blue-white, tongue and foam, a mild whimpering. And Maverick carried out his seventy-five-pound bull that day, out of the forest full of 'ōhi'a lehua and hāpu'u for two hours on his shoulders.

Harry O. carried the boar's head and Mr. Santos the meat.

I carried the guns and light gear. I watched my father walk alongside the bull trying to soothe it, Maverick's steady step, Mr. Santos's long gaze at his son. And in those last hours of our day, I listened to the reverberation of the quiet forest, the sure step of the hunters on the trail, the slow mourning of Maverick's dying bull.

Three

 The day Sheldon left for college in Honolulu, I celebrated.

At Elsie's Fountain, I ordered a large orange parfait, whipped cream, maraschino cherry, and macadamia nuts piled high. I sat on the red stool right in front of Elsie herself.

"When your brother coming home?"

"I don't know," I told her.

"I don't know or I no care?" she said to me, wiping the green Formica with a dirty dishtowel, leaving a greasy swirl around the fountain glass.

"Maybe both." And that was the sad truth.

Bunny spent the afternoon crying on Sheldon's bed like she was never going to see him again, and Mommy, our good mommy, consoled her with a trip to J. C. Penney for cap-sleeved tees. Bunny wanted every color for her denim overall dresses. She and Sheldon had sewn a mighty dozen or so.

At dinner that night, everyone ate solemnly. It was Harry O. who started our conversation. "Bunny, thank goodness you in that science class with Toni. Maybe she can get good grade with you there. You study together, okay?" he said to Bunny, whose rice balled up in a sad I-miss-Sheldon lump in her throat.

"How the hell you came up one science credit short, Toni?"

Mommy asked, slurping on the shoyu-sugar aku bones, then moving on to the brown-soaked fish head.

"This is a remedial class for seniors, Mommy," Bunny said before I could answer. "They let the ones without enough credits enroll with the sophomores. Maverick's girlfriend in that class too, right, Toni?"

I didn't answer and gave her a look instead. How the hell was I supposed to know? What was she talking about, remedial? "And how come you know about Lynette?" I asked her. "You been talking to Maverick?"

"Nooo," Bunny said in that sassy Japanese-girl tone that she perfected to an art form. "She's captain of the varsity cheerleaders, and at JV tryouts she was showing me her schedule. She know we close to Maverick, so she taking me under her wing. We close."

Bunny and Lynette were close to *everybody*. "I cannot wait till *you* go Honolulu to be close to your brother," I said to her. Mommy stopped scooping another paddle full of rice midair. Harry O. stopped chewing, chopsticks still on his lips.

"*You* going UH first, right, Toni? *You* going be there with Sheldon before Bunny, right? My three kids better get college degree, gunfunnit," Harry O. said. "You ain't going be bumming like those Santos boys, hah, kid?" He looked hard into my eyes. "No tell me you not getting your act together in school to go UH. Why you not taking science classes? Eh, what the hell's going on? By now, you should be in chemistry or physics, dammit, Toni."

I lowered my gaze. I thought about Maverick being tracked vocationally in school, and how I was tracked into classes like shorthand and business machines. I think my counselor thought I'd be an excellent secretary or bank teller.

"It's *our* fault, Harry," Mommy said at last. "We should've been picking classes for Toni, not her counselor. You know,

Harry, Toni get as much if not more brains than Sheldon and Bunny put together——"

Bunny's jaw dropped when my father nodded in agreement.

"But she get none of the killer instinct the other two kids have. *None.* She just like *you*, Harry. It's our fault," she said again as if I wasn't there, "for not being on top of this damn no-motivation kid. What for God gave her brains if all she do is sit on um every day?"

"Us, us, always blame the parents. That's Toni's fault for not having any interests, goddamn lump on a log. She no join clubs, take sewing, or piano. She no do nothing but lump around the shop with a bunch of old futs, and go movies every night. You grounded till you show interest in something. *Anything.*"

Bunny smiled and resumed eating.

"What's your hang-up, kid?" Harry O. said, pointing his chopsticks at me. "I no give a damn if you fricken Einstein reincarnated——no interests, no apply your brains, you useless."

I couldn't believe it. I managed Heads by Harry, answered phones, organized the bills, and rang up the register. I hunted with my father and knew plants and trees, endemic and indigenous birds and mammals, geology and geography from the miles we walked in the forests of the Big Island. I talked pig, goat, quail, and pheasant with the old-timers and learned the art of bullshit and storytelling. I painted game bird and mammal faces with expensive artist's brushes that I chose myself. Those were my interests. School learning for me took place in a capsule with no relevance to what I knew or cared about. And I was *just like him.*

I left the table quietly so as not to increase my grounding or get a slap to the side of my head with Harry O.'s chopsticks. Climbing up the back stairs to the living quarters above the shop, I watched moviegoers across the street pay Mr. Santos for their tickets, Mrs. Mei Ling scuttling around the concession in her slip-on stilettos, girlfriends in varsity jackets, boyfriends with Big Dips and popcorn.

Paula and Franjelica posed in the yellow light outside of Heads by Harry. Paula looked up and saw me leaning out of the window. "Where your brother?" she asked.

"Gone," I said.

"Too bad," she said, giving Franjelica an elbow to the side. They both laughed a silly inside joke. "So what, Toni, like suck a duck?"

"Suck your duck? Fuck you, Paula. I thought you cut off your duck? You guys better move away from the front of the shop. Harry O. just pau eating dinner, and if he see you guys out front—you the one going suck a stuff duck. What you hungry for? Mallard?"

"He blow my mind," Franjelica said, flinging her pink feather boa over her shoulder. "Fricken Harry, like his business hours should interfere with ours, no, Paula? We bring the men eyes to his stinken loser shop, no, Paula? And he lucky we like Shelly, and treat him like our sister, no, Paula?" The two hookers, swearing and swaying down Mamo Street, hustled toward Elsie's.

Bunny trudged into the room and laid out her clothes for the first day of school. "Get off of Sheldon's bed," she said to me. "He coming home, you know, and you better not put your smell on his bed."

I knew he'd be home, but for now, his not inhabiting a *single space* was exhilarating. I stared at the empty spot on the wall where Maverick's graduation picture used to be, full of O-rings of Scotch tape that Sheldon neglected to peel off the wall when he hurriedly packed the photo in his suitcase. I stared at Bunny writing in her stupid diary.

He'd be home. But he left a drawer full of his Sassoon jeans and Izod polo shirts, brand-new with the tissue paper still in them, left them at home probably because they didn't fit into his new college look. I claimed those jeans and shirts as mine, he being gone and all, jeans and shirts to last me the first two weeks of school without once repeating a color.

Harry O. told me that tigers lived in Pana'ewa. We were walking through rain forests covered with kūkae maile vines engulfing the native trees. The air was heavy with the stench of feces.

The tigers lurked in the forests that were overrun with green swords of yellow and white ginger, African tulip trees, and sweet waiawī. The honohono grass was so high that it came up to the fluorescent-orange hunting hat Harry O. wore everywhere since he started balding.

When I was seven, he'd take Bunny and me to get the dripping skulls of animal heads. "You wait in the Willys," he'd tell us. "Damn pack of wild dogs up that old house, and you know what else, right? The tiii-gggaaas," he'd say like a Vincent Price vampire taxidermist. "I treat you ice shave at Itsu's after," he'd always add, which was never enough to get Sheldon in the Willys, but enough for Bunny and me to grab a couple of Archie comics for the long wait and old dishtowels to cover our noses and mouths after Harry O. had hauled the heads into the back of the Jeep.

It was just me this time, now that Sheldon was in Honolulu and Bunny was at Kaiko'o Mall with Mommy for back-to-school shopping. And thankfully, there were no tigers.

I watched my father's head fade into the honohono grass as I waited in the old Willys Jeep. I sat there the same way I did when I was a child wanting to see him boil the sheep or goat heads in the fifty-gallon drum outside of the abandoned plantation house, light the fire for him, and sit by the burning smell of kiawe wood, raw wool, and old meat, the wild aroma of the boiling carcass stew.

Slowly I got out of the Jeep to follow the trodden path of honohono Harry O. left on his way to the abandoned house. I saw no piles of wild dog shit for me to estimate the approximate time of excretion, but near a clearing ahead of me, I saw Harry O. with a green garden hose, my father shooting water into Rubbermaid trash cans lined with garbage bags and hundreds of maggots inching their white translucent bodies along the insides of the cans.

"I was wondering when you would get the balls to follow me in, Toni," he said without looking at me. "All these years I been waiting. Where the tiii-gggaas?" He laughed, turning the spray of the hose on me, then spraying maggots off his own feet. A profusion of red seedlike maggot casings, black-ashen discharge, and the murky, rancorous smell of something dead made a river that led into a puddle near my feet.

"Check this out. Check out the eyeball. I don't know why the maggots never eat the eyeball. Look, the skull all eaten up like this, but the eyeball turn yellow like one devil cat eye." I stepped back from the smell, the maggots creeping toward my feet, all around us now in pools of yellow-green water. "Go over there and sit down." He pointed toward the broken steps of the old house. "You just as bad as your tunta bro . . ." He stopped himself from saying more.

Sheldon still bothered him. It was my brother he wanted standing by his side in the pool of maggot water. But I stepped closer, the air putrid and gamy, breathing in deeper until it smelled sweetly primal. My father looked at me for a moment. "Check out the ear," he told me. "See all the black egg casings that never hatch? Look like fat blood ticks all

lined up on each other, what you think? You like me pull
one out and smash um so you can see inside?"

"Yeah," I told him.

The smiling pig grimaced with its moss-rotting, blackened
molars, tusks dripping yellow water, and its long pink jaw-
bone still covered with strands of meat. Maggots poured their
fattened bodies out of holes in the skull, falling in clumps on
top of each other into the water. "I thought you boiled the
heads, Daddy? All this time, that's what I thought you was
doing back here."

"I never boil the heads long time already," he said to me.
"All that boiling brought the wild dogs. Just like I making
one giant stew back here, and they come around snarling at
me like I the chef and they the hungry ones. Flies, they just
squeeze their fat bodies into the trash can and one, two weeks
later, the maggots hatch, and eat the heads down to nothing."
My father spat into the foamy yellow water. When I was a
little girl, I'd spit too. And my father would laugh.

"Was hard dumping all that boiling water without burning
my feet, and catching the backsplash. That's why I dump the
heads in the trash cans. I tie um up good so the dogs cannot
take um. Dirty bastards, they eat rotten meat if they could,
but I cannot let them, eh? I saving the heads for the maggots."

I let it go silent for a long time and resisted a shudder as
Harry O. finished up the job. I thought he would make me
carry the head, pull it out for him from the dark cavernous
opening of the trash can. "You get balls, Toni?" he said after
washing down the entire carcass and the trash can.

"Yeah, I get balls, why?"

My father laughed a vampire laugh. "Okay then, girl with
balls." He paused like he was going to make me do it. "Open
that clean trash bag on the steps for me. No like stink up my
Willys, eh?"

I held myself up. He knew what I was thinking, that I didn't want to touch the pig head. But Harry O. dumped the head in himself, then carried the trash bag down the winding path of honohono, and into the sweet smell of the yellow and white gingers.

"Here," he said, pulling his pocketknife from his back pocket. "Pick some gingers for your mommy's kitchen. Cut the whole stalk." And so I did.

With the windows of the Willys open, the smell of wild ginger and pig head so rich my head swirled, Harry O. and I headed toward Itsu's for an azuki and vanilla ice cream shave ice, his treat.

In the Science II class that Bunny and I took together, the few loser seniors wandered in to the back of the room and slouched on the lab tables. The advanced placement sophomores sat upright in the front rows, textbooks jacketed with brown grocery-bag paper.

The highlight of the first week was the lab where Mr. Rocha taught us how to eat a concoction of dirt and crumbled Oreos we made in our beakers in case we ever got stranded in a desert.

Another highlight was the excursion we took every month. I realized then how differently the smart were treated from the average and the dumb. Giftedness was measured by the number of extras—excursions, guest speakers, films, and new, updated textbooks—a student was entitled to.

In Science II, we went to Punaluʻu Beach down in Kaʻū to see biologist Charlotte Forbes tag green sea turtles, to the Panaʻewa Zoo to feed the billy goats, to the Humane Society in Puna to clean dog cages, to the Geological Survey up at the volcano to clean Reggie Okamura's scientist-in-charge office, and the national park's Resource Management Division to observe the nesting nēnē goose and to pound fences.

All of these community connections culminated in a huge fourth quarter project for the Big Island Science Fair of endless slide shows, storyboards, and data. Mr. Rocha's students always beat out students from other schools on the island, some going on to place in the state and national science fairs. Their faces and projects graced the front page of *The Hawaii Tribune Herald.*

When it was time to select a partner—and I was no dummy about the *right* partnerships—I looked at Bunny with a beggar's face that said in expression only, "You and I, please, please, please. I can get the A I need if you choose me for your partner," but she turned her face and body toward a college-prepping Priscilla Tamura, and linked arms with her.

I felt Lynette Vasconcellos breathing down my neck. I think that in spite of the fact that she was Ms. Everything— cheerleader, homecoming queen, May Day queen, and Baddest Body four years in a row in the Hoss Elections, titles that any girl would want to possess in three lifetimes—we all knew that whoever partnered with Lynette would probably do all the dirty work, and then be forced to share half the credit with her.

"Me and you, Toni," she said at last. "I get one bad-ass idea."

"No way in hell" was my first thought, but before my second thought came to me, Lynette went on.

"Maverick and Wyatt hunting pigs up the Volcano National Park, right? So couple weekends when Mavs and Wyatt had to run the pig dogs, I went with them. And when Wyatt running the dogs, me and Mavs go in the bushes, and make out in volcano, how you like that? So fuckin' romantic poking in the wilderness. Only thing, the pili grass stiff and get stuck in my panty, shit, poke my ass and my choch all the way back to Hilo. But what the fuck, I still on the Pill, so I no give a fuck if a fuckin' grass poke my ass. Ai, he rhyme. So what, Toni? Me and you?"

"And what was the idea?" I asked her. I don't know why I asked her. If I had followed her tangent on the Pill or feigned deafness, but stolen her idea, it might never have begun. It was the pigs. It was Harry O. I knew I would please my father. I wanted the *idea.* The idea came with Lynette.

"We go do our project on pig eliminations in the Hawai'i Volcanoes National Park. No, what's the word? Emancipations?"

"Eradication?"

"Yeah, that's the one. Wow, so what, think you smart, hah, Toni? So what, you like partner with me?" She said this like it should be my honor to agree as she smeared a waxy coat of red lipstick over her juicy mouth.

And so it was. A pig project. Every day in science class that fourth quarter, it was me in the library, and Lynette in Jap bathroom smoking cigarettes before cheerleader practice after school. Me in the UH-Hilo library Friday nights, Lynette waiting in the parking lot with Maverick listening to Heatwave on his 8-track. Me talking into a tape recorder with the old-timers for my authentic field data, Lynette going to see *Xanadu* at the Mamo Theatre with Maverick.

I had a stack of index cards that Mr. Rocha showed us how to take notes on, spent days and nights in the library, and read article after article. But it proved to be quite useless compared to just talking story with Harry O. and his hunting friends—better than all my searches on the microfiche.

My conversations with them always started civilly enough

each afternoon when I'd ask my first scripted question and click the tape recorder on:

"What do wild Euro-Polynesian pigs do to the ecosystem?"

"So what if the goshdarn pigs are rooting up all the endangered plants?" Harry O. began. He was self-conscious at first, knowing the tape recorder was on, so he talked haolified. "By golly, that's our recreation, and my bread and butter, and I am against them killing my fun and my income. Maverick told me they cannot even haul out the pigs for the meat or to mount, nothing. They leave the pigs to waste there. Hey now, that's what I call harming the ecosystem." Harry O. loved to use better words than the other old-timers. "I can talk like them scientist guys, too. What you old futs think?"

Everyone laughed but Mr. Santos. "No hold nothing against my boys, eh, Harry O.," he said. "From what Maverick tell me, the damn pigs the one messing up all the plants. They no hunt the pigs, we ain't got forests."

I never had to ask a second question.

"Nah, not the kids' fault, that's the feds' fault. Goddamn feds coming in, and making like they God's gift to rules and regs and trees and bushes, sheez," Harry O. said quickly. This marked the end of civility, and as their voices rose, Harry O. passed out more beer.

"My boys get full-time work," Mr. Santos continued, defending his sons, "and they doing what they like to do for pretty good pay. And my Wyatt getting a paycheck without a damn diploma, how you like that? Gee, you think in this day and age, you need your high school diploma to get a good job, but eh, he working that federal job while I sitting in that ticket booth across the street," Mr. Santos bragged.

"We hold nothing against your kids. That's good they're getting paid. But you know what I heard?" Uncle Herb asked, always wanting to get in his two intellectual cents, which earned him the nickname of the King of Clichés for such wisdom as "reach for the stars," "go for the gusto," and "smell the proverbial coffee."

"The animal rights activists, they're on *our side,* because pigs have babies like bunnies, so Wyatt and Maverick are forced to hunt the fastest way, which is with pig dogs. And they have to leave the pigs there to save time, right? Sometimes the pigs aren't even dead yet. Now *that's* kind of inhumane, don't you think?" Uncle Herb added, and then laughed with the rest of the old-timers. "Inhumane, how do you like them apples? The animal rights activists are angry because one little piggy's bleeding to death in the forest. But hey, at least they're on our side. Inhumane is we cannot smoke the meat, right, Harry?"

"I thought they was shooting the pigs from the helicopter," Harry O. asked.

"How dense can you be?" Uncle Herb said. "Smell the damn coffee." Only he talked to Harry O. like he was still little brother. "It costs so much insurance and all that liability, gas, and pay the pilot, and only *one* shooter can go inside the helicopter. They waste my tax dollars when they do that. Sheez, I'd lodge a complaint to the goddamn President myself."

"Eh, Toni," Harry O. said to me, "turn off the tape recorder. I get one good idea for your project. Why not take in the pig head I mounted for Lionel, a couple of pig balls marble bags that I tanned last month, and tusk necklaces, stuff like that. Take in jawbones and tell how the Pa-kes grind up the bones for medicine. That's true, the Pa-kes cure arthritis with pig bone, right, Herb? I seen pig bones in a Chinatown shop. Show your teacher all the rotten pig teeth. And tell um about Kamapua'a."

Then Mr. Santos spoke. "My tūtū told me stories about the pig god. He was handsome, that Kamapua'a, with all his rippling muscles. And he like to make babies and eat and root. But the pigs my boys killing is not the Polynesian pig. They been interbreeding with the European pig for centuries. But, Toni, you teach the legends. I help you."

"Lots of hands-on. Bring Lionel in as a cultural expert. Teachers love that stuff. How do I know?" Uncle Herb postured. "I was a principal for twenty-two years, and I've been married to Mildred for what, twenty-four years, so I know a thing or two about what teachers like in student projects."

"Ho, the henpeck sonofabitch," Mr. Santos roared, "he remember the *exact* number of years he been marry. How you guys like that? How long you been marry, Niso-san?"

"Too damn long."

"See, Herb, you get ball and chain around your balls."

Without reacting, Uncle Herb continued, "Like I was saying, Toni, why don't you take in some smoked pig meat as samples . . ."

"And the pig feet ashtrays I made," Harry O. added. "You seen the ashtrays, Ute? Niso-san get couple of them in his store. I give you for your wife before you go home tonight. Tell her, 'Here, honey, I brang you some pig feet.'"

"Daddy, can I take pictures of you guys hunting?"

"Yeah, yeah, we go put on our army fatigues and paint our face black and green. What you old futs think?"

"No, let's just take normal photographs right here in front of the shop," Uncle Herb said.

Harry O. sighed. "Okay then, make sure the name Heads by Harry in all the pictures. So what, Toni? You for this pig eradication or you against it?"

"I don't know yet."

"You don't know? Toni ma dear, you *against* it. No ifs, ands, or buts, you hear me?"

"Yeah, you hear your daddy?" It was Mr. Ute, who hardly said a word.

"This kid, she always like be one martyr, that's what Mary Alice always says. What do you say to Mr. Ute, Toni?"

"Okay, Mr. Ute."

"Not 'okay, Mr. Ute,'" the old man said sternly. "You tell your daddy."

"Okay, Daddy."

"Thank you, Toni ma dear," my father said, first toasting me with his beer, then bowing deeply. When he was drunk, I always made him happy. A good martyr, all these years, even if only for him.

My father takes a picture of me, my long hair drawing breath in the wind. There is the mountain behind me, Mauna Ke'a, specter of white snow.

Mommy brushes Bunny's hair. Sheldon practices a smile in a hand mirror he brings from home.

I wear a little girl's red pinafore with lacy socks and white patent-leather shoes.

"Smile, Toni. Smile. Hurry up, Toni. You beautiful, ma dear. Smile. C'mon, dammit."

The sun in my eyes, winter sun, radiant and white, my breath is visible vapor in front of my mouth.

How beautiful would I be with the sun in my eyes?

He counts to three and I turn my gaze downward. A park maintenance man pulls up to a trash can nearby in a rusty Cushman.

"Eh, bruddah, take couple of shots for the Christmas card."

Harry O. makes *Mele Kalikimaka from the Yagyuus* photo-cards at Niso Camera Shop every year.

He gets off the Cushman. "Sure. Sure. One. Two. Three."

Sun in my eyes, I look away, toward the Bayfront, into the shade of the monkeypod trees.

For years, they accuse me of ruining that Christmas card photo. Harry O. makes a hundred copies for all the relatives and friends to teach me a lesson.

But in that photograph, I am the only one who looks beautiful, eyes wide and longing for shade, Mauna Ke'a, celestial, infinite behind me.

For a month, Lynette and I went every weekend to the Volcanoes National Park with Wyatt and Maverick. I remember the quality of the air and its clean slice through clothing and skin, the colic of cold. This project was *for me* —to take pictures and help feed the pig dogs; *for me*—to help clean the dog cages; *for me*—to bathe them and then run them.

I did all of this as Lynette sunbathed half naked in the bed of the truck. We chopped burlap-bagsful of romaine lettuce to feed the nēnē goose in the reserve while Lynette flirted with the haole rangers outside the goose pens.

Everybody at the shop jumped in on my project:

Niso-san developed all my pictures for free on expensive Kodak paper, enlarging the ones of wild pigs, and then teaching me how to use his Minolta with a zoom lens for even better shots;

Mr. Ute imitated the different pig grunts into a tape recorder for background sounds for my display—an hour of the old man pig grunting boar, sow, and piglets;

Mommy wrote recipes and created a display for the preparation of smoked pig meat;

Harry O. started a wild pig products storyboard for the tanned pig balls bags, pig feet ashtrays and gun racks, a huge boar's head, and tanned curlicue piggy tails made into key chains.

Bunny's project with Priscilla Tamura paled in the light of our family's concerted efforts. Her project, "Caffeine: The Body's Demise," consisted of serving coffee to the old-timers and taking their heart rates with a stethoscope before and after, and lo and behold, their heart rates increased after their morning coffee.

"This real intellectual stuff Bunny doing," Harry O. would say proudly. "All 'cause she going be the first doctor in the family. You know how doctors always researching what no good for your body, eh? You like me get some raw coffee beans from my friend down Kapoho? He get couple trees in his yard. Test what happen if you chew the raw bean."

"You croak, I think," Mr. Santos said. "Some test. Who like be Bunny's first ma-ke die-dead volunteer?" The old men cracked up.

My sister grinned sheepishly. After a while of this, Bunny knew her project was a big stinker. "I want to be your partner, Toni," she said one day in front of all the old-timers, Mommy, and Mrs. Mei Ling. "You doing most of the research all by yourself. I can help you if Lynette not doing her part. And if you and me team up, maybe we can take first place."

Bunny looked at Mommy and Mrs. Mei Ling like she meant this from her heart, to help me. "I can give Priscilla all my research and the whole project, which is almost pau anyway. I finished the display and the ten-page research paper."

"Toni needs help 'cause she has your good-for-nothing future daughter-in-law as her partner," Mommy said to Mrs. Mei Ling, giving her a playful body bump.

"Eh, no talk like that before come true. You know, Mary Alice, I don't know what Maverick see in that wāhine. I mean, she smart like a rock and she tita, tita, tita. I never heard such a rotten, filthy-ass mouth as hers. That's the trouble with boys—they no see nothing past the big tits and the legs spreading wide . . . and, well, what the girl see in my Maverick . . . well . . ."

"Nice ass," I thought.

"Hey, hey, hey," Mr. Santos warned, "not in front the kids."

"Best they know," Mommy said to him, "so these two ain't whores in the bushes with any Tom, Dick, or Henry." Mommy put her arm around my shoulders, coming in for the kill, I could smell it: "And, Toni, maybe you our martyr, but you ain't a whore. And I hope you let your sister be your partner. You know what Mommy always says, right? Blood run thicker than water."

The end all of the be-all was the blood and the water.

I wanted first place in the Science Fair, my picture in *The Hilo Viking* and *The Hawaii Tribune Herald*, framed on the wall in Heads by Harry—just me and maybe Lynette on the side taking her false credit. But tigers and sister, blood running thicker than water, there was nothing for me to say.

So it was Bunny, Wyatt, and me that next weekend in the back of the truck. Lynette and Maverick sat cut-seat in the front, two heads, one driver. Wyatt laid his huge body in the bed of the truck for the long ride to Volcano. He rested his legs on my lap and talked trash.

"Women, they just like pigs."

He monologued like he was on something that made him babble his two-bit analogies and philosophies: "Sometimes best you leave them there to die, 'cause you give them chance and they come crawling back to bug your ass. 'Take me back, honey. Give me second chance. I *never* fucking around on you again.' But if you let her die the first time you had her bleeding in the forest, would've been better for you. That's what I think."

"Oh, God," I said.

"Yes?" he answered.

"Wyatt, you're such an asshole," Bunny said.

"I have a huge black asshole. Thank you very much."

We did this every day of Spring Break until Lynette, the hypochondriac, sprained her ankle and couldn't walk from the truck to the dog kennels. Simultaneously, she got an allergic reaction to the sulfur from the volcano compounded with the pollen from the 'ōhi'a lehua in bloom.

So Bunny and Maverick rode in the front. Wyatt kicked me with his dirty boots to "Tell Maverick stop at Hirano Store," or "Light me one cigarette, Toni. My bag behind you," or "Cover me with that sleeping bag." Burp. Fart.

"Women, they just like pigs. You hunt um. You sniff um. You poke um. You leave um." I always rode in the back with Wyatt, my sister hopping in front with Maverick even when I got there first, squeezing her way to the door, and pushing on in. She'd turn and wave from the front periodically and I'd watch her laughing and joking with Maverick, easy bodies. Bunny steered at one point as Maverick reached for his sunglasses and cigarettes, the brush of his hand over her long arm, then a soda in a cooler by Bunny's feet and the momentary tango of their other uninvolved limbs.

"The way I think," Wyatt interrupted my staring, "is fuck it if they cannot take a joke, know what I mean?" He put his bush of hair into a ponytail and sucked his teeth.

"What the hell are you talking about, Wyatt?" I told him. "You talking bubbles."

He sat his bulk of a chest up and took off his shirt. "Feel this, Toni," he said, holding out his strong brown biceps to me. "C'mon, c'mon, cold, you know. I getting nipple hard-ons." And when I refused to touch him, he said, "Fuck it if you cannot take a joke. You get this upside your head." He acted like he was going to backhand my face but instead slapped his hand to his other hand by my ear.

"Eh, fuck off, Wyatt." He gave me a shove to the shoulder and lay back with his arms behind his head. He sneered at me and used my lap for a footrest. "Loser. Pig. Dropout. Ass-hole. Punk. Get your feet off of me."

"Ooohh, talk dirty, Toni, you turning me on, fucking boner the size of a horse dick, yes, yes, yes," an orgasmic crescendo in his voice. Maverick turned to see his brother jeering, prob-ably thinking we were having a good time together, as we turned into the park headquarters.

Every day of Spring Break and every weekend before Bunny started coming along as my inherited partner, Billy Harper, the chief naturalist's seventh-grade son, tagged along to help Maverick and Wyatt. Bunny stayed at Maverick's side, Wyatt with a joint hanging from his lips as he shot the dog shit from the kennels.

Billy Harper and I talked old times when he was a fifth grader in Mommy's class, practically living at our house in the days when Mommy took in waifs, particularly haole waifs, who were outsiders and pariahs in her classroom full of haole-hating locals.

She'd take them under her wing, underdogs she'd elevate to unsurpassed admiration from classmates who'd envy the special treatment, but underdogs who'd never forget her sav-ing them from the brutality of the other children. She'd hanai them the Hawaiian way—no legal documents but adopted by our family.

And one year, it was Billy, without his real mother and living with a stepmother and half sisters. Sheldon never liked the intrusion of children except for Billy. "Poor thing," Sheldon would say. "No cable or radio in Volcano Village, you know? What torture on poor Billy. And he's so cute, dammit."

Billy and I scrubbed down the dogs with coal-tar shampoo and warm water, Bunny shooting entire rolls of film on Maverick and Wyatt like she worked for *National Geographic*. Billy said to me one day, "You remember, Toni, the time we all went camping down at Waikini and Mrs. Yagyuu let me strap that big knife to my leg?"

"You thought you were a big-game hunter, eh, Billy?" He laughed easily, keeping the soap out of the dog's eyes, putting the excess foam on my arms, and cooing at the dog to keep her calm. "That's the place down Kahuku Ranch?"

"Yeah, well, remember we were driving out and we saw those three billy goats by a cave with the opening that went downwards? Man, I wanted to grab those goats by the horns badly so Mr. Yagyuu could mount me a trophy." Billy smiled softly.

Then he whispered something to the dog, who resisted a water-shake shudder. "Your dad went out of the car and Mrs. Yagyuu and I waited up by the entrance to the cave, and those goats started backing up butt first into the cave. So Mr. Yagyuu came back up and put his hands on his waist like this." Billy demonstrated Harry O. acting all macho and big-chested.

"Yeah, and then the three billies stampeded. The biggest one cranked my father in the ass and flew that old bastard up in the air like the Three Stooges." Billy and I laughed and laughed until Wyatt turned around and shot the cold water at the dog between us, causing her to bark and shake water all over us.

"Shut up, shit. We suppose to be working. You want this haole's old man come up here and give us shit. Fuckin' Ranger Harper, damn ugly haole always acting like we don't know what the fuck we doing. And wearing that stupid Dudley Do-Right hat. You tell your father *everything* I said," Wyatt taunted.

"You know, I've been thinking," Billy said after Wyatt stalked off. "Lucky thing I didn't follow Mr. Yagyuu into that cave, because I would've gotten a face butt." We laughed softly so as not to anger Wyatt again.

"Billy, you taller than Toni," Bunny said, walking over with Niso-san's expensive camera, pushing film into the pocket of the khaki vest she wore, muslin work shirt, tight Levi's, and hiking boots. She always looked the part of every part and today she was a *National Geographic* photographer, researcher, scientist on location in the lush, tropical, and exotic landscape of Volcano, Hawai'i.

"I haven't seen Mrs. Yagyuu for a couple of months now. I miss her——you," he said to me, then quickly, "I mean, I miss all of you. I wanted to take her out to the movies and go to the Fun Factory after, my treat. But only if it's an R- or X-rated movie."

"Yeah, right," Wyatt hissed. "I tell my father kick your sorry haole ass out of the theater, shit."

"No mind him, Billy," Maverick said, tying the dogs to the hooks in the truck. "He pissed at your father 'cause we been running this weekend duty for the last couple of months."

Bunny quickly changed the subject. "Come sleep over this weekend, Billy. Get *Everything You Always Wanted to Know About Sex (But Were Afraid to Ask)* at the Mamo. Me and Toni take you in." Bunny already started moving her body to the front door of the truck.

"Eh, Toni," Wyatt grunted, "come hold this nasty grey-hound. He like you, that's why. You get your rags or something? He can smell when you in heat. You in heat, Toni, you bitch?" Wyatt sniffed the air and then nodded an affirmative.

"Ooohh, gross," Bunny squeaked.

"He likes Toni because she keeps the soap out of his eyes when she bathes him." Billy looked at me with his deep amber eyes rimmed with dark eyelashes. "I'll ask my dad if I can stay the weekend with you. Are you sure Mrs. Yagyuu won't mind?"

"Mind? Since when do you worry if we mind when you drop in for one day, two days, a week?" I ask him.

"I missed you," he whispered again.

"You said that," I told him, then changed the subject. "I hope you don't mind eating fish head and bitter melon."

"My favorite," Billy said.

"Yeah, right," Wyatt said to him. "Haoles only eat bake potato and prime rib. I never seen one haole in my whole life handle the homegrown grinds." He leaned his arm against the truck right between Billy and me. "And how come *you* talk haole when you around this haole?" He moved around me like a wary wild dog, tiger eyes glaring at me.

Maverick gunned the engine and all of the dogs yanked forward and back to regain their balance, the scratch of dog nails on steel.

"What happened to Maverick's girlfriend? She came a couple of times, right, Toni?" Billy whispered to me.

"Why, what's it to you, hah, haole?" Wyatt said, flicking ash at Billy.

"Eh, fuck off, Wyatt," I said like I meant it.

"Why, what's it to you, hah, Toni?"

"Billy practically lived in our house the whole year he was

in my mother's class and the next year too. He's family to us. That's what it is to me."

"Oh, yeah? How can haoles be like family, hah?" Wyatt spat over the side of the truck and wiped a spit trail with the back of his hand. "Well, fuck it if you cannot take a joke, Toni. Haole-loving bitch." I saw Billy's face harden and his fists clench as I shrugged my shoulders and sighed.

"Maybe Maverick get new girlfriend, what you think, Toni?" Wyatt said, head-jerking to the cab of the truck. He watched me hard for a reaction to his remark. "They been laughing it up in there."

"So."

"You wish was you?" he said.

Billy turned, then looked at me. I met his gaze. I said nothing, but watched my sister flirt with Maverick like no Lynette, the cat's away, and the mouse didn't mind playing with fire. Lynette could kick my sister's ass to the moon and back with one leg tied to one arm.

"She better not," I said at last, more to myself than to Wyatt. "Maverick's taken." The truck yanked to a halt with Bunny and Maverick getting out to help untie the dogs.

"I been saving all the pig balls so your father can make me some bags," Wyatt said, hopping out of the truck. "And I been slicing off all the feet to make ashtrays for me and the boys. I get them wrapped in newspaper in the big freezer behind the theater." He took a Ziploc bag from the pocket of his army jacket.

"Ooohh, what's that?" Bunny squeaked in her acting-cute-and-dainty voice.

From the bag, Wyatt pulled some blood-hardened pig ears. "No need," Maverick said. "No need do that in front Bunny."

"Bunny? What was that?" Maverick didn't even bother to answer me.

"When the dogs think we looking for pig, they run faster, and we go home more early," Wyatt said. The dogs barked and howled, pulling at their ropes as Wyatt and Maverick released them one by one. The dust rose, fine Volcano dust into a northerly wind. I listened to the dogs crying their way into the brush, chasing a pig who had lost his ear.

Sheldon's collect calls started sometime into the second day after his dramatic departure from the Hilo airport. He cried fake tears, fake hugged, and waved and turned around at the top of the escalator.

He gave a theatrical last look at the entrance to the jetway, the swivel of his head, then body, chin held high, trooper that he was, Kleenex a gossamer scarf in his trailing hand.

Goodbye, goodbye. I shall return.

So Sheldon called us collect nearly every day.

Yet he spent Thanksgiving that first year away with a friend named Terry Tanaka on Maui. So much for homesickness.

He came home for Christmas to collect his gifts.

He spent Spring Break with another friend, Dale Nakamura, on Kaua'i.

He'd call some days, and I'd be the only one at home, so he'd chitchat with me. "So what," he said, "Bunny still pissed off at me for calling her a false Hilo townie?"

"Yeah, why? Why you tell her all that?" I asked him. "You eating your fingernails? I can hear you crunching something."

"No, I ain't biting no more and don't change the subject. Better that Bunny hear from me before she comes up to Honolulu acting like a hot shit false townie, when all she is is a country jack."

I thought about Bunny's new look, which had changed since Maverick started taking us to school, us and Lynette. I went along for the *moment of awe* when we pulled into the parking lot and exited the Jeep, how the gawkers associated me in their minds with Maverick Santos and Lynette Vasconcellos.

Bunny's new look was super-Shiseido calendar girl/Pola/Kanebo/Naris model with blue and pink eye shadow and false eyelashes to rival Lani Moo, the Meadow Gold Dairymen's mascot cow. Her lips puckered pink frost lipstick and she made Farrah Fawcett flips in her streaked-with-peroxide hair.

"Honolulu chicks make mincemeat out of chicks like Bunny from Hilo," Sheldon went on. "Even Pearl City girls are false townies to the Honolulu chicks." My brother was a sudden expert on everything Honolulu.

"Why, she look nice to us, kind of," I said. "And what's it to you, anyway? You don't even come home. You think you too good for us?" I stared across the room at Bunny's huge photo taken at the Kiawe Photo Studio, a photo session of model poses for the new look, cleavage, and an eight-by-ten for Maverick.

Sheldon squealed down the hall, "Terry, wait for me. I want to go to Zippy's with you guys." My brother was speaking perfect English! "Okay, Toni, I must go. Tell Harry O. I want fifty bucks for the dorm banquet, please."

"Ask him yourself."

"C'mon, please, Toni."

"No."

"When Mommy and Harry O. going Vegas for that American Association of Taxidermists convention? I have to ask him for some money before he leaves. If he comes back all pi-lut again, I'll never get blood from that stone, let alone fifty bucks."

"They leaving right when you pau finals. Mommy wanted you to come home so that you could run the shop. Me and Bunny got school till June."

"Well, I ain't coming home till after the first summer session. So you and Bunny run the shop. I'm coming, Terry, on my way," my brother said silky-voiced down the hall. "I have to go. Terry's cute, you know. Fifty bucks, okay?"

"That's a boy or a girl, Terry?"

"What do you think?" my brother asked. "No, never mind, don't answer that. I'll be right there, Terry. Ta ta, Toni."

The day after Mommy and Harry O. left for the taxidermists' convention in Las Vegas, I opened the shop at 6:30 a.m. with a hot pot of coffee and Holy Bakery apple pie with melted cheese for the old-timers. I answered a couple of early orders for stuffed birds. Uncle Herb took over for me on days when he didn't have ukulele classes at the senior citizens' center. I hurried back to the shop as soon as school let out because Bunny had cheerleader practice or student government meetings or May Day court rehearsals. I stayed open until 6:30 at night.

I did all of that for Harry O.'s promise to buy for me a good present from Las Vegas and split his winnings on the dollar slots. Every year at the American Association of Taxidermists convention in Vegas, Harry O. would gamble his money away to nothing and bring me home a T-shirt that said, *My Father Went to Las Vegas and All I Got Was This Ugly T-Shirt.*

I'd get that and a week's worth of Harry O. grumbling on and on about the rotten odds at the California and the Fremont Hotel. And all those goddamn rednecks from hick places like Hicksboro and Spoonerville who made Mommy and him sit by the kitchen door because they were Japs. And looking

at them, he always said, like they were the ones who bombed
Pearl Harbor. But the next year he'd go with Mommy for the
tax write-off, all-you-can-eat seafood and prime rib buffets,
and another shot at the dollar slots.

Their trip always came near the end of school, and this
year, to make coverage of the shop more difficult, Bunny
secured herself a place in the prestigious Junior Houseband
as one of the lead female singers, when, to tell the truth, she
could not sing to rival a bulimic frog.

On most of the numbers, the Junior Houseband let her play
the tambourine and mostly wanted her there for the look of
the popular Bunny Yagyuu gracing their band with her Dan-
skins binding big boobs, her stilettos hoisting long, tanned
legs. My sister looked hapa and everyone always asked if she
were half Portuguese, half Japanese. She looked like a tall,
auburn-haired Susan Anton, especially her lips.

"They're letting me sing 'You Light Up My Life' for the
opening number all by myself, you know, Toni," she said to
me one afternoon in the shop. Bunny leaned her elbows on
the glass showcase. "You coming to see the show?"

"How can I? Who covering for me?"

Maverick walked into the shop and stood behind Bunny,
leaning in toward her body. She breathed lightly, not turning
around. "So what, Bunny? Where the pictures you took of me
up Volcano? I like see. The pictures," he said almost into her
neck.

My sister's voice purred, "Upstairs in my bedroom. Come
up and get it yourself." I watched the turn of her face, the
movement of her hair, timed like a good movie love scene
starring who else, Susan Anton. "I put it in my panty drawer."
At the mention of panty drawer, Maverick nearly creamed
his jeans.

"I help you finish your project," Maverick said to Bunny,

who now moved her body to face his, his arms around her leaning on the glass showcase. "No need cook dinner, Toni. Me and Bunny going down Cafe 100. After I look. At the pictures." All of this was said with the two of them staring into each other's eyes.

Bunny sidled to the back door, turning back to look at Maverick as she mounted the back stairs, like Susan Anton giving her lover that come-hither-to-my-boudoir look, so easy and smooth like she was born to move with sexual grace. An hour later, the two of them still upstairs, I felt sick. I contended with Sheldon's obsession with Maverick, and now Bunny, who I couldn't understand.

Maverick was beneath her goal of marrying a college-educated haole so that she'd have a haole last name and hapa children. So that when Lynette walked into the shop, I was almost happy to think that my sister's ass might be kicked by the tita of all titas.

"Where Maverick, Toni? Wyatt said he came over here to look at the pictures *we* shot for *our* project." Lynette had a bad habit of getting the pronouns wrong whenever she talked about *my* project.

"You finishing up tonight, right?" she continued. "Maverick suppose to take me Poly Room to meet my cousins Angela and Chiquita. Then he suppose to rent me a room for my grad night party at the Hukilau Hotel. Who stay up there with him?"

"Bunny had to get the pictures. I had to stay in the shop. I can call them for you." My fingers trembled as I dialed the upstairs number. "Hi . . . hi, Bunny—tell Maverick—Lynette down here waiting for him."

Maverick bounded down the back stairs, still tucking in his shirt, which was buttoned crookedly. "Eh, babes, whassup?" he said, pecking her cheek. Bunny slinked down the stairs and stood at the back door of the shop. She let the spaghetti strap from her blouse slip off her shoulder, the damn actress.

"So what? I thought we was eating oxtail soup at Jimmy's tonight. And then we was meeting Angela and Chiquita down the Poly Room? So what, you showered already? You smell like a pig, honey." Lynette took a whiff off of Maverick's neck and pursed her lips, eyes tightening.

Maverick turned ever so slightly to look at Bunny. And then at me. "I picking up dinner for Toni and Bunny. We watching them till their parents come back from Vegas. Every year like that——we take care of them. Beforetime, they use to stay at our house. Sheldon too."

"Wow, what about me?" Lynette shoved Maverick in his chest. "You fuckin' acting like we never had plans. I like smash your face." Lynette's eyes caught the purple hickey on Bunny's neck way in the back of the shop after my sister moved her hair to cover it. "Eh, Bunny. Who gave you that muffler burn? I thought you and Cary was pau? And who was up there if your parents went Vegas?"

"I tell you after," Bunny said. "Toni has a big mouth, you know. She might tell my mother. I figure this hickey from Cary be gone by the time they come back from Vegas, if I ice it with one frozen spoon." Lynette and Bunny laughed so uncomfortably that I felt myself melting behind the counter.

"I taught Bunny that, Mavs, you better not ever forget," she said, staring right at my sister. Then coiling around to Maverick: "Remember the time we had the house all to ourself? The time my mother went my Uncle Big Boy's funeral in Maui? You sucked my neck and tits raw till I had three black-and-blue necklaces. Remember, babe? I couldn't walk good for three days from all the plunging we did." She was staking her claim as she sniffed his neck. "So what? What time you like Angela pick you up?"

I was so afraid. She knew. She knew everything. Lynette was fucking with everybody's head.

"I cannot go tonight, Lynette. I helping Toni and Bunny finish your project. Eh, babes, you getting the credit for this too, so better if I help little bit. You cannot grad without this science credit, right?"

Lynette looked nervous as she calculated whether we were on to her lazy science project sponge number or whether she wanted to kill my sister right at this very moment. "Toni," she said at last, "I staying here till my cousins go down Poly Room. You no mind, right, if I stay right here? They all came in from Kona for few days. I cannot dog them 'cause they my cuz, right? And Maverick can help you finish up. I mean, we showing our project at the Science Fair next Wednesday, you know." At least she had the deadline right.

Maverick moved toward the back door. "Lynette, start the project with Toni. Me and Bunny picking up dinner for my father and Butchie. They eating before the first show."

The two of them left through the back door. Lynette was no dummy and that's what scared me the most, knowing that she already smelled this every time we picked her up for school and Bunny got out of the front seat to give it up for her. Every time Bunny got dropped off at the shop after practice or rehearsal, Lynette waved a lazy goodbye, good riddance from the front seat as Maverick drove off. Bunny's every move and Lynette's seething ease with the whole matter gave me a rash.

A few days later, the whole fiasco of the Science Fair unraveled Lynette for good.

Maverick and Wyatt delivered the tape recordings of Mr. Ute pig grunting and the five huge storyboards with pictures to the school auditorium. We unloaded the full body mount of a wild boar, the hot rice and smoked meat cooked up by

Mrs. Santos in my mother's absence, the display items of tanned pig balls, tusks on leather strands, curlicue tail key chains, jawbones, mortars with ground bone, and the big sign that said, "PUAʻA MARTYRDOM: Hawaii's Feral Pig Threatened."

I basked in the ooohhhs and aaahhhs of the teachers and staff as they passed my display. Even Mr. Rocha had to eat his words. "The whole premise of preserving the wild pig is against my environmental stance," he'd said to me one day in class. "I mean, being part Hawaiian myself, I am fully aware of the Kamapuaʻa as native deity and all—but the preservation of our ecosystems for future generations should be of the utmost importance."

Priscilla Tamura's sorry "Caffeine: The Body's Demise" display got nary a second glance. Mr. Rocha and the science department began the interview portion of the competition.

I told Maverick, "Stay with Bunny and Lynette. *Please*. Wyatt driving me home so I can get our truck. Then we can take all this stuff home in one trip." I felt heat, Lynette's anger, and her mind made up to do something today.

So I made up my mind to do something too.

"Hurry up," Wyatt said, pulling at my shirtsleeve. "I like see *us* win first place. That's my hard-ass work in the pictures. I like them fuckas know they never let me grad but that's *me* with that fed job." Wyatt pushed my back toward their truck as I caught a last glimpse of my sister sitting uptight and tense on the stairs.

By the time I got back, Lynette and Bunny were standing on the far side of the auditorium for Lynette's last smoke before the interview. "I nervous," she said, taking a deep drag. "I get too much shit on my mind." She glared at Bunny.

"But what's more important is I have to grad. If I no get this credit, I ain't walking at graduation with my class. What if Mr. Rocha ask me questions and I don't know the answer? I looking sly at you, Toni, and you just pick um up. I try add in little bit to make like I know what the holy fuck you guys talking about." She dragged in deeply. "You that's why," she said harshly at Maverick.

"That's why I said to come up to the house last night," Bunny told her. "So we could practice a little bit. My mother and father not home and we could've stayed up late." Bunny paused and Lynette stared hard at her.

"What you said, Bernice?" Lynette confused me. She *knew* my parents were gone. She knew she needed the science credit. Yet she chose *this moment* to pick a fight with Bunny. It was in her face. She could not back down. "Your parents not at home? Then who the fuck was up there when I came to get Maverick the other night? Was just you and him up there the day I came, right? You ungrateful little Japanee slut." She shoved my sister against the rock wall. "I going kick your ass. You think I stupid, or what?"

Lynette threw her cigarette butt at Bunny. She hit my sister smack across the face. I tried to pull her off of her, but she turned on me. "And you," she said, slapping me across the head, "you covering up for your sister, you two fuckin' whores. I calling my cousins to kick both your asses."

Maverick, Wyatt, Mr. Rocha, and the vice-principal split all of us apart. The VP escorted Lynette off campus after Mr. Rocha whispered something in his ear. He knew that Bunny and I worked on every detail of the project and wanted us to complete the interview portion—to keep his winning record.

"You wait, Bernice. I coming to bust your face so that you never steal nobody else's boyfriend, you backstabbing whore. And you, Toni," Lynette screamed maniacally from across the street, "I thought we was close. You wait, I taking both you

Japs down. Maverick," she yelled, "I ain't pau with you
either."

Bunny wiped her bloody nose and dabbed at a fat eye.
Maverick and Wyatt leaned over the railing and Wyatt spat
hard, saying something about women, all a bunch of pigs. I
put my arm around my sister as we walked toward the judges.

After it was over, we loaded up the trucks slowly, all of us
expecting to see Lynette and her wild cousins turn into the
parking lot at any minute. "She ain't coming," Maverick said.
"Me and Wyatt can drop this off at the shop and tell your
Uncle Herb to close up. I going up Lynette's house after that."
Bunny started crying, her stupid purple hickey heaving in and
out on her neck.

"You fuckas all fucked up," Wyatt said as Maverick drove
the truck onto Waiānuenue Avenue.

"You deserve this," I said to Bunny. "We just need to make
it home and lock the doors. C'mon, hurry."

"I'm sorry, Toni. I'm sorry," Bunny cry-snorted. "I know
you like Maverick too, but I . . ." She stopped, knowing that
I seethed in the seat next to her.

"What? You don't know *nothing*. Never will." I waited at
the stop for an opening in the traffic. As soon as I pulled out
of the school and onto Waiānuenue, a car pulled up in front
of me, and one behind me. The front car slowed, and the
back car hit the rear bumper until we all three came to a
stop.

Lynette, Angela, and Chiquita rushed our truck, pulling
Bunny from the front, Lynette swinging and thrashing my
sister against the school fence. I felt a hand gripping my hair
as I struggled to close the window. I heard glass shattering
behind me as someone's fingers scratched for my eyes. I was
covered with tiny glass cuts. My sister scrambled to get away,

but Lynette took her by the hair and shoved her face into the fence again and again.

I reached under the car seat and frantically searched for the short-barrel 20-gauge that I stuffed there, knowing how afraid I was of Lynette, knowing there was no Mommy or Harry O. around, just Bunny and me—knowing blood runs thicker than water and tigers stalked everywhere.

My hand felt desperately for the old grip, Angela's hand full of my hair, as she pounded at the closed window. I heard nothing but the ringing in my ears, saw my sister's body going limp, and I pulled out the gun. I saw Angela running across the busy street, almost getting hit by a car. I got out of the truck, cranked my father's gun, and fired it toward Lynette. I aimed to miss. Dazed, I watched a scattering of ripped-out hair and screaming banshees. I staggered to my sister and held her, the gun falling beside my collapsing body, police cars, the VP, the sound of men's hard voices unintelligible buzzing to me.

There was an ambulance and handcuffs tight around my wrists in front of me. I touched a bald spot on my head and stared at drops of blood on the sidewalk. Hair, there was hair, swirling around us, hair, fine leaves and flowers on a trellis chain-link fence. The cool early evening, a gray-blue light on in a living room, a single lamp in a dark bedroom, this was the saddest time of day for me, the blue lights spinning.

Four

This headline appeared on the front page of *The Hawaii Tribune Herald*: "Hilo High School Sisters Take First Place in Big Island Science Fair." But I knew what they all wanted to say.

Bernice Yagyuu, grade 11, patch of hair missing, swollen face, mascara swiped in an arc under her eye.

Antoinette Yagyuu, grade 12, torn shirt, eyes afraid, and face lacerated.

This is how I knew my father loved me. Harry O., so proud but so pissed off, glued the article to a piece of cardboard, then put a thumbtack right through my head when he put it on the wall behind the cash register.

This appeared on page two, same day, in *The Hawaii Tribune Herald*'s Police Blotter, which was every nīele Hilo person's favorite gossip column: "Police charged a 17-year-old juvenile with felony possession of a firearm in an altercation outside of Hilo High School. The juvenile, of a Mamo Street address, fired a 20-gauge shotgun at another juvenile late Wednesday afternoon. Police said the victim, 17, of a Kaū-mana address, was treated for superficial injuries at Hilo Hospital."

Harry O. glued this article to a piece of cardboard, then put it up next to the other article with four razor-sharp ar-rowheads in each corner.

After the shooting, Mommy and Harry O. were still in Las Vegas, so Maverick and Wyatt came to get me at the police station.

Maverick spent the next two weeks at Lynette's side begging her to drop the charges against me, which she did eventually for a quarter-carat promise ring from Zales.

And Bunny pretended to be the true victim upon Mommy's return, her hickey faded to bruiselike coloration where "Lynette was choking me. That's why I have so many bruises on my neck."

Harry O. beat the shit out of me for "using my stinken antique mother-of-pearl pistol grip, fricken short-barrel shotgun to murder our neighbor's girlfriend. And making ass of our family with your goddamn nonsense printed in the goddamn paper, in the Police Blotter no less, for the whole goddamn world to see."

"Toni was trying to protect me, Daddy."

"Goddamn martyr."

On the Friday night after their return from Vegas, Mommy and Mrs. Mei Ling made pupus in our kitchen for the old-timers.

"Thanks, Mei Ling," my mother said, "for sending the boys down to bail out Toni." My mother couldn't stop saying thank you. But nobody ever thanked me for keeping Bunny alive. "Nobody in my whole family *ever* went to jail. I so shame over this," she went on. "You heard Kenneth Asato talking about me at bowling league last night? And Ethel Mizuguchi gossiping with Niso-san? Right when I walked in, she stopped what she was saying. That's how I know she was talking about me. Lucky thing Niso-san loyal to us, I tell you."

"Nah, was all in your mind, Mary Alice. And I never send the boys down the jail. They never tell me jack shit. No worry. People get short memory in this town. Like the time the county councilman's sister was in the Police Blotter for possession of marijuana. Was pau in one week. And Mr. Ute's nephew caught for shoplifting at KTA—eh, soon enough forgotten."

Aunty Mildred, Uncle Herb, and Harry O. talked story on the wooden benches outside Heads by Harry that night.

"What the heck got into Toni to do such an impulsive thing?" Aunty Mildred said. "It's something Mary Alice might do, with her hot temper and all, but not Toni. She's such a *good* girl. But doesn't it make the fact that she and Bernice took first place in the Science Fair dim in the light of a felony charge? And all the *hard* work you and Herb did for the project, Harry—what a shame."

"Sheez, Mildred, Harry and Mary Alice are taking this hard enough. Don't take away the pig project first place too, gee whiz. And, brother, take that thumbtack out of Toni's head from the newspaper article, for heaven's sake."

"You know what get me the most?" Harry O. said. "I cannot trust that kid anymore. And she never get into UH because of her messing around. This is just another example of her screwing up again. You know that damn kid going UH-Hilo this fall?"

"No," Aunty Mildred gasped.

"You're kidding," Uncle Herb said, acting like it was damnation to go to a second-rate junior college.

"Sheeeeez," Harry O. exhaled in utter disgust. "What get me is that Mary Alice is right when she says that Toni get more brains than Sheldon and Bunny combined. The kid was reading sixth-grade level in kindergarten, I no joke you. What the hell is wrong with that kid? You raise um the same, but just like she born to be one big loser."

"Don't talk like that, Harry," Uncle Herb said. "You want the kid to do a self-fulfilling prophecy on you? Look at Lionel's boy—the kid's doing A-OK now. And talk about a born loser, let's talk about Lionel's kid, Wyatt."

"Hell, maybe better for all of us if she right here where I can watch her every move. If I let her go to the big city, she go bananas up there. When the country bumpkins hit the big city, they run amuck." Harry O. looked at Uncle Herb, panicked, then rested his forehead on Uncle Herb's shoulder. "Ho, lucky thing she never blast that Vasconcellos girl's head off. You can imagine that? My kid be charged with murder?"

"It would be a family first," Aunty Mildred said, laughing under her breath.

I stepped out from Niso-san's camera store and waved at Butchie sweeping up the lobby of the Mamo Theatre. "You registered at Hilo College yet?" Harry O. asked. "How many credits you taking? Answer me before I slap your head in front of Aunty and Uncle."

"Nine credits."

Harry O. didn't really know about credit hours and what they amounted to, but I didn't want to be caught in a lie.

"Only nine credits?" Aunty Mildred harrumphed. "That's not even a full load, now is it, Toni? What are you thinking, dear? That's really a waste of your father's hard-earned money, I tell you."

"What? Not full-time?" Harry O. stood from the bench. "I gave you the money for full-time. How come you never pick up more classes? Next semester, you paying your own way, I tell you. What you thinking? I made of money? I get one money tree growing out back? Let me know if you seen a tree full of hundreds so I can harvest the bills. I cannot believe this kid," he said, walking over to me.

"Leave Toni alone," Mommy said, coming out of the shop with a bowlful of homemade pork rinds sitting on an oil-soaked paper towel. "Mind your own business, Mildred. I told

Toni to take what she can handle, and if that means nine credits, then so be it."

"So you think this kid can make good decisions, eh, Mary Alice?" Harry O. said. "I don't know what *you* thinking sometimes. You just as crazy as your crazy daughter." Aunty Mildred looked piously pleased with Harry O. on her side. "What, Mildred, how many more credits Toni need to make full-time?"

"Just one more class, but I'd make her carry fifteen credits, if I were you, just to keep her busy and out of trouble. Toni just needs to apply herself."

Everyone always told me to *apply* myself, teachers, counselors, Aunty Mildred and Uncle Herb, and especially Harry O. Year after year, the comment on my report cards was: "Antoinette needs to *apply* herself."

"Toni no need do nothing that you say or Mildred say," Mommy went on. "She do one thing wrong and you act like we should punish her ass for the rest of her days. My daughter has brains. We better start believing it ourselves." She glared at Harry O. "The Vasconcellos girl came down with all those tita cousins of hers. Bunny was all bust up, and me and you was in Vegas. Harry, what the hell you expected Toni to do?"

"Call the police like every other citizen."

"Easy for you to say," Mommy said.

"No, really, she should have gotten help from the office or called the police at least," Aunty Mildred began.

"And you, until I ask for your two cents, shut your mouth," Mommy said, pointing a mean finger at Aunty Mildred. "Call the police—yeah, right. Leave her sister, find a pay phone, call the police, then run to the office to call the principal, run back across the street. Stupid assholes—Bunny be dead by now."

"Assholes?" Aunty Mildred winced.

Nobody thanked me. I sat on the edge of the sidewalk with my face in my hands. I looked up at Butchie strutting across the street in his bantam rooster way. He lifted weights too much, making his arms look shorter and shorter, but he could strut. "It's Miller time," he said, Mr. Santos not far behind him. "We got time for at least two beers, Daddy," he said, turning to his father.

"Three," Mr. Santos said.

Butchie sat next to me. "Go get me one beer, Toni," he said, lightly punching my arm. I stood to get a cold one from the refridge in back. "You can fill in tonight for Herline?" he asked. "She getting morning sickness at night, cannot work. And shit, *Endless Love*, the line all the way to Helen's Fabrics."

"One more baby?" Aunty Mildred asked sassily.

"Her and Manuel expecting their second," Butchie answered as if not hearing her sarcasm. "And no, they not married. And no, they not planning a shotgun wedding even if this is their second baby. And yes, they just had Chastity. And yes, you all invited to the one-year baby luau at Mun Cheong Lau Chop Suey. So what, Toni, can cover tonight?"

"Yeah and tomorrow and the next night, and the whole week and the whole damn month if you need me."

"Yeah, Ma, Toni can cover," Butchie hollered across the street.

"Try ask Bunny too. We got slammed last night in the concession. Get me a Pearl Light, Butchie," Mrs. Mei Ling yelled back. "And watch your father so he only drink *one beer*, damn drunkard, think he Tennessee Ernie Ford with his goddamn 'Sixteen Tons' in the ticket booth and every time he come to the sixteen tons part, he looking straight at my ass and thighs. Think I don't know what you trying to say? Three beers and the old bastard think he Ricky Nelson."

"Okay, Ma. I watching Daddy," Butchie yelled, then winked at Mr. Santos. "Toni," he yelled to the back of the shop. "Get my mother one Pearl Light. She coming for one drink, and only one. Two and she think she Nana Mouskouri."

"She get the same ugly glasses," I yelled back to Butchie.

"Damn bunch of Portagee mouths," Mr. Santos grumbled, "yelling like they own this goddamn street. No shame, I tell you."

Harry O. laughed. Aunty Mildred clutched her handbag and put on her dark glasses to make sure no one recognized her amidst all the uncouth and uneducated. She shook her head disapprovingly and nudged Uncle Herb to leave.

Niso-san closed his camera shop and walked his old man's body to the wooden bench. "What a day," he said, sitting down nearest to the food and popping a daikon sushi in his mouth.

Maverick and Wyatt pulled up in their truck smelling like pig blood after a day's work. Wyatt leaned his huge arm out the window, lowered his sunglasses, then gave us an eyebrow jerk. "Howzit, family? Whassup, man? Bust out the brewski."

Bunny slipped in next to me, looking at Maverick, who in turn looked pitifully at me. "I can help you tonight in the concession, Toni," she said.

"Yeah, me too," Mommy said to me. "I be there for the eight o'clock show."

The paper boy passed today's edition of *The Hawaii Tri-bune Herald* to Harry O. for more of the town's bad news, clippings on cardboard for another family.

When I was ten, I remember Bunny fainting in the drying room for the stuffed heads. She fainted at the sight of her own blood. Not blood in general, gore she loved as much as I did—the gangrene of sheep entrails, blood from a carcass dripping maroon and melted red-chocolate, blood blossoms emblazoning a piece of cardboard in the garage.

Harry O. always placed the finished heads in a huge wooden box. Axis deer heads, buffalo heads, pig heads, goat heads, sheep heads, Hereford cow heads covered with snowy flakes of Borax stared up at us.

Sewing pins delicately held the skins taut. Clothespins and cardboard made for stiff and accurate bends in the ears. String crisscrossed eyes and noses like spiderwebs, tension created for alert hearing ears in this new glass-covered wilderness. My father twisted toilet paper into oval nostrils for drying. All of this we saw through the white-speckled, dusty sheet of glass over the drying boxes.

Yellow and green glass eyes that Bunny, Sheldon, and I stared at through the glass to see who would win in a staring contest. The dead heads always won, so we'd turn to each other for a challenge of the living. Sheldon always took first place.

The day of the blood, Bunny turned quickly toward me, her eyes sore already from losing to Sheldon, turning fast to retain the stare of a second-place winner. She swiveled her body toward me, then sliced her finger on the sheet of glass over the drying box.

I watched the quick dripping of carmine blood, significant individual drops over the stuffed heads. My sister held her dangling finger, the blood coming through the cracks between her other fingers. A slow wail and blood. She took a step toward me as I watched her face turn pale green, then white. Her eyes rolled back in the sockets and then she collapsed.

She screamed for Sheldon as she did when she first began to menstruate at thirteen. The reddened albumen from her body got on her hands and her inner thighs. My brother arrived yipping and yapping utterances of "Gross. Ho, the thick the blood. Mommy, where the pads? Mommy, Bunny's rags is coming out all Jell-O. Put the pad like how Mommy showed you, dummy," and laughing hideously at her clumsiness, watching and contorting his body to see the blood between her legs.

Mommy was on a petroglyph kick, and led the whole family on outings to remote petroglyph fields—to the Waikoloa paniolo, the horseman who told in stone how many trips he made around the island with circles around circles; and the pueo at Puakō etched in pāhoehoe lava with big owl eyes and a delicate bird's feet. Pili grass scratched our legs. The tiny green and yellow leaves of the kiawe stuck in Mommy's frizz; kiawe thorns wedged into our rubber slippers.

Mommy experimented with Crayolas, black and brown, the thick kindergarten kind, on bedsheets, unbleached muslin, and cotton blends. This time, I made Mommy's obsession fit my final ten-page research paper. A paper that would include extensive field data and visual aids.

The early morning of the last petroglyph expedition before I took my finals, Bunny dressed up as field scientist with khaki vest, Levi's, boots, and a cheap Instamatic slung around her neck for my visual aids. I drank coffee with Mommy like the real college student I was pretending to be.

Billy Harper walked in the back door of the kitchen without knocking, as always. Mommy excitedly read her *Hawaii's Petroglyphs: Field Guide for Beginners*, granny glasses clinging to her nose, already looking for her next conquest.

"Howzit, Billy?" I said to him. "Mommy, Billy coming with

us? How come nobody told me?" Billy walked over to Bunny rinsing her dishes at the sink, and she raised her cheek to him for a light kiss.

"Getting tall, eh, haole boy," she said to him.

He turned and wrapped his long arms around Mommy's neck and kissed her ear. "I miss you, Mrs. Yagyuu, my favorite teacher of all time."

"Hi, my best haole boy," she said, and then without blinking, "You using deodorant or what? Where's the Brut I bought you? And how you doing in school, Billy? Every time 'I miss you, Mrs. Yagyuu,' is really 'I'm not doing good in school, so I better butter you up before I land the bomb.' No try fool me. And how's your daddy and stepmother and all their kids?"

Billy didn't answer the barrage of questions but walked over to my side of the table, sat down, and stared at me for a while. He winked at me.

"What?" I asked.

"Nothing," he said. "Hi, Toni, I miss you too." He leaned his chin in his palm, stared some more, and finally kissed me too. Our legs touched under the table.

He looked at me and I looked at him, the amber flecks in his brown eyes intense. He felt warm. "I thought you was coming over to make us haole-style meat loaf and mashed potatoes last weekend," I told him. "We waited."

He put his head on my shoulder. "I was grounded. Grades," he whispered. "But you're still teaching me how to make oxtail soup, right, Toni? Me and you. Let's go grocery shopping at KTA when we get home tonight. I got some money."

I nodded and he wrapped himself around me. We all liked Billy's physicality with us, his open affection.

"Make him some scrambled egg, kind of runny, Bernice, and lots of hot rice with shoyu, ketchup on the side and don't let it touch the eggs. Did your stepmother buy a rice cooker?

Tell her Sanyo on sale at Longs and she doesn't need a coupon."

"What for? We never eat nothing but Minute Rice or Uncle Ben's that she makes in a little pot on the stove. Mrs. Yagyuu, you're the only one who remembers exactly how I like my eggs and rice."

"Don't butter me up," Mommy said. "I don't care if you the only one who knows where this Turtleback Cave petroglyph is. You better tell me how you doing in school. Right now."

"Not too good," Billy said at last. "Coach Cabingabang said if I don't bring up my grades in the third and fourth quarters, then I'm going to be back on the JV team next year for volleyball *and* basketball."

Mommy shook her head. "You the *only* freshman he allowed on the varsity squad and you messing up. How can you get that damn athletic scholarship he told you about? Six foot plus and breaking your ass for nothing. You make me mad, boy. You get your butt on the first Hele-On bus that passes your school and get to the shop, you hear me, Billy? Bunny can tutor you till your grades come up."

"What about Toni?" Billy asked, hitting my leg with his. "She's in college now, maybe she has some answers too, huh, Toni," he said, nudging me with his elbow.

"They ain't giving you answers. Toni can help by driving you home after we eat dinner, you hear me, Billy?" He nodded yes and smiled a rice-and-no-more-potatoes smile.

I still don't know who was happier—Billy or Mommy. Billy, who needed somebody like Mommy, unconditional with her biting, blunt, local kind of love, or Mommy, who needed someone to mold into another teacher's success story of which Aunty Mildred had none. Billy was part of our family, the kind of haole that wasn't a condescending mainland haole.

He was a local haole who took no offense to the word, was easy, and laid-back with his body.

"Okay, let's go," Mommy said after a long silence and Billy's quiet eating. "Bunny, go get my petroglyph bag and make sure I have enough pastel crayons. Oil-base, better than Crayola and nice after you iron it, no, Bunny? After you eat, you go look at the petroglyphs I framed in the shop. I selling them cheap, cheap, cheap, but I give you one free."

Billy dabbed his last forkful of eggs and rice in the ketchup, then got up to wash his dishes before turning to Mommy. "You think Helen might let me buy some unbleached muslin for cheap, Mrs. Yagyuu? I'm thinking maybe if you help me frame a petroglyph, I can give one to Coach Cabingabang's wife."

"Butter butt-licker, ass-sniffer," I told him as we headed out for the car, his hands on my shoulders guiding me to the door. "Don't push," I told him as the screen door slammed shut behind us.

"Brownnose haole," Bunny said, punching Billy's arm as she climbed into the back seat with Mommy. Billy rode up front with me for the long drive to Pāhala, past the forests of Pana'ewa full of invisible tigers, past redneck bikers at the one store and post office in Kurtistown, the smell of rock cookies and sweet potato manju from the Mountain View Bakery, the rain over fields of white ginger in Glenwood, fog hanging on 'ōhi'a like gray ghost fingers through Volcano, the endless blue over the black Ka'ū Desert, Mauna Loa, a white-capped, sloping purple dome, and expanses of sugarcane fields and macadamia nut trees.

"There, right up ahead by the Dip sign past the bridge," Billy said, "take a right. My dad brought me up here lots of times to see the cave and check the water meters." We rode deeper into the fields until Billy instructed me to park by a couple of orange spray-painted oil drums. "We have to walk in now, Mrs. Yagyuu. Not too far. I'll carry all the bags."

Mommy always appreciated Billy's filial concern for her welfare, a Japanese trait she claimed that she instilled in a haole, of all creatures. We crossed a deep, dry ravine with huge boulders, then skirted a basin dropping ten feet straight down to get to Turtleback Cave. I looked into the basin, imagining it full of churning water, a flash flood.

Billy spread his long brown legs across the tributary to catch us if we slipped trying to get across. He held our hands tightly, guiding us to the shallow opening of the cave.

On the cool, sandy floor, Billy took out a huge flashlight from his backpack and pointed its white beam into the recess of the cave. "See that tiny opening right there? Don't worry, Mrs. Yagyuu, my dad can squeeze his six-foot-four frame through it."

"Ho, the small," Mommy groaned, "I can't fit through that hole. My ass might get stuck. Then what we going do?"

"You can fit. Let's go. We'll push you till you pop in like a cork. I'm telling you, it's worth it to see these petroglyphs."

"Better be," Bunny said. "The petroglyphs are on a rock that looks like a turtle's back?"

"My dad said the stream that runs through this cave rushed around the stone, shaping it like a turtle's back. Thousands of years ago after landing at South Point, the Hawaiians migrated up here to tell the story of their lives. Pretty cool, huh?"

"Cool." I hated that haole word. But Billy amazed me—the way we spent hours talking about this and that. All the "cool" details he kept in his memory. Everything I knew, he knew a little more.

"Pretty soon, the petroglyph might erode, what you think, Billy?" I asked him. I said something to keep the walls from closing in on me, to relieve the claustrophobic tightening in my chest.

"Maybe in a couple of centuries the rubbings we make today will be worth a lot of money." Billy aimed the light toward the opening and squeezed through. Mommy followed after much protest and then Bunny. She turned toward me.

"You coming or what, Toni?"

I hesitated. I felt the musty mildew of the cave in cold sweat on my body, the sweet smell of moss and the damp dripping of water from the cave's interior. "I cannot. I getting claustrophobia."

"This is for *your* damn final paper, Toni," Bunny said. I sat at the edge of the cave and breathed deeply.

"What if there's a flash flood or something? We all cabbage in there. Mommy might plug the opening with her ass."

"I heard that," she yelled in a hollow, faraway voice.

"Wait for me." Bunny squeezed in, clutching the Instamatic to her chest. "Ho, the dark. Shine the light for me, Billy. Get bats or what?" My sister's final words were followed by ooohs and aaahs, holy-smoke's and oh-my-God's. They found the story etched in stone.

The dark cold of the cave pressing on my back, I saw Billy move through the tiny opening to get me. "I ain't going in, I told you," I said, mildly panicked. He put his hand on my back and stroked me reassuringly.

"Let's go sit out by the basin," Billy said. He held out his hand to me, then yelled into the opening, "We're right out here, Mrs. Yagyuu."

"Yeah, yeah, yeah," she yelled back. "Don't bother me. I busy."

Billy firmly held my hand out of the cave, and then we sat on the edge of the deep basin until I realized we were holding hands for too long.

"My dad's letting me breed pig dogs," he said to ease the slight discomfort. "I've got this whole genealogy going. Only thing, he assigned Wyatt to work with me, and Wyatt hates listening to my reasoning. He's really stupider than me about greyhounds being fast racers and Airedales sniffing the air for pigs—" Billy paused and turned his brown-golden face toward the top of the ravine. I noticed his eyes rimmed with dark eyelashes.

"Your real mother—was she Indian from India? Or was she Italian or Pakistan or something?" I asked Billy. He said nothing. The blunt local thing came out all wrong. He seemed injured and still.

He looked at my fingers one by one. "She's beautiful. I have a picture of her. I'll show it to you. She's why I'm this color," he said, holding out his arm to me in a way that asked for my touch. "I heard my Granny Harper tell my dad that I look like a sand nigger. Like my mother, I guess."

"What about pit bulls?" I said at last. Billy looked relieved. But he wasn't stupid. He didn't answer for a while, just to let me know.

"They should be bred in your dog lineage," I told him. "They grab good. Slow, but put in couple of terrier genes and you can sell some of the pups after you train them."

"I have this one male," he said at last, "him and some of his pups grab the pig's mouth the best, and a frontal attack means less kicks from the pig, right? So now I'm figuring that good pig dog traits are in his genes."

Our legs dangled over the huge boulder. He brushed a honeybee away from my hair. I rubbed a smudge of dust from his cheek. He reached for my fingers and held them on his face.

"How about Maverick's paper bull?" I said, pulling my hand away. "He might let you breed Smut Dawg? He used to grab balls good. He still mating but he pau with hunting."

"Who? Maverick or the dog?" Billy and me leaned into each other and laughed into the ravine until it echoed. "But you know who I really don't care for?"

"Who?"

"Wyatt. I mean, the guy's so disgusting. It has to be some anal retentive hang-up related to early toilet training, what do you think? And he forces me to call my dogs names like Linda and Lovelace. And then two other male bull-greyhound mixes, he named them Deep and Throat. And then Debbie and Does and Dallas. He's yelling at his dogs in the forest, 'Debbie Does Dallas! Deep Throat!' "

"Too many movies," I said to Billy.

"Freebie movies, and the guy burps and farts all the time."

"And he likes the smell of them both."

"Vanity." Billy laughed.

Billy Harper and I talked on and on over the edge of the basin, the blue expanse of sky, the wind sweeping down a dry riverbed. "Nobody's ever asked me about my real mother," he said to me that day. "Why do you think nobody asks?"

He looked toward the mountains. Indian from India probably, and haole from his father. We talked about dogs and genealogies, stories in stone, until he called gently toward Turtleback Cave, "I'm coming, Mrs. Yagyuu. Wait for me to get you. I don't ever want you to fall."

My mother took us on one last petroglyph outing. I had barely managed a 2.0 average at Hilo College, but it was enough to get me a transfer to UH-Mānoa. Bunny had been accepted into the freshman class. I would leave my home in Hilo for the fall semester in Honolulu.

I felt uneasy as we drove along the Hāmākua coast. The dying sugar fields looked sad, the waves beyond Laupāhoehoe Point were choppy and agitated. In Kamuela, the sunny mist through the pasturelands of Waimea felt cold. I slowly drove down the winding highway from the mountain to the seas of Waikoloa.

The heat waves on the leeward coast of the Big Island curvetted in front of us. They rose up through the soles of my shoes as we walked over fields of pāhoehoe, every clearing a blank sheet of lava rock. Mommy, Bunny, Billy, and I pressed forward toward the ocean. We walked for about an hour before we began to see small petroglyphs.

"There, that big ahu. It has to be the marker," Mommy said, her mouth dry and white. Billy ran ahead of us, far into the heat waves that coiled and rolled his shape. Through the pili grass and hopping to pull out thorns from his boots, he waved us all over.

When we caught up to Billy standing over a woman in stone, Mommy gasped and fell to her knees. "She so mighty. The book didn't say she was this big." Mommy touched the etching with her fingers, the woman with babies.

"I brought the white queen sheet, Mommy," Bunny said to her.

"How you knew, Bunny?"

"I didn't."

The four of us opened up the sheet, a sail, white trembling wings.

"Wait, we all need to lie down in her," Bunny told us. We all looked at each other for a moment.

"No," I said. "Feel her."

"She's pulsing," Billy told me, placing his hand in the space of the body. A quavering heat rose from the pāhoehoe. "She's so beautiful."

"But we can never be a part of this," Mommy said, moving her palm on the woman's head.

Bunny rested her face on the floating baby inside the woman.

Billy put his hand on the baby at the center.

And I sat beside the child coming out feet first who was painfully breeched and first into the world, her umbilical cord lying by the feet of her mother.

My father would miss me, though he would never say it. What we did as father and daughter, the miles we walked together for pig or pheasant or prawn, he wished to do with Sheldon as father and son.

The weekend before I left for college in Honolulu, Harry O. and I drove out to Honomu to catch river prawn and 'ōpae, maybe a frog or two. It was near evening. The sky faded from pale pink to a cirrus petticoat of lavender.

We wedged our small nets into cracks between rocks, the tributary of 'Akaka Falls rushing by. I steadied myself for the bursts of tiny 'ōpae bodies. Translucent gray 'ōpae, with black eyes, these tiny bites of river shrimps would be a prelude to the prawns and frog legs we'd eat later that night with a bowl of hot rice. My father loved the whole crunch of red-shelled 'ōpae bodies, sugar-shoyu-cooked.

He moved the fishing light into the crevices of the river-bed, as we looked for the red eyes of the huge prawns. We speared their flicking, snapping bodies before they dashed to the fine bottom sediment, their red eyes stunned by the light.

And we caught frogs. My father called this a poor man's delicacy; we'd eat everything we caught. The bag full, thick prawn feelers sensed air in a slow panic, and poked out through the fabric.

I cooked the ʻōpae for him and fried the frog legs like little wing dings. I sharpened the knife and sliced open the huge river prawns to drown them in the bubbling pan like coral butterflies, the brown butter in the brackish tender flesh of their bodies. My father sucked the loamy orange mush from their heads, butter-soaked and salty, the crunch of eyeballs and feelers deep-fried.

I walked out of the river that night with my father. He turned the fishing light into my eyes and saw no red glow as I ducked out of its beam.

"All the time like that, Toni," he said to me. They would be his last real words to me before I left for college. "No let them catch you stunned and stupid. You keep moving. Be one step ahead of them all. You *can* do it. You got brains. Keep them all in your dust." He slung the bag over his shoulder and shined the light to mark his step. I followed him rock over rock in the darkness, then took his hand to stride the distance to the embankment.

Five

**H**arry O. took no chances on Bunny and me in Honolulu. He rented a student-ghetto apartment for the three of us to share, sight unseen, overlooking the H-1 freeway. The heat of concrete and freeway was a dry heat, unlike Hilo, where my body felt sticky all the time.

This was better than spending all his hard-earned dollars on three separate dorm rooms and all the meal plans that Sheldon never ate, tuition, books, and the extra cash Sheldon always needed to do his laundry. He had stupidly admitted to using the vending machine outside his dorm for dinner.

My father lectured the three of us about monkeying around at the dorms all night. Aunty Mildred had filled him in on the nonsense that went on between coeds. He claimed that he'd be mounting three heads a day and a couple of birds till the wee hours just to keep up with the payments—but this way, he'd pay for only one phone and one monthly rent.

"But all my friends in the dorms, Daddy. That's not fair," Sheldon whined. "I told them I was coming back Mokihana dorm. All my friends got on the same floor next semester."

"Tough nuggets, Sheldon. Honolulu one big city and I want none of you screwing up in school. Think I never been around this world two times over? Think I don't know what go on when boys and girls live together? I wasn't born yesterday. Besides, I counting on you to look out for your sisters."

"Sheldon?" Mommy said. "Looking out for his sisters?"

Harry O. sighed. "Yeah, you heard me, Mary Alice," he said, all macho. "He the man of that house. He smarter and more responsible than he look. And smarter than he act. And a man, right, son? Sheez."

That afternoon, the three of us boarded Aloha Airlines to Honolulu. Mommy cried and honked her nose and hugged each of us at the airport. She talked about the empty-nest syndrome. We were to call her every day and were reminded that she'd be coming up Discoverer's Day to see if we were settled in. "You all coming home for Thanksgiving, you hear me, Sheldon?" she said.

He nodded like she was being a pain in the ass as Bunny and I sobbed along with her. The only other time I left the island was when I went to Baptist Summer Camp at Camp Erdman. Even then I was homesick the whole weekend.

I stepped into the apartment, tired from kicking boxes down the long hallway with a suitcase in each hand. The walls were lime green, and the bathroom a wallpapered orange, tie-dyed mess. Bunny flopped down on one of her boxes. I turned on the water in the kitchen sink. "We got nothing. No couch, dish rack, knife, potato peeler, nothing," I said, pulling open the drawers with mismatched roach paper dotted with the slide and slime of brown roach feet.

Sheldon yelled from down the hall, "You can share the small bedroom over there." Bunny and I looked into our room. "At least you have beds." Two mattresses left behind by the last tenant stood in poor posture against the closet. Sheldon yelled from his room, the air conditioner already on, "I want this hamajang desk. It's in my room anyway."

The whole apartment smelled like airplane exhaust. A fine, black dust seemed to cover every surface—the floors, countertops, bathroom sink, even the toilet.

We unloaded two cases of Top Ramen into the cupboard, Spam, Vienna sausage, and a five-pound bag of rice with a small cooker that Mommy bought on sale at Longs. An empty fifth of Kamchatka vodka sat under the sink; nothing but sugar cubes and solidified Folgers instant coffee in the refridge.

The emptiness of these rooms was a stark contrast to my life in the apartment above Heads by Harry. Everything that I was remained in Hilo. Here, I had nothing. When I shut the sliding doors and all the windows, the freeway sounded like the ocean, like water constantly gushing, except for the sweet car exhaust that burned in my chest.

That first day, I bought a fan from Longs for Bunny and me, lay naked after a cold shower on my mattress, and prayed for Thanksgiving. I cried until I fell asleep.

"Hallllo," Sheldon said into the phone, all sweet. "Uh-huh, uh-huh, when? My sisters have to come. My father might call tonight. And if they tell him I left them all alone, he just might kick my ass when I go home for Thanksgiving. Yeah, you heard right. I have to go home for Thanksgiving this year. But don't cancel the Lahaina trip because of me. Uh-hu, uh-huh. Okay, we're coming."

And then he laughed into the phone like they were talking about Bunny and me and we didn't know what was going on. He told whoever it was that I looked butch and had a bad attitude. And then he snapped his fingers when he mentioned Bunny, the man magnet all the fuckers up in D-Lounge would cream their jeans to talk to, his beautiful sister, Bernice.

I learned a lot of new things in college. It would be a

lifetime's worth of knowledge. I learned fast that I was no drinker at dorm parties that started on Friday nights and ended on the following Friday night. There was always a party in somebody's room—cases of baby Löwenbräu and Natural Light stacked in a corner and a cold pack already chilling in a Styrofoam cooler by the afternoon.

Myron was Sheldon's studliest friend, who introduced my brother to all of his studdly friends from Kaua'i, the island of the best-looking local boys. At a drinking party in his room, another 2 a.m. fire drill went off. Girls who slept in their blue eye shadow with Scotch tape on their eyelids for double-eye, Farrah Fawcett hairdos in stiff suspension, cooed, "C'mon, Myron. We have to go downstairs. Wow, just no invite us to drink, eh?"

I tried to push the Styrofoam cooler holding the door open inside the room. I pushed until its side caved in, a gush of ice water pouring out onto the floor of Myron's room. Drunk, it looked to me like the river where we caught prawns. I could feel the cool rush of ice water on my legs.

The girls screamed and the boys scrambled to catch the rolling beer as the Resident Adviser motioned for us to get downstairs. "Stupid Toni," Myron grumbled, "my fuckin' floor's all wet." They called him Destructo for a reason. He lifted the Styrofoam cover over my head and bonked me so hard that it cracked in half. Not so much that it hurt, but the crack was loud and I felt so ashamed when everyone burst out in fall-on-the-wet-floor laughter.

I came out swinging at Myron, a UH baseball player. He held my head with one hand, my arms flailing. "Sheldon, come get your sister. Ho, these Hilo titas, no can handle." Then he pushed my head out the door with one hand.

Always at those dorm parties somebody said, "Here, Toni, tank this Bacardi straight up, me and you." I had everything to prove to Sheldon and his friends, while Bunny sipped on her Tom Collins in the corner of the room, absorbed in attention, so many hands and eyes waiting on her every Cherry Blossom move. Long, tanned legs, and ass cheeks hanging out from ultra-tiny Dove shorts and shirts from Myron and his baseball friends cut right below her voluptuous honeydew tits. Hers was a halo of cascading golden-auburn hair. Mine was black, stringy, and I had tangerine-sized tits, at best. So I drank more. Never was I more out of my element than in the days I spent in Honolulu.

"Give Toni the Cuervo, Naks. Here's the lime and pass the Morton. Okay, boilermakers after the shot." The whole bottle gone by the morning hours, I sliced up the worm for us all to sample, counted slowly up to four people still upright in the room, grabbed a plastic cup and slid the pieces into it.

"Stupid fuck," a drunken Quinton said as he slammed his palm onto my back. "That was the spit from my Skoal in that cup. Didn't you see the brown juice I was spitting in there? No can handle."

I rinsed the pieces of worm in the ice chest water. "You eat the worm by yourself, Toni," he said. "The high just like mushrooms."

Always something to prove, I slid them down my throat, and sat there smiling to Quinton's "Ho, Myron, she can handle. Naks, check it out. Toni get balls. All right, now, you part of the boys."

Then I winced as a gush of water rose back up into my throat and mouth, burning upward, and before I could run to the bathroom, I caught the vomit in the scoop of my shirt.

My first semester at UH, I attended my lecture classes— sometimes. I decided to buy lecture notes from the bookstore, notes that belonged to some grad student with a big vocabulary complex, notes that didn't even make sense to me the night before midterms, too late, twenty chapters behind.

In the spring semester, I discovered Unit Mastery 100—psychology, sociology, and anthropology. I had no classes! Just read the chapter and go take the test, chapter by chapter, no lectures. I enrolled in one English class with Bunny on Tuesdays and Thursdays, and the rest of the week was mine. "I can read at the beach, if I like. I have no classes. I finally figured out this college life, what you think?" I bragged to Sheldon and Bunny.

"You think you're so smart, Toni, but you ain't," Sheldon said. "You think it's so easy to take Unit Mastery? This is Quinton's second semester trying to finish Psych 100. And he never taking another Unit Mastery again, stupid."

"Quinton's stupider than me."

"You might be smarter than all of us like Mommy and Harry O. always saying"—Sheldon smirked—"but you got no common sense."

"Or ambition," Bunny added.

"What's with ganging up on me?" I asked them. It felt sickly familiar.

"Sorry, Toni. Shelly, you want a Cup-O-Noodles?" Bunny asked from the kitchen. We hadn't eaten anything that resembled real food in the apartment since the frozen Ziploc bags of Thanksgiving turkey Mommy sent back with us had run out. "Shelly, you told Mommy that you double-enrolled at HCC and UH this semester?" Bunny asked, pouring boiling water into the Cup-O-Noodles.

"What?" I said, rolling over to turn off the black-and-white TV with tinfoil on the antenna. "Harry O. going kick your ass for going to that community college. How come, Sheldon? You have a high GPA at UH."

"Shut up, eh, you two squealers. Don't say nothing to

Daddy." He paused, looking mighty intelligent. "I double-enrolled 'cause I'm getting a business degree at UH and a cosmetology degree at HCC, same time. Watch out." He snapped his fingers dramatically.

"Eh, that's a good idea," Bunny shrieked. "I going do that too, okay, Shelly?"

"Okay, and we make Harry O. give us the shop and force him to retire. Then we open up our own hair shop—the best one Hilo ever known, better than Chickie's and Suavio's. And we make a shitload of money, not like Daddy—acting like he make all the bread when Mommy been busting her ass year after year to hold up the finances."

"Shut up, Sheldon. You don't know nothing about Daddy."

"*You* don't know nothing about Daddy. Open your eyes," he said, blowing at his noodles. "And the worse part is— Harry O. don't know nothing about *you*. I didn't tell him yet. Your fall grades came here, not Hilo. And, honey, if you didn't already know, you on academic probation, which means, you don't cut the mustard this semester, then, honey, you in deep, deep, maybe Hilo College-here-I-come shit."

I turned on the TV and lit a joint. "Yeah," I said, "and Daddy don't know nothing about *you* either."

"What you said, Toni? Speak up, bitch."

"You heard what I said. Wait till I tell Daddy all about you, *Shelly*." It was the only threat I had against my brother, who was brilliant in the area of mind games. I was defenseless. Tell my father about his late nights at Hulas, about his obsession with Maverick, about all the hairy old men he flirted with, and who went in and out of his room. And how much he cried.

"Toni, did you steal toilet paper from Sinclair Library like I told you?" Bunny asked me mid-drag to divert our attention.

She gave me the eye to *stop it*. I didn't answer but inhaled deeper on the joint crackling right in front of my face.

"Red eyes," I said. "Shine the light in his eyes. Stun the fucker."

"See, Bunny," Sheldon said, "she talking bubbles. And she don't give a shit about this apartment. Let's go to Shirokiyas and eat the free samples for dinner. Then come with me to Longs. Toni can stay home and get loaded like she always does. And if Quinton call, tell him we going Point After tonight. I have to buy foundation, Bunny," he whispered, "and then we simply must go Liberty House to check out the new Christian Dior eye palettes."

"Okay," Bunny said, all excited. "Toni, you like come?" She paused at our bedroom door. "Nah, no need. You act all dumb when you wasted. Eh, our English paper is due tomorrow, you know, Toni. You better sober up."

I had asked Bunny to write my paper for me. She did it all the time by simplifying her language after I had given her all the deep thoughts, theses, and supporting sentences for *both* our papers.

I turned to my brother. I felt mean. I hated UH, I hated Honolulu, I hated the apartment, I hated him for turning Bunny against me all the time.

"Why you buying makeup, hah, Shelly? I mean Paula. I mean Franjelica. Better buy the pancake foundation so you can hide your five o'clock shadow. Quinton might know that's you under your Christian Dior."

"You fuckin' little loser," my brother hissed. "Go goat hunting with your father and Wyatt Santos. The makeup's for my cosmetology class, okay?" he screamed in my face.

"Yeah, okay. I like going hunting with Daddy and Wyatt. As long I leave Maverick for you, right, Shelly? Try peacock blue, now that's a bird Maverick might want to shoot. Too bad you're a tom, you turkey. He pops one cherry in our house and now the biggest asshole in the same house wants Maverick to peanut-butter-pack him too. That's a first, don't you think, Shelly?"

Sheldon pounced on me, his hands squeezing tight around my throat. I couldn't fight him off, and at that moment I realized the physical strength of a man—even a so-called man like Sheldon. He choked me harder, his face in mine, until Bunny jumped him from behind and pried his fingers off my throat. He was sobbing, of course, and I was dying, but Sheldon lay his head on her shoulder, and then they walked out the door.

It went downhill from there. Maverick visited us at midterms, his first time on a plane since fourth grade when he came up with his 4-H Club and his prizewinning homegrown steer for the Hawai'i State Farm Fair.

"Eh, Toni," Maverick said. "When Bunny coming back from class? Eh, how come you no more class? Pass me that towel," Maverick said. "Your carpet blacker than the road. You get soda?" he said, peering into the empty refrigerator. "What's with all the damn S's on everything?"

"That's all Sheldon's food," I said.

"He marking his eggs and HoHos? What the fuck, man? You guys family. Wait till I tell Aunty Mary Alice."

"Drink his soda. As long as it's you and not me, he don't care. That's my Mickey's Big Mouth in the back. They ain't coming home for couple hours. After we pick them up from UH, we can get dinner at Grace's."

It was like being home again, talking to Maverick about Herline's secondhand Camaro and Wyatt's fling with Cecelia Saratoga. Mr. Ute's nephew was arrested for abuse of a household member, and Niso-san paid Butchie to paint his house.

Mrs. Mei Ling *earned* a new Ming's bracelet from Mr. Santos. And Mr. Harper gave Maverick several vacation days for being the crew leader with the most kills.

"Mr. Harper said to tell you that Billy the kid miss you. His grades ain't so hot again, something like that. Here"— he reached into his bag—"the kid said give this to you."

I opened the envelope. It was a black-and-white glossy photograph. A woman, a beautiful woman. And on the back, Billy wrote, "For Toni, because you asked. Come home soon. Love, Billy H." I put it in my pocket.

"What's that?" Maverick asked, reaching for the envelope.

"Nothing. You know what I miss?" I asked him.

"What?"

"Finding a clothespin when I need one."

"Hah?" Maverick said.

"I can't even find a safety pin. And juice in the fridge when I thirsty, laundry soap, loose change on the TV. I miss all of that—eh, man, I'm running to 7-Eleven to buy every little thing I had at my fingertips at home. Add up, you know? And my mother and father and all you guys. I never been called stupid more times than up here with Sheldon and all his jackass friends."

"Who calling you stupid, hah, Toni?"

"Never mind. Not worth it." He might have defended me then. He had been saving me all my life, and for the longest time it made me expect a happy ending.

"Here, Toni," Maverick said, opening his carry-on bag. "Smoke or snorts, what you like? I know," he said before I could answer. "We do some coke, four, five lines, whatever, and pick you up a little bit." Maverick tossed the Ziploc bag full of kolas to me. "Put this in your freezer. And mark the bag with a T."

Cocaine I loved, couldn't get enough, and Mickey after

Mickey, but not getting drunk. The next line never came fast
enough. But I never wanted to come down. I wanted my line
to be as fat as the next guy's line and got pissed off and
resentful if mine was skinnier. Maverick was always fair and
generous with me. In between lines, we smoked Kool Milds,
so that by the time Bunny and Sheldon stormed in the door,
nothing really mattered.

That long weekend, we hit all the discos with Maverick, who
to Bunny was a Hilo fish out of Honolulu water with his
Levi's, Red Wings, and flannel shirts. He was broad-chested
and bronze under the white T-shirt he wore beneath the flannel. His ass was fully rounded in tight jeans. She preferred
pale blond haoles in three-piece suits, scrawny Japanese townies in Angel Flights, and gold chains on hairless chests.

He looked good to me. All the waitresses thought so too.
Sheldon, who was all eyelashes at Maverick's side, pretended
to be *with him*. Bunny acted cold and uninterested.

At Moose McGillicuddy's, Maverick and I drank Long Island ice teas. Bunny and Sheldon had their Beautifuls with
Coke back. University girls with cigarettes, lip gloss, and attitude stood by the bar with glassy drunk eyes. I walked out
and barfed in the parking lot on the way to the car without
breaking my stride. Sheldon shrieked and Maverick rubbed
my back. Bunny walked ahead of us and pouted in the back
seat.

At the Point After and Bobby McGee's, Bunny danced with
haoles and townies and drank more Beautifuls all on Maverick's tab. We stood there in Sheldon and Myron's crowd,
Ralph Lauren Polo and Aramis mixed in with the Charlie
and Scoundrel crowd of false eyelashes and men watching
asses and cleavage, their crotches stuffed with athletic socks.
Waitresses in swimsuit tuxedos with tails sashayed by without

taking your order, thank you very much, if you weren't male and tipping. The lights in the fleshy, sweaty slaughterhouse spun, and I turned to see Bunny's mouth open wide like a cave and Quinton's tongue slide in.

"Who the fuck dropped their drink on my feet?" Bunny screamed all of a sudden. Maverick moved me aside and pushed people out of his way to get to her kicking, wet foot, her hero ready to wipe her with a cocktail napkin.

"You did, you dummy," I whispered to her, "that's your drink." Her hand still formed the C that held the snifter glass.

"Oh," she said, all cute. "Let's dance, Quinton. That's our song, 'Whip It Good.' Here, Toni. Hold my bag." They squeezed their way though the crowds of people, Bunny dancing like an oofing dog before she even hit the dance floor with Quinton pumping behind her.

Maverick crushed the napkin in his hand. He put both of his hands on my shoulders. Sheldon turned and glared at me with drunk eyes. Maverick whispered so close to my ear, I felt his warm breath, "We go do couple lines outside." I nodded. "Order us one more round, Sheldon," he said, taking my elbow to guide me out. "We be right back." A couple of townie girls watched us leave with sassy faces. They had been flirting with Maverick all night.

The lines were a sweet burn and a bittersweet drip. In the piss-soaked stairwell, I stared at Maverick. I realized that men like him needed women like him. He needed a trophy girl, one who would grace his side, one who the other men in the room could imagine fucking in the tangle of hair and long limbs, the smother of breasts—but she was his. No matter that she had shit for brains and a motor mouth like Lynette or was superficial and callous like Bunny.

"What?" he said. "One more before we go in?" He moved his hand over my legs.

"Maybe next time, *hero*," I said. I took the razor and cut the coke myself.

Maverick leaned back and laughed. "Wyatt was right, Toni. You one helluva motherfuckin' trip." I licked my fingers and he watched.

By the time we got back, Bunny sat on one of the stools, her body flopped forward, her face in her hands.

"Bunny," I said to her. "Bernice." I shook her shoulder.

She raised her head and said, "Where you was?"

"Eh, if you cannot handle, don't drink," I said to her.

"You should talk," she said.

"What happened?" Maverick asked.

"I dunno," she slurred. "First I felt my head going backwards. And then I was thinking: Don't let your head hit the table. All the drinks might spill on everybody. Better if I fall forward in my hand. So that's where my head went."

Nobody called *her* stupid. When the lights went on, Sheldon left with Myron's friends for another disco, as Maverick and I held Bunny up between us. "You think you can walk out, Bunny?" I asked.

"I can carry her," Maverick said.

"You have to *walk*," I told her. She stood, her legs wobbly as she took a few steps holding on to us.

"I can handle," she said, taking a few more steps. And then she let out a fart of tuba-blast proportions, the waitresses and bartenders turning to the obscene sound. "Phew, I feel better," Bunny said loudly, straightening herself up, poot-pooting out little farts as we walked out the door.

Back in the apartment, Bunny drooled facedown on her mattress with her heels on. Maverick shut the bedroom door. For Maverick and me in the living room, there were hunting stories to tell and relive, Lynette and the nice mother-of-pearl pistol-grip shotgun to laugh about, Sheldon's love for Nancy Kwan movies, pig stories, Wyatt stories.

"So Wyatt said to me, 'Tell Toni that Billy no come around no more, that good-for-shit haole, since she been gone. So no need come home.' And your father, he miss you, Toni, in his own way. He been talking about you taking us prawn hunting when you get home. Something about 'Keep them all stunned.' "

"What?"

"Private joke. That's what he said."

We coked out until five in the morning. Sheldon came through the door with a haole in a serviceman's tight and high haircut. Maverick and I feigned sleep, his arm over my chest on the black living-room floor.

We listened to the click lock of Sheldon's air-conditioned bedroom. "Bend over, Rover, let Jimmy take over." Maverick laughed. He turned to look out the glass sliding door. "Sound like the ocean, all them cars when you close your eyes, no, Toni?"

I nodded. "Yeah, with your eyes closed." We slept sharing a dirty blanket, no one waking the next day until the evening news, except once for the soft shutting of the apartment door at 6 a.m., the shadow of an unkempt serviceman slipping out, and Sheldon's soft crying in his room.

"**W**ho is who, Toni?" Sheldon continued playing his silly games. "I'm Modess and Stayfree, maybe Carefree too. 'Cause I know how to schedule my classes so I don't have finals back to back. Stupid, Toni, I told you not to take three Unit Mastery. Why you never listen to me? I bet you not even half pau in all three classes."

When I said nothing, he went on. "Bunny is Sure and Natural." The three of us were cramming the weekend before finals. There was no way I would ever finish the nine chapters I had left in each of my Unit Mastery classes. And no way I was telling.

"Toni is o.b., Tampax, Playtex Plastic Applicators without natural lubricant. You fuckin' stuck with three Unit Mastery tampons up your choch, honey."

It was true. I had nothing to say. He never even tried to help, going to the Point After and Bobby McGee's all night, every weekend, even on the weekends before finals, going to the beach. In his tight-ass Speedos, Sheldon said, "Don't read the whole damn *Othello*, *Hamlet*, *Romeo and Juliet*, and *Tempest*, stupid. Just keep reading the Cliffs Notes and show up for the final."

Right.

"Who is who, Toni?"

"Fuck you, Sheldon."

"You the rice bag rags, Toni. That's it, plain and simple. You ain't got nothing to catch all the blood that's going to spill." He rubbed some coconut oil onto his tanned shoulders. Bunny had no problem passing all of her classes. Sheldon had given her lots of little tips and advice. And she had listened to him.

I dozed off. I thought of all the haole old men, young servicemen, and skinny Asian boys who came late nights into our apartment after nights of drinking at the discos—Sheldon sending Bunny and me home with Myron or Naks at last call and going off into the night alone.

He'd slink down the hall, softly shut my bedroom door, and I'd hear the whir of the air conditioner humming on in his bedroom. By morning, my brother woke alone and acted like nothing went on, acting like his fake cheery yet bitchy self. Sheldon always kept his loneliness in check. So Bunny and I never said a word to him or to each other. For years it had been like that in our whole family. No one broached the subject. We kept our silence. My father kept his hope.

The sun smoldering overhead, the sound of the waves, Cliffs Notes covering my face, I remembered list after list of faves and stars, choice asses and best beards according to Sheldon, who Scotch-taped his preferences to the wall of the bedroom above Heads by Harry.

My father knew even then, though he secretly hoped it was Bunny or me.

This was Sheldon's I-love-haoles-with-golden-hair-and-beard phase, which lasted through *The Sting* and *Jesus Christ Superstar* and then into *Jeremiah Johnson*. Maverick Santos's senior portrait, in which he sported a slight goatee and mustache, was Sheldon's ultimate prize. My brother loved everyone who couldn't possibly love him. And out of no possibility, he wanted them more. Unrequited love. I learned *something* in that Shakespeare class.

After Sheldon's last final that spring semester, and several blenders of homemade Long Island ice teas in celebration, we did two things: Sheldon retattooed Bunny and me at 11 p.m., and then at 1 a.m. he took us all to the Wave.

On my ankle, over the tattoo heart he made me in eighth grade, he designed a cursive Y for Yagyuu with pakalana vines, dipping the fine needle wrapped in thread into the India ink. A cursive Y right over the eighth-grade heart that Mommy had found and told me to dig out of my skin.

"Mommy said to get that sonofabitching tattoo off of you before I tell your daddy and he rip um right off your skin," Sheldon said, trying to ease the pain of the needle with his impersonation of Mommy.

"I remember," I told him. I had felt close to him then.

"Well, we're doing this tonight to mark a milestone in our life as Yagyuu children. This is the first year we all lived together without Mommy and Daddy and we came close to it, but we didn't kill each other."

"And we all wasted," Bunny said.

"Right," Sheldon said. "And this time, Toni"——he paused as he poked deeper and deeper into my skin——"we won't have to poke the tattoo out with sour milk."

"Sour milk?" Bunny repeated. "What you did, Sheldon?"

"I had to poke the sour milk inside Toni's tattoo to dilute the ink. Then the heart disappeared, no, Toni?" He jimmied the needle to loosen more ink into the pore.

"That's how you took it off? When Mommy seen mine, I was so scared," Bunny said, "that I started to pick at my tattoo, and day by day I kept picking till it boiled up like a keloid and was gone."

"I never saw you do that," Sheldon said, "and I was right in the same house with you."

"Band-Aid, brah, Band-Aid." They laughed.

"There's plenty we don't care to see," I said. " 'Cause inside, we accept." I looked at my brother.

He gave me a small smile, so small it could've easily been forgotten.

Bunny's turn came next. She wanted a little Playboy bunny between her fingers. "Hide it with your class ring before Mommy make you dig this one out too," he said.

And there, on the inside of his left thigh just as he told us, two hearts with kite string and a banner interlocking them. "Put a cursive S. Practice on paper first. Curlicue like the one Bunny's drawing." I paused to look at Bunny's S on paper, then dipped the needle and injected the ink slowly into Sheldon's shuddering meat.

"Okay, now what?" I asked, and wiped my forehead.

"Okay, Bunny, practice a cursive Q for the other heart."

"Q?" she asked. "Who the hell is Q?"

I knew.

"For Quiet. For Quest. Or Quixotic. That's me."

Right.

Nobody said a word. Q was for some haole named Quince, I thought, or Quinton, who may have sat next to Sheldon at one of the dorm parties. Maybe their elbows touched, my brother making something out of nothing, my brother wanting. Q, for Queer.

It would be a heart whose contents sour-milked away at the shut of a door, a tattooed heart, sometimes empty, but never for very long, a heart changing shape and keloiding over, sheet of skin over shiny sheet of skin.

"One last fling," he said in the car on the way to the Wave, "before we slug out and die in Hilo this summer. I don't know why we can't stay up here since we have the apartment anyway and the damn junk car. I told Mommy I wanted to take summer school, but——"

"One last fling?" Bunny grumbled from the back seat. "How can I score at the Wave? All gay guys over there."

"Eh, get action for everybody." Sheldon paused. "The place don't turn real gay until about one. And, Toni," he said, looking at me, "at least try to give somebody your phone number. I mean, I want to tell my friends that all three of us scored, you know what I mean? You such a lump on a log."

"What's so important about telling your friends?"

"That's half the fun of scoring—bragging to the losers who went home with nothing." Sheldon and Bunny high-fived.

At the Wave, the deejay played mostly the Pretenders, the Police, Devo, and the Cars, not like the Sheena Easton and *Flashdance* soundtrack they played at the Point After and

Bobby McGee's. All the gay men hung out on the far side of the dance floor, some on stools with lovers between their legs, leaning on each other, and talking surreptitiously.

I scuttled behind Bunny and the two of us scampered like scared little mice. I felt like a homophobic, out-of-town hick, no place to park myself in neutral, and look and feel comfortable like a cool city person, the way I learned to blend in at the other discos.

Bunny danced with Sheldon, wasted and free of his studies. He gyrated his ass, arms in the air, swaying loosely back and forth. And when they played "Y.M.C.A.," the dance floor packed tight with bodies, shrieking, and fake oofing, Bunny came off the floor and stood by my conspicuously out-of-my-element side.

"Check that guy checking you out," she said. "Wait, wait . . . no . . . try . . . wait," she said, dragging out her words. "No . . . he's checking *me* out, how you like that?"

"Where, where?" I asked, swinging my head.

"Stupid, no make obvious," Bunny said, elbowing my arm. "The hapa one by the bar. Stupid, don't look, 'cause he looking straight at me."

"Which one?" I asked again.

"Over there," Bunny jerked with her chin. "The one with the brown spiked hair." Sheldon came off the dance floor.

"What? What?" he asked, sensing our estrogen. And then his eye caught the eye of the hapa guy. Bunny and Sheldon played coy for the next three songs, eye games, and acting as if they were having a good time with fake laughter, and punching each other's arms to ensure that the guy wouldn't think they came as a couple.

"I'm getting another drink from the bar," Bunny said at last, quite oblivious to Sheldon's interest in the hapa. He pursed his lips and blew her off with a flick of his hand. I

watched Bunny start a conversation with the hapa with more
fake laughter, her head thrown back a time or two and the
try-be-sexy swing of her thick long hair. She came back with
her drink, giddy, and said, "He asked me for my phone number. Score, brah, score."

Sheldon reluctantly high-fived her. "I'm going outside to
cool off a little bit," he said.

"Don't leave us, eh, Sheldon," I said to his back as he
headed first toward the bar, and then the door.

Bunny grabbed my hand and dragged me up to two guys
she said she knew from UH, straight, she was positive. "I was
in your history lab," she said to the bulky Korean one with
mild acne. "Dance with me and make your friend dance with
my sister." She still had her drink in her hand even onto the
dance floor.

"Dance with her, brah," the guy said to his oily-looking
haole friend, directing him to me with a macho head jerk.
The haole didn't even ask. He just pulled me onto the floor
for a dance that lasted until a slow song came on.

Bunny clasped her sweaty body to the bulky Korean as I
awkwardly smiled my way back to our standing spot on the
side. I craned my neck to look for Sheldon and felt relieved
by the tap on my shoulder. "Brah, I thought you went—" I
started before seeing the hapa.

"Dance?" he asked, and with one word, I knew he wasn't
local though his half-Japanese and half-haole look made the
Kramer's man-of-the-month posters outside the store at Ala
Moana look scrubby. I led him to the gay side of the dance
floor, away from Bunny, and after two slow songs, when he
asked, I whispered my phone number into Griffith Mueller's
Ralph Lauren-cologne-reeking ear.

I said nothing of Griffith, knowing that Bunny waited for
his call; neither did Sheldon. Because Griffith had asked him

for *his* phone number. What was Griffith thinking when the third number solicited that night was the same as the two before?

So that every time the phone rang after that Wednesday night at the Wave, the three of us jumped to answer it to the disappointment of, "Shelly," shove the phone to him, "Myron."

"Bunny," breathe out heavily into the phone, "Maverick."

"Toni," smirk and flop down on the beanbag chair, "Daddy wants to talk to you."

Until two days and two nights later, I picked up the phone. "Hello, may I please speak to Toni?" I felt wavy inside.

"Speaking, this is she," I said in perfect English. We talked for a few more minutes.

"Who's that? Who's that?" Sheldon whispered loudly at me. I waved him off with a deep furrow in my brows, the frantic flicking of my hand, and through clenched teeth still managed to sweetly say, "Daryl Hall and John Oates? At the Waikīkī Shell? When? Okay, seven o'clock then. 1601 Punahou Street. Bye."

I wafted toward my room, dropped onto my dirty mattress, forgot about three incompletes in Unit Mastery, answered no questions even with Sheldon and Bunny punching my back and ass for at least three minutes with "Who was that? Shit, tell, fucka. Who called you?"

And when the buzzer rang at 6:45 the next evening from the intercom downstairs and I left the apartment, I looked up from the parking lot to see Sheldon and Bunny leaning out of the stairwell to see who picked me up. "That's Griffith!" Sheldon screamed.

"Where?" Bunny yelled as she slammed him in the shoulder to lean farther out.

He opened and closed the door of his red Subaru pickup

for me. "Slut!" Bunny swore. "Fuckin' boyfriend stealer!" Griffith looked around to see who was yelling, shrugged his shoulders, and got into the truck.

Griffith was the first guy to glide his tongue in my mouth, which seemed ridiculous to me being that he did it to the chorus of Hall and Oates's "Kiss on My List," mistaking the word "list" for "lips." And thinking he was Rico Suave, his timing probably perfected as he listened to the greatest hits album at home. Every time the chorus came around, he sang and gave me the tongue with " 'Cause your kiss, is on my *lips*."

As we walked out of the Shell with our hands in each other's clothes, I saw Kennie Nakamura and Shari Sakamoto. It gave me supreme satisfaction knowing that they would spread rumors about seeing me with Griffith over the summer break in Hilo. I gave them one eyebrow jerk each and he frenched me right in front of them.

Griffith and I groped and probed each other in a studio apartment on Lewers Street that he had borrowed from a friend. I felt noble about not letting him poke me, which he had probably planned to Hall and Oates's "Had I Known You Better Then" from the *Abandoned Luncheonette* cassette he snapped on, as soon as he took the first bite of my nipple.

The whole night and into the morning, we made out, spit sloppy and covered with purple-black hickeys. We gave each other clumsy oral sex. He gave up a grand total of three spurts of sperm in my mouth that I nearly gagged on, more from the alfalfa-in-a-deli-sandwich taste than anything else. I've never really enjoyed a deli sandwich since. And hickeys on every crevice and angle of our bodies. When he dropped me off the following day a little past noon he said, "Babe, I'll call you tonight. Your kiss is on my lips."

My body was so pleasured, I overlooked his stupidity with

lyrics. I rode the elevator to my floor thinking about Griffith being half Japanese, half German, golden-brown stocky body, light hair, the pretty babies we'd make, a haole last name, and not going home to Hilo until every hickey faded, giving me time to go out some more with Griffith, and solidify a relationship. By this time I was walking down the hall, door key in hand—he could fly to Hilo, we could stay at Hilo Hotel and have sex, if I was ready for a commitment, if he loved me he could wait, write love letters every day, call long-distance—I turned the key, opened the door, and saw a floor-to-ceiling chicken-board partition in the living room.

They had moved me into a makeshift space that used to be the whole living room.

Sheldon's voice came from his room, the air conditioner on high hum. "I don't know why you wasted all your money on that wood from City Mill, Buns. Now you owe Fungo a favor for building that wall."

"One date to pay him back." She sniffled snot in loudly. "Kiss him, make him think I'm thankful. Fuckin' Toni, she stole the guy that was checking me out. I cannot believe."

"But you didn't have to put up the wall," Sheldon tried to convince Bunny. "Toni's suspended from UH for her proba-tion last spring at Hilo and her probation this fall. She screwed up big time this semester—she got three incom-pletes. She's suspended from UH, Bunny." I listened harder at the open door, not wanting them to hear it slam.

"So what does that mean then? The boyfriend stealer slut, tuna, bitch—she knew I liked Grif first—he was checking *me* out first."

"What I mean is that Toni going be packing up all her shit anyway when Mommy and Daddy find out from *you and me*, after we get all the grades, that she screwed up big time. I'm saying that she has to move back to Hilo. She's suspended from UH and even Hilo College. We come back to Honolulu for the fall semester, go down to the Wave, and find Grif for *you*. We can work at Helen's Fabrics this summer and save for an air conditioner for your room." Sheldon laughed and I slammed the door. They slammed their door.

I had Griffith. I knew he loved me the way he said it to me before each spurt. He made summer plans with me that night, where we would go and what we would do. All night, he talked about picnics at Kapi'olani Park, oh, we have to see Olomana at the Ranch House, and Kenny Loggins is coming in to town, what about you and me see the Pretenders with my brother and his wife, shit like that. Most men of the lying persuasion made those kinds of *plans* usually right before sex. Then they come in with the humdinger: Oh, we can drive out to the North Shore and watch the Fourth of July fireworks and get a bungalow at Kuilima or just camp out under the stars in the back of my truck. Stupid men love clichés.

I fantasized in my spare moments. He could transfer to Hilo College. Dorm. Ship his truck. We could camp at Kawaihae under the stars, of course. South Point. Hilina Pali. All my high school friends would be jealous, more so since Kennie and Shari already started the rumors. I wanted to walk in the Kaiko'o Mall with Griffith on a Saturday morning near Christmas. I thought all of this out after the first night of sucking and groping.

So that when he called three long *ring-phone-ring* days later, and after that one call, four days later after my "Operator, please check if my line's working," I flew home to Hilo.

No phone number or address in Hilo asked for or given in our last conversation. No last date the night before I left. No more calls. No last-minute visit to the apartment to say goodbye. No dozen roses the last hour, the last half hour, the last fifteen minutes before Naks arrived downstairs for the three of us. No hapa running toward the departure gate, no last embrace. I don't think he even knew my last name.

I longingly looked back at the terminal as we boarded, thinking I'd see Griffith's hands full of roses pressed to the glass window, me running back to hold him, as he lifted me up off the ground spinning me around and around. Nothing.

"He ain't coming, Toni," Bunny said on the stairs to the plane, the hot air rising and people pushing behind me. She laughed. "That's what you get, slut," she said to me as I stepped aside at the bottom of the stairs to let a tourist couple pass me.

Love, some love. Fading yellow-green hickeys, one drunken date, a Daryl Hall and John Oates concert T-shirt on, they caught me, all of them, stunned and stupid. I turned to see my nine boxes taped and sealed moving slowly up the baggage ramp.

S i x

The sun in a cane field. I was nine, sitting there in the sodden heat, and with the keen funneling of my hearing, listening for Sheldon, Bunny, Maverick, and Wyatt. Butchie supervised us, without our really knowing. We waited that afternoon for Thanksgiving dinner at Aunty Mildred and Uncle Herb's old house in Pepe'ekeo.

After we pummeled each other with rotten guavas, Mrs. Mei Ling yelled from the back door, "Butchie, get those damn kids out of the cane. Uncle Herb got six more months before the harvest, gunfunnit."

"Where you want them to play, Ma?" he yelled back.

"I don't care. Anyplace but the damn cane field before Herb has nothing to show for his two years of growing that goddamn sugar. Use your fricken brains, Butchie, before I give all you rotten kids dirty lickens."

Butchie motioned once with his head for us to follow him. He led us to Uncle Herb's garden down the road, which was full of sweet potato vines, bitter melon, chiso plants, tomato bushes, and long eggplant. He brought the slingshots we had made the summer before with guava branches.

This was the slingshot I'd sanded to a fine grain in Harry O.'s shop, its rubber tubing taut. We had practiced in the back alley behind the kitchen, hitting soda cans with stones. By the end of that summer, I could slingshot a bull's-eye of Diamond Head strawberry soda at the top of a soda-can pyramid twenty yards away.

We ran down the potholed road, past the old Pepeʻekeo Community Center and the grove of eucalyptus trees. I waved at Mrs. Freitas, who cleaned reindeer horn leaves from her lawn. Wyatt shot his stones at our feet. I lingered behind to gather them up.

Butchie whispered to Bunny and me to slink quiet and low next to him by the wooden fence. He moved the honohono grass aside for us to see. The pheasant stood in front of the sweet potato patch. "Shut up, Wyatt," he scolded, "before I broke your ass."

"What? What I said? Shit, was Sheldon the one talking. You fucka," Wyatt said, punching my brother's arm, then shoving him to the ground.

"What, Butchie, where?" Maverick asked, moving his way between the bodies wedged next to Butchie. "I cannot see."

"Move, Sheldon, my bradda like see. You deaf, hah?" Wyatt said, shoving my brother's skinny body out of the way. Bunny began to whimper. "Shut up, Bunny, you damn crybaby. Go home cook rice," Wyatt said.

"Get blood," she sobbed. "You stupid pig. I going tell my mommy."

"Shaaadaapp," Wyatt said again. "Go home—never have no crybabies on the fuckin' Ponderosa. Suck the blood or beat it." He turned to Butchie. "Let me shoot the pheasant, Butchie."

"No, not you." He slapped Wyatt's head. "Toni going shoot. Come, Bunny, no cry. Tell Wyatt, 'Yeah, never have crybabies on the Ponderosa, but never have no pigs neither.' "

"Had. Hop Sing made barbecue ribs, so had pigs," Wyatt muttered softly because *nobody* talked back to Butchie.

Butchie moved his brothers out of the way. He wanted to let the girls shoot first, complaining that his brothers and Sheldon were all a bunch of plugs. He gestured toward a red pheasant head. There were two of them.

"I see him, Butchie," I said. "The one by the cucumber vines, right there?"

"Yeah, hit him in the head. You hit the body, he just get stun, then he shake um off and fly away." Butchie moved Bunny closer to the fence. He held my shoulders in front of him, and I shrugged his hands off of me. "We can pluck it and make a fire outside the garage. We put that bird on a spit for our own Thanksgiving," he said into my ear.

"Go, Toni. There, his head stay up," Butchie whispered as I raised my slingshot and fired—a whole barrage of stones following mine and whizzing through the sweet potato patch. "Fuckin' stupid ass," Butchie yelled to Wyatt, who began firing his pocket full of stones. "C'mon, Toni, right in the head, quick before he fly."

"I got him," I screamed, as Wyatt rambled over the fence. "That's mine," I yelled, trying to squeeze through the posts.

"Ai, ai, he still alive," Wyatt yelled to the rest of us running through the garden. "Hhhaaahhh!" he screamed at the bird while waving his arms. The bird flew off unsteadily as Wyatt continued to scream, scrambling around for stones. He picked them off the ground and flung them wild and hard.

The stunned Chinese ring-necked pheasant, a torrent of plush copper feathers, hurled itself into a barbed-wire fence behind the sweet potato patch. Its eyes and mouth were pierced, the beak was gaping and soundless. Wyatt grabbed for the bird, its body fluttering, shivering in a frenzy.

"No, stop it. That's mine," I said again. Wyatt yanked the bird's head off of the barbed wire and twisted its neck in front of my face. When he turned away laughing, I loaded my slingshot with a stone from the garden and fired it at him.

"Oowee, my asshole, you fuckin' Toni," Wyatt said, first grabbing at his ass, then turning and charging at me. The pheasant flopped in his hand. He lowered his shoulder and slammed me hard. My head jerked forward, then my body snapped back, whiplashed.

I saw green venetian blinds, vertigo lines, and through the shifting lights and grilles, I saw my brother looking down at me, screaming at Wyatt, throwing stones and handfuls of red dirt at him. Sheldon touched my forehead with the back of his dirty hands and softly said my name. Wyatt walked back to stand over me, glowering, larger than his physical self, to spit in the dirt next to my face.

Sheldon told me later that they plucked my pheasant and a fat Chinese turtledove that Maverick shot on our way back to the house, plus a wild chicken that Wyatt jumped on outside of Efrem Garcia's row of marungay trees. He had bitten the neck of the chicken with his bare teeth and spat the feathers and blood out of his mouth.

Sheldon also told me that Butchie roasted all the birds on a long spit over a campfire. We sang "Kumbaya" and "Happy Trails" into the dark. Then Butchie made us all eat the stringy wild birds right off the spit, our own Thanksgiving, Ponderosa style. Bunny gagged with every bite, but the boys forced her to finish her portion of each bird.

I remembered none of it.

Maverick picked his teeth with a huge kiawe thorn. He sat next to my sister, who gave him pieces of pie off of her plate when he asked. Butchie rubbed the huge tankobu on the back of my head. I would be one of the boys that day for the hit I had taken from Wyatt, a "fuckin' Pop Warner second-string linebacker," who watched me and gave me an eyebrow jerk of mockery.

Wyatt took savage bites from the chicken. He sat there with his legs spread, and yanked at my arm when I tried to move away. He wiped his hands and mouth on his shirt. I was repulsed by him, but also drawn to his seductive anger, a kind of sickening, naked attraction.

I rode home in the Willys Jeep that night, and on the rise past Pāpaʻikou, I could see the orange glow of the streetlights below us in Hilo town. I smelled my hands, and then the odor of molasses from the sugar mill wafted through the open window. My sister slept, as Sheldon hummed "Kumbaya." The smell of blood lingered on for days. And this I don't remember but I know—Sheldon forced Wyatt to let me carry my pheasant home.

Harry O. knew nothing of my suspension from the university. I made myself his pal, his little buddy, gofer, second mate, a garut, an apprentice, and shop janitor. I took no job that summer but helped out all day, every day, in Heads by Harry. I answered the phones, took in orders, greeted customers, and prepped their game for the freezer. I picked up doughnuts from Robert's Bakery before six-thirty in the morning, perked the coffee for the old-timers, and asked for no wages.

It was the summer that KIKU-TV, a Japanese station in Honolulu, began running a samurai series with subtitles, called *The Yagyu Conspiracy*. Harry O., Harry Osamu Yagyuu, the samurai-descended taxidermist himself, said, "So what if we get one extra *u* in our name? Yagyuu, smell the same as Yagyu, if you ask me."

Nobody had asked. It was my father's story that some haole clerk in immigration at the turn of the century spelled his father's name wrong right off the damn boat. It was the government's fault that our family tree was changed forever.

"Eh, samurai is samurai," Harry O. would say. "Just like ninja was ninja——but the Yagyu sword style, that wasn't no ninja shit."

Mommy always rolled her eyes by this point in Harry O.'s tirade. "The Yagyu Shingate School was the official one of the Shogun Iemitsu. This was in the Tokugawa Era. It's in all the history books. Think I joking, eh? Just wait and watch."

"He's right, Mommy," I said this time, backing up Harry O. I knew the grade slips would arrive any day now. "Ninjas was in a lower class than serfs. I learned that in my History 151 class." I turned the channel to 13 and watched the end of a Tomoe Arare commercial.

"Why you on his side, Toni? Damn garut, cleaning up all the maggot skulls and rotten skins. And when the hell you plan on getting a summer job? Daddy ain't paying you nothing this summer. You have to help us out a little bit and pay for your own books next semester."

Wyatt and Maverick came in the upstairs door with a wheezing Mr. Santos behind them. "Ho there, Yagyuus," he managed to say in half breaths. "I cannot handle the back steps, shit. Where the poops, Mary Alice?"

"Mary Alice this, Mary Alice that," Mommy said sassily. "Eat, eat, eat, that's all you old futs think about. The pupus tonight is boil pipipi and 'ōpae. You brought up the beer from the downstairs refridge, Toni?"

"Aw, Mommy, the show's starting in a little while. And why we eating pipipi for pupus? How we supposed to read the subtitles, take out the meat from the shell with the sewing pin, and eat without poking our lips?"

"Eh, wise ass," she said, "why don't you make the pupus every goddamn Friday night of your life? I making double pupus with all you nuts watching this damn Japanee show after your happy hour downstairs. And Mei Ling's doing double duty across the street with Butchie. I'm going to Mildred's house play acey-deucey."

Mommy grabbed at her purse. "Sheldon!" she yelled through the back window upstairs. "Bring up the Bud in the big freezer right now before it explodes in there. And hurry up. Their *favorite* show is about to start."

Sheldon bounded up the back stairs and passed all the men a beer, then placed his ass in the crowded living room right next to Maverick, who moved a little closer to me. "Maverick, I cannot see," I told him. Everybody was drunk already from the late Friday afternoon spent outside the shop drinking and talking story with Niso-san and Mr. Ute. Maverick smelled cleaned and bathed. Wyatt still wore his pig-hunting fatigues with no shirt and sprawled himself out on the floor with a throw pillow folded in half under his head.

"I be Juubei, Samon, and Juubei's father tonight," Harry O. said.

"All right," said Wyatt, already drunk and unable to read the blurry subtitles. It was usually the one most sober who read subtitles, and Harry O. was the *best*, drunk or sober, with the Japanese kind of gruff, macho samurai talk with a Toshiro Mifune accent.

"Toni, you be Akane," Wyatt said. "She so fuckin' bad, that Sue Shiomi. She was Sonny Chiba's karate student, you know.

You seen her in *Dragon Princess*? Fucka was good, and my father ordered the dubbed one, no, Daddy?"

"Eh, Harry, you saw Sue Shiomi in that movie?" Mr. Santos asked. "She kick that Doberman's ass. That's real stuff when they karate-chop dogs. How they can stunt that?"

"Use a stuffed Doberman. Shut up, the show coming on," Harry O. said. "Make the TV louder with your toe, Wyatt. Eh, if the Imperial Courtiers come on tonight, you be all of them, Sheldon." Harry O. passed the pincushion and the bowl of pipipis to Mr. Santos. "Good luck, brah. Don't poke your mouth."

All of us always said the opening monologue aloud, which was the same for every episode, memorized by everyone in the whole room except for Sheldon, who went to the Poly Room Disco on most Friday nights. Tough and mean:

"The secrets of the Yagyu sword style . . . [dramatic sha-kuhachi music] . . . shall emerge triumphant in every battle . . . for we possess the secrets of the Yagyu . . . if your enemy interferes, slaughter him . . . if your brother interferes, murder him . . . if the gods interfere, forsake them . . . if the Buddha himself interferes, renounce him . . . for we are the protectors of the Shogun and that is our destiny!"

We all hootaed and high-fived at the end of the monologue as KIKU-TV played the same Shiseido cosmetics commercial ad straight from the sixties. I leaned forward to take the bowl of pipipi from Mr. Santos, and Wyatt poked his toe under my ass, which made me squirm.

And then the show began with the eerie shakuhachi music. Harry O. spoke as Samon, Lord Yagyu's second, not so rugged, but smart son. "For the sake of the clan, Juubei-sama, Father says we must avenge the magistrate for the murder of Lord Nakaya. The scoundrels are beating the rap! Justice must pre-vail!" The subtitles always read like corny clichés and we'd ham it up even more. I slid the bowl of seashell pupus to Maverick.

I spoke as Akane, Juubei's karate-expert but ninja-trained sister. "But, Juubei-sama, what of his beloved wife and child? The heir is a blessed first son and his mother most admirable. The clan minister pressured Magistrate Yamamoto. The minister is utterly vile and evil." I stuck my tongue out at Wyatt, who flipped me the bird. He poked the sewing pin in his teeth and sucked air.

Harry O. spoke as Juubei, big brother, big hero: "The wrath of the gods will strike him down, the wrath of my sword, the honor of the Shogun is at stake——the truth shall be upheld in the Yagyu's revenge! Come, faithful retainers of the Shogun Iemitsu. We must stamp out the scum! Culprits! Cads! Rats! Hurry, we go!"

We never missed an episode. Nothing stood in the way of missing one piece of the serial's story line that summer.

Mr. Santos began ordering more samurai movies to play at the Mamo Theatre in spite of Mrs. Mei Ling's complaints that the draw was small and not worth the run. "Shit, honey, one, two nights max. Please," he begged in front of all the old-timers, who were regulars at every showing of a samurai movie.

"Tuesdays, only then," she grumbled. "Every third week of the month. And, Ute, you better bring your wife and sister-in-law, eh," she commanded. "And Niso-san, you better not give me none of this 'I too tired, I going home' after work shit, you old futs hear me? And no freebies. That's money I losing for your damn samurai movies."

"Wow, Ma," Wyatt said. "Like we losing that much money, shit. And, Daddy, *Bushido Blade* no count, right? 'Cause had haoles: How come get haoles in every main movie about Japan? Like Richard Chamberlain was Anjin-san in *Shogun*, and now he in that movie with Toshiro Mifune and Sonny Chiba——" Wyatt stopped, looking at Sheldon.

"Why, I like Richard Chamberlain. He handsome, so what? He bring star quality to those damn barbarian Jap-ugly Tojo wannabe Westerns," Sheldon said from the doorway of the shop.

"I rest my motherfuckin' case," Wyatt whispered.

"Wyatt was the first one there with his sekihan from Aka-fuku Manju when we had the *Shogun* potluck," Sheldon said to no one in particular, "so I don't know why he grumbling."

"Fag," Wyatt muttered. Mrs. Mei Ling slapped his head hard with a backhand. Wyatt got up and stalked into the shop, shoving aside my brother with his leg. "Move, asshole." Sheldon didn't even respond, but sauntered down the street to talk to Franjelica leaning on the wall outside of Elsie's Fountain.

I finished sweeping the floor behind Harry O.'s worktable and began Windexing the glass showcase when Wyatt leaned his steamy arms on the glass. "Stupid, you cannot see I trying to wipe? Move," I told him. "And don't come around here after work unless you take a bath. You smell like rotten pig teeth." I kept bitching at him to lead in to what I really wanted to know. "And by the way, what's the scoops with Maverick?" I asked him. "Where he been?"

"You never hear?" Wyatt said to me. "He checking out Heather Sugimoto. Eh, she Miss Kona Coffee this year. What, bummers for your *whole* family my brother get girlfriend?"

"Eh, fuck you, okay, Wyatt." I slammed the dirty towel on the glass showcase.

He grabbed my arm hard. "I sorry, Toni." He wouldn't let go even as I tried to shake free from him. His touch felt warm as his large hand loosened its grip.

I yanked my arm away from him. "What? Was hard to say? You sorry, yeah, right."

"No, I sorry," he said. And then it was quiet. He ran his fingertips over the glass countertop. "Eh, my father ordered *Yagyu Ichizoku Inbo* for tomorrow night, you heard? You coming?"

"Yeah, why? Me and my daddy coming."

"He not coming. They going up Laupāhoehoe Reserve with Cardoza tomorrow and they coming back late. That's what my father told me. They want my mother to run the movie one more night, but she said, 'Tough shit, life is full of choices.'"

"Why can't they just no go hunting on Wednesday?"

"Cardoza cannot get them in the reserve anytime they fuckin' please." Wyatt paused. "Me and you, Toni, we the only ones left from the *Yagyu Conspiracy* gang. Harry O. and my father like know what the whole fuckin' Yagyu story is from beginning to end."

I picked up the glass cleaning towel and made it into a whip to snap at Wyatt's ear. "Why, mental," I said, whipping the wet tip right next to his face. "Why I have to go with you? You cannot read the subtitles, eh? Then try be sober before the damn show, shit."

Wyatt stood there silent, staring hard at the glass showcase, as he leaned on both arms spread wide. He rubbed his goatee and bottom lip with one hand. I felt sick and sorry. I knew the answer to my own question. So that when Wyatt said, "I *going* be fuckin' drunk. 'Cause tomorrow Mr. Harper, up the park, he said after work, we going— Fuckin' chick, all chicks, fuck you, fuck um all. I thought you was small kine all right, but no—"

"Okay, okay, okay," I said, pretending anger and attitude

so as not to let Wyatt know what I knew. It all made sense
in that one moment, him not graduating and hating school,
teachers, counselors, and cutting all the time except for football season, not taking the GED and flunking year after year.
"I meet you seven o'clock," I said without looking at him.
"Inside."

"Why, so nobody see you with the *other* Santos brother?
Fuckin' Maverick poking every goddamn squid in town, in
alphabetical order, and he already on Heather Sugimoto. And
to you blind motherfucks, he one *nice* guy. Nice guy, eh, my
brother? Love um, fuck um, and leave um." He shook off his
momentary jealousy. "Fuck it, if you cannot take a joke.
Seven, then, near the front, so I can see my babe Sue Shiomi
right in my face."

He turned and walked toward the band of afternoon light
in the door of the shop, his hair long and golden-brown curly
in the sunlight. He stopped to look at me with the barest of
smiles. "And no be late before I kick your ass, and your brother's ass, and your father's ass too," he said. "I take on your
whole Yagyuu clan." He laughed mean as he spun a beer
bottle cap out onto the middle of Mamo Street, Wyatt who
couldn't read.

And so I read to him the subtitles of the entire movie. Wyatt
Santos sat alone on the far left of the theater, not looking
back for me while I stood below the projection booth, con-
templating an escape out the side door and through Juanito's
Barbershop.

I moved sideways into the row he chose. He put his hands
on my hips and let his fingers linger across my ass.

"Fucka, don't touch me, shit. And where's your shirt?"

He passed me a fifth of Beefeater as soon as I sat down
next to him. It was nearly empty. The movie came on, and

we started saying the opening monologue aloud to a couple of old Japanese men's "Ssshhh, yakamashi, dame yo."

But Wyatt stood up and said the rest of the words with a mighty and drunken gusto. "This is my fuckin' theater," he said, beating his bare chest. "Don't like it, there's the door." Somebody clapped for him. He flopped down in the seat next to me and laughed.

"C'mon, read," he said, giving me an elbow.

"Shhhh!" someone hissed.

I leaned over next to Wyatt's face, my hand cupped toward him, the sweet reek of gin and Aramis from his pores. "The ninjas have stolen the dead Shogun's heart and Lord Nakaya has it in his possession. It is our destiny to protect his heart." He leaned back and breathed in my hair.

My shoulder pressed to his. "I am prepared to commit seppuku," I read in his ear as he moved toward my neck. He was smelling me. "That is my karma." I finished. Akane, Juubei's sister, backwards ninja-jumped over a house to escape the evil Imperial Courtier Okinishi. Wyatt moved his heavy arm to the backrest behind me, and I settled my uncomfortable and tense body into the space.

And as my mouth whispered subtitles into his ear—"Only one man is born to this by the blessings of the gods. You are this divine man"—I felt his fingers on my arm, his rough, hard fingers lifting the sleeve of my shirt and brushing my skin underneath it. My breath short and shallow, he moved his hand over my neck. He swept his fingers under the neckline of my shirt, on my bare shoulder, a slow, light sweep over and over.

"Hirano-sama, you are held in high regard for venerating the honor of your brother." I could barely go on. He took my hand and placed it on his thigh, moving my hand upward. I wanted Maverick and in many ways played this out as a perverse secret that Maverick would one day stumble upon. His pig brother took me from him and now he could defend me against his *own brother*.

"He does not deserve your benevolence, the scoundrel." Wyatt leaned his face into mine. I felt his tongue moving in my ear, deeper into the hole, the cracking warmth of flesh, and then he began biting me. "I follow the path of no return." His hand slipped under my shirt.

The credits started rising on the screen. The lights went on and I pushed him off of me. I got up to leave. I would run if I had to. Wyatt slumped in the seat and buttoned his jeans.

"Your father read subtitles more better than you any day, Toni." I stopped at the end of the aisle. We didn't look at each other.

"At least you took a bath," I told him.

"Only for you," he said, mean. "*Shogun's Ninja* next month. Same time, same row."

"Good, I send Harry O. to find you. He the best, right? I tell him to sniff you out. Just follow the gin fumes."

"Good," he said. "Then I no need bathe after work."

"Good," I said, and left.

I crossed Mamo Street into the damp moth and rust of the summer night, walked up to my bedroom, and leaned out the window. I watched the traffic lights blink yellow and red on the corner. Elsie locked up her fountain down the street. The fluorescent lights in the Mamo Theatre lobby flicked off, while the lights in the office upstairs illuminated Mrs. Mei Ling's small money-counting figure. Finally, the Mamo Theatre sign, which was missing a lightbulb in the O, fizzled and zapped off.

The phone rang.

"I scored a bag of dope," he said.

"So what? Big thrills," I said to him.

"And some coke," he whispered.

"So—"

"I meeting Maverick down at Isles. He just called." I stared out of the open window. The rain slid through rusted holes in the gutter and onto the wet street.

"Maverick and who? Heatner?"

"No. Sheila Wakida, I think."

"Sheila? That fuckin' tuna," I said. The line went still. I saw Wyatt's shadow move to the open window above the lobby, the bedroom he shared with Maverick. He leaned on the frame and looked at me leaning out of my window, his face distorted by the lurid street and blinking traffic lights.

"So what, then? We go Isles. My brother on the W's," he said. "Almost the Y's. One of you Yagyuus get chance pretty soon, maybe *you* this time." This felt so secretive, almost incestuous because of the closeness of our families, our own incompatibility, and our long history of verbal and physical brawling.

"You go inside Irene's Liquors and buy me one bottle Tanqueray. The cashier lady still carding me, that fuckin' obasan."

"You made her granddaughter pregnant in eighth grade, you stupid shithead."

"That too." Wyatt laughed at the memory. "So what, you coming with me?"

"Maybe," I said.

He rested his face on his bare arms and stared down at the street. "Get *plenty* coke," he said. "For Maverick and some of the pig boys." He looked up. "And you and me."

I sighed heavily. "Yeah, okay then."

I watched Wyatt Santos cross the street. He still had no shirt on and his Levi's zipped but unbuttoned. He pulled his

flannel jacket over his thick arms, lifted his hair out from
under the collar, then disappeared around back to the kitchen
door. I listened to his light footsteps up the back stairs.

"That you, Bunny? Sheldon?" Mommy called from the living room.

"Me, Aunty Mary Alice," Wyatt called to her. "Toni and
me meeting Maverick them down Isles. Short kine."

"Oh, okay. She's in her room. If Sheldon meet you guys,
tell him Helen called, and said don't be late tomorrow. Damn
kid, think life is one all-day, all-night party, then showing up
late for work."

"I slap his head for you, Aunty," I heard him say right
outside my door.

I stared at the dark marquee and didn't turn around. I
waited for the slow turn of the doorknob, the opening door
purling light onto the floor. Wyatt slid inside the blue-black
of my room, his tall body leaning on the door. His finger over
his lips, he walked toward me, took off his flannel jacket and
let it fall to the floor; he moved himself on top of me without
words.

I cannot enter a room anymore without the knowledge of
this night. And every time we inhabit the same room, I feel
his pull and the weight of his look. There is one man in a
lifetime who will do this to you: make you feel his eyes from
inside your clothes and skin. You wait for the solitary moment
to feel the touch of a hand on your body and without words
he moves you to some naked, repulsive darkness to eat you,
layer by layer.

Harry O. and I stand on a pu'u past Hilina Pali. We are
alone on this goat hunt, together.

The silvery velvet liko drips dew into the broken bark of the 'ōhi'a. I pull my army jacket tighter around me. The summit of Mauna Loa swoops down, amethyst-tinted in the morning wind. I can feel the pulmonic beat of a crater bird's wings above as I speak to my father.

"Daddy, I flunked out. I don't know what to do. I cannot go Hilo College. They suspended me for one year."

He fires once and stalks off half running into the pili brush. I am not far behind him. And then he shoots again, into the billy's head. Blood spatters on my boots and pants.

He skins the goat while its body is still beating. He pulls hard with his knife, angry. He stabs at hide and flesh, making careless incisions. Stiff black goat hair dries in blood on his arms and hands. He throws the head and skin near me; goat legs dangle flimsily. Then he bags the meat in a bleeding rice bag that he throws over his shoulder.

He wraps the head and cape around his neck. "You break my heart, Toni, you know that?" he says in a cold monotone. "I thought you had brains." He walks ahead of me. "Maybe somebody hunting out of their area mistake me for a goat."

Sheldon and Bunny returned to Honolulu for the fall semester at UH. I took a job at Hilo Hattie's, a mu'umu'u factory in a broken-down Quonset hut in Hilo's industrial area. Busload after busload of tourists streamed in, their faces smelling like coconut oil, wearing aloha shirts decorated with palm trees or huge hibiscus blossoms, and tacky black socks with vinyl sandals.

I was hired as the official lei hostess. Clyde Morton, my boss, said that I didn't have enough experience with cashiering, no sales pizzazz for the floor, and not enough sewing skills for the factory. But I qualified for the minimum-wage job of hostess.

"Give the customers a nice shell nei, offer them a cup of Kona coffee in your best English, and pour it, of course, then offer them a macadamia nut butter brickle sampler from the koa bowl near the entrance. Make sure the ti-leaf lining in the bowl is fresh. And smile, smile, smile if they lean toward you for a nice peck on the lips. See if you can get those stains out of the coffee decanter, tacky, awfully tacky when it's empty. And, Antoinette, make sure your mu'umu'u is always neatly pressed. You're on the front line. You're the first person our customers see and it's important to make a good first impression."

I was also in charge of the tiny tape recorder under the coffee table that played fabulous Hawaiian tunes of wartime yesteryear like "Everybody loves the hukilau. The huki, huki, huki, huki, hukilau. Everybody loves the hukilau, where the laulau is the kaukau at the hukilau." And my favorite: "I'm a little brown gal, in a little grass skirt, in a little grass shack in Hawaii . . . through that island wonderland, she's broken all the kane's hearts . . . it's not hard to understand, that that wahine is a gal of mine."

Taped songs in a Bing Crosby croon droned on about swaying palm trees, balmy breezes, grass shacks, maidens in sarongs with exotic blossoms in their hair, two or three brown maidens for every man, colonialism, charlatanism, romanticism—all in the name of capitalism.

But I needed a job. I needed the money.

"Aloha and welcome to Hilo Hattie's, where Hilo Hattie does the Hilo Hop. My name is Antoinette. May I offer you some complimentary Kona coffee and macadamia nut butter brickle sampler? Mahalo."

To me, it beat working downtown in the Green Onion Lounge or waiting tables at Jimmy's or Mun Cheong Lau for all of my family and friends to come down and make me serve them beer or tea for a five percent, *we're family*, tip. I'd see nobody at Hilo Hattie's but tourists, no classmates to run into with their "Eh, what's up? So . . . what you been up to, Toni? I thought . . . you went college? *This* what you doing now?!"

I'd be content with Clyde Morton, haole boss, so easy to hate, territorial salesladies with red lips and glasses hanging on chains, rows and rows of matching coral and shell necklaces, bracelets, earrings, rings, and pins.

I dusted koa pineapple serving dishes, koa monstera leaf dip trays, carved tikis of naked native women, warriors, and major Hawaiian deities, lava crucifixes, fat-tummied Buddhas, and lava tiki key chains with red rhinestone eyes like the one Peter Brady bought, getting cursed by a tarantula on his bed when there are no tarantulas in Hawai'i. I wiped monkeys carved out of coconuts, shells-in-acrylic penholders, and tropical shell night lights. I arranged coffee mugs alphabetically.

Barbara—Palapala.

David—Kawika.

James—Kimo.

Susie—Kuke.

Gifts perfect for the in-laws, everything stamped *Made in Hawaii*, which was another capitalist lie. Everything was made in the Philippines, Taiwan, Malaysia, Singapore, or China by sweatshops full of children.

Harry O. made me take the Hele-On bus home from work as further humiliation. I had to stand at the bus stop and wave my hands in the air, a human fan in a pleated caftan, for the bus to stop for me. That's how one used public transportation in Hilo.

But then Maverick and Wyatt started picking me up in the pig truck on their way home from work. Wyatt would jump out, run to the koa bowl for a fistful of macadamia nut brickle, and throw a couple of unopened cans from under the table to Maverick in the idling truck.

It was humiliating riding in the back of the truck with a couple of dogs who barked in greeting and slobbered all over my muʻumuʻu uniform. Clyde Morton stood with his hand on his hip at the main entrance, clipboard poised, pretending he was writing me up for something like maybe being a little too low-class for Hilo Hattie's.

He made all the old Japanese salesladies, the Filipino seamstresses, the Portuguese janitor ladies, and the Puerto Rican baggers get dropped off and picked up in their beat-up Batmobiles at the back entrance. All the yuppie haole and Japanese accountants and bookkeepers he let through the front or side doors.

Wyatt stole cans of butter brickle, bags of Kona coffee, and Mr. Coffee filters, and finally the whole koa bowl full of brickle crumbs stuck to a shiny ti leaf. One drunken Friday afternoon on their way home from work, Wyatt tucked it under his arm like a football and ran back to Maverick in the truck, whereupon Mr. Clyde Morton fired me right in front of Hilo Hattie's.

"And don't you ever ask me for a reference of any sort. You have a poor work ethic and lack professionalism. I'll make sure you never find work in the tourist industry in this town again." He huffed his pink-faced self into the Quonset hut, deducted every stolen item from my last paycheck, and had me charged with theft. The police drove up to the shop that night to arrest me, but no evidence.

We consumed all of it, except the bowl, which Wyatt flung out of the truck and into Ice Pond.

I was back in the shop between jobs. Harry O. had not spoken a sentence to me for several days. "What next, Toni?" he finally asked me one afternoon. He meant job-wise. He meant arrest-record-wise. He meant my-whole-life-wise. He meant, how would I fail next? I didn't know. I shrugged my shoulders. I had failed him, in some ways worse than my brother, who in Harry O.'s eyes was a failure as a man.

"You don't know?" he said when I shrugged again. "That's what I thought you said."

Maverick had started coming in to the shop at 5 a.m. to help Harry O. open up. He sat with him for the first cup of coffee and the first bird skinning of the day before leaving at seven for his pig job.

"So what, Harry O.," he'd ask, "same incision no matter what kind bird?"

My father gave a guttural "Um," meaning yes. "And watch how you sever the leg from the body."

"Where, try show me?" Maverick would ask.

"Right . . . here," my father would say gently, showing Maverick how it should be done with a flick of his knife.

After work, Maverick would watch the finishing varnish of a deer nose, the black painted in to the deep recesses of tear ducts. "So how you got the small veins by the eye? Ho, look real. Eh, Harry O., you always put veins?"

"Um. Anybody who *apply* themself can only get better and better at what they do." He looked at me. "But quitters never prosper, know what I mean, boy? And brains is just a pile of intestinal goop if you never use your head." Maverick nodded.

On weekends, he watched as my father skinned hides on the sawhorse in the back alley. "How much salt you think you use? About one pound per skin? Half pound?"

"Um," he replied, real Pat Noriyuki Morita monosyllabic Japanese master samurai sensei style. The aged revered master questioned by the guileless neophyte, Master Po and Kwai Chang Cain, Charlie Chan and Number One Son, Lord Yagyu and Yagyu Juubei.

"So what, brah," Harry O. said to Maverick one afternoon, "like learn my trade? Like apprentice?"

"Yeah, Harry O.," Maverick said, nearly falling off the stool. "I was wondering when you was going ask. Oh, jeez, if you ever *was* going ask. Would be my honor to apprentice here."

"I got no number one son to take over this business for me. Might as well be you. You like family to me. Sheldon, sheez." Harry O. sighed. He glanced at me sitting behind the register. "Sheez," he said again, shaking his head. "What I going do? I think the boy mahu."

My jaw fell open. Maverick swung his head to see my reaction. "He so tilly," my father said. "Broke me up, I tell you, when the boy act faggot."

"Me and Toni," Maverick said, "we like learn from you. You like, Toni?" he called at me across the shop.

"She don't know jack nothing," Harry O. said before I could answer. And my answer was yes. "This her motto—not shit for brains but brains for shit. Besides, this ain't no women's work. This ain't for Toni. This is a man's work. Go down Helen's Fabrics ask for Bunny's summer job. Toni *going* back school," he said to Maverick.

"Why, Toni can handle," Maverick answered. "Me, Toni, and my brother Wyatt, please, Harry O.? You got nothing to lose. We catch our own game, and then we help you, no pay, no nothing while we learning. And then what, say sixty-forty? You make sixty percent off us. All us three."

"You been thinking this out, eh, Maverick? Eh, boy, you get gumption. That's what I like to see in one apprentice. That's what I like about you—you know how to *apply* yourself."

I was the one who had gumption.

All those years of hunting and hanging around the shop table, getting the skulls, washing out maggots, organizing the trays of glass eyes as soon as the bubble-wrapped package came in from Van Dyke's. I even named them: Sandy Duncan, Big Horn for Ute's pet sheep, Sammy Davis, Jr., Chinee, Japanee, Beloved Fern, Pueo for birds, and Mr. Fung, my seventh-grade counselor injured by a five iron at Hilo Municipal.

I sampled bottles of Crimson Blaze, Scarlet Sin, and Ruby Passion Cutex at Ben Franklin because he was too embarrassed to test them on his own fingernails. He painted Ruby Passion on the chukar beak and chicken faces that same afternoon.

I melted slabs of Parowax and red crayons for him over a Bunsen burner in a Niblets can, adding in the carnation-pink crayon, the flesh crayon that was never the color of anyone's skin that I knew, and once, on a whim of genius, I melted a piece of cornflower crayon which gave me the right, rich color of a boar's gaping mouth. I watched my daddy paint the hot wax over the papier-mâché he formed into a tongue in the mouth of a boar with twisting tusks, watched as I jotted down the exact combination of colors for the next pig.

Gumption. I had more gumption and heart than Maverick Santos any day.

"Okay," Harry O. said to him. He startled me. "Classes start anytime you here. Important stuff I save for the weekends, if can. If, I said, if. I running a business, you know. Tomorrow, tanning. Lesson number one. Tell Wyatt no be late. I put my money he going be the best at this. Toni, go get the totan from under the building. We pickle-bathe the hides this afternoon."

"Okay, Daddy."

Maverick looked at me and raised his eyebrows in the local gesture of *I did good*. Again. He needed to stop saving me. I couldn't wait for another round of women and alphabets.

Maverick, Wyatt, and I left for the trash bins down at Isles to look for strays hungry enough to approach the old fishermen who went there day after day and night after night. A small menpachi on a full-moon night, a small halalū or 'oama when they ran through the bay, fish tossed over their shoulders to the cats.

I had called the one vet in town, Dr. Fulton Myles, for specimens from his lab. He told me that I needed to pay him five dollars per cat carcass.

"Five dollars per cat?" Wyatt said. "Shit, if we wasn't doing him a favor for disposing his damn dead animals, yeah, I can see he charge us. Five dollars? That's more expensive than top sirloin per pound and we ain't eating them fuckin' cats."

"Let's trap mongoose or something," I said.

"They filthy stink," Harry O. said. "Just like rats. Not that I want you to use cats. Why no wait till Ute go Lāna'i for deer?"

"I cannot wait that long," Maverick said, looking at Harry O. "Plus, I was reading the taxidermy book and said to use small animals."

"Gumption," Harry O. said, turning toward me, raising his eyebrows.

"Eh, more cheap if we go down the Humane Society and get couple cats," Wyatt said. "We name um in front the cat guy and act like they already pets."

"Go offer Dr. Myles a tan cat hide to replace the stupid toupee he wearing now. Maybe he give us sale price," Maverick said.

Mommy sat down at the table with her mug of after-dinner o-cha with bits of popcorn and tea leaves swirling to the bottom. "You guys make me sick. What the hell you think you doing, gunfunnit? The damn animal rights activists be crawling up your ass if they ever find out you're behind this nonsense, Harry. And it's a misdemeanor on top of that."

"Why, that's not me. That's the kids. You guys ain't going finger me, eh?" Daddy laughed nervously. "They only going do few cats, what the hell? We keeping the feral population down. Maverick's right. They should start small when they learn tanning, Mary Alice. They cannot learn on cow hide or sheep hide. Uh-uh. Too big. Eh, you one teacher—suppose to give positive experience, eh?"

"Don't give me that shit. I tell you, you spending a couple nights in the county jail for this and I letting you rot there for being stupid, you damn Harry."

Wyatt and Maverick planned to catch two cats for each of us to learn tanning. Wyatt would throw the small net over them as they came from the trash bins for the open can of Starkist, a mild skirmish of arched backs, neck hair stiff in the air, and feral hissing before he shoved them into rice bags, claws piercing the fabric, legs kicking. We even had our choice of colors.

"We should drown um when we get home," Wyatt told me while Maverick took a leak by the trash bin. "You ever seen cats drown? I did. He stare at you with his glassy eye, and the mouth open and close like he sucking for air, but that's water going down his lungs. And he fighting and clawing all the way, so you hold his head down. The eyes no close when he finally ma-ke." I felt sick. "Here, Toni, you better drink some of this." He handed me a bottle of 151 Bacardi. "Straight up, me and you. To us."

"To *us*? Yeah, right. Dream on." When I took the bottle to my lips, Wyatt tilted my elbow up and my throat opened for the burn of rum rushing down my neck. I wiped my mouth with the back of my hand. He held me against the truck and tipped my head back with his hand to take the rum off my neck with his tongue, his mouth moving toward the back of my neck.

"Eh, what you fuckas doing?" Maverick said, walking toward us while zipping up his jeans. "What's going on, man?"

"Toni," Wyatt said, giving me a sharp shove, "she one pig." I shoved him in the chest. "All the Bacardi went down her face. Never like waste. Here," he said as he passed the bottle to Maverick, who raised an eyebrow at me.

We sat down on the pier and passed the bottle around. From the pocket of his flannel jacket, Wyatt pulled out a joint wrapped in a matchbook cover. I knew I would need anesthetizing.

I drank deep from the bottle, the keen amber swelter of rum in my chest. Rum, bottle, lips, hands, joint, always two hands going at once, passing left and right.

Wyatt lit a cigarette for us to share. Maverick was zoned out, lost in space somewhere over Mauna Keʻa. Then Wyatt pushed my legs apart with the easy roll of his hands and the bottle of rum pressed hard between my legs. This seduction felt sinister in its secrecy.

Maverick sat right next to me.

Breath of rum in my hair, breathing and pivoting the bottle, I felt the splintery wind off of Hilo Bay. I smelled the sharp brine of brackish water. I listened to the muffled thrashing of cats in the bed of the truck.

Wyatt tanned the best, just as Harry O. had predicted. Thick, hard hands, the quick slice of meat off of deer, sheep, or cow hides. He worked his skins clean and even. He eased the stiff hides through the breaker, his hard hands impervious to the sting of the pickle bath, the pounds of salt seeping into every cut, pore, and hangnail. His fingers massaged the tanning oil into the cured flesh like a lover.

Soon Maverick graduated to head mounts. Harry O. taught him the old way of molding papier-mâché on a skull, reconstructing the facial features of the animal with a sculptor's intimate hand. We were not to learn on the prefab urethane head forms which eliminated creativity; we were to see with the eyes of God that Harry O. often spoke about as we worked. Maverick finished a baby goat he found in a nanny's womb, and positioned her in fetal rest with an infant's tilt of the head and wondering eyes.

I learned about birds, slowly slicing skin and flesh, keeping the body dry, and feathers unsoiled by blood or body fluids. I put my knife down and gently pulled the ears from the head with my fingernail. I never nicked the eyes, and I know my father marveled at the elegance of a woman's hand. I positioned legs, wings, body, and head, then perched the mount on an 'ōhi'a log. My first real bird mount was a chukar; I made him noble and magnificent with a proud excelsior chest. This I learned from Harry O.

I taught the Santos brothers how to sew. Wyatt tanned pig balls, goat balls, sheep balls, buffalo balls, cattle balls, and deer balls, which we sewed into coin bags pulled taut with strips of leather.

We never killed another cat.

I brought out some smoked marlin and sekihan musubi from the kitchen. Mommy was behind me with a bowl of home-made namasu. Harry O. followed with the tall stools from the shop. "You seen what Wyatt made?" he asked the old men. "Look, all my stools get padded cowhide cover now. My friend Hubert Nariyoshi slaughter his cow and gave me the hide. Wyatt is good with his hands, you know. He make the skins tough when he tan, then he pull tight when he upholster. Eh, the kid has a big future in Heads by Harry, Inc."

Mr. Santos and Mrs. Mei Ling crossed Mamo Street with Herline's third baby, Tabitha. "Eh, Herb," Mr. Santos said to my uncle, "you seen what my boys been make with Harry? Toni, go get me and Aunty Mei Ling one beer. Come, come, Herb. You the skeptic one, eh?"

Mr. Santos passed Tabitha to Mrs. Mei Ling. "You see this how clever," he said, pointing to a mount on the wall.

"What's that?" Uncle Herb said. "It's just a bunch of mounted deer asses with what, the tail up like he's about to take a dump. So what? That's not very clever."

"I mean, the possibility is endless," Mr. Santos said. "Who would ever think my Wyatt be good at something, no, Harry?"

"He mean, but he one hardworking kid," my father said. "And good with his hands, no, Toni?"

I said nothing.

"I kid you not, Harry. That's exactly what Mr. Harper told me when I seen him Vulcans basketball at the Civic. My boy Wyatt, he one merciless hunter, Harper tell me, but the boy is there every day, on time, ready to go. Remind me to tell him his boss no like him slicing off the pig balls and the feet. What you guys making with the pig feet?"

"You see," Harry O. said.

"Gun rack, ashtray, lampstand, what? Make coatrack with all kine different feet."

Maverick walked into the shop full of grime from work. Wyatt followed with a Heineken in his hand. "Eh, who brought the Heinees?"

"Me," Uncle Herb said. "Drink up. They were on sale at KTA."

Wyatt gave me a head jerk. "So what?" *Yagyu Conspiracy* tonight? What a day, no, Mav? Stupid Harper's number one, scrub-ass, hopeless dog got bust up today. And where was the boss? Up in the helicopter with his stupid kid Billy. His dog all bleeding. I had to stitch his ass in the forest." He looked at me. "Lucky thing you taught me how to sew, no, baby?"

"Eh, no be 'baby'ing me, shit."

"What I saying? Stupid me. Sue Shiomi my babe," Wyatt said. "I full of dog guts, fuck, all his slobber all over me. I going shower."

"Wait," Harry O. said. "I want to say something in front your father, mother, and Aunty Mary Alice. Herb, try wait——" Wyatt stopped in the doorway and spread his arms across its width. "We in a new phase of Heads by Harry," he began. "We Inc. now, and you boys been the reason—the way you work like hell, no grumble, learn fast——"

"What about Toni, Harry O.?" Maverick asked. "She did mostly all the birds."

"Well, that's what I wanted to say tonight to all of you before we go upstairs for *Yagyu Conspiracy*. I made up my mind." Mommy looked on, angry at Daddy. "And you shut your mouth, Mary Alice." Mommy turned and stormed out of the shop.

"Eh, what's going on?" Maverick asked. Wyatt kicked his boot on the doorframe and refused to look up.

"You boys continue working with me. Business as usual. But Toni—" He paused until I looked him straight in the eye. "If she don't go back Hilo College this fall and get a business degree so one of you clowns know what the hell is going on in the books, it's over for her. You hear me, Toni? Don't be a half-rate businessman like me."

I knew this was hard for him to say to me. "But Bunny and Sheldon getting business degree, Daddy. They can do the books." I came out from behind my shop table and stood next to Maverick.

"Bullshet. You do your own books. And who said they coming home Hilo after they pau UH? Trust nobody. Not even your own brother. That's the way of the Yagyuu."

"Oh, fuck," I said. I couldn't believe he was going to rely on a television cliché in this moment. "I guess I have no job. Again." I kicked a hole in the dry wall. "What I going do, Daddy?" Everyone looked uncomfortable.

"You heard me," he said softly. "Go back school, Toni. What I says goes. You get your choices."

"Eh, Harry O.," Maverick said. Wyatt stared out the door. "Nah, just coast. Maybe Toni can go community college book-keeping like Pearly, no, Uncle Herb?"

"Sheez, that's a huge waste of time," Uncle Herb said. "If I were you, I'd force her into a four-year program. Otherwise, you're just a lousy bookkeeper. I think you heard your dad, Toni."

I slipped out from behind Maverick, took off my work apron, and laid it on the counter. I pushed past Wyatt, who occupied the doorway. "Where you going?" my father yelled. "I not pau with you yet. Get your ass back in here."

His words trailed off as I headed up the street. "And don't

think you coming back *my* house tonight to watch *Yagyu Conspiracy*. And don't think we going tell you what happened to Juubei. Toni. Toni, get your ass back here."

I turned around once by Kaya's Pawnshop to see Maverick following me up Mamo Street, but even to him, I had nothing to say.

Seven

Two successes befell the great taxidermists.

The first involved Maverick and Wyatt, who drove all the way to a garage sale in Kamuela, where an old haole man sold them a whole body mount of a puma, mouth open, ready to pounce. His ear was ripped, his fur splotchy, his tail crooked, and he rode to Hilo in the back of the truck.

Maverick restored the broken ear with leftover wild goat hide, patched the holes in the fur, repainted the tear ducts, nose, and open mouth, changed the glass eyes, added veins to the neck and face, and straightened out the tail. I nodded when I thought he was adding an artistic touch.

Harry O. sold the puma at triple the cost to the Orchid Isle Auto Center, where it still waits mid-spring to pounce when you go to buy a Ford.

The second success involved Harry O. Someone who walked into the shop one day turned out to be a production assistant for the movie *Black Widow* starring Debra Winger and Theresa Russell. For the scenes in the palatial mansion in Kona or some unnamed Hawaii-ish beachfront locale that Theresa inhabits after she black-widows her most recent lover, who FBI agent Debra Winger has also fallen for, they needed a Chinese ring-necked pheasant to sit on the grand piano. They also requested a boar head, a Moloka'i safari antelope, a mouflon, and a shark mount for the wall in the lover's trophy room.

These were mounts that Maverick and Wyatt worked on while I watched.

Two hundred dollars plus residuals every time they showed the movie on TV or cable—Harry O. would get a check for twenty-five dollars, to be split sixty-forty with the Santos brothers.

Harry O. let *the boys* deliver the animals when the *Black Widow* crew filmed their police station scenes at Hilo Intermediate School. And there in our shop, framed next to the thumbtack through my head in the Science Fair newspaper article, an eight-by-ten color glossy of Maverick holding Debra Winger, and Wyatt holding Theresa Russell, signed "To Heads by Harry, Thanks for the Gorgeous Animals, Love Ya! Debra Winger and Theresa Russell."

It made me sick.

Sheldon graduated from UH that spring to the fanfare and adulation of all his relatives and friends, a double major, so to speak, a bachelor's in business management and an associate's in cosmetology from Honolulu Community College.

In Sheldon's honor, Mommy threw the biggest block party in the history of Mamo Street. Aunty Mei Ling ordered all of his favorite movies and played them for free on the night of the party and then ran the movies for the next two weeks. *The World of Suzie Wong* with Nancy Kwan and William Holden, *Jesus Christ Superstar* with Ted Neeley and Hawaii's own Yvonne Elliman, and *Flower Drum Song.*

Sheldon was riding high on the night of his party, so he demanded, "Float me a loan, Daddy. I want to open my own bad-ass salon down Kaiko'o Mall. Eh, what I learn in business is, you like make big money, then you risk big money."

My brother was drunk, I was sure. Hadn't he noticed his growing invisibility to my father? All those nights since he returned home, out late with the boyfriends—Harry O. sat on his favorite chair till two in the morning, making it clear that he knew more than he wanted to know about Sheldon.

I'm not a dummy. I know exactly what's going on. I might never change you. But that doesn't mean I need to approve of your flamboyance.

"So what, Daddy?" Sheldon pressed, sassy-ass and curt.

"Go for it, Harry O.," Mr. Santos encouraged with a punch to my father's arm. "Ha-ree, Ha-ree, Ha-ree," he started chanting, and everyone else joined in. "The boy been make you proud. Now your chance give him the wings to fly, brah. What is faddas for?"

"How much you talking, Sheldon?" my father asked. It was *two* of us he was disappointed with and he seethed a low anger.

"Ummm." Sheldon pretended like he was thinking this out for the first time. "I'm talking you loan me twenty grand. That's the least I need to get what I want in the salon. I don't want no cheesy-ass, hole-in-the-wall, downtown Hilo, rat's-ass shop with faded pictures of hairdo models from the sixties on the wall taped to cover the damn pukas. No, I want one upscale, high-class, big-bucks, no-whammy salon."

Sheldon planned to travel to New York City with Bunny after her graduation to check out chic salons and bring a "concept" home. "None of this naming the salon after yourself like all these Hilo guys do," he said. "Ours going be something chic, like Funkytown Inc. or PYT, for Pretty Young Thing, something like that."

Harry O. burned through Sheldon's fantasy. "Twenty thousand fricken dollars? Where in hell's name I suppose to get that kine money, hah, Sheldon? I like you tell me since you the man with the plan, damn kid. I put you through school and now you like bleed me dry some more. Highfalutin punk with your stupid nose in the air. Who you think you, hah? Gunfunnit, you think money grow on trees? You show me the tree out back where the hundred-dollar bills growing and I harvest um myself." My father stopped to see his friends around him, jaws agape.

He quickly changed his tone. "Maybe you marry a rich *girl*, you get set for life. Mommy, what Dr. Morimoto said about his last daughter, Mona, the one at MIT? Perfect for Sheldon, no? Something like that he been tell my wife."

Perversely, Harry O. was rubbing Sheldon's face in some unreality. If my brother was a bloody laceration, Harry O. was a handful of rock salt.

Mommy shook her head and sat down next to me on the sidewalk as the yelling went on. "Not in front of everybody," she whispered to herself. Then she got up and walked over to Sheldon. "He's mad 'cause you mahu, but you're my boy, Sheldon," she said to him. Mommy never waited for my brother to come out of the closet. She burst right in. It was her way, and it eased my brother's pain. He turned dramatically to follow her inside.

Sheldon would come back to his block party to have a couple more Löwenbräus, look at his name lit up on the marquee across the street, "The Sheldon Yagyuu Film Festival," carry a six-pack of baby Millers and a bag of pork rinds to the Mamo Theatre to watch the second showing of *Flower Drum Song*, and ask Butchie to play it over and over while the drinking raged on outside on Mamo Street until four in the morning.

I walked over to the theater with Sheldon's corduroy futon

before I went to sleep that night. I found my brother curled up in a chair, Nancy Kwan spreading his favorite songs over his sleeping body, singing to him in translucent Chinatown bliss.

Sheldon ended up renting a chair at Chickie's Chop-Choppers. Mommy and I never heard the end of all his daily "*hairstylist* not *beautician*" drama.

"You know, Mommy, that stupid gaudy manicurist, Roberta Figueroa—I tell you, I cannot handle this. Wait till Bunny work with me. At least I get somebody to roll my eyes at when Roberta come in with her thick-ass, long acrylic fingernails, all bright pink with stupid fourteen-karat-gold charms on her damn three-inch-long pinky fingernails. Oh, gimme a break."

"She was your student?" I asked Mommy as she rinsed the chawans and small breakfast plates in the sink.

"Yeah, maybe she was Mommy's student," Sheldon said before she could answer, "but she wasn't forcing everybody in third grade to make fingernails like her, and wearing her goddamn bright clothes, plenty Rainbow Brite eye shadow, and fuchsia lip gloss. And she forever talking with her hands, for irritate me, shit."

"You taking this too damn personal, Sheldon," Mommy said. "Like Roberta's wearing that lip gloss to send bugs up your ass. Go with the flow. The *real* reason you all huffy is 'cause your father never dish out the money." Mommy wiped her hand on her T-shirt and sliced a beautiful persimmon at the table for us to share.

"Yeah, maybe," he said, taking a vicious bite of the fruit, "maybe I wish Daddy would just accept—" He looked out the back door of the kitchen toward the alley and the KTA parking lot. "Oh, fuck it."

Then, to keep himself intact, he continued bitching, always good at keeping denial in its proper place. It was easier taking his anger out at the world. "That lazy fucka, Lorilei Ushijima—she rents the chair across of me, right? Well, that fucka never likes to wash towels, even when Chickie tell her *to her face*, 'Wash the towels, Lorilei.' What the hell she thinking? The damn towels ain't going wash themself.

"And then yesterday, we ran out of towels, and I no like look stupid in front my customers, right? So I folded the *dirty* towels that was not too wet, until I had time to wash and dry one batch. No can, I tell you."

"Ask Chickie if he like Toni come down be receptionist for him," Mommy told Sheldon. "She needs a job bad. When you planning to look for a job, Toni?" Mommy felt sorry and never really bothered me, not until now.

"I don't know."

"Chickie has a receptionist. But that's not the end," my brother went on, oblivious to my unemployment. "And there's that asshole Aurora Kubo, who grad two years before me. Forever butting into my private conversations with my ladies. Always adding in her damn two cents.

"So—my customer's telling me that her daughter's half-popolo, half-Pa-ke ex-boyfriend from Guam still coming around after two and half years of breaking up in San Francisco after she got her degree in accounting—I like be nice, so I tell, 'Eh, maybe he still love her, Harriet, 'cause your daughter has a college education, eh?'

"But no! Aurora butts her nosy ass in and tells my customer, 'Tell him to get lost, the loser. Just tell him to beat it,' she says. 'Be direct. And your daughter cannot be weak—

tell her be stronger on the inside.' Ho, Mommy, I tell you, she irritate me too."

"Go wash heads for Sheldon, Toni, and clean his station. He'll give you some of his tips, no, Sheldon?" Mommy said, trying not to be pushy. "Or go back part-time Hilo College, go easy, easy, six credits. As long as you in school, I think Daddy don't mind supporting you."

"Who he hate more, Mommy?" I asked. "Me or Sheldon?"

She gave no answer but a cold glare. "He don't hate you," she said softly.

"And then," Sheldon went on, "oh, try wait. No—I don't want to split my tips, sorry, Toni," he said, pseudo-sympathetic. "Mommy, I don't have enough clientele yet. Maybe when Bunny and me open our own shop, if we ever do, Toni can work for us.

"See, the trouble is, I don't have regulars, so they forever asking me, 'Oh, how long have you been doing hair? Are you familiar with *this* type of hair?' I like tell um, 'Nah, what you think? I been working on asshole haoles for all my years in beauty school. I figured out a long time ago how to cut your damn hair. In fact, you're such a cocky-ass rich haole bitch who think you better than me, I going cut your hair all crooked!' That's what I want to say."

My brother looked at me. "He hate *me*, Toni, always did, but now, he not shame to show his true inner feeling. You and him, Toni, you close, always was—only thing, he fucked about both of us now."

Mommy shook her head. "No kidding." She knew Sheldon's assessment of our father was correct. Then she covered up. "I mean, no kidding about the haoles thinking they better than us," she said, nervously missing the point to ease our discomfort.

"Just like Clyde Morton," I said to Mommy. "I'll send him

a coupon for a free haircut and when he go Chickie's to cut his hair, Sheldon can give him the bobora special—chawan cut straight from Tokyo."

"Who's that, Clyde Morton? Oh, never mind. Eh, that's not all. Right before closing last night, in comes this young local chick, and Chickie tells her we almost pau, but me, I desperate for clientele, so I tell Chickie I'll do it.

"Then that tuna busts out a picture of this pretty haole with fancy hair and she tell me she like look like the picture. I tell you, people no realize that the haole in the picture get one personal hairstylist who take two hours to make her look like that, plus one more hour for the face.

"And me, I tell her, 'Oh, that's *really* difficult to achieve for the *everyday* person. I can make your hair like that, but for you to do that every day will definitely pose you some *major* hairstyling dilemma. There's tons of mousse here and gel there and tons of spray here.' What I like do is cut out the damn face from the picture and say, 'Now—you *still* like this hairdo? You sure? That's what I thought—you wanted her face, eh?' "

Maverick and Wyatt walked in through the back door. "Whassup?" Wyatt said to Mommy, who passed him the last slice of persimmon. I was relieved to see him. The possibility of our conversation heading *anywhere real* had ended. "So what, Toni?" he said, kicking my leg under the table and throwing the whole piece of fruit in his mouth.

"So what, what?" I said back to him, not wanting eye contact. He pressed his thigh to mine under the table. Sheldon reached over to Wyatt's long hair and rubbed the ends between his fingertips.

"Oh, jeez, are you in dire need of a deep conditioning for these damaged ends or what? You've got some gorgeous natural curls here," he said, grinding Wyatt's hair between his fingertips like sandpaper, "but obviously no concern for shine or vitality. Your hair's absolutely too brittle. A weekly hot oil treatment, maybe?" Wyatt jerked his head out of Sheldon's reach. "Free deep conditioning and *head* massage with a cut, darling." Sheldon winked at him.

"Pass," Wyatt said. "I use Prell or Suave, whatever on sale."

"Oh, heaven forbid, an off-the-counter product, such poverty. Well, no wonder. Mommy, that's why I tell you, you simply have to be a snob when it comes to the products you put in your hair. You clearly see here a case of somebody who wants to achieve a certain long-maned look, but don't know how to maintain that look, so he comes out looking damaged and tangled. Simply tacky."

"You lucky I ain't listening close what you telling, Sheldon, or I might have to broke your ass right here in front your mother," Wyatt said, standing up.

"So what, Toni?" Maverick said.

"What? What?!" I said to him.

"What?" Mommy said.

"I asked Mr. Harper if he would give Elwin Tanaka's pig-hunting job to you," he said." 'Cause Harper busted Elwin taking home one piglet too many to fatten up for luau later. And Harper said he know Aunty Mary Alice 'cause of Billy, this and that, Billy love her, thanks for all your support of his son, blah, blah, blah."

"But," Maverick said, sitting down next to Mommy, who poured him a cup of coffee, "Mr. Harper said Toni get good chance if she apply. I like persimmon," he said as Mommy got up to cut another one from the counter. " 'Cause it's big-time federal regalations to hire minorities. And Toni's minority, first, 'cause she one girl, and second, 'cause you guys Japanee. So what, Toni?"

I rested my chin on my folded hands, thinking. Maybe I could make Harry O. happy, for now, with gainful employment if not yet a college degree. "You guys get good benefits, right? And pretty good pay."

"Pretty good? We get the *best* job. Outside all day, no paperwork, plus the money we making from taxidermy," Maverick said, then stopped, looking at me. "As far as I concern, I have a federal job. That's it. Bottom line. And I in charge of two of the four crews, so I make sure you out in the field with me and Wyatt."

Wyatt leaned over and whispered in my ear, "I like you come hunt with me." I was sure at that moment that everyone in the room knew about us. He breathed on his shades, which hung from a rubber tubing around his neck, and wiped them with his shirt.

"What you whispering?" Sheldon whined.

"Nothing," I said.

"Go, Toni," Mommy said. "See, even Wyatt take care of you. You ain't got nothing to lose. Or you planning on slinging burgers at Woolworth's lunch counter? Tell Mr. Harper I said thanks and tell Billy I'll take him go see *City of the Living Dead* this weekend. And tell Billy he can sleep over. Only him like spooky movie around here."

Wyatt got up to leave. He was circling me, smelling me. Maverick gave him the head jerk to leave and he pushed the back door open with his foot. "I take care of you, Toni," Wyatt said, my mother nodding her thankful approval.

I got up slowly and walked toward the open door. Maverick reached over my shoulder from behind to stop the door from slamming into me. "Go with Wyatt up the headquarters 'cause the boss waiting to interview you."

"What if I told you no?"

"You never tell me no, Toni," Wyatt said, turning to face me.

"Not you, you stupid asshole. I was talking to Maverick." Wyatt laughed and put on his sunglasses.

"Don't be a stupid fool all your life," Maverick said. "I staying to help Harry O. with the peacock Moniz just brought in from Pu'uwa'awa'a Ranch. Wyatt take you. Harper's in his office. Wyatt!" Maverick yelled to him.

"Shit, I know, I know. I was there when he told you all that. Why you acting like you the only one know all this shit? Fuckin' like make big man with the plan. Was *me* the one told you to hire Toni, fuckin' hero. Was *me* wanted her there with—us." Wyatt turned to me. "Baby," he said, "you the first girl pig hunter since they started killing all them pigs."

"Fucka, I ain't—"

"I know. Sue Shiomi my baby." He gave me a shove, then put his big arm around my neck. I nearly fell over. "What, *The Killing Machine*, Tuesday night?" I jerked myself from his grip and he pushed my back again. "Sonny Chiba, Henry Sanada, and Sue Shiomi—you and me?"

"Eeeww," Sheldon said, standing behind Mommy at the kitchen door. "What's that all about?"

"Nah, nothing. Not what you think. The two of them been going samurai movie long time, you know that, Sheldon," Mommy said. "We family with them."

"Yeah, right, Mommy. Open your eyes. I could smell the testosterone in the kitchen, and believe me, if anybody can sniff out testosterone, it's yours truly. Well, if Maverick going movies with you guys Tuesday night, then I like go too," he yelled from the doorway as if he was doing all of us a favor.

"Yeah, well, if *us* let *you* come," Wyatt said, leaning out the window on my side of the truck, "then we *all* get free deep conditioning at Chickie's, Shelly."

"Stink ass," Sheldon said, flipping him the bird. "Trim your own split ends, fuckin' brittle and lifeless needing a few lessons in hair care and manners from *Maverick*," he yelled.

I turned to look at Mommy. She had on that face, her unreal face. That *oh heavens* face. She looked so sad.

Don't be sad. I'm not as fucked up as it seems, I said to her face with my face. She waved as Wyatt screeched out of the KTA parking lot behind Heads by Harry. Mommy turned and went inside.

My very first day at the Hawai'i Volcanoes National Park I knew the pig-hunting job made me sick. Not the 'ōhi'a forests or the sky, a multifaceted blue, or the winds' textures, the silver-black shades of the landscape. Nor was it the rain or thick fog I sat in for hours waiting for it to pass. The job itself made me sick.

Once, Mr. Harper told Wyatt and me to train the new dogs since Debbie, Dallas, and Lovelace were being retired for "severe injuries sustained" in the last few, rainy months.

"Wyatt, I'm entrusting this to you and I want it done soon, son, very soon, or the crews will be short on dogs."

"I hate when he call me son, that motherfuck," Wyatt said, stalking off to the kennels with me.

The very day Mr. Harper gave us this task, Wyatt and I trapped some baby piglets from a sow he had just shot. I thought it was for him to steal and sell at the Open Market down at the Bayfront, until we got back to the park to get the new dogs, Sue, Shiomi, and Juubei.

Wyatt drove Billy Harper and me up past the nēnē goose sanctuary with the dogs. I sat close to Billy so that the gearshift wouldn't be between my legs. Billy Harper was really the one in charge of the breeding schedule, though Wyatt wanted to believe otherwise. He parked the truck and we all got out. Billy had taken one of the piglets out of the burlap bag and was holding it like a baby.

"Stupid haole fuck," Wyatt said, grabbing at the piglet. "Don't let the dogs loose, Toni," he yelled at me.

"You not my boss. Don't yell at me. You always telling me what to do and you better stop it, asshole," I yelled at him.

Then he talked directly to the pig that Billy was carrying. "Since you got the first and only love you ever going know in your whole life from this haole punk here," he said as he grabbed the crying piglet, "you be the first to die." He squeezed the piglet by the scruff of its neck.

"What're you going to do with the piglets, Wyatt?" Billy asked.

He hated Billy. He hated the way we talked. He hated Billy's ease in his own body the same way he hated it in Maverick. He hated Billy's father. He hated haoles in general. He hated Billy's relationship to our family. He hated Billy and me sitting in the movies. He hated Billy at our kitchen table, Billy in the shop, Billy's pictures on our TV.

"What you going do about it, hah, haole? You one environmentoist? Go tell your daddy. He the one told *me* to train the new dogs. C'mere, Sue, here, Baby Sue. Shiomi, Juubei." The three dogs wagged their whole asses around Wyatt. "Hold them back, Toni, and don't let them go till I say, you hear me?"

"Yeah, why, what you doing? Wyatt, no get stupid, eh. You ain't doing that pig-ear shit, hah?" I watched him reach for his buck knife. "No, don't cut the ear, Wyatt."

"Hold them back now, Toni. Billy, you fuckin' hopeless haole, come help Toni. Shit for brains." I looked at Billy and shook my head.

"I knew we shouldn't have come with him, Toni. I don't like the way he talks to you. You deserve way better treatment. I would never——"

"Oh, shut the fuck up," Wyatt said. "Get your ass over here, haole, and bring your bitch." He jerked his head toward me.

"See what I mean, Toni? I don't spend my summers here at the park to be in your intolerable company, Wyatt," Billy said, "and furthermore, I resent the way you——"

But before Billy could finish, Wyatt, in one sharp stroke, cut off a hind leg of the first piglet. It screamed in a voice I felt in my whole body. The dogs barked and jumped in mad circles, yanked back by the ropes that burned my hands. Wyatt let the baby go shrieking into the brush.

"Hold the dogs," he yelled, "hold the dogs." He took the severed hind leg and rubbed it hard on the dogs' muzzles, in their mouths, around their noses, their eyes and jawbones. "Smell me," he said. He took the ropes and released them.

I heard the piglet's wail in the ʻōhiʻa forest, the barking of the three young dogs on its trail, us behind them. Before this, there was the pig without an ear, and now, the pig without a leg. The crying stopped; the barking turned to a frenzied whining. We caught up to the dogs waiting, breathing hard and hanging on.

"She be the best," Wyatt said, pointing at Shiomi. "You good girl, you grab the mouth," he said to her. "Man, I have to work hard on this hopeless fuck," he said, pointing to Juubei. "Stupid, why you going for the balls, hah?" he said, kicking at the dog. "You like this pig's daddy come kick you in the head?" He moved the dogs aside, grabbed the piglet, and sliced off its head. "One less for me to catch," he said, slinging it in the bushes. "Eh, haole, how many more piggies you get in the truck?"

"Three," Billy whispered.

"Tree?" He wiped his knife on his pants and whistled for the dogs the way he whistled for me from the street when we went to samurai movies.

"Tree, hah?" he said again, walking ahead of us, laughing. He threw his knife into the ground. "Talk some more, Toni, talk it up with your boy. I like hearing you laughing it up with him, talking all those big-ass words like I don't know what the fuck you saying," he dared me as he stalked off on the trail. "Let me see you act up some more behind my back. Tree more piggies, right, Billy boy?"

"You heard me," Billy said, choking back his tears. I started gagging. Billy rubbed my back, and then I threw up on the grass. He put his hand on my hair. The wind rustled in the trees. I could feel the rain coming again.

"Next," he said, turning around to face me, his eyes shifting over the landscape of my body.

I *knew* this job would be hard for me even *before* Wyatt drove me to my interview. But my father's ever-growing definition of "This ain't no women's work" burned inside me.

My third day on the job, I sat forty-five minutes waiting for a boar to die before Maverick found me sitting in the brush. He stabbed it to death, sliced open its stomach, and pulled out all of the innards—blood and entrails steaming out onto the lava rock.

I vomited between my legs. The other hunters in this crew, Pocho Robello, Ringo Ferreira, JoJo Masaki, and Wyatt Santos, sat down around me for a good laugh.

I was shit to them from that day forward, but I couldn't quit. My father might not have talked to me for another year. I couldn't fail, again. And I was statistically important—Mr. Harper needed my female, Japanese, minority status for federal monies and did everything to encourage my performance on the job.

So after consultation with Maverick, Mr. Harper let me hunt with Billy when they split our crew. Billy was the only one not caught up in the macho, keep-up-with-the-boiz shit. Even Maverick had a hard time when it came to *the boiz*. Billy would look out for me the way that Mommy had watched out for him. And she was right. He was filial, a trait she instilled in a haole of all creatures.

Billy loved to use his grandfather's .30 caliber carbine of World War II vintage. He had four smart dogs—Airedale-greyhound mixes that he named Tybalt and Mercutio, because he thought he was literary after reading Shakespeare in seventh grade; Rambis for Kurt Rambis of the Lakers, who to him was the best white boy in the NBA; and Sally for the song "Lay Down Sally," the only Eric Clapton song he knew by heart. Billy's dogs never grabbed a pig in total abandon. We took Juubei and Sue along too.

Billy also never forced me to shoot. I was content to walk along with him side by side through the forest of uprooted trunks, grasses, and pig shit. We hunted in a recently fenced-off acreage so ravaged that it seemed like a mucky pigsty with trees. He carried my rifle for me all day. I packed our gear.

I was about to tell Billy what Harry O. had taught me long before, that the sounds of the dogs' barking told a hunter whether they found a big boar or a small one. But Billy broke into a run when his dogs began barking. We already knew from the deep, guttural pig grunting that we had a huge one.

We listened to the big boar from a small hill full of staghorn and ginger. Billy approached it from one large tree fern to another on the side of the hill. He motioned for me to stay at the bottom, and I was grateful. For a moment, I relaxed myself into the sweet humus of a hāpu'u fern.

I looked for Billy from behind the tree trunk. Up on a small rise, I saw the thick-necked pig, ample shoulders, his wily eyes searching as he sniffed the air, his sense of smell highly developed. With his huge snout, the boar lifted the bottom of a hāpu'u and ravaged the soft pubic earth of earthworms and slugs, the sandy sod caught in a delicate system of roots, a littoral memory. I hid from him, pressing my back against the fibrous trunk.

When I turned, he was gone, and for a moment I thought he was circling me. I smelled fresh pig shit and urine upwind, brackish pools of semen. I glimpsed a sudden movement on the other side of the rise, and watched the boar's supple ass and engorged testicles retreating into the underbrush of 'ākala. He lifted his snout and smelled the Hawaiian raspberries, amused, as though he knew I was watching him. And then he stopped and looked directly at me.

"Billy!"

The sound of a stampede. Dazed, unprepared, I knew enough to brace myself behind the huge trunk. The moment unfolded slowly as the boar hauled three hundred pounds of furious muscle straight for my tree with the dogs in pursuit. With one frenzied swing of his snout, the pig hurtled the hāpu'u.

The entire trunk thrust into the sky, my body swung in the same direction as I held on to the hāpu'u. I felt the dull thud of my body on rock as I landed. The dogs barked and snatched at the boar, who backed up into a nearby fallen kukui tree trunk, yellow tusks wet with mucousy saliva, preparing for a fight.

"He's only fighting 'cause his backside's protected," Billy said to me, out of breath. He quickly helped me off the ground. "See, he can fight them coming from the front or sides but he's weak from the back. You remember that, okay, Toni?" I nodded, and he dusted me off, then pointed me toward my rifle.

By the time I looked back, Billy had approached the boar from the front and shot it in its snout. The dogs celebrated around him. Kind words, the sound of three hundred pounds of animal expiring air and fluid. I walked away, Billy behind me.

Billy turned back. "He's gone, Toni," he frantically said.

"What?" The smell of fresh blood and pig excrement, Billy motioned me to move on through the grove of kukui to hunt for the pig, the one so amused by me, lusty mucks of trampled 'ōhelo, rutted patches of 'uki 'uki fruit, silver-thin pa'iniu rosettes unearthed and provocative.

Billy and I worked our way to the far north of the acreage. The dogs were tired and depressed from following trails that led to empty pig havens, ditches with prints, the musty pig scent the dogs smelled, to me, a pungent, wet dankness of pig and sod.

I looked around. Our singularity on this landscape suddenly frightened me. I realized that each tree and stone, each plant life, wind, and animal possessed an equality of significance in this place. Billy and I were two small foreigners on this landscape. Yet we had presumed our dominion and shot the pig.

The fog ushered in a heavy rain. "You have a raincoat, Billy?" I asked.

"No, but I have a couple of garbage bags. You want one?" I took the bag from him and tore a hole in the bottom for my head. Billy secured it around my waist. The dogs scrambled and barked at the fencing. "What, boy? Tybalt? Toni, let's get them over the fence. The pig's got to be up on that hill over there."

"Nah, better not. Let him go."

"Him?" Billy asked. He took my fingers in his and tried to warm them up. "C'mon, let's go. We've finally got it." To Billy, this job was a daily passion play of conquest: hunt, forest, fear, and deliverance. I wanted to go home and take a bath.

"Him, the boar," I said. "It's not for us."

"Huh? We have to. It's our job."

"No, not this time."

"We can't be too far behind it." Billy led me by the hand up a hill of pāhoehoe covered with grass. "This is weird, Toni. I shot it in the face."

"Maverick going get mad with us. Just stay in the area," I told him.

"One less pig to hunt tomorrow, Toni. Besides, it has to be half dead. Look at all the blood we followed," Billy said to me, managing a small smile. "Plus, you know what? One of the rangers told me there's petroglyphs right up past the north fence." He hoisted the dogs over the fence. "I think I know where it is. I got some ribbon in my pack so we can mark our trail. We can bring petroglyph stuff tomorrow and get the rubbings for Mrs. Yagyuu. She can't ever come up the federal access roads, you know. C'mon. Just mark the trees best you can so we can find our way back to the pickup point."

I hesitated, knowing that I was being pulled along, led into the forest deeper and deeper by the boar who circled me with his semen. But not wanting to be left behind in the fog, I quickly tore at the orange ribbon, haphazardly tying the plastic pieces to branches as I sludged through the rain.

"We supposed to be on the northwest side by five," I yelled at Billy. "Where we stay? Northeast or northwest? They going leave us, Billy. Billy!" I yelled as I followed the barking of the dogs. "Where the hell is the compass?"

I stopped, tied a ribbon to an 'ōhi'a, then walked slowly into the waiting forest. I followed the barking and Billy's weakening voice. "C'mon, Toni," he called. He carried the radio. I heard it break, then static, then clear.

I called for Billy. No answer. The fog was so thick, I could barely see my feet. And then, feeling utterly lost and alone, I sat still on a small ridge, waiting for Billy.

Somehow he found me, having turned back on his own trail. Shivering and afraid, I finally understood how the coming of night meant danger, a timeless genetic imprint.

"Toni," he said, putting his hand on my shoulder, "everything's going to be okay. Let's follow the ribbons out." The ribbons. I had stopped tying them to trees, but I knew where I might have ended. "It's five-thirty, but they'll wait. Lots of times Pocho and Ringo came in late and they waited." Billy helped me off the ground.

"But we can't see shit. We have to wait till the fog lift." The dogs whimpered in the cold. The plastic bags we wore flapped in the wind. "Call them on the radio. Tell them we got lost."

"But, Toni, we might never hear the end of it, you and me. Like the time the physical science aides got trapped on Hilina Pali, the whole park heard the girls yelling for help over the radio and everybody ragged them till—" Billy paused and shook his head.

"Call them," I said to him. "I don't care what the fuck they say. Please, Billy." Reluctantly, he held the radio.

"Maverick. This is Billy."

Static.

"Maverick? Billy Harper. Come in."

More static.

"We're out of range," he said at last. "Quick, before it gets dark, let's follow the ribbon out to the north fence." I led

Billy foot in front of foot back to the place where I thought the ribbons ended.

But then I stopped. "Oh shit, Billy. Look at all the ribbons." Yellow, orange, and red ribbons flailed in the winds.

"Huh, what? My father's division's supposed to have orange ribbons. What's going on?" Billy grabbed on to one of the ribbons and pulled it from the grass. "Think, Toni. Did you tie it to the *grass*? Where did you stop?" It wasn't a scolding or a plea. "Can you remember your last tree?"

"This way. I think this way. They supposed to take off the ribbon when they walk out, shit, what the hell is this?" I stopped myself from the panic in my voice. And then a wave of cold air rolled in from Mauna Loa, the moon a slit in the deep, graying sky.

Billy grabbed my arm. "We need to get ready for tonight," he said. And he suddenly wrapped me inside of him. He held me for a long time. A pig laughed from the viscera of the forest. "It's okay, Toni. It's like we're camping at Kahuku Ranch. Except. Except . . ." He looked around. "No fire, no Mrs. Yagyuu, and no hot dogs. Six cold dogs. Help me get them together. Here, these trees over here might protect us better."

After settling the dogs down—in the humus and soft soil beside a series of hāpu'u, Billy and I dug a shallow trench. The cold was piercing; my gloves were torn and my hands were sore. Billy buried me first in the soil, then covered himself. The two of us, his body curled into mine, his arms and legs wrapped around me, his warm breath in my hair. I felt his hands inside my clothes.

When the rain stopped, the wind no longer whistling through my ears, the night grew eerily still. The sound of the winds was now distant in some faraway treetops whirling. A tall finger of 'ōhi'a, the only movement in a strange draft above us. Light shifted from tree to tree, gray-lingering-black, then swift to hide. A dog growled; another whimpered. Something bristled against my dirty face. I turned deeper into my chest, Billy deeper into my warm neck.

Billy's sudden words broke my darkening fear. "I loved my mother very much," he said to me. And although his words seemed absurd, they stilled me, so I followed them.

"I still got the picture you gave me. Why did she look so sad?"

"I don't know."

I started panicking. "We don't belong here. The trees, yeah. The birds, yeah. The pig belongs here, but not us."

"I'll bring you home, Toni."

"Get ghosts, Billy. I feel them. Remember the time Harry O. took us fishing down South Point and we was walking back at night with the kerosene lanterns? I swear I was following your light and your voice. They didn't want us there too."

"But when we found you, you were sitting by the beach house at Ka'alu'alu. Why were you there?" He put his crossed arms over my bra and his cold hands under my armpits. "You found your way back to the campsite."

"I heard you calling my name. You and Mommy. I thought I was right behind you."

"There're no ghosts here," he said, his breath on my neck now. "I'll keep you right here with me."

"Tell me something."

"I made sixteen last May," he began.

"Twenty-two," I told him.

"I know how old you are," he said. "I always knew there was six years between us." We said nothing for a while.

"Always was six," I said. "When you was seven in Mommy's class, I was thirteen. That was the year my father *lost* me in the mountains above Honoapo Mill. He wanted me to prove that I could find my way back to him. I marked my trees, I marked my stones, but I was going in circles."

"Did it get dark?" he asked me.

"Yes." I began crying. "These places, they want to humble me, but I don't know how——"

"You be an equal part," Billy said to me. "No more and no less."

"Kind of fucked, coming from a haole."

"We're all haoles to this place," he said. Strange night sounds tittered, movement in the brush. A single tree faded back and forth.

I placed my hands over his.

"When I was thirteen, you were nineteen," he said to me. "When you left to go to UH with Bunny, I wrote you so many letters. I never sent them. I felt—— I called Mrs. Yagyuu every day. I was—— Do those six years still matter?" he asked.

"Yeah, they matter." I felt him push his groin into me hard, rubbing and pushing, his legs trellised onto mine, a low moan. "Stop," I said. I knew from long before that Billy and I were about more than this pulling of our human selves into the lure of kukui and ginger, strange southerly winds coiling about the understory and treetops.

I felt his lips on my neck and then he stopped. "My mother's from India. They met at Berkeley and she got pregnant." I said nothing. "I want to go to Berkeley when I graduate," he said at last.

"What happened to her?"

"She had me and went home to her father. She left me with my dad. Help me with my classes this year, Toni."

I had so many questions. But with Billy, I had the confidence that we'd talk again and again, around and between the subject of his mother. With other men, there'd be a stupid urgency. I'd want to know everything in the moment because there might never be another chance. But Billy and I learned to dance together early, and on this night, he wanted me to walk him off the dance floor and out of this spotlight.

"You got AP classes?" I asked him.

"I got kicked out of all my AP classes. I can't play volleyball or basketball unless my grades——"

"How come? You fucked up fourth quarter?"

"Yeah, big time. But the athletic director's letting me practice 'cause he said to Coach Cabingabang, 'Lucky this haole didn't go to St. Joe's.' "

I laughed. I didn't feel as afraid anymore. "Every class, you know, Toni."

"Not that I want a compliment, but you sure I'm smart enough to help you?"

"Only you can talk to me. And Mrs. Yagyuu."

"That's not smartness, you know." I told him.

"It's *something* to me." Sue moved in close and licked my cold face. She settled herself down. "I can't hunt with you anymore once school starts. I'll tell my father to let you go out with——"

"Maverick," I said.

"He'll watch out for you. You remember what I told you about Wyatt——he's weakest from the back. From the front, he can see us coming."

"But you said that about——"

"The pig. Don't you see, Toni?"

All the time, all those days in the field and even when he was a kid, we anticipated each other's thoughts. "Six years," he said again, reaching under my bra, his hands warm on my cold breasts. I moved my fingers into his massaging hands. "Every day after school?"

"I'll pick you up at the ramp after your practice."

"My dad won't let me get my license till I prove myself

academically, jeez. He said I might have to catch the Hele-On bus to my senior prom next year at the rate I'm going."

"Stay over on school nights. You can't go back Volcano every night after we all pau tutor. Mommy don't mind." For years, my mother had always set up a folding mattress for Billy next to my bed. He had his own futon in our house and a summer quilt she made for him in a Singer's night class.

"My dad doesn't mind if I stay over either," he said.

"Get all A's and he cannot complain."

"Okay," he said.

"I going miss you, Billy."

"Back to you, Toni."

From Billy I learned that love is easy—to truly *like* a man, remarkable. A boy whispered my name that night, the spirits dispersing in blue lights, flickering shades, a lone dog howling, 'ōhi'a limbs, māmaki leaves, a finger-flutter of 'a'ali'i clusters in the constant motion of this forest, and Billy's face leaning in to mine, his hands on my body, such wonder in touch—all this in the spine of the night.

Billy moved into the room I shared with Sheldon. He slept on Bunny's unoccupied bed and lived out of a small suitcase until I gave him two of my bureau drawers. We went to J. C. Penney for ten new pairs of BVDs to commemorate the space I created for his underwear. He playfully leaned into my body in the empty aisles of the department store. We shared a blueberry freckle at Treasure Island and he licked the melting ice cream from my fingers. We bought Rod McKuen cards for each other at the Book Gallery, skin in constant but discreet contact.

"He got no mother, that's why," I heard Mommy tell Sheldon one night. "Between Toni and me, we raised a good boy. Poor thing, you know. That stepmother of his, she not mean, but just like the boy invisible."

"Don't I know the feeling," Sheldon muttered.

Billy became my best friend. We Christmas-shopped at Edith's Dress Shoppe, MJS Music, and Kurohara's, fifty-fifty, for friends and family. He wrote one list for the two of us. Billy and I chose new curtain material at Helen's Fabrics, which he sewed in his class Industrial Arts: The Home. He made us a huge bowl of saimin that we ate while watching late-night TV, lying on the floor, our bodies under the soft futon in the dark living room.

"Billy and his father was constantly moving. He only married the stepmother a few years ago," my mother told me over a hot cup of o-cha one night. "You know, the father was climbing up the ranks, so you go where the feds tell you to go. Poor thing, the kid. He pull the real mother's side, so was hard, the father told me, 'cause the boy look half-breed."

"Oooh, but that hapa look is so *in* here," Sheldon whispered, blowing on his hot tea.

"Yeah, in—but when he opens his mouth, he still talks like a haole," Mommy said. "That's why Wyatt always picking on the boy."

"That's not the only reason," Sheldon muttered.

I had no time for Maverick and Wyatt. I didn't do coke at Isles with the boys, never stayed for drinking parties after work, and never watched them mount or skin animals. I never sat outside to shoot the breeze with the old-timers and, worse, never served another pūpū or beer.

"That fuckin' haole," Wyatt said to me at work one day. "Good he had to go back school. The motherfuck had the nerve to tell me that after he pau college, he coming back to be my boss."

"What you said to him?" Maverick laughed.

"I said, 'Kiss my left nut,'" Wyatt said, grabbing his crotch. "Toni did. And she loved it, no, baby?"

"Fuck off. He ain't no typical haole," I said softly to Maverick so as not to draw attention to him. "Get haole haoles and get local haoles."

"He ain't no local haole," Wyatt snapped. "Why you always whispering, hah? To me, even those so-called kamaʻāina haoles, they fuckin' haole to me. You wait till I tell your father all this shit, Toni. He need one good laugh."

I had no time for my father. I never shared a cup of coffee with him before work, never even brewed it. I passed on the morning doughnut from Robert's Bakery. I never answered the phone for him, prepped the game, dusted heads, or Windexed counters to curry favor with him.

"Billy was telling me he like learn taxidermy," Harry O. told me over dinner one night. "You teach him, Toni. What the hell, I could use another hand. The kid been working hard in the shop, clean the toilet, scrub the sink. You use to do all that, Toni."

"Until you fired me. I sorry, Harry O. I too tired after work——"

"And you know, Mary Alice, the boy contacted the Nature Conservacy on Molokaʻi about their pig eradication programs, how you like that? Him and the father like me go Molokaʻi with them. We can making one side trip to hunt axis deer. And me, how long I wanted to see the Deer Man of Molokaʻi. He my competition, eh? And a tax write-off. Damn, that kid is smart. What a good son that Mr. Harper has."

"Right," Sheldon said, rolling his eyes.

I had so much confidence in myself and in Billy that Sheldon's snide remarks blew past me.

*Cute ass. He's a fag, trust me. Only fags can wag like
that. Baby mind. Virgin. The talk of Hilo town. So shame.
Mommy's blind. Harry O., stupid. All he need is one night with
Franjelica or Paula. Or me. Immature. Big dummy and her
little buddy.*

The only time I ever experienced friendship like this was
with Billy. He knew all the people I talked about at work
and understood the nuances of my work relationships with
depth and insight. He helped me figure out what not to say,
what to say, why and how. He helped me unwind and put
things in perspective all the time.

"Don't stop, Toni," he said. "Don't cut it short. Why do
you always do that? I want to know everything from the
beginning to the end. So he said—"

"I do that all the time, yeah?" Billy sprawled out next to
me on the living-room floor.

"How come?" he asked, tracing the bones in my hand.

"I don't cut short with Mommy or Bunny. Only with men.
They like me to summarize. Like if I don't get it all in during
the commercial, then no sense even starting."

"Not me," Billy said, moving close to warm up his feet
with mine. "Okay, from the beginning—"

I went with him to the movies, except for every third Tuesday's samurai movie. He caught on to jokes fast.

I picked him up from school every day even after his stupid
jock buddies began asking, "Who's your old lady?" and meant
it.

I brought him home and into our room, where we folded
laundry, read the liner notes and lyrics off our favorite Carly
Simon cassettes, organized baby photos in shoe boxes, or ate

li hi mui and wet lemon peel until the roofs of our mouths
went raw.

Billy ate backyard Japanese plantation food with my family, spicy gobo, bitter melon and bacon, nishime, and fried
mochi with kinako and sugar.

I tutored him every night in the kitchen. I figured, with
all I learned from *his* classes that I missed the first time
around, maybe I could get in to Berkeley too.

"We can be roommates," he said. "I cook, I clean, I do
laundry. Look, we study well together already."

"When boys don't have a mother," Mommy chimed in,
"they really learn to fend for themself, no, Billy?" He nodded.
"This boy been doing everything for himself since he was
small. That's what impressed me about you," she said to him.
"One time I asked the class bring in one picture of a typical
family day. The one you brought wen' broke my heart."

"What was?" I asked.

Mommy looked at Billy for a long time. "Was a small,
dirty-face boy without shirt in an old Winnebago," she said.
"The family was camping, but I knew there wasn't a mother,
not even stepmother. The boy was by the stove holding a
frying pan. He was showing the pancakes he made for him
and the father. And he was smiling for the camera."

Billy got up from the table and leaned over the kitchen
sink. "It's my turn to do the dishes," he said.

My mother walked over to him and placed her hands on
his tall body. "That's why I brought you home with me. Time
somebody take care of *you*." Billy turned and wrapped his
arms around my mother. "So you stop messing up in school
before I give you dirty lickens," she said, patting his butt.

He made fresh Kona coffee every morning with the grinder
he bought from Kino's Secondhand Furniture.

He baked bread and Betty Crocker's Light As A Feather

muffins, which he insisted we eat with Darigold butter and his homemade 'ōhelo berry jam.

He baked a thimbleberry pie for me.

My mother adored him. They went to *The Exorcist*, *Halloween*, and *Friday the 13th*. Nobody loved a horror movie as much as Billy and Mommy.

He massaged her shoulders with strong, untiring hands.

They went fishing at Isles, continued their search for elusive petroglyph fields, got interested in collecting old bottles, and challenged each other's corn chowder recipes. He bought her a Crock-Pot.

"You're lucky I'm haole," he said. "Only haoles cook with Crock-Pots. Man, tonight's corn chowder's gonna——"

"Broke the mouth!" Mommy finished.

She brought him along to play acey-deucey at Aunty Mildred's one Friday night a month and let him smoke her long cigarillos.

Billy discussed environmental issues with my father——the eradication of pigs from the Hawai'i Volcanoes National Park, the impact of the geothermal plant in Pohoiki, the release of hawksbill turtle hatchlings at Punalu'u beach, the federal protection of palila honeycreepers versus the eradication of mouflon sheep on Mauna Ke'a, the nēnē goose propagation efforts, the breeding of the nearly extinct 'alalā crows on Maui, and Jim Plunkett's Cinderella Super Bowl victory.

"You know, boy, better you major in botany, I think," Harry O. told Billy in the shop one afternoon. "That's what the reserve manager told me when us went Moloka'i. What her name was?"

"Joan Yoshioka. Man, she was tough, wasn't she, Mr. Yagyuu? The way they hike down in Pelekunu Valley. I thought I'd die of exhaustion, but I didn't want to look like a wimp in front of you and my dad. And her."

"You? Jeez, she put me to shame." Harry O. wiped his hands on his pants.

"And she has that tiny little voice like Bunny. But remember when we talked to that woman working with the preservation of hawksbills in Kaʻū?" Billy asked.

"Yeah, Charlotte Forbes, John's niece. What about her?" I watched my father's proud face as he talked to Billy.

"Well, she told you that she majored in biology, right, so I thought——"

"Double major?" Harry O. high-fived Billy, making a white cloud of Borax around their hands. "And get a PhD so that you at the top of the GS pay scale. Gumption, my boy. Gumption. There, your daddy came," he said, pointing out the front window. "Go get his things, Toni."

I hated to see him leave with his father on Friday nights. I waited for him on Mondays. My body churned to be near his, his fingers lingering on my face, the warm press of his hand and the sweet smell of his skin as he reached over from his bed to say good night.

The six years between us mattered at work.

It mattered every day.

Pocho Robello went on for days. "Help! Maverick, help! I no can kill this little piggie. Oops, I drop my rifle. Oops, I forgot my knife. Aw, where my liddle buddy? Oh, I forgot. He only eleventh grade. Had to go back to school. Aw shucks, forgot your bullets, Toni? You plug. Use your government-issue tampons."

I wanted him dead. "Fuck you, Pocho, you eighth-grade dropout with too many kids and that fat, stupid Japanee wife of yours, you sarcastic, big-mouth, pea-brain Portagee."

"Cunt, why no just quit already. Maverick, make her quit."

Wyatt interrogated me at least twice daily. "Why that haole fucka living with you guys, hah, Toni? And why the fuck you no drink with the boys no more? No, Maverick? Fuckin' Toni, when the last time you smoke with us? What, Toni, where the fucka sleeping?"

I glared at him and dared him to go on. So he did. "Eh, no tell me—eh, boiz, Billy Fucka, Jr., stay sleeping with our Toni here."

"Not."

Hoot. Hoot. Hoot. Yi-haa. Ooot. Ooot. Ooot. A bunch of fucking redneck brownies.

"Like you even give a shit," I said to him.

"I going have to broke his fuckin' ass for the sake of the clan." The boys laughed and high-fived Wyatt even if they didn't know what he was referring to with his samurai talk.

"I seen you with Cecelia Saratoga," I said to him. "And I heard Harley Ann Feliciano was down at Isles making out with you last Saturday. She married to your cousin, eh, Pocho?"

Wyatt's eyes glazed over. "You fucking the *boss's* son, Toni. What's with that? Maybe I gotta broke *your* ass first."

"I drink to that. Tonight, after work."

"I can watch?"

"Fuckin' haoles, they no can."

"Know-it-all summabitches."

"Billy Fucka, Jr.? And Toni? Bwwaa-haaahaaa."

"He know where his dick stay or what, Toni?"

"What you do for foreplay, play cribbage?"

"Eh, the haole the starting center Waiākea High."

"So?"

"I thought he went St. Joe?"

"Eh, we go play Kill a Haole Day. That's what my uncle

them did in the sixties, brah. Go school and yell 'Kill Haole Day' and all the braddas start throwing wherever they stay. Any haole. Fuckin' kill um all."

"For what?"

"For fun."

"What else?"

For Ringo Ferreira, everything he said came down to his self-proclaimed massive dick. "Why you never call us on the radio if you was just north of us? You wanted to camp overnight, eh, sleep over kine? Cradle robber, you, Toni. Nah, you know why? You never had none of this Portagee sausage yet. Thirty years been growing strong," he said, squeezing his balls tight in his huge hand. "You *never* go back to your little link once you taste this sucka, what you think, boiz? He fat. He fat. And fuckin' juicy. What—like try, Toni? Fuckin' oily like chorizos," he said, unzipping his jeans.

I looked the other way. Pocho grabbed me by my face and tried to make me look at Ringo, who was taking off his pants. Maverick slapped his hand off my face but said nothing to either of them. Wyatt chuckled.

"I getting *sick* of you," I yelled. Wyatt knew I meant him. Not once did he defend me.

It was like this every day since I'd gotten lost in the forest. For some reason, I felt mute. I even allowed old fut JoJo Masaki to rag on me. "But that's not the worse part—fuckin' Toni," he said. "The whole damn park, the rangers, the geologists, the firemans, the Park Service, eh, the whole goddamn world up the volcano know you got lost. Even up Volcano store the waitress was talking about you."

"They called Civil Defense, Maverick?" Ringo asked. "Harry Kim came up the park?" Maverick shook his head.

"You the first, that's why," Wyatt said to me. "You and

that fuckin' dumbshit haole wannabe hunter, biologist, dog breeder, scientist, know-it-all dickhead."

"And what's this I hear you fuckin' fucking the haole too?" JoJo asked. "You wanna lick some dick, you go for a man-size meal. Come sit your ass by Uncle JoJo and Uncle Pocho—we get cooking big time, little girl."

Every day it got clearer to me that it wasn't about me. I was a body there. They talked big and bigger for each other. It could be any hole, any crevice, any slit. I was just a conversation piece.

Maverick always took the middle road. "For real, Toni? The haole living with you guys? Not that I mind, 'cause that's Aunty and Uncle business. But to me, the one thing I do mind is that when you one of the boiz, you need to hang with the boiz, know what I mean?"

"No. I don't know what you mean. What you mean, Maverick, hah?" I said, pushing him out of my way.

"Whoa."

"Look out."

"Gettin' mean."

"Bitch."

"Fuckin' poosh um back, Maverick."

"No chick lay a finger on me without getting two slaps to the head."

"Means you better fuckin' show face at the party tonight," Wyatt said, grabbing my arm, then spitting into the dirt. "Even if you and Aunty Mary Alice was driving out to Kohala for Billy the Fucka's game, fuckin' bench warmer, no, Maverick? How come he never go out for football? No can handle, that's why. You better get your fuckin' ass to the party."

"How you know where Toni was going be tonight?"

"Yeah, Wyatt—how you know?"

"What, Wyatt—checkin' out Toni or what?"

"Hooota, Wyatt, action, brah, action."

"Spread um, Toni, here come bradda Wyatt."

"Answer them. Why the fuck you care?" I dared Wyatt to tell them, tell Maverick about what we had been doing.

"Nah. She ain't my type. I no go for Jap bitches with rotten attitudes who think they better than you, when they just as fucked, out somewhere in nowhere-land."

"Fuck you, I no go for losers."

"I no go for cunt I can get *every* night without even asking."

"I no go for pigs." He got up and grabbed me by my hair. I fell to my knees but would not make a sound.

"Nah, Wyatt, small kine."

"Why you getting all up tight?"

"Eh, what's going on?"

"Yeah, you only do that to your old lady."

Wyatt let me go, but I came back, fingernails flying for his eyes. Maverick got between us. "No, stop," he said. "Toni, they throwing the party for the guys who helped rescue, I mean *look*, for you and Billy. I joke you not. That's why they making the party up Nāmakanipaio 'cause everybody coming. They almost called Harry Kim at Civil Defense."

"I told you," Ringo whispered, "they wen' call Civil Defense."

Maverick pushed Wyatt away. "You get something going with Billy, Toni? Since when?" Even Maverick was jumping in. His half-assed approval catapulted the boys into more leering. They harassed me the rest of this day as our crew readied for the party—slicing huge slabs of red fish and picking up beer at the Kīlauea Military Camp's commissary, chopping cabbage, making pork adobo, and pot after pot of rice for musubi, turkey tails roasting, macaroni salad, and smoked pig meat.

So when Maverick lit the first joint on the last beer run up to Nāmakanipaio, I sucked deep, ready to blow it all off. They all guessed my secret, my innermost secret: *my Billy, haole lover, sicko cradle robber*, and I thought they were all dumber than me. I drank my first beer. Then the next and the next. I was determined to keep up with the boys tonight as I had wanted to so badly at the dorm parties with Sheldon's friends.

Within an hour, people began arriving with food, pupus, ice chests full of beer and hards, homemade pineapple and dandelion wine, rhubarb pie, and 'ōhelo berry pie—haole granola-ish stuff. More food arrived with the coming of dinnertime. I knew this was an all-nighter.

I was already nursing my beer, dumping some out when the boys weren't looking. But if the fire we sat around was the sun, I was Mercury on full-tilt orbit. I was next to Maverick with the pig hunters, the local physical science interns, and the young ranger from Nā'ālehu. And I stayed quiet and still so that the conversation would never veer my way. I sipped my beer slowly until Pocho Robello proposed a toast.

"To Toni Yag—what's your last name? To Toni. Us all here tonight drinking and smoking," he whispered, " 'cause she the only pig hunter who got lost in the forest with a haole loverboy and got all these other haoles with they bee-badees bunch up they ass over it, so that we could get one whole day off to make the food and fuckin' get loaded tonight. Suck um up, braddas, to Toni."

"Tank um, Toni."

"Drink, fuck, that's your toast."

"Boilermakers next. Where the Bacardi?"

"Put hair on her chest tonight."

"Fuckin' drink, pussy."

Heads turned from the pavilion. I poured the beer down my throat and nearly gagged. "I gotta piss," I announced as I wrapped the army surplus blanket tightly around my shoulders and staggered off toward the bathroom to vomit. Wyatt waited against the wall.

"Fuckin' get guts left or what?"

"Fuck off, prick. You guys all a bunch of assholes."

"Going be one *long* night, Toni."

"Go drink with Harley Ann," I told him. "I like go home." I leaned against the wall and slid down to a squat.

"That's just the start. 'Cause everybody going rag on you tonight. You the man, know what I mean?" he said as he reached into his jacket pocket. "You better do some of this shit with me. Make you last long. All night, you know that. You ain't going home till pau." He flicked the bag. "I got enough for me, you, and Maverick, and that's all, so no be sucking in your boogas and wiping your nose with the back of your hand when we go back, eh? And hold the first one down. No puke um out and fuckin' waste." He sat down next to me.

I knew what was going on, how we waited all night for the solitary moment that would bring us together, alone, under the orange light outside of the rest room. I knew he would come, and in many ways, I asked for him to follow me.

"Okay," I told him.

"And no be drinking in between the times the boys telling you toast and all that shit. Stupid, just make pretend. Those fuckas so wasted, Maverick too, they don't know if you fake drinking or what. But you ain't faking them out when they tank."

"Why? Why they doing this to me?" I pleaded with Wyatt.

I already sounded drunk, and if I continued talking, it would get dramatic. So I gathered myself. "Why are *you* doing this shit to me?"

"They like you quit, Toni. Maverick been taking shit for you from the boiz and the boss. Every day, 'Why no fire the bitch, Maverick?' Every day, 'How's Toni doing, son? I'm depending on you.' The boiz cannot stand when you on their crew. They might get injured 'cause you so fuckin' lame out in the field. You one fuckin' pussy. That's the word out on you in all four crews. You history, Toni, 'cause they all like you gone and they going keep at it till you crack. Me—"

"Yeah, what about you, you fuckin' asshole prick?"

He laughed. "Come." Wyatt grabbed my upper arm and led me through the trail in back of the rest rooms way in the back of Nāmakanipaio to a dry spot amidst the kukui and 'ōhi'a. He trampled some stalks of ginger with his heavy boots. "Put the blanket down, shit, like you so cold."

He lit a joint laced with cocaine while he cut up the coke on a small mirror with his hunting knife, fine, fine dust in four fat lines.

"Make mine smaller," I said. "I no like do all that. I might puke."

"That's yours," he said, pointing to the thickest line with the tip of his knife. "You need it." He smoked the joint as I stuck the rolled bill in my nostril. I licked my fingers and snorted them to get moisture into my nose. I sat there, drunk, stoned, coked out, thinking about Billy, and listening to the senseless laughter around me.

"No think about him," he said.

"Why?"

" 'Cause it's enough to make a pig laugh," he said, throwing his head back for the sweet drip.

"And how you know what I thinking?"

"This is why," Wyatt said. "You think about me from now on and only me." And he reached for me from behind, dragged me toward him, and spread his legs around me. He moved his strong hands under my clothes. I felt him biting my neck, my back, and then the side of my face, covering my body with teeth marks.

He devoured me, piece by piece, rooting and scavenging into the crevices of my body, so that when Maverick came drunken-stumbling through the ginger, Maverick looking for his share of the coke, Wyatt and I were too far gone by now; we continued on, dazed and bestial.

He stood there for a moment and watched our naked bodies, Wyatt's low moaning. Then I heard the slow unzipping of Maverick's jeans, his work boots' heavy fall, the slip of his arms from his shirt, the weight of his heavy jacket on my feet, then the warm press of his body against my backside, his erection probing and wet.

Wyatt pushed Maverick. "Eh, wait, asshole. Your dick touching mine," he managed to say.

"Move," Maverick said, shoving him back as he entered me from behind, Wyatt groaning and pulling out his long slide of a shiny penis to make room for his brother.

"Fuckin' prick," Wyatt said as he began suckling eagerly at my breasts.

The world has no rapture to offer that can compare to my night with the two brothers. I thought of Billy. It was what I wanted with him but would not make happen. I wanted to blame myself because I was wasted, I was drunk, I was vulnerable, stupid, and horny.

I've never experienced such pleasure since, this slow wave, a tidal motion of bodies and hands, the heady contrast of cold and warm, the ocean of semen that poured out of me into my hands, dripping between my fingers.

Maverick zipped up his jeans, then draped his jacket over my naked shoulders. He did two lines, then wove his way through the brush to get back to the party. Wyatt sat stooped over a small mirror, naked beside me, divining up another gritty line.

Eight

**O**nce Bunny graduated from UH in accounting and HCC in cosmetology, Harry O. and Mommy sent her and Sheldon to New York City to visit swanky Fifth Avenue hair salons. They would stay with Mommy's second cousin Donald in Hoboken, and take the bus every day to the Port Authority bus terminal. There would be taxis, dinners at Sardi's, and Broadway musicals like *Cats, Starlight Express*, and a remake of *Dreamgirls*.

Sheldon *had* to stand outside of Jackie O.'s apartment building, order a drink in the *lounge* in the crown of the Statue of Liberty, and drop a marshmallow mini from the Empire State Building. He also just *had* go to Battery Park, where Madonna sat in *Desperately Seeking Susan*, see Wall Street, where fine young men in business suits strutted by, walk SoHo for the artist in him, stand respectfully outside the Dakota, home of John Lennon and Yoko Ono, head up to the Bronx Zoo for the visiting Chinese pandas, and back down to Rockefeller Center in the hopes of glimpsing Bryant Gumbel.

Before leaving for Honolulu, where he would meet Bunny, Sheldon cleaned out Mommy's sewing room and moved out of our bedroom. "Before Bunny moves home, Billy, you get off her bed, you hear me? Stupid Toni, why you sleep head to head with Billy? You not shame your boyfriend in high school? Baby mind, never did grow up from high school, big dummy. That's what whole damn town saying about you."

"Billy ain't my boyfriend and I don't care what everybody saying. And don't tell us what to do," I spat back. "And I ain't the only one they talking about from this family," I hinted at Sheldon. "All the *boys* you been hanging with— I wouldn't talk."

"Yeah, butt out, Sheldon," Mommy said. "You're moving out, so mind your own business. Boyfriend, girlfriend? Billy and Toni? Oh please, that would be incest."

Billy wouldn't look at me. On many occasions, he had come very close to betraying my mother's trust in him. Yet I wouldn't sleep with him. Mommy always told me, "Once you have *it*, you'll always want *it*." And though she's been right 99.9 percent of the time, this time she was wrong. I'd already had it many times and many ways, but I never crossed that line with Billy. The loss of control, the neediness, the obsession—how much worse would it get? Billy looked at me.

Mommy moved a soda box full of rolls of waxed linen and beads off of her lap. "Billy," she said, startling him. "Can you take me up Volcano to pick some more of this orange fungus for our macramé pendants? I running out."

Billy took the box from her. "And I'll pick up more of these amber beads from Ben Franklin after school today. Do we need more Varathane for the fungus?" Mommy nodded and took some money out of her wallet.

Mommy glared at Sheldon. "Toni *finally* can be a big sister to somebody, that's all. And you and Bunny kind of reject Toni. And it gets worse when the two of you gang up on Toni. And Billy's finally getting his act together. Maybe he'll make it to college on scholarship after all. He just needed a family to take care of him."

"Well, Billy can always move in with me," Sheldon said, winking at Billy. "Solve everybody's problem, no, Billy? Separate beds, of course." Sheldon gave me a sarcastic smile.

"Please shut up, everybody," Harry O. complained. "I said *please*. Not every night they show *Banacek*, and *Baretta*, on Channel Four. And who Sheldon been hanging around with?"

"Never mind, Daddy," I said. "You better get ready and change clothes if you going to the Civic." Billy moved himself between my legs.

"Massage my shoulders before I go to the gym, Toni, please."

"Massage my shoulders, yeah, right," Sheldon said under his breath. "Come here, Billy. I massage you——head first," Sheldon whispered.

I had had enough. "Back off, Sheldon, before I break your ass. Fucking shoving shit in my face all the time."

"Knock it off," Harry O. complained.

"You going to the game, Mrs. Yagyuu?" Billy asked. "Pass me the baby oil, please."

"I not going," Harry O. answered. "I watching TV, I said. Oh, you was talking to me? Toni, try call Wyatt. He called little while ago. I forget tell you. If he coming over, remind him to bring up the beer. Sheldon, who you was with last night?"

"Oh, just some friends from the shop. Who's taking me to the airport?" Sheldon whined.

"Girls?" Harry O. asked.

"Sometimes," Sheldon mumbled.

"Huh, what?" Harry O. asked.

"Yeah, sometimes they girls, sometimes they——" he said.

"Good," Harry O. muttered under his breath.

"Who's taking me to the airport?" Sheldon repeated, this time stomping his feet.

"Me," Billy said, rotating his head from side to side to get any pregame kinks out of his neck.

"Oooh, I get you all to myself. But you only have a learner's permit. You not supposed to drive at night, no, Mommy? You lucky you cute. You get your damn way all the time in this family. When I get home from New York, I simply must shape those eyebrows of yours. You definitely have that Brooke Shields look, but you do need a good shaping."

"And a deep conditioning too, okay, Shelly?"

"And pick up some real Baltic amber beads for Billy in SoHo," Mommy said, nudging Billy with her elbow.

"Toni's coming with me to take you to the airport before the game. More down my back, please," he said to me.

"Why?" Sheldon grumbled. "She'll only get in our way."

Billy lifted his arms up on my knees. "And we'll be back to pick you up after that, okay, Mrs. Yagyuu?"

"Fine. Where did you put the varnished fungus?"

"No call him Shelly, you haole boy," Harry O. said.

"Don't call him haole boy," Mommy said to him.

"And, Daddy," Sheldon added, "I simply must insist on dyeing your hair with a really good salon product when I come home from New York. That Grecian Formula's making your hair purple in the sunlight."

"Try smelling his oily pillowcase," Mommy said, pinching her nose.

I got up to use the phone. "Wyatt? This Toni. Bring beer up for Harry O. You coming up to watch TV with him? Basketball. Civic Auditorium. Me and Mommy. Billy them against Hilo. No, you cannot, 'cause you treat Billy like shit. I said no. I ain't thinking about *it*. Was nothing. Yeah, you heard me, was nothing. You better not. Keep your mouth shut. No. I didn't. He don't know. You better not, Wyatt. Yeah, bye, asshole."

I hung up the phone, and a few minutes later Wyatt bounded up the back stairs with the beer. "I ain't staying, Harry O. Nah, one beer, then. My father coming up after the eight o'clock."

"I'll be out of the shower in a few minutes, Sheldon," Billy said.

"Flush your face down the toilet while you at it," Wyatt muttered.

"Hurry up. I might miss the plane of my lifetime. Get it, Daddy?" Nobody responded. "I'm going on an airplane and this is a chance of a lifetime, so *plane of my lifetime*. Ho, nobody can take a joke, this damn family."

Billy came out of the shower. Wyatt stretched out on the floor next to me. "C'mon, Toni," Billy said. "You ready, Sheldon?" He helped me up. Wyatt hung on to the bottom of my jeans.

"Eh, what is this 'You ready, Toni?' shit? Where you going, Toni?" Wyatt asked, all pissed off. "I thought us was going watch TV with Harry O.?"

"*Us?* Not even. Let go of me. Billy and me taking Shelly to the airport, then we coming back to pick up Mommy."

"No call him *Shelly*, sheez."

I looked back at Wyatt. "Why? You like come basketball with us? I thought you had to meet the boiz at Isles? You never said nothing about TV, bullshitter. What am I saying? I told you, that you cannot come with us to the game, 'cause you treat Billy like shit."

"So. I can come if I like. You ain't my boss. Free country. Aunty Mary Alice, I can come?"

"Fine. Fine. Toni, you bought carton passion orange juice for Billy after the game?"

"Yeah, I put it in the downstairs freezer. You can wrap um in tinfoil for me, Mommy?"

"Toni, let's go, Sheldon's waiting," Billy yelled from the back stairs.

"Toni, hurry up, shit. Billy cannot drive without your license. And I don't want to miss my plane of my lifetime. Bye, Mommy. Bye, Daddy. See you in two weeks."

"Be good and no spend all your money, eh, Sheldon. And give half your traveler's checks to Bunny."

"Toni, what the fuck, man?"

"Toni, don't forget to pick up me and Wyatt."

"Toni, where the goddamn remote?"

"Toni, I said, what the fuck, man?!"

"Toni, how come you no tell Wyatt what going on?"

I will always remember the way Billy ran up the bleachers before every game to kiss Mommy and me—pregame superstition. Then he'd take off his chain for me to hold and lay his jacket across my lap.

At every game this season Mommy yelled at the refs, "Juice, brah, juice! Where your glasses? What?! You get eye problems or what? How much the other guys paying you, hah, ref?"

At this game, Wyatt leaned back against the bleachers behind us and hit me in the back with his knee whenever Billy made a mistake. "What a panty. Fag. Haole plug."

"You made us proud," Mommy said to Billy afterwards. "We never had one athlete in our very own family to cheer for, no, Toni? Maverick and Wyatt maybe, but not the same as Billy."

Once home, Billy showered again. I rubbed Shower to Shower powder on his back. Then we talked about the game and the coach.

"He really needs me at center," Billy said, lying on his stomach and clutching his pillow under him.

"But at small forward, you can impress the college scouts," I told him. "Coach Cabingabang's looking out for you. Did you see your father in the stands?"

"He's mad at me for not going home with him tonight."

"He your only blood, you know." I never thought I'd hear myself use the blood guilt trip, but I meant it.

"He says I'll never be fully accepted by the locals here even if your family calls me a hanai-son. I'm not adopted legally —that's what my dad always tells me. I'll be a haole as soon as my back's turned. But that's exactly the point. I *am* a haole, so what?"

"Maybe we should invite him over for dinner."

"I'll make him some nishime," Billy said, turning over on his back. He reached his hand out to me. I placed it over my neck and he splayed his fingers over my collarbone. "Good night, Toni." Every time he touched me, I reminded myself that it could get worse. The first step, the next step, and I wouldn't be able to stop myself. I put my hand over his.

At every game that season, I watched Billy play intensely. Number six—to commemorate the years between our ages— had his following of admirers: a tiny Japanese chickie-poo cheerleader who was always at the top of the pyramid of screaming cuties; Japanese false townies with false eyelashes, Kleenex boobies in padded bras, and Lee Press-On Nails; a Japanese/Dutch/Irish/Cherokee Keywanette cutie pie with Jolen peroxide head hair, arm hair, upper-lip hair, and a fabulous collection of high-heel Famolares; a Chinese student government treasurer who plucked her fuzz and toe hairs— this according to Sheldon, who bikini-hot-waxed her at the salon; a Korean singer in the Houseband who thought she was Linda Ronstadt; an Okinawan/Filipino/Spanish flutist; a messy bilevel shag volleyball player; and a former lesbian DECA secretary.

I wasn't playing with a full deck. I knew it every time Billy looked for me from the court or the bench, the turn of his face, a wave, and I felt myself throbbing between my legs. I was a sicko, I was sure, a stupid high school cliché, only worse, because I graduated six years before him, yet wore his chain, held his jacket and bag, and readied myself to run next to the stretcher and wail like Bunny if he ever broke a leg. I was a sicko who mentally logged all the girls who called for him at home, the girls who waited with him before I picked him up every day, the ones who wrote him letters that he reluctantly let me read.

Sheldon thought so too. Aurora Kubo, who rented the chair next to his at Chickie's, told him that her cousin, Emerald Hiramoto, who had worked at Lanky's Bakery since we were in the tenth grade and was a little bit smarter than an ear of corn, went to the Pāhoa High School Sophomore Banquet with one of the bag boys from Pick 'n Pay.

This was the same Emerald I laughed about for years when I once ordered from her at Lanky's, "Six apple turnovers, please."

"Cherry?" she asked.

"No, apple," I said, thinking I was missing some inside pastry joke.

"No apple, right? So it's cherry." She ran around behind the greasy glass counters like a recently beheaded chicken.

It had gotten bad for Emerald, Aurora told Sheldon, who then told me. " 'Cause my stupid cousin, she was nuts for a fourteen-year-old kid. And how old was she? Twenty-three and baby mind like you cannot believe. So his parents was all against her, right? I mean, c'mon now. A twenty-three-year-old chick going with their tenth-grade son?

"So they ground him from going out, so that he cannot see Emerald. But my stupid cousin, she park way down the street and run in the dark to the kid's house, and then, she climb in the kid's bedroom window nighttime. How you like that, Shelly?

"Now that's what I call immature. Fuckin' no can handle guys her own age, so dominating one small kid's mind. Plus, they oofing. More, they all emotional attach each other. She was dorky in high school, you remember? But now, she get the big man on campus. Give her some kine rush, I think."

"You heard about my sister?" Sheldon asked meekly.

"Nah, which one?" Aurora said, feigning *first time I heard this* tone of voice.

"Antoinette," he said.

"Nah, yeah, small kine. That's why I was telling you all this, Shelly. What's with Toni?"

"Why, who told you, Aurora?"

"Da kine, what's his name? Came in yesterday. He your client but he walk in and you wasn't here. No, not Maverick—everybody remember Maverick Santos, that hair and that fine, tight ass. The other brother. Yeah, Wyatt, the mean sonofabitch. He told me *all kine shit* about Toni. He fucking good-looking too, you know what I mean, Shelly? Ai, I never did hear even half the shit he was telling me through the grapevines, I no joke you. How he know all that about Toni?"

Sheldon chewed me out for embarrassing him with Aurora, who knew everything about everybody in Hilo and never hesitated to spread the news. And he was curiously mad about what was going on with Wyatt and me. Sheldon was mad for nothing, because really, *nothing* happened after the night

Billy and I were lost in the forest. But I could never tell him about Wyatt and Maverick.

"And so what?" Sheldon drilled me one Sunday outside the shop. "You going to the Winter Ball with Billy? The class voted him Junior Dreamboat, so he has to go, you know."

"He didn't ask, so I ain't going," I told him.

"But what if he ask?" Sheldon whined. "Oh, this is a fuckin' shame for the family. And don't tell me this is the same as when Butchie took you prom. That's not the same, 'cause old guys check out young chicks all the time. But you hardly ever see old chicks checking out high school boys, unless you get half your marbles in the fish tank growing moss like Emerald, know what I mean?"

"But what if he ask? What I going do?"

"Tell him no. Just like that. No."

"He going be hurt."

"Tough shit."

This time I would have wanted to go.

Grow up.

I would have cared about my dress, my shoes, my flowers, lingerie, lipstick, hair.

Get a life.

I would feel excited getting ready as I pulled long red gloves over my hands.

Reliving high school days?

Take a prom photo for Mommy.

Get a grip.

And slow dance to the theme song like I meant it.

"There's Pio, I must be going. Ta ta," Sheldon said that Sunday afternoon.

"Where you going?" I asked.

"Cruising," he said.

"I can go with you guys? Where you going?" I asked again.

"Four Miles, and no, you cannot come. 'Cause when I with Pio, and I pouring out my heart and soul, I don't want you there rolling your eyes at me like I'm the big-ass cornball of the century or something."

"Hah, *you* and *Pio?*"

"I never said that. Just friends. Like *you* and *Billy*. And you better not tell Harry O. nothing, you bigmouth, 'cause he thinks I'm going out with a Pia, not a Pio. You know, like Pia Zadora? Pio! Hooey, honey, try wait, no. I get something upstairs for you," my brother said, leaning into Pio's Prelude like a hooker.

Pio Pratt was one of the drummers from Sheldon's halau. For a long time, Sheldon liked haoles and haoles only, but Pio looked like Maverick. He'd done his hair twice, tinted it a fabulous ehu-henna for free and bought new Centerline rims for Pio's Prelude with sunroof. He had come home with little hickeys between the scrawny hairs on his chest. Sheldon was somewhat distracted.

"Okay, wait now," he said, skipping into the shop door, then turning back to Pio. "I was at Liberty House yesterday, and Ralph Lauren Polo was on sale, and came with free eau de toilette with over-thirty-five-dollar purchase. I picked one up for you. I'll be right back." His voice sounded one octave higher.

"Eh, Toni," Pio said to me, giving me a head jerk. This was not an effeminate man, but there was a gentleness in his voice. "You looking good. So what's the haps?"

"Whassup, Pio?"

"How you like my hair?"

"Nice."

"Shelly did um," he said. "Free, of course."

"And so what? You treating my brother good?" I joked with him.

"What you think, Toni? Would Shelly have it any other way?" Pio laughed as he surveyed all the freebies that surrounded him.

"Okay, now, Toni," Sheldon said, breathy and caring when he returned with Pio's gift in hand, "you remember what I said. N-O spells NO. Make it your motto: *I do not have moss growing on my marbles.* Your time is past. Okay, Pio—up, up, and away," Sheldon snapped. "And tell me the whole scoops on Wyatt later. Bye, Toni." To Sheldon, we were all bit players in the ever-evolving drama of his life.

Billy looked older in his all-white Junior Dreamboat tux with a red rose boutonniere from Ebesu's, a red-blood metaphor for my bleeding heart. He held a red rose wrist corsage in a plastic box for the tiny Japanese chickie-poo cheerleader who was always at the top of the pyramid and picking him up at our house since he had no license. Mommy flashed snapshots of him from all angles.

"My last child's going to the Winter Ball," she said. She made me take shots of her and Billy. She never prom-posed with Bunny, Sheldon, or me.

Harry O. raised the volume on the TV. "Here, haole boy," he said, giving him a twenty-dollar bill. "Go Hilo Drugs and buy you some profalactic for the submarine races."

Billy walked down the hall and into our room. Sheldon had just finished styling his hair with a sweet laminate. He smelled like Shower to Shower. When I found Billy, he was sitting on the edge of his bed.

"What?" I asked him. "Cara Shinsato coming, you know." I looked at the twenty he kept creasing with his hands. "Harry O. wants you to go crazy with her."

"Stop it, Toni. Why haven't we——"

"Cara's on her way," I blurted. I looked at him for a long time. "I would lose too much," I began. "And you're only sixteen."

"So?"

I sat down next to him, our legs touching. "Mommy wants you outside for more pictures," I said, banging his leg with mine.

Billy moved himself away. "You're confusing me," he said. And then he looked at me with sad eyes. "I would've gone with a third trumpet player in the band."

I said nothing for a while. "Second trumpet."

"Second, then, I would've gone with a second trumpet if it were really up to me and not up to you, you know, Toni. Just as friends, no big deal," he said. "Is that why you're mad at me? Is that why you won't—— You're playing some kind of game with me, aren't you?"

"Shut up," I said. The perfect boyfriend I had made him into was beginning to mildly irritate the shit out of me.

"This kind of meant something to me, you know," he said. "Not like we're playing wedding or nothing like that. Just something nice I wanted for you being my, my——"

"Shit, I must be your buddy, right?"

"My best. I asked *you* first. I wanted you and me, tonight to be the first time we——"

"Billy! Cara came," Mommy called from the living room. I got up to open the door. Billy jumped up after me, but held the door shut. We stared at each other. But I wouldn't do it. I wouldn't cross that line. So he held me, kissed my ear, and whispered, "I'll be home by ten." He put the folded twenty in my hand.

I sat on the bed by the window and watched Billy walk around to the driver's side of Cara's red Camaro. He raised his eyebrows and shrugged his broad shoulders. Then he waved at all of us above Heads by Harry. Mommy and Harry O. watched him leave from one of the living-room windows, Sheldon and Bunny in the other, a regular Waltons scene. I leaned on my hands, keeping a smile on my face, until the Camaro turned the corner of Kīlauea Avenue and drove out of sight.

I looked across the street to Wyatt's room. He stood there putting on a T-shirt. I almost called out to him. He leaned his body out of the window. "Eh, Cecelia, baby, wait. I coming down right now."

He stopped and looked straight at me.

After one week of fact finding, Sheldon and Bunny came up with their concept: *Purple Rain/A Salon.* They nixed PYT, for Pretty Young Thing, because it was too close to PTL, Jim and Tammy Faye's club.

"Purple Rain's way cooler, you know, 'cause purple's for you know like, regal, intriguing, insane, and stuff," Bunny said with her new haole accent. "And rain for, well, oh my God, what else, dude? Rain's for Hilo, babe."

It was like that with Bunny—*she was who she oofed.* And now, she was haole from the Bay Area for her yard landscaper boyfriend Rolf, whom she met at the Poly Room.

When she dated Tim Huntington, a navy man from Atlanta, "Gee-aw-gee-ah," she was talking in a Southern drawl, which of course she couldn't get right. "Tiii-iiiyym! When ya'll comin' home for some suppa?"

Said to her redneck haole boyfriend from Texas one Christmas break, "Well, my mama made us some nishime fowa dinner. It's like, well, kinda sorta like a Japanesey stew?"

This before the oof of her life, one Adam Chalmers from Princeton, a period when she uptalked and irritated the shit out of everyone in earshot. "Well, I'm like, I don't know if she'll appreciate it? Because I'm very sorry, but I can't help if I've matured and grown a lot since getting my degree? And if she can't handle it, then Toni should get a life? And I don't know how to speak pidgin anymore? Know what I mean?"

In between each haole, Bunny went back to Maverick and back to sounding like her old self. "Toni, get a grip," she'd say. "The boy loves *me*. You had Griffith, big deal, came to nothing. I have Maverick. If I tell him, he marry me tomorrow."

"Talk is cheap."

"No cheaper than the life you need to go and get."

I took her words to heart. I got a life and quit the Park Service. Just like that. When, having lunch out in the field the last day, I refused to get up and walk to the truck to get the jug of ice water for the boys, Pocho called me "fuckin' lazy jackass cunt" one time too many.

Just like that, I dropped my gear, threw my lunch and my rifle at him, and headed for the access road. I took off my army jacket and flew it at Wyatt.

Once I hit the main road, I heard Maverick's government-issue vehicle hauling up the road behind me, so I stopped and turned. "What the fuck? Where you going?" he yelled from the cab.

"What the fuck? No, fuck you, Maverick. You see this?" I said as I gave him the bird. "Says . . . fuck . . . you."

"Eh, c'mon now, Toni. All in fun. You need the money, and the benefits. Get in. We go talk things over with Pocho. Pau already," he said, reaching over to the passenger side of the truck and opening the door for me.

"No," I said, "it ain't all pau . . . you guys all pau, as far as I'm concern. I reporting all your sorry asses to Mr. Harper. I telling him all the fuckin' cunt crap you guys been saying to me and all the shit you guys did to Billy."

"Toni, c'mon. No make like that. Cool your jets. Think this through little bit."

"No, I telling him everything." I picked up a rock and threw it at the truck. "But you no need worry, Maverick. You never say nothing, right? And Wyatt too, right? That fuckin' asshole. Both you guys. Especially you—*you never said nothing*. No worry, I not mentioning your two names, just Ringo, Pocho, and JoJo. So fuck off," I said as I continued my march to the office. "But I should report Wyatt just for fun, that pig-ass creep."

Maverick drove the truck slowly beside me. "Pocho get three kids, you know, and they living in the basement of his mother-in-law's house up Waiākea Uka." He threw my jacket out of the window. "Put that on. Too cold for just undershirt. And Ringo's old lady expecting her second kid, and the first one had bad asthma, you know, and needed one special breathing machine. And JoJo one of your father's oldest customers, all his sons and son-in-laws, his brothers and uncles them, you know, Toni."

"You and my lousy father can go suck a duck."

"No say that about your father."

"Why? He like you more than me. So fuck you and fuck him. Firing my ass and giving it all to you and that pig brother of yours. Look what it got me," I said, holding my arms out. "I back at nowhere, taking shit off of a bunch of low-life knuckleheads."

"Toni!" he yelled at me, mean. The truck came to a halt. Maverick got out, slammed the door, and grabbed me by both shoulders. "You listen to me. Get in the goddamn truck." He tried to shove me inside. "You ain't going say nothing, Toni. This me. This Maverick," he said, slamming his chest. "I asking you to think about all the shit I done for you over all these years and all the years to come. I going do some more. We ain't pau yet, Toni. You and me, we been—man, we been *everything*." He paused and remembered that night. I knew by the way guilt and pleasure came across his face. "Know what I mean, Toni? You listening?"

I tilted my head back to stare at him. I nodded slowly and pursed my lips.

"So you go in to Harper today and you quit. Whatevers. But for me, *for me, Toni,* you better not say shit. That's my boiz, and they fuckas, but they heart always stay in the right place. We been friends since small kid time."

"Yeah, but we been friends long time too."

Maverick put his arm around me. "I sorry, Toni. I never try stop this. I sorry." He stroked my hair. "There was nothing they ever said that if they said just one time to Herline or Bunny, I would've put their face through the windshield. But I always think you can take it. And I the one who hired you—just like they was blaming me. I have to work with them tomorrow and the next day. And Wyatt too, he could've said something. But he has to work here too, you get what I saying? I couldn't make like I was going easy on you . . . I sorry. Now get in."

I moved away from the truck. "I want to walk." I heard the engine start. "Your sorry means shit to me. You was adding in big time, punk," I yelled at him.

"That's what I said. I was adding in my two cents too. I said sorry, jeez, Toni. What *else* you want from me?"

Maybe it was my one moment to grab at the golden hoop. It was a moment that could've changed the course of lives. It was a moment that, for years later, filled me with mild regret.

He wanted *me* to say it.

I want you.

"Kiss my ass," I said.

"Okay, when? Not like going be the first time. I mean, yeah, let's do that. You promise, Toni, you ain't going say shit?"

"Yeah, yeah, yeah." I continued walking. "And my sister don't love you, you dummy. My brother loves you."

"What about you, Toni?" Maverick yelled at me as I walked further down the road. "Who your hero?" I felt myself tightening up inside. I stopped walking and turned around to face the truck inching along behind me.

Maverick had given me two chances.

"Nobody," I told him. "Me," I whispered.

Bunny was full of stories of her travels during college with her haole boyfriends that Billy and I were forced to hear. As she stuccoed on her makeup for a Friday night at the Poly Room Disco, we listened to her latest jaunt before her return to Hilo.

Pio Pratt had been driving Bunny and Sheldon everywhere in his fully loaded Prelude, most of the first-class accessories —the leather dash cover, the lambskin seat covers, the Pioneer four-speaker system, Hurst shift, and three bottles of Juicy air freshener—purchased by Sheldon.

Bunny readied herself for a double date with Pio and Sheldon, who was swathed in layers of Ralph Lauren Polo, beginning with the bath gel, splash, aftershave, and then spray cologne. Bunny wore a high-maintenance hairdo—full of Paul Mitchell Freeze and Shine. Her date for this double was Maverick Santos.

"Thought I'd give *the boy* another chance," she said gratuitously, putting a fake Madonna mole on her upper lip. She slipped in and out of an indiscernible region of a haole accent. But as her story got more heated, she'd rip out the pidgin, catch herself, and apologize.

She was telling all of us about her ex-boyfriend Leif. "So Leif and I went to Benihana's of Tokyo in Cupertino to eat lunch. I was PMS'ing real bad and wanted to eat some teppanyaki."

"Even her Japanee words get haolified," I said to Billy. "Tep-pun-yakky?"

"I heard that," Bunny said. "So what—do you want me to go on or what? I can't help if I don't speak pidgin anymore. And don't hate me for being better than you by elevating myself via my language skills."

"Yeah, yeah, go on," said Sheldon, who loved living vicariously the life of a so-called world traveler and oofer of all flavors of men.

"So me and my man sat at one end and two ladies sat across the Mexican teppan cook who no could even fly his fuckin' spatula in the air, ooh, sorry."

"For what?" I said.

"Anyway, these two ladies, about a hundred eighty pounds each, mind you—well, let me me describe what they looked like. The first one had thin and stringy hair but set in hot rollers—know what I mean, Shelly?" He nodded. Billy and I looked at each other and shrugged our shoulders. "She wanted to give the *appearance* of *volume*," Bunny shouted at us.

"This better be going someplace," I said.

"Like you get someplace to go," Sheldon said.

"We're going for a ride," Billy said, trying to defend me.

"Oh, wow," Sheldon gasped with both hands on his face. "Gag me with a spoon. Toni has plans. Oops, only plans with a high school boy. Go on, Buns," he said as he waved his hand.

"So then, this blonde, or a likely facsimile, did her makeup okay, if she was one drag queen for one skanky Las Vegas casino. And holy shit, she had fuchsia lipstick with pot-o-gloss on top! Oh, sorry."

"For what?!"

Sheldon, by this time, was rolling on the floor. "And then, and then?" He looked at Billy and me. "You have to be a vogue hairstylist to appreciate this chic humor, shit. Like *Mirabella* and *Mademoiselle*"—he pointed at himself and Bunny—"New York and London"—he gestured with his sassy face—"SoHo and Fifth Avenue, and *Cats* and *Les Mis,* versus"—he paused—"*Seventeen* and *Cosmo,* Hilo all they seen, Mamo Street, and the Hilo Playhouse doing *Oklahoma!* for the third time." He smirked at Billy and me.

Bunny rolled her eyes and went on. "So the second one, let me tell you, had dishpan-brown hair. Her bangs were thinning like Joy's and she had big gums like Joy too."

Bunny still burned up over the fact that Joy finished in economics at Berkeley and was on to UCLA for law school a full year ahead of her own graduation from UH.

"This ain't going noplace, Billy, let's go," I said.

"No, don't go. Okay, here's the California story," Bunny whined. "So these two, they're regulars. They don't even need to open the menu. The Chinese waitress comes around to take the orders.

" 'May I have two grilled chicken luncheon specials? And can you make it *all white meat*?' I mean, I wanted to say, 'Yeah, right, you fat fuckin' no-shame pigs.' "

Billy and I looked at each other, and he grabbed for the car keys. "Maverick wants you to pick up a cold pack of Bud before you go down to Isles, Toni," he told me.

"Maverick?" I asked him.

"Okay—so you don't understand, right? Well," Bunny went on, "the chicken special is the cheapest thing on the menu and they get the nerve ask for all white meat. Oops, sorry. And I ask you, Shelly, for what? They're watching their weight? I think not. And that's not the end."

"What *is* the end? Is it in sight?" I expelled all the air from my lungs in utter disgust. I didn't understand why Bunny cared so much about such asinine matters and why Sheldon wanted more.

"Then the wagon full of raw stuff comes around and the fat-ass, skanky *hole* on the end says, 'That's all white meat for us, right?' "

"Nah?!" Sheldon said, acting like he knew exactly where Bunny was coming from, when he was just as lost as us. "And then, and then?"

"That *is* the end," Bunny said.

"Oh," said Sheldon in that moment of uncomfortable non-comprehension.

"I mean, yeah, yeah," Bunny said, "I wanted to tell her, funny, eh, you shameless, stuck-in-the-seventies, fucked-up, fried-hair piglets."

Sheldon caught on, somewhat, and began to laugh for real. "No shame whatsoever," Bunny continued, "that's my motto for California. Let me tell you, Shelly—I don't rip on people on purpose, they make me do it." Bunny rubbed a red coat of matte lipstick on her yawn of a luscious mouth.

"I know what you mean," Sheldon said. " 'Cause I bet from the time the two chicks sat down you thought they was Hele-On bus drivers, eh? And then they had to act stupid."

"That's why when we saw Leif in New York, I really fell apart, Shelly. He said I was too judgmental. He just can't see our background. You know how we all rip on every Pa-ke, yobo, Jap, flip, borinque, popolo, haole, Portagee, and Hawaiian in our own house. But really, when we see each other at church or the mall or KTA, we're all 'Hi! How you been?' I mean, we all think we're basically better than the next guy, that's the problem. Us Japanese even think we're better than Okinawans and Ainu and they're Japanese too. All us damn locals crumbing around the floor for the same crumbs."

"Not like they not ripping on the Japs in their house," Sheldon said. "I mean, *everybody* hate the Japs. Excuse me for living. Even we hate us, and we Japs. That's why we all rather have hapa kids, so the blood mix—we no like be pure Jap no more."

"But we all like each other," Bunny said. "Never mind. I'm glad I got that off my chest."

"Got what off your chest?" I reached for Billy's arm and looked at his watch. "I wasted, what, thirty minutes here listening to you for nothing."

"You see how she is?" Sheldon said. "She never did change, no, Bunny? If anything, Toni got worse. She got no job again, no college education, no nothing going her way. Mommy and Daddy so shame of you, Toni, I cannot even tell you what they been saying. But begins with LOO and ends with ZER."

I got up and moved toward Sheldon with the TV remote in my hand. I flung it at his forehead and it landed with a hollow thuck. "You fucka," he hissed, and shoved me so hard that my whole body hit the living-room wall. Billy got between Sheldon and me.

"Me and Bunny was going hire you to help us with wedding side jobs, but now—" Sheldon said, nostrils flaring.

A horn tooted from the street below. "Shelly," a voice wafted up. "You ready?" Pio asked. "Chauncey and Nigel wen' call me from the Hukilau Hotel. They said they meeting me,

I mean *us*, at Poly Room. Quick, I have to save chairs for them."

Sheldon leaned out of the window and giggled while waving. "We're coming," he crooned as he dramatically snubbed me. "Oooh, Bunny, Maverick's looking good. Oooh, he's a hunka-hunka burnin' love if I ever seen one. Where he got those bad-ass threads?"

"I picked them out for him at Kurohara's. It was part of our deal. I'd date him only if he let me dress him, know what I mean? Next, I shape that hair of his and those thick eyebrows, and that goatee beard thing he's got going, has to go —unless he agrees to let me shape it so he can look like the Polynesian version of George Michael, you know, WHAM? Then it's a different matter, wouldn't you say, totally different head."

"Totally," Sheldon said, hooking his arm with Bunny's as the two of them proceeded to the back stairs. He turned to Billy. "Don't do anything I wouldn't do," he said. " 'Cause my sister might want to do it too. And that's statutory."

"Faggot," I muttered under my breath.

I looked down at Maverick on the street below. "Bring the cold pack down Isles for Wyatt, Toni," he said. "Tell him I not coming down tonight. And the boiz start talking shit, you tell me what they said. I fuckin' broke they ass."

"You no learn, no, Maverick?" I yelled at him. "We been *everything*, that's what you said to me, right? I tell you what—one thing I never been was a motherfuckin' stupid ass like you."

"Oh yeah—I wouldn't talk, Toni," he yelled back, all macho. "Who's that standing next to you, your fuckin' small brother?" Bunny bounced up to him and wrapped her arms around his waist. They kissed hard, with him looking up at me.

I laughed and flipped him the bird. "See what I mean, you stupid fuck."

"Yeah, fuck you too, Toni."

Once when I was seven, my father and I went riding into the Waiākea Forest Reserve to see Tino Medeiros, his rancher friend, who purchased seventy acres of land bordering the Pana'ewa Forest.

My father put a Pepsi for me and a 7-Up for him on the cool side of the truck so we'd have something to drink after seeing the huge enclosure the rancher devised to catch wild pigs.

We watched the pigs with binoculars as they entered a small trapdoor for the evening's garbage of moldy bread and spoiled fruits. Sows and piglets first, the boars, more wary, waited outside for darkness. Then Tino Medeiros closed the trapdoor.

"In the morning," my father told me, "he let all the pigs out. Maybe twenty, maybe eighty pigs in there. So they trust, right? And anytime Tino like pigs, they all fat and trapped, so he catch them easy. Smoke pig every day if he like."

We hiked back to the truck for soda. But my can was empty, the top unpopped. When we got back to the shop, Harry O. filled an old paint can with water and submerged my empty Pepsi can. No air bubbles.

"Was full when we left. What you figure? Who drank your soda? Maybe was the Kamapua'a sick and tired of moldy bread and rotten papaya. Tell Daddy how that legendary pig wen' suck out the soda without opening the can when you figure this out, okay?"

Till this day, my father placed that Pepsi can on his work-table to remind him about blinded belief.

I never figured it out.

What you see is not always what you get.

My father loved me, I came to realize, in his way.

Even after I quit my job as pig hunter at the national park, I knew he loved me. He spoke calmly to me. "As far as I concern, I done lecturing you, Toni. I tired of wasting my breath."

I knew it from his withdrawal from the family into the TV. "No sense beating a dead horse, right, Toni? Pass me the remote."

He spent fewer hours in the shop. "Make yourself useful and finish this bird for me."

He drank coffee with me in the kitchen downstairs, long and into the midmorning. He never yelled at me.

I was a loser and a fuck-up, so he gave up. I was the pheasant whose wing would never sit right. As far as he was concerned, I never made the right choices. A feather that never fell right on a finished mount. I was smart but without common sense. No excelsior stuffing. So I was his little pal again, no expectation, no disappointment whatsoever.

I saw this whatsoever love in every sip he took from the mug I bought him when I was seven, World Class Hunter. On his face I read his words, "Why wouldn't you just leave Hilo so I wouldn't be reminded of your sorry-ass state? What are you going to do? What now? What will become of you? I cannot support you the rest of your life. Get married. Be somebody else's problem. What is your problem? Where did I go wrong? I wanted something better for you. Something better than *this*. Is that too much to ask? What in God's name did I do to deserve a daughter like this one?"

I give up on you.

On my face, I wrote, "You fired me. You apprenticed Wyatt and Maverick Santos. You shamed me in front of our family and friends. You even wanted me to teach Billy to be a taxidermist. I wasn't even good enough for *this*, yet it was good enough for you. Daddy, I fucked up. But you fucked me over."

I listened numbly to the stories he retold from my childhood, one every day over coffee with Granny Goose on the AM radio in the background, as my father began trying to help me find clarity. New eyes, clarity of vision was what he wanted to pass on to me.

I held the empty Pepsi can in my hands one day in the shop. "Still empty," I said to him, distracted by someone walking in front of the door.

"What you see is not always what you get," he said to me. "Mean for good and bad."

"Hah?"

"You never did figure it out, no, Toni? That's the whole trouble with you." My father brushed a light coat of Borax off of his hands. Loose quail feathers fell to the floor.

"One time," he said, "this Filipino guy from Kea'au brought in this huge Cuba fighting chicken. Was all muddy and full of blood. The guy wanted me to finish the job in two weeks but I told him that one big bird like that take at least one month to dry." He wiped his hand on his apron.

"I finish the quail for you, Daddy." He looked at me for a moment. He knew I had been angry at him, yet I had been willing to work in the shop. He moved out of the way. "And then—" I asked.

"So I ask the Filipino, 'How this bird wen' ma-ke?' He told me that the chicken belong to his girlfriend and she went Vegas, but her brother never feed um. He let um go find his own food.

"So what's wrong with that?"

"Wait," he said, "the chicken was blind and so this other rooster been fight um and kill um. See, the chicken was blind since birth, so the Filipino guy told me, his girlfriend fed um by hand every day for six years. Can you imagine that?"

I wound a light string around the body of the quail and, with a tiny paintbrush, overlapped the feathers, weaving them into place. "Tilt the head to the right, or what, Daddy?"

"Yeah, up little bit more."

"So what with the blind chicken, then?"

"I told the Filipino guy I mount um for him with nice glass eyes. This bird who no could see to defend himself in this life might as well see in the afterlife, know what I mean? But he tell me, 'No, make the eyes close, 'cause the chicken was blind.' "

"What you did then? Why didn't he want a nice job to remember his chicken?"

"That's what *you* need to figure out, Toni," my father said. "The guy told me, 'Us like remember the way the chicken was from the time was small. That's what was nice about this chicken. Not the way he got all bust up, but the way he was, when he was his true self.' "

"Maybe he trust too much," I told Harry O. "Always had a hand giving him the mash. He thought everything would be cool when he got kicked out to fend for himself in the yard. But it wasn't." I held the empty Pepsi can in my hands. "I could never make it in the big yard too, Daddy, the way you want me to—" I felt a knot tightening in my chest.

My father let me off the hook. "So, I did a nice job for the Filipino guy," he said slowly. "I made the beak slightly open like the rooster was just about to crow. I made the chest real proud and tall. But the eyes. I left um shut."

"What you see is not always what you get. Better not to look," I muttered.

"Turn it the other way, Toni. Turn yourself around. Daddy know you can. I know you been thinking I gave up on you. In plenty ways, I did. But you know what? In the end, I cannot. If somebody no believe in you, your own family even, then who going?" My father turned and walked out the back door. I heard him sanding an 'ōhi'a stump for the next bird sprawled and defrosting on the shop table. "You just have to open your eye," I heard him say. "Open your eye, that's all."

My father finally apprenticed me in the shop. This was the world he never wanted for me. His children were too precious for this kind of labor; this was the world I longed to inhabit because it inhabited me.

I sliced open the chest of a kalij pheasant and sprinkled a handful of Borax onto its sinuous pink flesh. I never detached myself from what I was doing as my father had told me. I let this art possess me. I listened when the chuckle of the bird who whistled on the slopes of Mauna Loa sang for me.

I slid my fingers into his body to separate the skin and flesh, his blue back feathers scintillating in contrast to his long white chest feathers. I felt for his legs, scaly, blue-gray, and hard, and I cut them free from the body. For the first few days, I often looked up at the clock, thinking about my old job, marking time by my memory of days with Maverick's crew.

With a delicate cut, I severed the wings from the nape of the bird and worked my knife to its neck. On Mauna Loa, I once listened to a kalij pheasant as he flapped his wings against his body, the sound of my mother whipping the wet laundry in a brisk wind.

Harry O. showed me how to skin close to the base of the skull and then turn the head inside out by peeling it from the meat. With my fingernails, I lifted the ears and eyes from the face. I freed the coat of feathers from its body of flesh and held the skinned bird by the head, dusting the Borax from its formless body with a lover's caress. I never removed the brains with my father's brain-and-eye hook.

Hanging the carcass from a hook behind me, I judged the size of the body according to this kidney-shaped mass of flesh covered with fat purple flies. Into the twine-wrapped excelsior body I hooked wires for the neck, wings, and legs.

Harry O. showed me how to gently hold the bird's limp neck in my hand as I eased the neck wire into the base of the head until it entered the brain cavity, wrapping toilet paper and twine around the wire to approximate a neck. I added another layer of fine kapok, and here Harry O. and I differed from all of the other taxidermists. With their thick necks and proud chests, our birds looked magnificently noble.

Even on the days I felt nauseated from the chemicals, I continued working. I slid the wing wires into place, then moved the leg wires along the shinbone until they protruded from the bottom of the bird's feet. Harry O. always drilled holes for me into natural wood perches, and after sewing the chest cavity shut, I positioned the pheasant slightly crouched with wings spread open and beating in some distant forest. I elongated his beautiful neck and opened his beak to allow for his chuckling twitter.

I always saved the eyes for last. I rolled molding clay into the eye socket and affixed the red-orange pheasant eyes so that they looked straight at me. I wove the feathers into place and gently arranged the plumage of white feathers on the head. He needed to dry before I put on the finishing touches of varnish and nail polish. I passed the bird to Harry O., who'd inspect my work, nod slowly, then place my finished mount in the drying box gallery of birds.

I was tired, so tired. I slept at seven o'clock after helping Billy with his school projects. Sometimes I didn't even bathe. Billy pulled my blanket over me and started stripping our sheets and pillowcases twice a week.

I mounted half the jobs. And thinking that we had lots of items that might be of use to other artists and crafters, I had a contract with the Ali'i Feather Lei Shop owner, to whom I sold pheasant pelts. I also had a contract with a baseball cap distributor and asked Wyatt to make our first design, Pheasant Phlight, Heads by Harry, Hilo, Hawai'i. I sold Harry O.'s photographs of indigenous birds and mammals to painters, writers, scientists, and universities. I always reminded myself of the difference between commerce and art.

Wyatt, Maverick, and I made pig feet, goat feet, deer feet, and buffalo feet ashtrays. I made deer thermometers by embedding them in forelegs. We made reindeer footrests with the antlers as legs and stretched the tanned hides over foam padding for the upholstered tops. I made peacock fans with handwoven lauhala handles.

Billy and I took over the books. He'd come into the shop after basketball practice and sit on the edge of my worktable. He stayed over even on the weekends to help me put the accounts in order. Late at night, Billy and I pored over the books. In that darkness illuminated by a single light, our bodies close and legs entwined, he found that over the years, Harry O. had let many, many debtors slip by. The invoices unpaid amounted to hundreds and hundreds of dollars.

The next morning, I asked my father why he never collected those bills. "They all living off welfare and cannot even

feed their kids and you want me to collect every last cent?"
Harry O. said. I was feeling lousy again and not holding my
food down. I took a deep breath and shook my head.

"Then I'll do it myself," I told him.

"Not easy, you know. I was in Longs Drugs yesterday, and
I seen this Puerto Rican guy I stuffed a big mouflon sheep
for maybe fifteen years ago. Me, I forgive, but I never forget
when somebody owe me money. He never did pay me, that
dirty bas-ted. So I follow him down the vitamin aisle, and I
give him stink-eye. He cannot even look at me. Fifteen years,
I tell you. That's his guilt."

"Who you kidding, Harry O.?" I asked my father. "He still
has that damn sheep on his living-room wall. Guilt? That's
happiness that you never collected. I get them to pay." I
looked at Billy, who nodded in agreement.

"Eh, haole boy," Harry O. said, "thanks, but no, thanks."
My father patted Billy's shoulder.

"But, Mr. Yagyuu, you and Toni work so hard," Billy said.
"It's like giving your art away for free."

"Mind your own two cents, son," Harry O. told Billy.

"Highlight all the more recent ones," I told Billy, "maybe
back two years."

"Eh, Rambo," my father said. "No get stupid, eh? If you
going big time like this, why not hire the Rex Steve Collection Agency down by the old police station?"

"But costs money, right?"

"That's what I mean," Harry O. said. "Sixty-forty. By the
time you go through all your trouble, you might as well been
move on and make money by mounting." My father looked
at Billy. "And you," he said, "you better listen to me. Keep
out of this before somebody shoot your head. I might have to
stuff you for your father."

"What's wrong, Toni? You look green," Billy said to me.

"You feeling all right? Maybe you have the flu." He pressed his hand to the back of my neck. I rested my head in his hand and closed my eyes.

I breathed deeply. "I feel green." He stood up behind me and I let him move his hands over my neck and shoulders.

"You know, last year," my father began, "I sent a Christmas card to one of the damn punks who owe me money, and inside I been write, 'You owe me $100 for the pig head.' You think I seen that money? No. So I told the guy's father. Nothing. So I went to the meat department at Sure Save to tell him to pay up, dammit, but no help. I talk to the head butcher heart to heart, but no help. I went to Sure Save meat department once a week and talk loud, 'Eh, Randy, you owe me hundred dollars,' loud, in front all his co-workers, and still no help. What I get? Ten dollars here, ten dollars there. Big deal. That's why I say, some people have big problems and a half. Let um go."

My father took a bite out of an oil-hardened sugar doughnut and leaned over my shoulder. The sugar fell on the books, leaving instant oil puddles. He wiped the sugar off of his lips. "Pour me a cup of coffee, Toni," he said.

"This is really a matter of thousands of dollars, Mr. Yagyuu," Billy said at last, circling the final figures.

"You get basketball practice, haole boy?" Harry O. asked. "Do I hear Mrs. Yagyuu calling you from upstairs?" he said, cupping his hand to his ear.

"No, we've got a game tonight, and no, I'm picking up Mrs. Yagyuu from her quilting class at five."

My father sighed heavily. "You know what get me, Toni? The kid is right. I work so goddamn hard on these animals. You know all the details go into one damn mount. To me, I am one artist. We all artists, us taxidermists—George Lee, the fish man from Kapahulu, he the best fish mounter I ever

seen. Jimmy Lee—nobody beat his whole body mounts and
sheep head. Roland Lum, Clayton Ueda, only few of us left.
And the man in Kaunakakai, Narikiyo, he make the deer look
so alive, so sad, them eyes he make. I never seen a deer look
so damn real. They take us cheap." My father slurped his hot
coffee. "Sugar, please, Toni ma dear," he said.

"Let me figure this out, Daddy. Me and Billy."

My father stared at the messy books he'd kept and shook
his head. "Yeah, but you tell me your plan before you get
out there and get your goddamn heads blown off. And start
with the damn Chinee guy from the mainland."

Billy scanned the books. "Where? Oh, here. The goat? This
was just last month. Michael Kwok?"

"Damn Pa-ke said the goat not worth the full amount. And
I rushed the fricken job too. He living up Volcano Village.
That asshole, he tell me he no like the goat in the end. He
tell me, 'This goat's smiling at me. Look at it from this angle.
I don't want it. It's smiling.' "

I tried to subdue my laughter. But I burst out all of a
sudden. Daddy put his coffee down and motioned for us to
follow him into the shop. He pointed at the goat on the wall.
"He smiling at you?" We held in our laugh. My father looked
at us behind him and laughed at last. "Oh, what the hell, I
should've made the tongue stick out at that Chinee bas-ted
too, no?"

I hired Maverick and Wyatt to collect for us and paid them
fifteen percent plus what they already made doing their side
jobs in the shop. I short-listed three debtors a week, beginning
with Michael Kwok, who nearly shit his pants when Maverick, Wyatt, Pocho, and a few of the hunting dogs went to his
little cabin in the village and pounded on his front door.

Butchie stayed in the truck in case there was big trouble,

which usually there wasn't. They all looked unshaven with windblown, tangled hair, mokes with dark glasses, a cigarette dangling from the corner of the mouth, and hunting clothes covered with blood. Butchie drank a Heineken; the dogs barked. A rack of rifles was visible through the windshield.

They never paid Pocho, who came along for the potential sport of busting up somebody's face. They paid him in bentos, raw fish, and cold packs. And Daddy wanted Butchie to handle all the transactions once the boys got the client in the mood to talk payment—all cash.

I began collecting fifty percent up front from new customers and let the regulars do business as usual. We had aunties coming in for loose feathers and T-shirts for their favorite hunters in the family, all original designs by Wyatt. Painters and teachers purchased the photos. High school boys bought shark teeth and boar tusks on black leather cord necklaces. My mother's petroglyhs and macramé fungus necklaces went over big with the artsy-fartsy crowd, as she called them. Bosses from downtown businesses bought deer asses for office gags. A couple of reindeer sold every Christmas as Rudolphs with blinking red nose lights. We sold a lot of leg lamps on tri-foot stands.

I opened my eyes one day and we were in the black.

Mommy could retire from teaching at last. "We're throwing a big retirement party for me," she said. "And a kanreki for Harry O. He turns sixty this year and Japanese say he going be in his second childhood. What you figure, Toni? Sun Sun Lau, the whole restaurant?"

I opened my eyes one day and saw my hands moving over the open chest of a pheasant, not impersonally, as my father had instructed me. I felt the pulsating spirit of the bird that seemed to rise up and hover, as I took it all inside of myself.

Daddy said this was true art, not a painting or a poem, inaccurate and prone to interpretation, but breathing life into flesh drawing breath. I let my own wonderment remain inexpressible but for the tilt of a head, the turn of a wing, a chest proud, beak open and ready to crow, eyes closed on a blind chicken but seeing in a new life.

Nine

Sheldon breathed Pio.

He made sure we all knew that this was no unrequited love like all the others in his past. This was real, reciprocated, never mind that all of Sheldon's tips and half his salary—which would've gone to rent anyway—in some way, form, or manner, went to the *Pio Fund*. And Pio was gorgeous, the gorgeous among us deserving of gifts and flowers.

Sheldon bought car accessories to rival the Love Bug. Sheldon bought cassettes for mood music. He bought colognes and clothes from the Men's Shop, special-ordered expensive gel and mousse, finishing spritzers, and semipermanent vegetable colorants. This was love on a two-way street, of this my brother was sure.

No wonder his distraction when Mommy asked for the fifth time if he was picking up the red shirt she had selected for Harry O.'s kanreki from the lady at Ah Mai's.

Sheldon used to play deaf-ear all the time when he was a kid. He was good at playing those "army games," as Mommy used to say, but he wasn't playing this time. He simply hadn't heard. It must've been sex, a lot of sex, making him oblivious. Even the pimples on his back were clearing up.

My mother grumbled about having to plan her own retirement party and my father's kanreki party. Mommy got up from her stool on the sidewalk, walked over to Sheldon, and slapped his head.

"Shit, no pupus for us tonight," Mr. Santos said, watching the whole escapade unfold. "Wyatt, go up Elsie's Fountain and tell her make us sushi and teri sticks. Mary Alice get her rags or what?" he whispered to my father.

"That's right," Mommy snapped from the front door of the shop. "Eat dirt. All you old bas-teds."

My mother sat down. Her nostrils flared as she shook her head slowly. I dusted my hands and put the paintbrush full of red enamel into the can of turpentine.

"Mommy, I have everything planned," I said to her. I explained how I had called Akafuku Manju for the pink mochi on top of the white mochi for the centerpiece on the head table. Mrs. Akagawa said she'd make a big red onaga with a daikon fishnet and rose radishes and lots of sekihan. I already ordered the cake from Robert's Bakery with the turtle and bamboo designs for long life and endurance.

She nodded a tired nod. "What gets me," she said, "is how the Japanese only celebrate a man's second childhood. The women get nothing. That's downright chauvinism. We push out all them damn babies and reduce our life expectancy. We ma-ke by the time they celebrate. Why should I throw a funeral buffet when I not going be there to eat, yet I the guest of honor?"

"No kidding," Bunny said, coming into the shop and leaning on Mommy's shoulders. This gesture gave my mother some comfort. My sister was in charge of the decorations and, with Sheldon's help, the program and entertainment.

"And Harry O.'s been folding the thousand and one cranes every night. Niso-san and Mr. Ute helping him," Bunny said.

"They folding now?" Mommy asked.

"Yeah, almost finished," Bunny said. "Sheldon said he's

making the folded cranes into a big design. What did he say he was making, Toni, love or good luck?"

"Happiness, I hope," Mommy said.

"Harmony," I said.

Sheldon walked into the shop. "How come I have to pick up the red shirt?" The slap on the head must've affected his hearing. "You always giving me the garut jobs."

"How can you be a garut when you don't do nothing?" Mommy asked. "He cannot even pick up a goddamn shirt without grumbling and you expect him to finish a whole thousand and one crane design?" My mother glared at Bunny.

"You act like I'm hopeless, sheez," Sheldon said.

"You are," I said as he snubbed me.

Not thinking, not doing, not being anything but Sheldon Yagyuu looking through the eyes of love.

"Pio's helping me," he said, dropping Pio's name into every sentence and situation. "And Pio and me almost finish with the invitations and seating arrangements. I know who hate who and which aunty and her entourage need be sitting by the kitchen door way in the back. I got it. Don't worry." He dramatically did a double snap and an around-the-world for emphasis.

I put all my tools away and followed the three of them back out to the street, the cool of the late afternoon, and the drift of people to the lobby of the Mamo, fluorescent lights flicking on one by one.

Maverick passed me a beer and I sat next to him on the sidewalk. "Whassup, Maverick? How the pigs been——" But before I could finish, Bunny sat on his other side and draped her hand between his legs. She whispered something into his ear and he laughed.

I took a deep drink.

"Whassup with you, Toni?" he said to me at last.

"I been feeling shitty, like nauseated."

"All the chemicals," he said. "You doing too much business. Save the pig head from JoJo for me. I coming in to skin um tomorrow."

"Good. I wanted to make the pig smile at JoJo, that flabby jerk." He looked at me and shook his head.

"Let um go, Toni, let um go," he said. "Wyatt said he starting the two birds the Honolulu guys brought in on Sunday. Stay thawing or what?" Bunny nibbled on Maverick's earlobe.

"I took them out at about twelve. And when you and Wyatt collecting from the haole guy up Kaūmana?" I asked. He pushed her off and she suddenly stopped mid-bite. I watched Bunny and Sheldon sneering at me from the corner of my eye.

"Tomorrow," Maverick said. "We been trying to catch that asshole early in the morning up his house. Fucka ain't answering our phone calls, nothing. And every time we go down his job site, he hiding or something. We see his truck, but he dig—fuckin' Wyatt, all nuts already. He putting his nose to the haole's tracks to sniff that asshole out."

Bunny fake-smiled at me.

Then Sheldon chimed in. "Eh, he not *yours,* okay? He Bunny's."

Bunny backed him up with a look.

"He ain't mine. But you, Sheldon, you *wish* he was yours."

Sheldon smiled meekly at Maverick.

"Your mouth, Toni, I swear." It was Maverick. "You too much." It broke the moment of a perverse spotlight on Sheldon.

"You're terrible, Toni," Bunny said quickly. "You're always lying about Sheldon."

"Yeah, you evil mouth," Sheldon said, relieved. "Even Pio said I better watch out for you even if you my blood."

"I hate her when she drinks," Bunny said. "She gets so vile. I don't know what becomes of you, Toni, it's like we're not even related."

My sister was full of shit. In between haoles, she was back-pedaling to Maverick again. I was embarrassed being related to her. He'd take her back and never learn a thing about being second trumpet. Then she'd get bored with him and shove his ass aside for the next haole passing through Hilo looking for immediate cultural acceptance by screwing some-body brown or yellow.

Billy sat down next to me on the sidewalk. "You was sup-pose to call me to pick you up after practice," I said. Billy took the beer from my hand.

"Martin Medeiros brought me home. I thought I'd give you a break."

"I know but," I began, "I wanted to pick you up, then go down to—"

Billy leaned over and whispered into my hair. "Let's walk down to Ah Mai's and pick up that shirt for your dad."

Sheldon rolled his eyes. "And when you come back, you said, right, Billy?" Sheldon cooed at him. "Tonight's the night I work on your hair at Chickie's, right? 'Cause I closing the shop and you said you hanging out with me, right, 'cause Pio's working in Kona and I might get lonely, remember?"

I looked at Billy and shook my head. "Why?" I asked him.

"He's right. I promised," Billy said.

"So?"

"I'm not going home tonight," Billy said. "Shelly's going to give me the whole nine yards—wash, cut, style, eyebrows, then treat me to the teishoku special at K K Tei, right? It's not like you and I were planning on spending twenty dollars at Hilo Drugs on——"

I stared at Billy. His mind games didn't perplex me, they crushed me. And then they made me mad at him.

"You damn kid been pissing off your father," Harry O. said to Billy. "Pretty soon I going claim you on my tax. And this boy can put away the groceries. Ho, he can eat!" My father laughed with the other old men. "Think you one Yagyuu or what?"

"He one haole," Wyatt said, spitting on the street. "And haoles ain't nothing but fuckas. All of um. I don't know why you even letting him live in your house. He come over and you open your doors. 'Hey, man, come on in.' What the fuck is that?"

"Fuck off," I said, mad at Sheldon, Wyatt, Maverick, Bunny, and Billy for making plans with Sheldon. "You guys all go to hell and die."

"Now, now, kids."

The old-timers yakked on:

"Kids?"

"They never been change."

"All these years, shit."

"Still at each other's throat."

"Damn filthy language. That's what I cannot understand."

"And Toni the worst one."

"When you going open your eye and see, hah, Toni?" Wyatt said to me.

"I see you."

"No, you *never* seen me, Toni. *Never.*"

"I do. Pig." I looked at Wyatt hard.

Then he stood up. I thought he was coming at me. But he charged at Billy, grabbed him by the front of his shirt and yelled, "You, fucka. You the one making things hard. Go back where you came from."

Maverick got between them and shoved Wyatt off, then put his arm around his brother's neck, whispered something to him, then hit him in the chest with his open palm.

Wyatt stalked off across the street. He threw his beer can at the taxi stand next to the theater and the yellow liquid streamed down the totan walls of the lean-to garage like urine.

"Your boy get one hot temper, Lionel," Harry O. said, walking into the shop.

"Toni driving him nuts," Mr. Santos answered, slowly crossing the street.

"Kids," muttered Niso-san.

"Forget the last show tonight," I said to Billy. "The pig going be in the projection booth."

"You the one making him crazy, you know, Toni," Sheldon said. "Why you acting like you get something going with Billy?"

"What he care? I have nothing going with Billy. You guys all deaf or what?"

"Deaf maybe. But we ain't blind," Sheldon said to everyone there. "You had something going with Wyatt, no lie."

"Hah?" Mr. Santos said, stopping in the middle of Mamo Street.

"Toni and Wyatt?" Harry O. added. "Cannot be."

"He hates my guts," Billy said, slumping down onto one of the empty chairs. "Toni——" He paused. "You really have nothing going with me? I thought——"

"Mind your own business, Sheldon," I said to my leering brother. "Nothing's going on between me and Wyatt either."

"Billy is my business," Sheldon said with a dirty smile. "Pio and Billy." My brother looked at Billy and winked. "Always was from the time he was small, no, Billy?"

He didn't respond. I felt edgy. And then I glanced at Harry O. He grimaced at my brother and ever so slightly shook his head.

"I just have to stay away from Wyatt for a little while," I told Billy. He stood up in front of me. "Though I don't know how, when he coming in tomorrow to work on those birds."

I tried to wrap my arms around his waist. He pushed me off. "Nothing, huh? Maybe I should call Cara tonight."

"Oh, stop it. You're my best, best friend," I told him. He looked uncomfortable.

"Back to you, best buddy," he said sarcastically.

"Billy, when you come up to Chickie's," Sheldon said with obvious pleasure, "leave your best friend in her cage. I mean it. You can call Cara to join us at K K Tei. I'll show you Pio's modeling portfolio." Sheldon yelled up toward the open window for Bunny to give him a ride back to the salon.

Billy and I started walking down Mamo Street. When we turned the corner at the KTA parking lot, Billy stopped. I held out my hand to him, but he turned back toward the shop. I cut through the back alleys of downtown Hilo to Ah Mai's alone.

He smelled clean and young. He held his white palms to my face, and I breathed in a smell I will remember for the rest of my life—the smell of sun-stiff wash, a favorite blanket on a cold morning, a shirt worn, the body gone, but the smell still there for years.

I woke him up. I made him breakfast. I bought his deodorant on sale with coupons. I took him to school. We knew each other with the ease of an old friendship. But it was getting older by the minute. I knew how to turn things around. How to make him emotionally and physically attached to me. I could do an Emerald Hiramoto. And then it seemed all wrong.

I felt crazy and talked about. I *was* talked about, but for nothing. Billy was greeted every morning by the same horde of cheerleaders. "Wave bye-bye, Billy."

They called him every night.

"Hi. Is Billy there?"

"Is this Billy's mom?"

"May I please speak to Billy Harper?"

"Could I leave a message for Billy?"

"Did Billy come home from practice yet?"

"Please tell him Cara called. That's Cara Shinsato, his prom date. Thank you."

I felt him slipping. The same thought kept running through my mind. *Just spread your legs, Emerald.* Instead, I asked him to call me from the pay phone during his first recess. It was just me in the shop, and I felt sick. I looked toward the clock, hands moving painstakingly slow toward ten, every day.

If he called me at lunch, I'd rush up to the school with lunch and sodas and drive us to the Bayfront. Then I picked him up at the gym. I did his homework. He did my book-keeping. He bathed. Then I bathed.

I was a step away from becoming Emerald Hiramoto, a pseudo-child-molester sicko.

I had lost myself in him and him more so in me.

My mother told me years later that somewhere inside of himself, Billy decided to forge an identity apart from me, apart from all of us here on Mamo Street.

I had to laugh. It was the sex.

"Mrs. Yagyuu, it's not about wanting to be local," he tried to convince her. "I could stay with you, all of you, for the rest of my life. Is it supposed to be this easy? I mean, is somebody's life just mapped out like this? And Toni and me, I want. But she doesn't. I'm confused——"

"Hah? Listen, Billy," she said to him, "you have to get all you can out of *one* life. I don't ever want you to turn around one day and say we kept you from doing your thing. But regret, that's a bad thing. And worse is blame. Besides, Toni shouldn't be leading you on, for heaven's sake."

"My father's talking about a transfer to Alaska or taking a post in the regional office, I don't know, it's just talk. I could stay, right?"

"Or you could go."

"Because Toni and Wyatt——" Billy said to her.

"What about Toni and Wyatt?" Mommy asked.

"They. I think they. Never mind. I've been everywhere with my dad. He's my only blood."

Billy left to pick fungus with Mommy and later they stopped by Ben Franklin to buy some amber beads.

Billy and Martin began to hang out more frequently, and I was jealous—and angry for being so. Cruising, picking Billy up some mornings, and, more often, bringing him home after practice. They went to dances in the gym, drove down Banyan Drive, went to the movies and Pizza Hut with the in crowd of jocks and cheerleaders.

They drove around in Cara Shinsato's red Camaro, Billy wedged between Jamie and Jewel, the Hashimoto twins, like human bookends. After the games, they'd head for Wailoa State Park to hang out or go to a hotel party on Banyan Drive.

From this time on, Mommy and I went home alone after each game. He'd slip into his bed around one in the morning, the sweet smell of liquor on his breath. I pretended to be asleep.

The nights Wyatt still whistled for me from the street to read subtitles for him—two Tuesdays a month now—Billy would watch me from the window. Wyatt draped his heavy arm on my shoulders and flipped Billy the bird behind my back as I shrugged his arm off of me.

Wyatt drank Southern Comfort and I felt the brush of his breath as I read to him in the dark theater. He would find a reason for us to go upstairs or to the projection room. I went knowing what would transpire between us.

Afterwards, he'd force me to go to Isles to drink and smoke with the boys, "good for business," hang with Maverick and two crews of pig hunters. Cecelia, Harley Ann, and now Lynette Vasconcellos, their "old ladies," would work their way toward Wyatt as they flicked ash in empty Bud cans.

Wyatt's hot temper with the boys was never directed at me, which was his apology for the way they treated me when I worked with them. He dropped me off on the street, grabbed my ass on the way out of the truck, and I'd say, "Fuck you, Wyatt."

And he'd say, "You promise? Next Tuesday, Toni."

Later, I'd climb into my bed. Billy pretended to be lost in sleep.

We lost ourselves anyway. We should've slept together. It would've made things clear. Instead, we distorted our friendship. And in my life, desire and compatibility of spirit never again manifested themselves in one male body.

Two weeks later, I went to see *Streetfighter's Last Revenge*, starring Sonny Chiba, with Wyatt at the Mamo. Billy was working on a science project at Cara's. Wyatt was already drunk. I drew my knees to me when the theater darkened.

"Cold?" he asked. "Try wait." Wyatt went bounding up to

his room and came back with a light quilt. He draped it over my lap.

"No put um between your legs and make um stink. That's my blanket. I coming in tomorrow after work to start the pig feet ashtrays."

"Yeah, whatevers."

"No close the shop is what I saying. Wait for me. Here, drink. Lighten up. What's with you, man?" He put his hands under the blanket, warm, rough hands, moved it over my thigh. "Relax," he said, tapping my leg. "There, Sonny Chiba. Read good. There Pocho and his old lady. Eh, there Harley Ann——"

"Stop calling them old ladies, shit, they have names, you know. That's what I hate about you guys. Everybody is their old lady, their old lady. My old lady this, my old lady that. Rowena. Her name is Rowena Ah Chong. So what about Harley Ann?"

"Nothing." Wyatt found my hand, wound it with his, and pulled it to his chest. "Fuck um if they cannot take a joke. Shit, you no more your rags, eh?" The movie started. "Read, Toni. Read good."

We met the boys afterwards at Isles. Wyatt's quilt was still wrapped around my shoulders. Butchie sat down next to me. "How my brothers been treating you, Toni? Which one you like me give dirty lickens?" He laughed.

"Sheldon," I answered.

"No, that's *your* problem. Him and Pio Pratt going strong, eh? At least it's love. What more you can ask for in this life? Bunny just came down with Maverick. His 'old lady,' he tell."

It made me sad. Even my beautiful sister was somebody's old lady. "Where is she?"

"Over there by the truck."

I turned to my sister's swing of long hair, a coy laugh, still the center of every guy's attention with her hickey-laden body, skintight jeans, and soft pink fuzzy sweater.

"I going back school, you know, Toni," Butchie said to me. "Me and you, we go back UH-Hilo. Herline told me easy and she get kids. She went the scenic route, so what? She almost pau in accounting. I going major in Hawaiian studies. I mean, the theater is good, but there's more, you know what I mean? That's why your pops all hu-hu with you. They wanted more for us kids."

"Yeah," I said. We held each other. "I'm happy for you."

"Here, Butchie, smoke?" It was Wyatt. "Move over, Toni, get some dodos over here." I moved over toward Butchie, who dragged deeply on the joint. We shared a bottle of Tanqueray. "Eh, there's that canoe coming in the bay. There"—he pointed— "see the small light?" I saw nothing.

"This your blanket, eh, Wyatt?" Butchie asked.

"Yeah. This my—my date tonight to go see Japanee movies. No, Toni?"

"Date, yeah, right." We all laughed.

The three of us were the last to leave Isles that night. Butchie closed the car door for me. "See you guys at home," he said. We sat there, Wyatt and me, in intimate silence.

We took the long drive back to Mamo Street and he parked his car behind the theater. There was a long pause. I didn't want to go to an empty room, the lights off in the house and Billy not home yet.

Wyatt said nothing. He reached behind me to lock the door and eased me out through his door. His huge arm around me, he led me up the back steps of the theater to the rooms above it. Down the hall to the room he shared with Maverick, Wyatt hung a wire hanger outside the door before pushing it shut. "He know what that mean," he said.

In the light from the street, it was the way he placed his

hands on my naked belly, sat there astride, touching my entire
body with such gentle hands, lifting my arms, smelling me,
the way I could smell the musk of his hair, see his eyes close,
hear his slow moan, feel his slow entry.

"No think about him, Toni," he said, licking away the tears,
drinking fully, lips on eyelids, the warm move of his huge
naked body. I slept in this lover's largeness, this lover who
never turned his back to me. "Next, next Tuesday, Toni?" he
said as he pulled me near.

In the morning, Mrs. Mei Ling yelled, "Wyatt, phone." He
picked up the line in his room.

"Yeah, whatevers. For you," he said, holding out the phone
to me.

"Me?" I mouthed silently. I stopped gathering up my scattered clothes, hopped on one foot to put on my panties, and
grabbed the phone. Wyatt watched me, arms folded behind
his head.

"Hello?" No answer. "Who is this?"

"You don't have to drive me to school." I looked out the
window, curtains sucking in, blowing out, and saw Billy's
shadow pause.

"Billy," I whispered.

"I don't get it, Toni," he said at last. "You sleep with everybody else."

We were in the car on our way over to Sun Sun Lau for a
combined celebration, Mommy's retirement and Harry O.'s
kanreki.

"You three circalate tonight, okay?"

Mommy wanted Bunny, Sheldon, and me to "mingle, mingle, mingle. If all those people coming to celebrate with me

and your father, the least you can do is talk to *each* guest, small kine, so they don't think we're all stuck-up and throwing this party for their monetary gifts."

It would be a long night.

"You hear me, Bunny? Stay away from Maverick."

"Yeah, Mommy."

"You hear me, Sheldon? Pio can take care himself."

Harry O. shook his head and exhaled a blast of disgusted homophobic air.

I nudged my brother. "What? What? Yeah, I heard."

"You hear me, Toni?"

I said nothing.

"And, Billy, you help Uncle Herb and stay away from Wyatt. Toni, you hear me?"

Billy hadn't spoken to me for days. In fact, he had gone home for the last few nights. "It would be my pleasure," he said in a smug haole way.

"We have *five hundred* people, plus the crashers *we know* going come, Mommy," I said.

"Your father and me cannot do all the mingling by ourself. Toni, you heard me?" she asked again. My mother was tense. "You planning to get all loaded, hah, Toni? That's why you cannot do your father and me just one favor on this, our one and only special night till the night of our funeral, hah?"

"I'm mingling, Mommy," I said at last.

Mommy cranked her window open hard. "Damn kid, only think about herself. And no college degree, that's what gets me." The truth was finally out.

So it was my mother who had really wanted me to finish school. All those years, she had used Harry O. to exert guilt and pressure on me. I'd listen to him. I would please him.

But in the end, I couldn't.

My father looked at me in the rearview mirror. He told

me with his look that everything would eventually be all right, that Mommy was overreacting and just wanted the whole night to be perfect. His look, so suddenly a part of this moment in our lives, startled me.

"Toni—you make sure Pio Pratt and his mahu friends sit by the kitchen," Harry O. said. "Expecially that damn Franjie and Paul, those two damn tuntas always selling their body outside my shop."

"Funny, very funny," Sheldon said to him. "Mommy, make him stop teasing Pio and my true friends," he whined.

"Shut up and listen to your father," she said as Harry O. grinned.

At the door of Sun Sun Lau, Mommy and Daddy greeted all the guests. All of us wore red, including Billy. Mommy was in a ten-strand pakalana, and Daddy in a double maile. There was an endless line of family friends, neighbors, customers, downtown merchants, taxi drivers, the barber next to the theater, Elsie's entire fountain crew, hunting buddies, Mabel Otsuji and her school of fashion design, Efrem Garcia, Mrs. Freitas, Melvin Spencer, Chickie's hairstylists, county councilmen, the mayor, Park Service people, schoolteachers, custodians, cafeteria workers, principals, friends of our friends, and friends of our relatives.

"I never know we knew five hundred people," Sheldon whispered to me after hugging the three hundredth person in his floozy, fake hug, fake smile, light tap, tap, tap on the back way. "I sick of my smile already," he said while still in the act of smiling. "I have a fuckin' headache. Hiii, Mr. Harper! Mrs. Harper!" Fake smooch. "Billy's helping out my Uncle Herb behind the bar."

"Come in, enjoy! Get plenty beer."

"Hi, thanks for coming."

"Hiii! Mommy, look, Helen came! And the fabric ladies too!"

"Hiii, you guys . . . ooh, gimme hugs!"

"Hiii! Nice to see you."

And mingle we did.

Billy and the Santos brothers busted their asses behind the bar. Maverick cooked bags and bags of smoked pig, goat, and sheep meat in the kitchen, shiny sizzling meat in aluminum trays. Billy sliced sashimi and neatly lay the translucent red layers on beds of ogo and shredded daikon. Uncle Herb mixed the drinks and acted like the mayor of Hilo, all of them acting:

"Long time no see!"

"And the wife?"

"And the kids?"

"And the grandchildren?"

"And the new car?"

"And the job?"

"And the dogs?"

Into the fifth of nine courses, I signaled to a mingling Sheldon across the huge restaurant to start the program. Of course, he *insisted* on being the emcee. And with a wave of his hand, his entire hālau took the stage. Maverick played bass, Wyatt the guitar, Butchie danced, Sheldon's kumu hula sang, and then Sheldon himself kicked off his espadrilles to dance in the front row.

"For Uncle Harry and Aunty Mary Alice," Maverick said into the mike as the hālau began their second number. I breathed deeply. The night was half over.

"And this next song is dedicated to my mommy and daddy," Bunny said into the mike with a cry-coming-on, quivering voice. " 'Cause love will always keep them together."

Bunny and Sheldon sang to the flip-side instrumental, after I shoved the tape into the recorder by the mike on the podium. Deep into the lyrics, Sheldon stared at Pio throughout the whole song, wiping tears from his eyes even as he boogied.

"And now," Sheldon began melodramatically, "I want to call to the stage, my Uncle Herbert Yagyuu, my daddy's big brother, who will give the banzai toast from the guests to my loving mom and dad. Let's give them a round of applause."

I stood by the bar exhausted. Billy passed me a stool and a Spanada wine cooler in a plastic cup. It was his first gesture of kindness toward me in weeks. But he turned to pour a drink for Cara Shinsato, daughter of county councilman Andy Shinsato. She had decided to hang out at Billy's side for the whole night.

Uncle Herb made his way to the stage. He adjusted the mike, which squeaked and squawked as he hit the head with his palm.

"Testing. One, two," and he cleared his throat. "I'd like to wish my brother, Harry, and my sister-in-law, Mary Alice, ten thousand good wishes from us, the guests, here tonight at this kanreki and retirement party." Uncle cleared his throat again.

"They deserve this. You all know what I mean. Harry and Mary Alice have been a friend to all of us here tonight. And for those of you who've never experienced the Yagyuu hospitality—come down to Mamo Street one Friday at pau hana time. Have a couple of beers with the boys, right, Lionel? Ute? Niso-san?" The three old men held up their beers and toasted my mother and father.

"Mary Alice makes delicious pupus if she isn't on the rag." Uncle Herb looked at Harry O. and smiled. "So now, as the Japanese say, we all need to take home some bad luck tonight, just a little bit, so that the only thing left for my brother and his wife is good luck in this lifetime." Uncle Herb raised his beer.

"Fill up your drinks and stand up." Then Uncle Herb yelled in his deep baritone from his ki, way down below his chest, *"Yagyuu-kun, banzai! Banzai! Banzai!"*

The guests thundered back, *"Banzai! Banzai! Banzai!"* Maverick popped a bottle of Mommy's favorite Asti Spumanti and poured the foaming champagne into glasses on the head table.

Sheldon took the mike again as the cheering and clapping died down. "And now," he started, "I take great pleasure in calling my sister, Antoinette Yagyuu, to give the banzai from the family to the honored guests."

I glanced at Billy. "This wasn't in the program." I looked back at Sheldon and shrugged my shoulders to signal, "No, you moron, what are you doing?" But it was too late. Everyone was turning around to look for me.

"Toni?" Sheldon said again innocently. "Let's give my sister a round of applause."

"I cannot."

Billy stepped in front of Cara. "You can, Toni. Listen," Billy said to me over the noise. *"Raihin no shokun,* then *banzai.* Three times, that's it."

Billy held out his hand to me. He was about to walk me to the stage when Wyatt came out from behind the bar, wiped his hands on his apron, pulled it over his head, then made me take his arm.

"Move, punk," he said to Billy while giving him a shove in the chest. "C'mon, Toni. Everybody looking." I looked for Billy, who sat on my stool, an angry Cara at his side. We started walking to the stage. And then Wyatt whispered to me, "I would've made you one good prom date."

"You wish."

"I did," he said.

"And then what?" I asked.

"Then I smoked a joint."

"Figures. Take off your shades. Nighttime, stupid ass," I whispered as we neared the head table. *"Raihin no shokun, raihin no shokun,"* I thought to myself over and over.

Wyatt stopped at the stairs that led to the stage and waited there. I looked at everyone from behind the podium—Bunny with Maverick holding her from behind, Sheldon checking his notes, then staring at Pio and blowing him secret kisses, Pio, meanwhile, far more interested in Chauncey and Nigel, Wyatt with his shades back on, Billy, my Billy. I searched for him but he was gone. I looked at Mommy and Daddy.

"On behalf of the Yagyuu family," I began, "I would like to thank each of you for coming." Sheldon signaled me from behind a potted palm to *relax, relax.* "My mother and father will now enter their second childhood with your blessings. They can go Vegas when they like," I stammered on. "No need to work anymore. Now my daddy can see Japan like he said he would one day. Do what they like, when they like. Brunch at Elsie's at ten. Don't need to worry about us kids anymore. You take it easy now."

I raised my beer. "Fill up your glasses and stand up, please." I saw Billy heading out the door with Cara. *"Raihin no shokun, banzai! Banzai! Banzai!"* The guests shouted *"Banzai!"* three times in response. Billy stopped for a moment, then left holding hands with Cara.

Wyatt filled the glasses at the head table. "Easy on the Asti, Aunty Mary Alice," he said to her. "Suck um up, Harry O.," he said to my father, passing him the bottle. My father took a long drink and passed the bottle back to Wyatt.

"To Heads by Harry, Inc.," he said to Wyatt. "Call your brother to the front."

The bottle of Asti tilted for a long drink, Wyatt finally said, "Hah? Why?"

"You heard me, son. Call your brother."

"Mav!" Wyatt yelled toward the bar. And with a swoop of his big arm, called Maverick to the front. "Come." Maverick bounded through the crowd of people. Sheldon began shuffling through his notes.

"What's Daddy doing?" he mouthed at me. I shrugged my shoulders. Sheldon hustled over to the mike and whispered into Harry O.'s ear. My father put his hand over the mike and told Sheldon to beat it, this was *his* night and don't forget it.

Sheldon, not to be bested even at what wasn't a party thrown on his behalf, took the mike. Then leaning in, he rushed, "And now, my father will say a few words on behalf of him and my mother. Okay, all yours, Daddy."

"Testing, one, two, three." Old-timers always tested the mike like they distrusted technology. Then Harry O. blew into the mike to make double sure. "Thank you all for coming from me and my wife. We like you stay 'cause Michael Hara and Pacific going play some oldies after this. And I get plenty pig feet ashtrays and heads to give away with the lucky number—dendrobiums, mochi, sheepskin, any kine. My son going draw the lucky numbers pretty soon."

My father motioned for Sheldon to come back up to the stage, me too. Then he scanned the room for Bunny and called her up with a tug of his index finger. "Maverick and Wyatt, come stand by my kids," he said. "I want to say this in front all these people tonight as my witness."

I turned to Mommy to see if she had any idea where this was all heading. She rolled her eyes and shook her head.

"See, all my life, I had Heads by Harry, and you all been

my loyal customers and friends. See, now—I going pass the torch to my daughter, Toni, and her two partners, Wyatt and Maverick Santos." The three of us looked at each other and Wyatt raised both clenched fists into the air. The two brothers bear-hugged each other.

" 'Cause since the day my daughter came home flunk out from UH, till today when I been pass things over to her small kine, she been double my business with her two partners. That's why now I can retire. But I tell you all something. And you my witness. Was Lionel's two boys who been *take care of business,* if you know what I mean. So from now on, this Heads by Harry, Inc." The audience clapped and cheered.

"I not pau," Harry O. said, leaning into the mike. "Testing, one, two. This *my* party, shit, gimme a break." Sheldon and Bunny faded into a bizarre background color.

Green.

My brother crossed his arms and Bunny sat down in the empty seat beside Mommy. "But," Harry O. said out of the blue, then paused to look at both Sheldon and Bunny.

"Toni and the boys ain't having no Heads by Harry, Inc. till the surveyor come in and split the shop space to make two shops. See, all you guys my customers and friends. I like you come down to the other shop I going open down Mamo Street, Heads by Bunny."

Bunny looked at Sheldon. "Chickie been good to my kids," he said, looking at the hairdresser at the table next to the stage, "but my kids both get business degree from UH, so I figure this the time for them try their wings."

My father looked at Mr. Santos and they toasted each other. "So I like all you old futs come make permanent wave and dye your hair from that old fut blue to black. And you makule old bas-teds dump out your Grecian Formula. My son said turn your hair purple from oxidation and all the wāhines laughing behind your back when you go out in the sun. We give you small discount. And all you men better dump your barber, unless the guy is Juanito's next to the theater, and give my kids your business. This the two owners," he said proudly, "Sheldon and Bunny Yagyuu." My father put his arms around both of them.

Then my father turned to Maverick, Wyatt, and me. "That's the only way I giving you the shop," he said to us with his hand over the mike.

"Whatevers, Harry O.," Wyatt said with a macho handshake and men-style hard slaps to the back. Then he bear-hugged my father.

"That's cool with me," Maverick told my father, then hugged him inside his huge arms. "Thanks, Harry O."

"Toni ma dear?"

"Okay, Daddy." My father kissed my forehead.

"Drink up, everybody!" my father said. "Kampai! To Heads by Harry and Heads by Bunny, Inc.!" Michael Hara and Pacific began playing on Sheldon's cue, opening with a Tony Orlando and Dawn medley of "Take a Message Maria" and "Knock Three Times."

Sheldon ran to get Mommy and Bunny to dance, as my father and I danced his old-fashioned way as if he were pumping gas, Mommy complained.

The guests began to leave after the lucky numbers were all drawn. All of us still danced as the band played on. Billy never came back.

I slow-danced with my father that night. And he told me quietly about artistry and the artist's hands I inherited from him along with the business. He reminded me about keeping my emotional distance from the animals. "A scientist you are," he said, "no, *creator*—in no other art form does the artist attempt direct re-creation of life."

He looked at me and smiled. "And never mount someone's pet no matter how much they beg you. And let some debtors go if they living off of food stamps" but want a beautiful pheasant for the shelf.

In spite of his emotional distance, he had deep, inherent love for animals. "That's the only way to survive in taxidermy day to day."

I don't think he wanted the song to end. "Taxidermy been good enough for me. So how can it be anything but good enough for my daughter?" He wanted to feel close to me and tell me everything about his life work in the space of an old love song.

Because to tell me at that moment was to hold me.

That Christmas was an incredibly lucrative time at Heads by Harry, Heads by Bunny, Inc. Mommy woke up early to make espresso and fresh banana poi cake for Heads by Bunny customers, and a Mr. Coffee carafe full of Yuban for the old-timers to have with their staple of glazed doughnuts from Robert's Bakery.

She receptioned for the person irritating her the least, which meant, even in her retirement, she was back and forth between shops every other day.

The days she helped me, she wore her double-knit shorts and *Heads by Harry, Hilo's Finest Taxidermy* T-shirt.

The days she worked for Bunny and Sheldon, she wore her Liberty House mu'umu'u, nylons, matching pumps, and pearls.

Sheldon custom-designed the aprons he and Bunny wore to compliment their figures and deemphasize their problem areas. This he had learned years ago as a graduate of the Mabel Otsuji School of Fashion Design.

And he designed their window display, "Walking in a Winter Wonderland," complete with spray-can snow.

In Heads by Harry, an axis deer got a red-light nose and game birds got little Santa caps.

In Heads by Bunny, Sheldon and his sister wore the faux red-and-white fur Santa caps alternating with haku lei of tinsel and garland.

"Just like one of the Keywanettes, remember, Buns?" he said to her.

"Pretty good for a rat's-ass, hole-in-the-wall downtown dive, eh, Sheldon?" Harry O. said to him one day as he was having his hair dyed black.

"Pretty good," Sheldon said.

The contractors had built a little window between the two shops so we wouldn't have to walk all the way around to talk to each other. I never appreciated the perm solutions and acrylic nail bonder that wafted in, while they complained about maggot and decaying meaty odors.

Franjelica and Paula, honest now by day thanks to Sheldon, apprenticed their four hundred hours for licensing in nails. Training as makeup artists under Bunny, the three of them made a killing selling Noevir, Pola, and Shaklee cosmetics, doing demos at night like Tupperware party ladies.

All the ladies on Mamo Street went for extravagant acrylic nails—Herline, Aunty Mildred, Elsie and her fountain help, Helen's Fabrics yardage cutters, and finally Helen herself. Mrs. Mei Ling wanted three-inch candy-apple red nails with fourteen-karat gold decals under the top coat; cousin Pearlie was ready and willing for anything free, and so was Mommy.

Even Frankie Bobo got a weekly pedicure and manicure

from Sheldon. I saw Harry O. watch my brother file the old man's fingernails. Sheldon caught him staring. My father shrugged, then half-smiled at Sheldon.

That Christmas, Billy's father took his whole family to visit the folks in Flagstaff. "Tell Toni I'll be back for the rest of my things," Billy said to Sheldon as he cut his hair in Heads by Bunny.

"What? When did he tell you this?" I asked Sheldon.

"I don't remember. Maybe a couple of days ago. Go check our appointment book. You were picking up some skulls with Wyatt." Sheldon smiled and fluttered his eyelashes, mocking me. "Whatever you did, you made the boy very upset, Toni."

I had nothing to say. Billy was right. Though I did not necessarily sleep with *everybody else*, I slept with Wyatt. I had been calling everywhere for Billy until I became a nuisance. I had called his house, Cara's, Martin's, and even the Park Service, thinking he'd be working part-time with his father.

The few times he came by the shop after the big party, he spoke to everybody but me. I got angry at the stupid mind games he played. To get back at me, he took Bunny to the movies, spent time laughing in the salon with Sheldon, went turkey hunting with Harry O., and old-bottle hunting with Mommy. He went home every night. After a while of this, my pride kicked in. Fuck him. I can play this game too. I played my game with a samurai's silence.

Then one day, Billy was gone. No goodbye, no nothing, no Merry Christmas, nothing.

It felt odd being so alone. Bunny stayed over across the street with Maverick. The hanger on the bedroom door, Wyatt slept on the couch.

I had a lot of empty time. So when Maverick and Wyatt

got home from pig hunting, we worked in the shop until ten at night over a couple of six-packs of Heineken.

"C'mon, Toni," Wyatt would tell me, "drink your share." But half a beer made me burn from the inside out; then my head got hot, so hot that I perspired cold sweat. I turned the a/c thermostat up every night until the two of them put their work jackets on. I knew what was wrong with me, but I refused to face it.

"What's up with the weight, Toni?" Maverick said to me one night. He didn't look up from the half-skinned axis deer.

"And lightweight. No can handle no more," Wyatt said. "Pass me the hook needle, Toni. And since you putting on the pounds, maybe you should come back in the field with us. What you think?"

"Nah, not in her state," Maverick said quietly. He knew. But he thought it was Billy's. He moved his finger into the empty eye socket, then looked up at me.

Oblivious to the innuendo, Wyatt pressed on with his work. He poked the needle into the cape of the goat's hide and pulled tight his first stitch; it broke with a snap. "Shit."

"How come you mounting that lady's silky terrier, Toni?" Maverick asked.

I looked up from the black paint on my brush. "What? What did you said?"

"Eh, stupid," Wyatt said, "you wen' paint tears on the dog's eye." He stabbed the hooked needle into his table. "Pass me the black nylon thread, Toni."

"You all right, Toni?" Maverick asked.

"Eh, you notice, Mavs, that ever since that fuckin' haole been go with his father, Toni been more cool head."

I looked at them.

"What, Toni?" Maverick asked. "No stare, shit, you making me all nervous."

I shook my head. I didn't know which one of them had done this to me.

"Tell me what the old lady told you guys, Toni," Maverick said. He wanted to change the subject, sensing something more was at stake.

"Tell him what the old lady told you, Toni," Wyatt said, knowing it would make me look stupid.

"You tell him," I said. I brushed the wispy gray hair out of the clay-filled eyes of the silky. "What kind eyes should I use for this dog, Maverick?" I asked. He knew I had something to tell him. "Goat? Baby fawn? That's close. Nah, I better special-order. Where my mother put the Van Dyke catalogues?"

"So this fuckin' Toni," Wyatt began, "the old lady come in couple Sundays ago and look like she came straight from church with her Bible, her church kine pāpale and all. She tell Toni if she can do one rush job for Christmas. So this Toni, she tell depend on what, like us had that kine time with all the back orders. So the lady, she step outside to her car and bring in this stupid dog in this basket all wrap in one blanket like one little baby."

Like a little baby. I counted back the days to the night in the forest, and right before that, my last period.

"Then I step in 'cause you know how Toni been lately, since the haole wen' split, and I tell the lady, 'Nah, we no do pets. That's our number one policy. He not going look like your dog was in real life, and you going blame us, when us not God. We cannot make him look like his old self again. Nah.'

" 'I pay double the price,' she tell. And this Toni, instead she shut her mouth, she ask the old lady how the dog wen' ma-ke. The old lady tell she was at Bible study and all them old Jehovah's ladies went Dick's Coffeehouse after was pau, so she came home late. And by the time she came home, her brother-in-law, one alcoholic fucka work down Glover, came home all drunk and step on top this small runt dog."

"Nah?" Maverick said, laughing.

"I know, brah. I wanted to bust laugh right there, but no, Toni keep on making sad face at the lady like she was feeling all sorry and she was going do the job." Wyatt poked the hooked needle into the top of his goat's head and reached for the scissors.

"So I told the lady," I said to Maverick, "I'll do it, as long as you promise not to cry and get all sentimental, and she promised. She hugged that dead dog like was one . . . one . . . one—"

"Baby?" Maverick asked.

I nodded but refused to stay there. "When I was working on the dog, you guys no do this? Look for the injury, like that? I didn't see nothing external, and no sickness in the internal organs, but had some mean-ass blood clots on the back end and muscle bruises on the back part."

"Think you Quincy, hah, coroner?" Wyatt said.

"Like a baby?" Maverick said, looking at me. The window between the shops flew open. Bunny stuck her head into our shop.

"Maverick, go and bathe. Hurry up. We're going to the Poly Room with Franjelica and Paula." Now that she was back with Maverick, her haole accent sounded forced.

"Okay, gimme twenty minutes. Laters then, Toni. What about Sheldon, babes?" Maverick asked, pulling off his apron and quickly straightening up his tools.

"I fixing up the orders and the books," Sheldon yelled from Heads by Bunny. "But thanks for asking, Maverick, you honey-glaze ass." Wyatt looked at his brother, batted his eyelashes, and pretended to barf. Maverick flipped him the bird.

"So what, movies, Toni? *An Officer and a Gentleman.*" Wy-att came around behind me and held me inside his upper arms so as not to get Borax from his hands all over me. "No need the haole," he whispered to me. "Not next, next Tuesday yet, but what the fuck, who counting days, hah?"

"Me," I said.

"Hah?" He let me go and dusted his hands over the trash can.

"I cannot," I said, putting my knives away. "Sheldon and me going over our books too, shit, you no record nothing right. The books all screwed up."

"Fuck, Toni. You hopeless," Wyatt said to me, walking over to the sink in the back and then squeezing the last of the PHisoDerm into this hands. He burped long and loud. "That's dedicated to you, Toni." He stood by the back door for a second. "You know why the haole stay in Flagstaff, right? The father transferred. They had the party already. You was invited. How come you never come? Everybody else was there. Except for you Yagyuus." He kicked the back door open and it slammed shut.

I turned off their lamps, then washed my hands. I sat on my stool. "Sheldon?" I could see his outline through the window.

"What?"

"Sheldon?"

"What?!"

"You heard that? Mr. Harper transferred. They had the party and everything already. Eh, Mommy and Daddy never go, right?" I asked him.

"No. I didn't hear nothing. How come Billy never tell us? Look bad, eh, he live with us and we don't go to the goodbye party. What's with that? What did you fight with Billy about?" Sheldon was feigning innocence. He knew something. He poured himself a cold cup of coffee.

"He didn't even give me a chance to fight with him," I said. "It's one thing for him to leave me out. Fine by me. But not Mommy and Harry O. What they did to him? Only treat him like their own."

"Better than their own," Sheldon muttered.

"Wyatt's lying," I told Sheldon. "He don't know shit. I mean, if Billy was really leaving, he would. I think he would. And Mommy, what about Mommy? I know Billy. We would talk."

"Wyatt know. All the park guys know everything about everybody. You know that, Toni." I sensed restrained pleasure in his voice.

"Sheldon?"

"What?"

"Sheldon—"

"What?! I busy. I like go out too, you know."

"I think I'm hāpai, Sheldon."

"Hah? From who? Billy? Oh no, Toni. He's only what, seventeen, right? So that's why he left."

"You think Wyatt's right? The Harpers moving? What you heard? How you know Billy moving? He not moving. He going to UH-Hilo."

Billy had put aside UC Berkeley for UH-Hilo. He'd wait for me to get enough credits after reenrolling with him. We'd transfer together. We'd be roommates. Staying in Hilo was the plan. He wouldn't even have to dorm. He'd live with us. Late into the night, we'd mapped out our lives.

"What you mean, what I heard? What *you* heard? Fuck, you only sleep with Billy, shit."

"It's not what you think. This isn't Billy's," I said, placing my hand on my stomach. "How you know Billy moving, Sheldon?"

"One thing at a time. Has to be what I think. Who's the father, then?"

I couldn't tell him. My mind scrambled to change the subject. "Sheldon, why you not going out with Pio tonight?" Through the window, I saw him take off his glasses. We said nothing for a while. Absorbing the words we exchanged through the window, Sheldon and I never looked at each other. I asked him again. "So how come you ain't going out with Pio?"

" 'Cause I making him think."

"Think what?"

"That love is a two-way street."

"You're good for Pio."

"According to him, I ain't. I'm too possessive."

"Well, I would be too, the way he was acting all hands with those haoles from London. What was their name?"

"Chauncey and Nigel," Sheldon said. "See, Bunny saw all of this too. I thought was all in my mind. That's what Pio trying to make me think. Like I was overreacting, fuckin' flirting queen making me all nuts and then telling me I'm insecure."

"You're worth more than all the shit you buy for Pio. Take it all back." My brother turned off the lights in his shop and sat under the lamplight over his desk.

"How many months, Toni?"

"I counted back three. Don't tell Mommy and Daddy, okay, Sheldon, promise?" He stared out the glass window.

"Who the father, Toni, if not Billy?"

"Shit, me and Billy, we never did it, not once——"

"What about Griffith then, you did it with Griffith?"

"What are you talking about, Sheldon? What he get to do with this?" I threw my pencil on the books.

"No, I just asking. Did you fuck Griffith Mueller?"

"Why? What's that got to do with now, hah?"

" 'Cause."

" 'Cause what?"

" 'Cause *I did.*"

"Fuck you, Sheldon. You fucked Griffith, yeah, right." I put my face in my hands.

"That night at the Wave, he took all our numbers. I bet you didn't know that. And after he dogged you out, me and Bunny went back to UH the next semester. Was business as usual. The whole semester, Griffith and me, we——"

I felt sick, him winning, always needing to win over me. "Bunny know this?" I asked, mean. I looked at my brother. The fluorescent lights from the theater marquee made his face green.

"No." His voice was soft. "She don't know shit. Nah, maybe she know, but she never said anything to me. Just like you, Toni."

"Asshole, what Griffith said about me?"

"Like he wants to talk about you when he has his tongue halfway down my throat and his hands inside my pants. Then his mouth all over my——"

I stood up at the window. "You fuckin' lie, Sheldon. You wanted him from me so bad. *Everybody* you want from me. Even Billy. Instead of making things better between us, you laughing it up with him in the salon. You think I deaf? Why you like that, hah, Sheldon?" I threw the pencil at his head. "Or what, two years from now you going tell me that all the time I was with Billy, you was fucking him too?"

"Maybe——"

"What?!" I flopped back onto my office chair.

"Maybe I did and maybe I didn't. Billy too. I got him drunk enough a couple of times. If I wanted him bad enough, he would've gone along for the ride."

"How the fuck you know?"

" 'Cause I can smell testosterone a mile away. Trust me, honey."

I put my face in my hands.

"I won, Toni, that's why I did it. I won."

I felt wounded. "You won nothing," I said to him. Everything went still but for the hum of the air conditioner. "You still wake up by yourself. Love ain't only on one side. It has to come back. And it doesn't come back with expensive presents. You are by *yourself*, Sheldon. Every morning and every night after they pau with you, they go home."

I heard my brother crying the way I had heard him through the walls of the apartment in Honolulu.

"You're a bitch, Toni." My brother blew his nose. He threw his Kleenex on my side of the window.

"Oh, yeah? And what you going do about it?"

"Nothing," he said. I was ready to stab him with my work knife. " 'Cause I'm a bitch too."

I couldn't believe it.

I heard the marquee lights buzzing off, on, then off. Someone ran across the street. It was Wyatt, his hands tucked in his jacket pockets, running through a light Hilo rain, orange rain, static in the streetlights. He rapped softly on the glass door.

"Who's that?" Sheldon asked.

I got up and opened the door.

"You hāpai, Toni?" Wyatt asked.

I stared at him.

"Maverick told me you pregnant, that's true?"

I shrugged my shoulders.

"From that fuckin' haole, hah, Toni?" He poked at my chest with his finger.

"Who's that?" Sheldon asked again.

"How many months?" he yelled at me.

"Three," I said. "No, not him, stupid," I said, helping him out of his jacket, then shaking it off on the sidewalk. "I three months."

"No call me stupid," Wyatt said to me. "Three months?" I watched as he began calculating the days in his mind.

"That's you, Wyatt? Toni, don't tell him shit. He going tell everybody."

"Eh, mind you own business," Wyatt said to Sheldon. "Was I fuckin' talking to you, hah, bitch? Before I come over there and broke your ass, motherfucker."

"My sister is my business," Sheldon said softly.

I lowered my eyes and Wyatt moved me to the chair. The bell on the door of Heads by Bunny tinkled, then Sheldon came through the front door of our shop.

"Oh my God," Wyatt said, slumping on the dirty floor at my feet. "Me? That night? The time you quit the job? Was me and you? But Maverick—him too." He put his face in my lap.

"What? What? Tell me, Toni." Sheldon pulled up a chair. "Maverick and Wyatt? What's going on?"

"What I going do? I your business, you promise, Sheldon? What I going do? Daddy going kill me. He going hate me. No can, not now, when things finally good. You don't know how long I was waiting for him to be all right with me. I so fucked up. He going take back the shop from me. I have to get rid of it."

Wyatt stood up and pulled me to the sink. "Wash your hands, Toni, right now, and shut up. You ain't no fuck-up.

Believe me, you ain't nothing close to——" He squeezed and squeezed the bottle of PHisoDerm, finally opening the top and shaking water inside to get one last wash.

"No, Wyatt, you ain't a fuck-up." I ran my fingers under the water.

"Oh, shut up," Sheldon yelled at us. "You both fuck-ups, but who ain't, right?"

"Daddy ain't."

"Wanna bet?" Sheldon said. I looked at him. My brother patted the chair for me to sit down. "What do *you* want to do, Toni?"

"Get an abortion."

"Kind of too late," Sheldon said. "You too far gone. Going be a major operation. No can. Going cost in the thousands when you get rid of it late."

Wyatt took my hands and covered his face with them.

"Stop crying," I said. "You want our parents to force us to get married? And what if this baby's not yours? Could be. Could be Maverick's too——" I stopped.

"And what? That would be better for you?" Wyatt said, swiping his nose on his arm. "So you force to marry Maverick?"

"How can that be?" Sheldon asked. "Oh . . . wait. Don't tell me . . . you three didn't do what I think you did. When? How? *Why?* Don't answer that. I don't want to know. No, I want to know. Oh, jeez." My brother rested his forehead in his hand.

"That's why. I'm getting an abortion. Make things more easy."

"You heard me or what, Toni?" Sheldon yelled.

"No, Toni. Fuck, I like slap your head," Wyatt said. He rolled the office chair he sat in closer to me.

"Why? You not Catholic. What you care for, hah?" I pushed him away. He got up and kicked the chair against the wall.

"See, that's what I said about you, Toni. You never *seen* me. Never. Open your eye. I no like marry you, fuck that, but I no like you kill what's mine. Look around. Look what's in this room."

"Maybe it's *not* yours."

"Maybe. But still *ours.*"

"Go get a blood test," Sheldon said.

"Me and Maverick same blood type. That's what the Park Service guys told us in case get emergency." I rested my face on Sheldon's shoulder. "Let me talk to Maverick first. See what he say. No do nothing stupid, eh, Toni?"

"When are the Harpers leaving?" I asked Wyatt softly. "You know this for sure?"

"Yeah, I sure. They gone already. The house empty."

"What?" Sheldon said.

"Some of the boys went help them load the heavy stuffs." I said nothing.

"That's haoles for you, eh, Toni? You help um, you feed um, you fuck um, and they no tell you shit when they bag."

"They never *did* it—what do you know, Wyatt? Tell us." Sheldon asked for me. I was breaking apart.

"I heard this right before Thanksgiving."

"Thanksgiving?" Billy had known for a long time.

"The big boss was thinking about taking a job up at a national park in Alaska. More high the pay. Or the regional office in Flagstaff. They get family there or something, right? They no more family here. You fuckin' kidding yourself when you think of haoles as family. And in the end, I think they went Alaska. So much for family, eh? They gone, Toni." Wyatt smirked. "Why, you going miss your small kid boyfriend?"

"He ain't my boyfriend. They went to Flagstaff, Arizona, right, Sheldon? To visit family? And he coming back for his things?" He nodded.

"Then what is he—to you?"

I looked up at my brother. "I don't know."

But I did know.

"Don't tell Billy nothing, you promise, Wyatt? If he gone he never need know nothing about this."

"Why? You no like the haole know you low enough to fuck pig shit like me, hah, Toni? He *know* already. Why you think he never say shit to you when he left? He gone."

"He's not. He got stuff upstairs. I just don't want him to think I'm a—"

"Whore."

"He asked me to pack his things," Sheldon said.

"He history, Toni." Wyatt moved into the darkness behind his own worktable. "He already *know* what you about, that smart little Billy boy."

"Stop it. Shut up. Wyatt, you asshole. You no more feelings inside you for my sister?" My brother pulled me toward him and stroked my hair, my brother who I thought incapable of love. "You my business, Toni," he said over and over until I believed him.

Years later, I understood. The impossibility overwhelmed him. My brother placed his hands on the plane of my belly and wept, my body, not his, capable of creation.

T e n

 **B**illy left his story in my room. He had haphazardly packed some of his clothes and toiletries, but he left behind all of his trinkets and effects. For a long time, this made me think he was coming back for them.

He spoke to Mommy the following Christmas Eve. Somebody saw Mr. Harper on an NBC Nightly News. Cara Shinsato had gone on to Berkeley. Maybe they were roommates. About a year after Billy left, Martin Medeiros came in with a mouflon head and said that Billy had called; he had even written him once or twice. He was attending the University of Alaska—Fairbanks.

The New Year's Eve after Billy left, I went upstairs and put his things away. No more sleeping in his clothes, looking through old pictures and yearbooks, holding on to someone else's prom paraphernalia—a class ring, school papers, letters, novels, music, or antique marbles.

The year he lived with us, he had stolen his social studies textbook after a school-wide shortage of books. I thumbed through its pages. I found there, in Harry O.'s handwriting, a Christmas card he had given to Billy.

Dear Haole Boy,
    Mele Kalikimaka (Merry Christmas). I found this poem.
One day when you pau college, tell me how this guy knew

*about taxidermy. I would of ask Toni but you know how
that story goes about Toni and college. She touchy and she
don't listen. So I give it to you to figure out for me. We
confer after the holidays.*

DODO

by

Henry Carlise

*Years they mistook me for you,
chanting your name in the street,
pointing grubby fingers.
Today in the Natural History Museum,
Dodo, you look the way I feel
with your sad absentminded eyes,
your beak like a Stone Age ax.
Even your feathers dingy and fuzzy.
What woman would want you for a hat
with a name like* Didus ineptus?
*Where could you go?
Wings too small to fly
with feet too large and slow.
You were not very palatable.
Men slaughtered you for sport.
Hogs ate the one egg you laid each year.
Sometimes I think I know how it feels
to be scattered all over the world,
a foot in the British Museum,
a head in Copenhagen.
To be a lesson after the fact,
an entity in name only
and that taken in vain.*

*You listen to me, haole, don't be a lesson after the fact.
Don't let this be you. It was almost me. Merry Christmas, Holiday Cheer, and all that jazz, Harry Osamu Yagyuu*

The Christmas Billy left, Mommy separated all of our presents and put the stacks on our desks downstairs. We would
not celebrate, because of Billy's departure. But she was the
one who had told him about regrets and blame. Maybe he
had listened to her.

My mother came into the shop in her red muʻumuʻu.
"You're going to Uncle Herb's for dinner, right?"

I shook my head and absentmindedly tore at a rip in Bunny's gift to me. Mommy put a small box at the top of my
stack.

"Present from Billy to you, Toni. I found it in my room."
She sat down next to me. "You said anything to him before
he left?"

"No. Did you?"

My mother wiped a tear from her eye. "So unlike that boy.
I thought he was just thinking things out. I never thought
he would do something like this," my mother said. "Even
when he was one small boy, have you ever known him to up
and leave, no goodbye, no nothing?"

"You mad at him, Mommy?" I asked.

"Sometimes," she said, "but in the end, no. He's just a
mixed-up kid. Was all the adults who screwed up. Open the
present."

I lifted the top off of the box. "A jade bracelet?"

"Way too small for you, Toni. This is for a baby." My
mother gasped and put her hands over her mouth.

"What? What? It's a pendant, Mommy," I said to her.

"Kind of clunky, eh?" she said sarcastically. She looked me over up and down and stopped in her gaze at my belly.

"I know what he thinking," I said to her.

"What? You better speak up, Toni. What you did to Billy? Now you the one making me mad."

"I know."

I put the bracelet back in the box. Bunny tooted the car horn and yelled for Mommy. They would be late for dinner at Uncle Herb's. My mother stood up. "This is getting more and more bizarre as the days go by, I tell you." She stood at the back of the shop. "One day, maybe you'll have a little girl who can wear it—but better not be Billy's."

I rested my face on the stack of presents on my desk. "He's gone, you know, Mommy."

"I know. I ain't stupid. That's why I said, what you did to him?"

"We did nothing." And that was the utter truth.

I hunt with my father the day after Christmas. I tell him everything. "Daddy, I reenrolled at UH-Hilo. Me and Butchie. He going Hawaiian studies and I going wildlife biology."

Harry O. touches the silvery velvet liko, the dew in the broken bark of the ʻōhiʻa. "You ain't a lesson after the fact, that's why. You make me happy."

"Huh?" In that moment, what he says to me makes no sense.

We stand there together on the slope of Mauna Loa, the amethyst morning wind pushing in a rain and rolling fog. There is a sound to this in the tip and tilt of trees.

"Daddy, I pregnant. Daddy—"

He puts his gun down and drops his pack at his feet. "Who's the father?"

"What's the difference?"

"Big difference to me. Who's the goddamn father?"

I watch the tip and tilt of trees.

"You're so out of it, Daddy."

"Since when is disappointment old-fashioned? That's age-old, you no think so? I thought you was pau with screwing up. How the hell you so smart and no more one ounce of common sense?"

I smell the sweet, sweet grass, feel the sweeping brush. I watch my father's back. "Make your choices good ones, Toni," he says, not looking at me. "How come I cannot make you see?" He slowly fades into the forest as he heads east toward the road.

The trouble started as soon as Sheldon told Bunny.

Mommy told Daddy, who already knew.

Mommy told Mrs. Mei Ling.

She told Mr. Santos.

Wyatt told Maverick.

Maverick told Bunny, again.

All of this happened in one day. It was a workday, a Tuesday, pau hana time. Through the window between our shops, the yelling started.

"You're a bitch, Toni. Why you fuckin' around with *my* Maverick for, hah?"

"See, Toni," Sheldon cried, "see what you did to Bunny? Now what? I tell you what. Now her *niece* or *nephew* is her future children's *half sister or half brother.*"

"We was all drunk."

"I hate sluts who use that excuse," Bunny screamed as she overturned a rollaway cart full of perm rods. "I was wasted.

I lost my memory. I didn't know what I was doing. Yeah, right. Not *once* in my whole life, wasted and crawling out the door, I still knew *exactly* what I was doing."

"Yeah, don't give us that shit, Toni," Sheldon added with his arms around the grieving Bunny.

My mother came in the shop through the back door. She slapped my head, then threw at me a box of surgical gloves to handle the chemicals.

"Toni, I'm telling you," my mother started, "this takes the goddamn cake. What you was thinking? Who's the father, Maverick or Wyatt?" she asked.

I shrugged my shoulders.

"You better think fast 'cause you marrying that baby's father. I don't care what you say. You giving that baby a legitimate last name. You know how screwed up kids get when they illegitimate? They messed up for life. I know. I wen' teach thirty years and I seen those messes with my own two eyes. When kids abandoned by their own flesh and blood—look at what happened to Billy."

The truck pulled up. Maverick bolted into Heads by Bunny and Wyatt into Heads by Harry. He looked my mother in the eye, then tossed me the folic acid and multivitamins the doctor prescribed.

"You damn kid," my mother ranted on, "you not going be selfish like all them housing girls, sleeping around and pregnant. Every kid has a different father. You raising this baby in a stable nuclear family with mother *and* father."

A hysterical Bunny pounded on Maverick's chest. "Fuckin' man-whore, you're the worst one. It's over with you and me, Maverick. Go fuck my sister. But wait in line behind your brother Wyatt."

"That's not mine," Maverick said to Bunny. "Cannot be mine, babe. They lying."

Wyatt pushed his way to the window between the shops. "Eh, fuckhead, you was there, the night this baby came in Toni. Why you trying to deny, brah? What's your trip?"

Maverick came through the front door. "Eh, shithead," he said, shoving Wyatt in the chest, "you was there first, unless my guys swim faster than your guys, which I fuckin' doubt, that's yours."

"Yours, asshole."

"Yours, you motherfucker, I never shoot."

"Eh, I told you this morning, dickhead," Wyatt said, "could be *mine* or *yours* and you said, 'Yeah.' How come now you fuckin' acting like no way, hah?" Maverick could not look at me. " 'Cause Bunny cannot handle? That's why you lying and telling you never shoot? Shit, brah, no lie. You something else." Wyatt sat down.

It was at this moment that my idolatry of Maverick Santos ended forever.

"You opened your legs," my mother said to me, "and one of you or both of you laid down," she said to Maverick and Wyatt. "So we going do the responsible thing and do what is right by this child. So—it's either one of you, right? You get the same blood type?"

Wyatt nodded.

I breathed deeply and shook my head.

"It's going to be one of these boys, Toni. Wyatt?" my mother said. He looked the other way. "Toni, you always liked Maverick, now's your chance," she said through gritted teeth. "You going pick, Toni, *now*."

My sister wailed from Heads by Bunny. "What you talking about, Mommy? Stop it!"

My mother closed the windows between the shops. I thought about Billy, how I had lied to him and how he had left; I was wearing his clothes. How was I any better than

Maverick? What if Billy had done this with Cara? I would have felt betrayed to the very core. He was gone for good.

"My other girl," Mommy said to Maverick, her head jerking toward the closed window, "she would've made your life miserable. You don't want to live like that."

Maverick said nothing. I took a deep breath and shook my head. My mother looked at me, betrayed also by my decision to tell Harry O. first.

"Well?" she said to me. "There's no abortion and no adoption because there just won't be, over my dead body. I tell you, Toni, you break my heart."

"C'mon, Aunty," Wyatt said, "we been like family all these years."

For a moment, Mommy seemed perplexed and then she must've conjured a picture in her mind of the three of us doing it in the bushes. "That's the whole trouble," Mommy said, "don't you think so? We family. And Billy," she said to me, "he knew. How could you do this to him, Toni? He's just a kid and you leading him on like that. He was a big part of this family and now look what you done. He left because of you. I no blame him."

"Don't you ever say another word to me about Billy." I stood up and walked over to her. "I not marrying him," I said, pointing at Wyatt. "And I not marrying him," I said, pointing at Maverick. I stared at Maverick and shook my head in disgust. "Who's my hero?" I said to him.

He stared right back at me. "That's not mine," he said.

"Say it enough times," I said, "pretty soon you believe your own lies."

Mommy sat down and began crying. "Oh, no, we're another broken-home statistic. This is so shame for the family. The whole town going be talking about us. How can I look anybody in the eye? And poor Harry O., so shame, I tell you. We never be able to hold our head up in town. From now on, *you* do all the grocery shopping," she said to me.

"We *all* raising the baby," I said to Maverick and Wyatt.

"Fuckhead," Wyatt said.

"Dickface," Maverick replied.

"This baby has two fathers," I said to them. "Don't force anybody to get married, Mommy."

"My mother going be here any minute now to shove that up my ass," Wyatt said.

The room went still.

"Mine too, Aunty Mary Alice," Maverick said after a long moment of quiet. "Maybe mine."

"Me and Maverick, we can raise the baby with two daddies. What you think? I been thinking about this all day," Wyatt said to me.

Things shattered in Heads by Bunny. The crying got louder until Sheldon screamed, a full-blown melodrama. Car tires screeched out of the parking lot. Sheldon ran up the street.

"Fucka run like Jerry Lewis, no, Toni?" Wyatt said.

"Prince in *Purple Rain*," I said.

The front door flew open against the rain as Sheldon heaved and sobbed into the shop. "Mommy! Mommy! I don't know what Bunny going do. C'mon, we all have to go find her." His panicked eyes scanned the room. "What are you guys waiting for?"

There was a calm. No one was drawn into the maelstrom.

"It's always about *you* and *her*, no, Sheldon?" It was Maverick. It was enough to shut my brother up for a moment. He would not rescue them again.

My mother blew her nose in a Kleenex, then straightened up her shirt. "Two daddies?" she whispered at last.

"C'mon, Mommy! Come with me find Bunny! Who knows what she might do in her state of mind!"

"The baby be lucky," Mommy said, ignoring Sheldon. "Let me *try* talk things over with Mei Ling and Lionel. I cannot promise nothing. And I *try* talk to your father, Toni. But looks like this your straw wen' broke that camel's back."

"He not mad at me," I said to her.

"You're right," she said, "he not mad. He feeling same like Billy." Mommy stared at Sheldon. "Don't worry, son," she said. "Bunny's too vain to kill herself."

Sheldon slumped into a corner of the shop, drew his knees to his chest and sobbed loudly.

"Eh, get a grip, asshole," Wyatt said to him.

"And don't anybody ever refer to this as a mistake," Mommy said, pointing her finger at all of us. "God no make mistakes. And this baby better never think it was a mistake, you hear me?" Mommy sat down on my office chair and glared at Sheldon.

Bunny dramatically reentered. Maverick stood up. He looked at me as though, for the first time in all those years, he finally understood what I had been telling him.

He didn't even say her name. "I opened my eyes and what I seen—"

My sister fell into him, expecting him to hold her. He stepped back. "You using *this* to break up with me? No do that to your sister. She your blood. What's the matter with you? I never was good enough for you."

Maverick turned and looked at me. Softly he said, "I not good enough for you either."

"Fuckin'-A," I said, nodding.

"Shut up, Maverick, stop it," Bunny screamed. "Why are you making me the bad guy? I'm the victim here."

"You go your way," he said, pushing her off. "Find you one good haole."

"Two daddies," my mother said. "And two of the best grandmas," she said of herself and Mrs. Mei Ling.

"We been through worse," Maverick said to my mother.

"And a grandpa who going let this child go wild in the concession, grumpy old fut," she said about Mr. Santos.

"Nobody's kid get free ride," Wyatt said, imitating Mr. Santos's gruff voice, "unless they related to me."

"And Harry O.——" Mommy sighed. "One day, he take um hunting and stuff this child a beautiful pheasant himself."

I stepped outside of the shop. The living room upstairs was dark, except for the gray-blue flickering light of the television. My father looked down at me from the window.

My labor went on for twenty-eight hours. Mommy and Mrs. Mei Ling stayed there with me. Wyatt, somber and still in a corner, listened to Herline, who told him to get a warm compress or smoke a cigarette or get a cup of coffee. Every time the big contractions came, I scratched and dug into the wall with my fingernails. The women sobbed in empathy. Wyatt tried to put ice chips in my mouth.

Then Wyatt, tired by the twenty-sixth hour, approached the bed with his fifth cup of coffee and kicked its leg by mistake.

"Fucka," I snarled, "watch where you walking. Think I having one party over here, shit? C'mon, I dare your fuckin' macho ass to trade places with me. Let me shove a watermelon up *your* asshole and see if you can handle when somebody tell you, 'Relax. Get a grip.' Grip this," I said, flipping him the bird.

Herline told him to get me another towel for my forehead. Wyatt returned, shaken and sleepy.

"Fucka," I snarled, "this towel's cold as ice. Cannot use

warm water, shit? That's the whole trouble with you and your fuckin' brother who got me in this shit to begin with. I swear, men ain't the stronger sex. And where Maverick? You guys good for nothing but sex 'cause you think with your head without brains, ass wipes."

"Your mouth, Toni, I swear," Maverick said from some dark corner. Labor made me both more honest and vile.

"Somebody get this out of me."

"Somebody make the bitch in the next room stop SCREAMING!"

"This is it for me. No more babies, no more sex."

"Why YOU no trade places with me, hah, always acting like you so tough. Brah, you *nothing*. You don't know PAIN."

"I ain't *ever* having sex again."

"You nothing, you heard me?"

"No look at me."

"Billy! Billy!"

"I can yell his name if I like."

"Stop staring."

"Somebody *help* me."

In the twenty-eighth hour, I went alone into the delivery room. I wanted no coach, nobody to hold my hand.

A girl.

I named her Harper Santos Yagyuu.

"Who ever heard of one girl with three last names?" Wyatt grumbled. "I going call you Hapa," he said, moving his big, rough hand over the soft head of hair. He learned from a pretty haole nurse to swaddle her tightly in the hospital's pink receiving blanket.

"She get your mouth, Wyatt," Maverick said as he peered over Wyatt's shoulder.

"Thank God ain't Toni's vicious mouth," Wyatt said to Maverick. "Eh, where you was, brah, all that time I was taking all the raps from Toni?"

"After that 'think with your head without brains and shove a watermelon up your ass' shit, I went in the waiting room with Harry O. I no can stand see Toni in pain." Maverick kissed the baby's forehead.

"My father was here?"

"The whole time," Maverick said.

"That's Toni's nose," Wyatt said. "Good. Little girls no need huge honkers."

"She get Maverick's hair. Light brown," I said.

"And all this time, us thought was Sun-In, hah, Mavs?" Wyatt said. "And what's wrong with borinque hair?"

My father came in with a bunch of mixed anthuriums he must've picked from Mr. Ute's yard. He took the baby from Wyatt and held her swaddled tightly and sleeping.

"The two happiest days of my life," he said, "was when I brought you and Bunny home from the hospital. No get me wrong—the *best* day of my life was when I had my first boy, but we was so scared, never know how to take care one baby, me and Mary Alice."

My father looked at me. "I have another happiest day now." He said to the baby, "Going be the day I bring *you* home."

I heard my father whispering to Harper. "You go college, now. That would make your grandma happy." He looked at me and I understood him.

Wyatt snored in the next bed as Maverick finished my bland hospital breakfast. Sheldon sat in the only chair in the room, channel surfing.

The first night I brought Harper home, I realized that mothering was not instinct. Unlike animals in the wild or Billy's pig dogs who whimpered ever so mildly as they pushed out green-black sacs of babies, we lost the ability to know, and this terrified me. We never lose the ability to fear.

What have I done?

I cannot handle this.

Who am I kidding?

How the hell am I taking care of this baby?

I'm going to kill this baby.

I'm going to drop her.

Support the neck?

Is she breathing?

She stopped breathing.

Somebody help me.

A kindness not forgotten, my mother slept with me that first night. "You think Billy would've helped me?" I asked her. She said nothing. "I *know* him. He would've been right here." She woke at two with me and at four and at six. She checked Harper's diaper and her kimono to see if she was wet.

Always check the clothes. Might be wet too.

My mother watched the clock for me—ten minutes per breast, burped her in between, then put the baby down.

When Billy's best dog Sally whelped her first litter, we camped out at the kennels for twenty-four hours straight. Billy brought warm food to her every three hours, then filled the empty dish with water. In the wild, the male dog would do all of this.

What have I done?

I never left the upstairs apartment. I wanted no visitors, no gifts; everybody was so intent on seeing the new baby. Oily hair, still in maternity clothes, flaccid belly, gray-faced, rock-hard breasts, I continued bleeding, bleeding, bleeding.

The blood smelled metallic. The walls closed in on the crying and the boredom. I was tired and so afraid of the utter help-lessness I felt.

Harper cried at one in the morning; I got up bleary-eyed and undid my bra holding milk-heavy breasts. The bedroom door opened slowly, and Wyatt walked in with the pitcher from the hospital and its matching cup.

"Drink this whole thing," he said. "Every time she suck, you have to replace the liquid fast."

"How you know? Who told you?" I just wanted to succumb to the anxiety and panic.

"I read in Herline's tits book." He paused to put the water down. "Yeah, I can read, sometimes." He glared at me. "Had plenty pictures, okay?"

"I didn't mean——"

It was Wyatt who helped me adjust Harper's body; my efforts were frantic and awkward. "Football style," he said. "That's what the book said. I like that—maybe she play powder-puff football, no, Hapa? Be one linebacker like your Aunty Lynette."

"I cannot do this shit," I told him.

"You can. Twenty minutes per. Move your arm. Lean back little bit." He pressed my shoulders into the back of the chair. "Relax. Whoa, hurry up. Ho, your tit shooting milk. Okay, ready, set, go. Hugest to the max, your tits. And black. Used to be nice skin color, how come?"

"I don't know—why don't you go read your breast book and tell me why my tits came black."

"Your areola," he said as Harper sucked and sucked and sucked. "Ho, my baby latch on good, eh, Toni? That's what the book said, 'latch on.' Relax, no sweat. Drink the water."

Wyatt leaned back on the bed and propped himself up with

three pillows, burped and farted, and turned on the TV to WTBS. He memorized the whole twelve-to-five in the morning lineup after a couple of weeks.

"Lucky thing they five hours ahead of us," he said to me at her 2 a.m. feeding. "This what the haole must watch in the morning before he go school. That's what I think."

"What haole?" I asked. "Never mind, I no like know. Just shut up about him, okay? Punk. And don't be calling her Aunty Lynette."

"I said drink your water before you piss me off."

He burped her. "Always have to make sure the big one come out or they get gas and going cry more. Herline's advice. She double degree in accounting and early childhood, you heard? What the hell, she had plenty experience." He raised his eyebrows and shrugged. "Eh, she handle three kids. She the sexpert, know what I mean?" I leaned back in the rocker and breathed.

When Harper turned three months old, Sheldon moved out. Bunny moved into the vacated sewing room.

Babies cry.

"Make her shut up."

Babies occupy the center spotlight.

"Am I invisible or what?"

He moved out and into Pio's house in Kaūmana. Pio had played with his British lovers, and then he came back. This would be true of Pio for years. Sheldon, in the meantime, would come back home, and then in a couple of weeks, he'd be back to Pio with an illusion of well-being.

Pio was a good person, it's true. *Anyone* who could tolerate Sheldon for the number of years Pio had must've been a tragically wonderful person. It was love. And like all love, involved a measure of infidelity and rust for the honeymoons to shimmer.

Mommy carried Harper around the living room. Harry O. ran the shop for me. "I better go start lunch. Did Harry O. put the portable crib in the kitchen, Toni?" Mommy asked while handing me the baby. She left down the back stairs.

"I not moving out 'cause of Harper, you know, Toni." I said nothing. "I just wanted you to know." Sheldon had not been welcoming at all to the baby. It saddened me.

For a while, I thought it was the friend-has-baby guilt trip. The baby comes and changes the friendship.

You ease out of the friendship no matter how deep.

Before I had Harper, I didn't even know what kind of baby gifts to buy, so I'd buy nothing and start the cycle of guilt. I wouldn't visit. I wouldn't call. The guilt deepened.

"I mean, if Pio tells you something like I said I couldn't stand all the crying and shit—I said that 'cause I wanted him to let me—"

"Move in with him. That's what you always wanted even if you cramp his style."

"Not true," Sheldon whined. "You don't know Pio's true, ultimate self. At least I have *somebody*. You no more—"

"I have somebody, Sheldon. I have Harper."

My brother sat down on his box. He glared at Harper with contempt.

"I made this baby, Sheldon," I said.

"Big deal. Look where it got you. A prisoner in your own house. No sleep. No life. No sister. No husband. You look like shit. You made yourself eighteen years of trouble. So don't give me that bullshit, Toni. You the unhappiest person in this whole house, except for that screaming seed of yours." Sheldon wiped his eyes.

"Then why are you crying, Sheldon?" I said to my brother through clenched teeth. A minute passed.

"Nothing, why?" He wiped his face with both hands.

The years seemed to surge into this one moment.

"This body is *mine*," I said. "This *body* made this baby." Sheldon began crying more. "I have *somebody*. You can never take this from me."

I watched my brother cry. He cried for himself. And now, I know, he cried, too, for me.

"I like Pio," I said to Sheldon at last. I would be the one to let him off the hook. "He has his ways, but he's a nice man. Just hope he not all itchy forever. It'll pass."

"You think so?" Sheldon said, looking up at me. In many ways, it was always about Sheldon Yagyuu. And this diversion to the center of his world brought comfort to him.

"Guarantee," I said.

"How long you think all his shit going on?"

"I don't know, Sheldon. Maybe till he doesn't look so good anymore. Depends, too, on if he has a big-ass chronic itch or regular itch that pass with age."

It was an itch that would pass.

Sheldon picked up his box of clothes. "Go for Maverick," he said to me. "Now's your chance. You always wanted him, no lie, Toni."

"I don't need to go for him," I said to Sheldon. "Like I told you—I have Harper. Maverick has a long ways to go. He like his women stupid and gorgeous—he has to keep coming to somebody's rescue, Sheldon."

"Too bad about Billy." I didn't like the way he said this. "See you later, Toni," he said, not once looking back at me or the baby. I listened to his heavy step down to the parking lot.

I prayed for love, for Sheldon, to be bestowed upon him in

some measure. I prayed that he love himself, accept himself as a person worthy of love, the body he inhabited, good enough.

Wyatt bought a Gerry baby walkie-talkie and installed one in my bedroom and one in his bedroom across the street. The crying brought him over every night. I'd peer down out of the window and see him striding over in whatever he fell asleep in that night—on muggy nights, just jams.

Our routine set, he brought up the pitcher of water as I changed the diaper full of mustardy goop, by which time he set the pitcher down and finished the job, wiping Harper's folds clean and pink shiny.

I washed my hands. He changed the kimono, swaddled her tightly, positioned me, positioned her, filled the cup with water, and started the clock. He watched WTBS until he burped her, sang and rocked her to sleep, and then put her in the crib. Then he fell asleep on Bunny's old bed until the next feeding.

One night, after Harper had gone down, he caught me rubbing kukui nut oil on my belly. I thought he had fallen asleep. I cried about the stretch marks, red and ugly tears in flesh, my skin ripped apart in huge rivers.

"No matter, Toni," he said to me.

"Don't look. I told you you could look at me, hah?"

"Why, I seen your tits how many times, shit. Like I never seen your stomach too. And how you think we got Harper?"

"You wasn't looking, you was drunk and coked out of your fuckin' mind. It's so damn ugly," I said to him.

"Eh, fuck um if they cannot take a joke," he said, walking over to me as I stood in front of the bureau mirror.

"I still look four months pregnant," I said.

He pushed me toward the rocking chair as I started buttoning up my shirt. "Wait," he said. He held my shirt open. "You never get lost again, Toni. You get your map right here." He slid his finger over the great rivers of red skin. "Fuck um, Toni. Took nine months make Harper, going take nine months get rid of this big-ass flab."

He had a way with words, this man.

"You can believe," he said, *"your body made that baby."*

Such simplicity. He looked into the crib. "You and me— well, maybe Maverick. So fuck it. Go sleep. She going wake up in three hours. And then what? We all fuck up from crying over stretch marks? Get a grip."

I watched him pull my heavy futon over his dark chest. I followed his deep breathing and covered his feet, which were never under the blanket. "And put on something decent when you come over, eh? Shame, you know, when you go home in the morning half naked and all the old futs sitting out there having coffee."

He mumbled. "Fuck it if they cannot take a joke."

When the hanger was outside his bedroom door across the street and the Gerry was turned off, he'd send Maverick over. But Maverick would come for one early feeding and then act like he'd done some humanitarian, beyond-the-call-of-duty favor for me.

"Harley Ann separated from Pocho's cousin," Wyatt told me one night as he flicked past an episode of *Mannix.*

"Like I care. You see somebody in this room who gives a shit? I don't." I put my finger over my lips to shut him up as I put the baby down.

"No, I no see nobody who gives a fuck, so I getting my loving, fucking, whatever, elsewhere, thank you very much." He pointed the remote to the TV and stopped on ESPN.

"So you trying to say? That she separating from Pocho's cousin because she's in love with you?" I sat down in the rocker.

"Love? What that? Yeah, love, maybe. Why?"

"And you proud? And that damn Lynette called here for you tonight." He laughed. "She know this your baby, right? What's with that?"

He enjoyed this dance. Whenever he thought he had me, he went to Harley Ann. When Harley Ann thought she had him, he went to Lynette Vasconcellos. From Lynette, he went to Cecelia. From Cecelia, he came back to me. I wanted no part of this but felt a kind of needy attachment to him in my postpartum delirium.

"I told her to fuck off," I said, "he's with Harley Ann."

I looked at Billy's picture on my bureau and then the sad eyes of his mother.

I was a lesson after the fact.

"Eh, my heart bleeds. You made your bed," he said to me. "Now come lie in it with me." He slid his hand on the bed and patted the space beside him. I threw a container of Vaseline at him.

"Clean up your shit." The yellow slime, cunning smooth, smeared the wall.

"Better than nothing," he said as he oiled up his hand and lowered his pants, his other hand on the remote control.

I went back to work soon after my postpartum depression left.

"Took me long to figure all this out," Harry O. said, looking up from the half-glasses he was now forced to wear.

"What?" I asked.

"This taxidermy thing." I watched him move single chest feathers on a Japanese blue pheasant with long tweezers.

"If I was patient, if I cared, maybe every mount I made would've turn out better. Took my time, no demand too much, take things slower the better. Feel—for the bird, that is. Was the best I could do."

"Daddy, you all right?" I asked him. "You want a beer?" He lifted the feather horns on the bird's head and nudged the glasses up his nose.

"I was the one who told you to be impersonal, Toni. But you never was. And that's what made you a good taxidermist. Better than me. How much you cared, you poured it all back inside the animal. Was *never* about being impersonal. What was I thinking all this time?"

Harry O. looked at Mommy singing and dancing with Harper out on the sidewalk. Then the old-timers held the baby on their laps one at a time.

"I learned from my mistakes," he said to me. "You too, you better learn from your mistakes. And I might sound like Uncle Herb, but follow your heart. Your brain, he lie to you all the time. Here, I show you—you get one skull. You don't know whether you have one goat skull or one sheep skull and you put the wrong horns on the wrong skull. You never listen what your heart told you. Before you know it, you have a mouflon with a billy's beard." He took off his glasses. "Every little thing I did meant something."

"Everything came out okay, Daddy."

"In *taxidermy,*" he went on, "you not God. I not God. In the end, we cannot control—" He put his tools down and wiped his hands on a dirty rag. "A taxidermist is one artist but not like one regular artist. Them other artists can make mistake and make it part of the canvas.

"With us, it's like somebody took a piece of the sky and

shook it up—stars, moon, sun—then they ask you to put it all back together.

"I should've known I could never achieve perfection." My father breathed deeply and stared out the back door. I watched him for a long time.

We had all disappointed him.

"To make everything exactly the way I wanted it was the challenge," he said at last. "You hear me, Toni? The *challenge*. And in the end, I look at my work. Was the best I could do."

I followed my father out of the shop. He took Harper from Uncle Herb and then went by the window of Heads by Bunny.

"See that two manicurist, Hapa?" He pointed at the glass. "They not wahines, you know, they mans. When you grow up, you no be whores like them."

"Harry!" Mommy scolded.

"I not pau talk to my granddaughter," Harry O. said. "Well, Hapa ma dear, they use to be streetwalkers and bring down the property value on Mamo Street, but now, 'cause of your Uncle Sheldon, they earn honest living making fake finger-nails for all these wahines."

"I tell you, you nuts, Harry. Shut your mouth," Mommy whispered through clenched teeth. "Lionel, get this senile old bas-ted a beer."

Sheldon stepped out of Heads by Bunny. "Smoke break," he said. "Shit, I have so much stress." He lit his cigarette.

"Say hi to your niece," Mommy said to him.

"Hi," he said, exhaling smoke.

"No be blowing in the baby's direction," Harry O. said. "Here, Toni, take her upwind."

Sheldon dragged deep and turned his gaze toward Frankie Bobo walking up Mamo Street. His head down, he walked past the old men outside of Heads by Harry. Sheldon took a last drag and held out the cigarette to the old man, who took it from him without looking up.

"Nails, eight o'clock," Sheldon said, Frankie Bobo waving him off. "Franjelica." The old man waved again without looking.

"I simply cannot stand pilau hands," Sheldon said while opening the door to his shop. The gold bell tinkled. Sheldon sashayed back inside.

Frankie Bobo looked back at my father, who had watched the whole episode unfold. Their eyes met.

"Somebody shaking up your sky, Daddy?"

He smiled at the old man, who smiled back at him. My father waved tentatively. The old man walked on.

"Was the best I could do," my father said to me. "Not perfect, but when I look at my work——was the best." He stared into the glass window of Heads by Bunny, I imagine at my brother's back, his flailing arms telling another drama-filled story, or tweezing his eyebrows in the mirror. "Pretty good," Harry O. said to me, taking the baby from my arms. "It's all pretty good, no, ma little dear?"

When Franjelica and Paula completed their four hundred manicurist apprentice hours under Sheldon, Harry O. sent flowers to Heads by Bunny. "F and P, Earn an Honest Living. No Loitering Outside Heads by Harry."

His son, the *best* day of his life, the best he made from a shaken sky.

What helps me are miles and miles of snapshots. Harper's life recorded like a visual diary. Every movement was an event.

First smile. I laid a thick baby futon on the living-

room floor. She looked at me and cooed a sound like "Errr."
Harry O., who had been watching *Good Morning America*,
ran for the camera.

Harper finds her toes. I watched this epic struggle. She
wanted those sweat-sour linty toes so bad, she drooled.

I love my chichi bottle. After I weaned her, I made eight
bottles of Similac a day. I packed a bottle for her everywhere
we went, but I didn't mind. It beat busting out my tit in
public.

Gerber's rice cereal and applesauce. Mrs. Mei Ling snapped
this one. She gave me her blender to make the applesauce.
At first, I mixed the rice cereal with breast milk. Just the
thought of it made me think twice when I played "Watch
me eat, Harper. This tastes good."

Tooth. The first one came in a crooked, serrated nub. I
rubbed her gums with my finger and froze wash towels from
Woolworth's for Harper to gnaw on.

Haircut. She had a chichi bottle in her mouth as she sat
on my lap in Uncle Sheldon's station. He's in the picture
posing too.

Sitting up. I watched her at a Lili'uokalani Park picnic. She
sat like a squat toad with her legs spread. There is a picture
like this of me.

Rolling over. I clapped for her, so she did it until she got
dizzy.

First bee sting. Wyatt snapped a whole roll of twelve on
screaming and crying, boogers hanging, red eyes, and me
blowing on her foot after I pulled out the sting.

First Christmas. I dressed her up as Santa Claus.

First Girl's Day kimono. I dressed her up like an imperial
courtesan.

And we took rolls of pictures with Papa Maverick. Daddy
Wyatt had all but moved in with us upstairs after Harley Ann

temporarily reconciled with her husband, Cecelia found a divorced cop, and Lynette nearly killed him with a kitchen knife for his lack of commitment. But he continued to prowl.

They took her to get the skulls from the gallon drums up in Pana'ewa. Wyatt carried her in a baby backpack to see the maggots.

Maverick took her to the Merrie Monarch parade to wave at Uncle Butchie's hālau, Uncle Sheldon, and Uncle Pio. See the pa'u riders on horses, the satin holoku on the riders and magnificent lei.

She sat with Grandpa Lion in the ticket booth on nights the three of us worked late in the shop and Nana Mary played acey-deucey at Aunty Mildred's. She fell asleep in the projection booth while Uncle Butchie worked.

Hāpuna Beach. First bikini. Sheldon sewed this for her from fabric I picked at Helen's. He made a matching bikini for me. Luckily, I was the photographer.

Running our bird dogs with Daddy Wyatt. He let her hold the skinned pheasant pelt wrapped in newspaper. He let her reward the dogs with a bit of Milk-Bone from her pocket.

Sundays at Lili'uokalani Park, Maverick scooped up nets full of 'ōpae for night fishing, the buzz of the portable air pump in a bucket, Harper's hand in the tickle and leap of 'ōpae antennae.

Grandpa Harry walked with her across the bridge to Coconut Island on the day he bought her a red parasol from the National Dollar Store. I took a picture of them both turning. Mauna Ke'a, a white specter of snow behind them, the old man carried the girl with the red umbrella.

I knew these pictures.

Harper in Popo Mee's stilettos.

Nana Mary Alice and Daddy feeding the ducks with Harper.

Daddy Wyatt and Harper at NAS keiki swimming lessons.
Papa Maverick and Harper at Seven Seas Luau House.

She was the girl who ran ahead of them along the breaking tide, the girl who ran through the staghorn and wild orchid, the girl in the pictures.

Smile, Harper, smile.

The winter sun blazed radiant and white.

Sun in her eyes, she looked away, toward the Hilo Bayfront, into the shade.

Beautiful eyes, wide and longing, this is the shot I chose to enlarge and frame at Niso-san's.

"She not even looking at the camera, shit," Wyatt grumbled.

She looked away, Mauna Ke'a celestial and infinite behind her. She was mine.

Bunny intended to outshine Joy at her wedding, and even in the most froufrou fuchsia gowns that Joy had selected for her bridesmaids, I was sure my sister could do it. Summer after summer at Mabel Otsuji's School of Fashion Design paid off with a tuck here, a lowered bustline there, and a slit up the thigh.

Joy's ultimate wedding marked her betrothal to Dr. Clinton Motomura, young psychiatrist-in-residence at the Hilo Medical Group. Joy, attending law school in the fall, BS, MS, and soon to be JD, would be married to an MD with a BMW and a new home on Sunrise Ridge, along with membership at the Hilo Yacht Club.

Heads by Bunny was paid in full to do makeup, nails, and hair—Sheldon, Bunny, Franjelica, Paula. I was paid to wash heads, remove and paint nail polish, apply foundation, other basic garut jobs that I didn't mind doing for the tips.

"Let's go eat, Sheldon," Bunny said after a last-minute consultation with Joy over the phone. "At Dick's Coffee House. The fuckin' wedding's tomorrow. We better eat and sleep."

"I have to trim Harper's bangs. I don't want her running around the shop tomorrow when we all busy." Sheldon yelled through the window, "Harper, come. Uncle Sheldon wants to cut your hair." She climbed up on the desk to the window between the shops and tried to hoist herself over. "Use the damn door, gunfunnit. This kid looking more and more like Maverick every day."

"Lucky her," Bunny remarked. "Hurry up, Harper. Aunty Bernice is hungry and you're holding up Uncle Sheldon. Toni, where's Maverick?" she yelled through the window.

"He went to get Brenda down at Redondo's Meats. They going to her brother-in-law's housewarming." Wyatt cleared his tools and walked to the sink in the back.

"Can you beat that?" Sheldon said to Harper as he hoisted her through the window. "Your Papa Maverick's marrying the stupidest false townie chick ten years older than him who works at Redondo's Meats as a part-time receptionist, looks like your Aunty Bunny's older twin, and wears a mu'umu'u from Liberty House every Friday."

"Shut up, Sheldon," Wyatt said. "Hapa, Daddy going take a dump and then pick up dinner for us. What you like eat?" he asked me.

"Daddy," she said, reaching her hand to him.

Sheldon tried to hold her still. "He making doo-doo, shit. Now, don't move your head before you bleed, damn kid."

I walked over to the window, my hands filthy with grit. "What time you like me be here tomorrow, Bunny?" I asked my sister.

She was crying. "Early," she managed to say as she moved behind the curtains where they stored their hair supplies.

She would marry soon after Joy, marry a local haole deputy prosecutor, her customer. Be Bernice Cutler. Sheldon was man of honor. And Bunny was happy for the two years they stayed married. Bunny with a haole last name, for two years, one up on Mrs. Joy Motomura.

Weddings in Hilo all started with the bridal party entering the Koa Ballroom at the Hilo Naniloa Hotel to the theme from *Ice Castles* called "Looking Through the Eyes of Love."

Guests tapped their water glasses so the bride and groom would kiss.

A slide show documented the couple as children, teenagers, graduation photos, the college years, and the coupled years, with clichéd music like "We've Only Just Begun." Let us not forget the one obligatory sunset shot, couple hand in hand, waves washing their footprints. And then one last picture, a kiss as the sun goes down in an orange haze.

Guests tapped their water glasses so the bride and groom would kiss.

A petite maid of honor gave a cute speech. After she sat down the emcee added, "She's still single and available, all you young men! And the best man, Clinton's big brother Elton, he's a doctor and single too!" The best man talked about how the wonderful couple met, then courted, and how the wonderful Clinton proposed so romantically to the supersweet Joy at Hy's on Valentine's Day with two dozen long-stemmed roses as Audie Kimura sang *their* song, "Up on the Roof."

Guests tapped their water glasses so the bride and groom would kiss.

Joy tossed a bouquet that nobody jumped for, so it fell to the floor, forcing a rethrow.

Clinton tossed Joy's garter belt. Wyatt wrestled Butchie to
the floor for the traditional hundred dollars tied to the garter
with ribbons.

We listened to thank-yous from the bride and groom to
Aunty This and Aunty That for helping with the flower arrangements, centerpieces, the thousand and one cranes, and
wedding favors.

Clinton nearly cried, "And to Mom Mildred and Dad Herbert Yagyuu . . ."

Joy did cry, "And to Mom Evelyn and Dad Gerald Motomura . . ."

Together they sobbed, "For your love and support throughout the years, for guiding us and being there through the
good times and the bad, we really cherish you with all of our
heart." This, the one organ they now shared.

This was about the time I wanted to gather up as many
wedding favors as I could, snatch the centerpiece, and head
home. But Harper was boogieing with her second cousin Nathan, the ring bearer, as Mommy rushed around snapping
pictures of her.

My mother moved toward us. "Mildred said she saw Billy
Harper."

"What?" I said.

Bunny slumped in the chair next to Sheldon and Pio; Franjelica and Paula hustled off to powder Joy's nose and touch
up her lipstick. Sheldon swiped his thumb under Bunny's lip
to clear a line. "Eh, Mr. Ute said he was talking to Billy
outside."

"What?" I asked her.

Sheldon broke in. "Fuckin' Aunty Mildred made me touch
up her makeup after the wedding ceremony and the damn
picture taking. She's not even the stinken bride. No can, I tell
you." He looked at me.

"Who saw Billy?" I asked.

"Probably isn't true," Bunny said. "Mr. Ute was drinking plum wine all night."

"That damn Pearl," Sheldon whispered to Bunny, "get the nerve to ask me to make her look as skinny as possible when who she think me, God? I don't think so, honey. Three hairdos and five pounds of dark contour under the chin later and she still look like Mrs. Jumbo, the pachyderm matron of honor. I'm so very sorry."

"That's him, eh?" Pio said.

Maverick's gorgeous fiancée, Brenda, stared blankly into the crowd.

Bunny rolled her eyes at her.

Wyatt and Harry O. hustled behind the bar.

Butchie worked the pupus with Niso-san.

Uncle Herb slicked and schmoozed with the rich in-laws.

Mr. Ute sat with a glass of plum wine on a high stool near the bar.

Mr. Santos and Mrs. Mei Ling sat with Herline and Manuel. Chastity, Buddy Boy, and Tabitha played the video games in the lobby.

Harper ran back to our table in her white patent-leather shoes.

"Go dance with Papa," I told her.

Brenda rolled her eyes.

I watched the two of them move to the dance floor, my baby laughing under the spinning lights.

And there, in the back of the ballroom, I saw Billy Harper. Couldn't be. I pulled Bunny's froufrou sleeve, "That's Billy over there, Bunny?" I whispered in her ear.

"Where?"

I pointed.

"Nah. But yeah, kind of looks like an older version of him.

That's not him." My sister squinted her eyes and lifted her head above the crowd. "That *is* him. Toni, that's Billy. What he doing here?" She looked at me, and then at Maverick and Brenda. She looked toward the bar at Wyatt. "Go, Toni. I'll take care of things," she said.

I shrugged my shoulders; my breathing quickened. "Nah, I going home. Get me out of here."

"Go," she said. "Go talk to him." She surveyed the table. "Anybody need another drink? Brenda?" Bunny pulled me to my feet. She nudged me along from behind. "Now."

It would not be easy. He never wrote, he never called. I could've gotten on a plane and found him, found his address, a number, that would have been easy. But I hated him, and loved him. I fucked up, not him. So they all blamed me. Then I blamed myself. I turned to leave.

Billy walked across the room in a man's body. His legs were no longer lanky and awkward; his chest was full, his face still smooth. He dodged a little boy with two cups of punch. Then he was in front of me.

"Hey, there. How you doing, Toni?" He half reached for me, half hesitated.

I shook his hand. "All right, I guess. And you?"

"Fine——" Billy stared at the floor. "No, not fine."

"Good, I mean, well, when you came home? Not home, I mean, back here?"

"I'm home," Billy said.

"Right."

"Where the heart——"

"Oh, please. Uncle Herb's the King of Clichés. Who you? His court jester?"

He looked at his hands. I looked toward the door in the uncomfortable silence. "I transferred all my credits to UH-

Hilo," Billy finally said. "I'll be continuing here next year."
My eyes moved to the back of the room. Billy's followed.
Wyatt walked away from the bar and sat with Butchie.

"I just finished my first year," I told him. He raised his
eyebrows and smiled. "Wildlife biology. Maybe I see you
later—on campus." I turned to leave.

"I'll be down at the shop after registration." Wyatt, with
Harper in his arms, walked toward us. Billy's eyes fixed on
the jade bracelet. "Your baby, Toni?"

"You knew."

Billy glanced away, looking down. He nodded slowly.

Wyatt nudged my back with his elbow. "Tell him your
name," Wyatt said to Harper.

"Har-pa," she said, resting her head on Wyatt's broad
shoulder, then reaching out her arms for me to take her from
him.

"Hapa," he said, correcting her.

"Are you still pig hunting?" Billy asked.

"Funding getting fucked up, so I studying for my GED so
I can get me one fireman's job up the park. Captain Fuller
said, so long I get my diploma, I got chance." I gave him a
dirty look. "Your father sent in a good rec for me."

Billy moved uncomfortably. "Wow, that's great. I didn't
know my father—"

"He all right. You guys all right," Wyatt said. "For haoles."
He took Harper from my arms. "Where the other bottles,
Toni?"

"In the cooler behind the bar," I told him.

"You brought extra diaper?" Wyatt looked at Billy. "This
one still need bottle to go sleep. But better bottle than tits, I
guess." Wyatt turned to me. "I going put her down in the
car. And you," he said to Harper, "getting too big for this

chichi bottle shit." He flicked the empty bottle that hung like a pendulum from the nipple between her teeth.

"Shit," she said.

"What I told you, hah, Hapa? I said only daddies can say bad words, right?"

"Stay with her, eh."

"Yeah, yeah," he said, leaving, but not before goosing me and whispering, "Tell Lynette where I went."

"Still the same?" Billy asked.

"No. Kind of, but not really. He's a good father, co-father, Maverick——" Billy looked confused.

"Maverick *and* Wyatt?" Billy sat down on an empty chair. I sat next to him. "You named her Harper?"

My father winked at me. He held out his hand to Billy. "Howzit, haole man?" Billy rose and hugged my father. "So where you been? That's the thanks we get for feeding you, housing you, clothing you—no can even send one damn Christmas card, say goodbye, nice knowing you, nothing——"

"Fuckin'-A," I said. Harry O. winced.

"I didn't want to be a lesson after the fact," Billy said to Harry O. My father half smiled at him. "I know how it feels to be scattered all over the world."

"An entity in name only and even that taken in vain," Harry O. finished.

"You knew what it meant," Billy said to him.

"And now, you know," my father said. He squeezed my shoulders. "We confer at the shop, haole man," he said as he walked away.

Billy moved his chair to face me, then sat down again. We stared at each other for a long time as he held my hands. I pulled my hands away and crossed my arms. His face had changed. There was a hardness in his jawline; guilt played across his lips. He breathed deeply and closed his eyes for a moment. "Toni," he said, "I lost myself here. You know, I blamed myself."

"Go fuck yourself. You left, asshole. So much for all that bullshit we talked about. You know what, Billy——" I got up and started walking toward the door. I wanted to go home.

"I *chose* to leave," he said, following me. "I knew what was going on between you and Wyatt. You know it still would've been easy for me to stay with your family. But I would've been a joke."

"So?"

"Toni, I was still in high school. Mrs. Yagyuu, Sheldon, and I talked. And I knew about the pregnancy——"

Mommy approached from one side, Bunny and Sheldon from the other.

"Come down to the shop," I said to Billy. "We confer. You confer with everybody else, punk."

Everyone moved in for a final dance.

Mommy took Billy in her wide embrace.

"My haole boy came home."

Sheldon and Bunny joined in the hug.

Harry O. walked over to us. He looked at me and then he looked at Billy. He held out his hand to me. I danced with my father on this night. He took my face in his hands. "You be okay. Listen, just listen," he said, placing his hand over his heart. He wanted to tell me everything in the space of an old love song.

I walked out of the hotel lobby and stood in the middle of the wet parking lot. I found comfort in the varied smells of Hilo rain, evocative and abundant. Standing in the orange glow of a streetlight, I heard a joint crackle from the darkness and turned to its sweet glimmer. "Hapa fell asleep in the truck." He drank deeply from a bottle of gin as he leaned on one leg bracing his weight against a concrete pillar.

Billy approached on the sidewalk.

The heart and the head seldom share in these times.

"I one fuckin' good father," Wyatt said. "Let's go home." When I didn't move, he said, "Do what's right by Hapa, Toni, you fuckin' hear me?" He started walking to the truck. "Get your ass in the truck with your daughter." I followed him. What would everyone say if I didn't?

"Toni, wait," Billy stammered.

I thought about Billy's mother's sad eyes looking toward India in the photograph I still had, now Billy's eyes. "But I came back," he said to me as though he knew what I was thinking. "She left me, but not a day goes by without her thinking about me. And I know I'll be in her thoughts until the day she dies."

"So you took the easy way. You came back," I said without even looking at him. "You so arrogant, typical haole."

"No," he said. "They're both the same way—not a day has gone by or will go by without a thought of you." The boy Billy Harper might've sat on the curb and cried. The man Billy Harper just stood there in the rain.

Listen.

"Get in the truck, *now*. Eh, you better listen to me, Toni, before I fuckin' snap." Wyatt threw the bottle onto the road, shattering across the wet surface.

Billy held up six fingers and winked. "Second trumpets make the best music."

"What the fuck you talking about?" Wyatt seethed, grabbing my wrist and pulling me to the truck. "C'mon, we taking our baby home."

"I left that card for you to find, Toni. Harry O. wanted you to know too. Don't be a lesson after the fact."

"I going fuckin' kill him," Wyatt said. "Talking that motherfuckin' hyperbolical shit again like I don't know what the fuck is going on." He yanked open the door. "Get in." He pushed me hard. He reached for his baseball bat.

Open your eyes.

The wedding reception had ended. Mommy and Harry O. walked out with Mr. and Mrs. Santos. They each carried an orchid plant centerpiece. Sheldon, Bunny, Franjelica, Paula, and Pio paused in their trek to the Poly Room. Mr. Ute and Niso-san belted out an old Japanese song, "Tsuki ga, deta deta. Tsuki ga, age-ta. A yoi, yoi!" Uncle Herb, a mighty baritone, joined in as Aunty Mildred helped Joy into a waiting limo. Maverick put his arm around Brenda, who stood near Harley Ann and Pocho's cousin. Lynette stood with her hands on her hips. Butchie threw two cases of beer into the wet bed of the truck.

He looked at Wyatt, then at me. He glanced at Billy. "Shall we party on?" he said to all of us. "You know where I going be. To Mamo Street, Wyatt, my man," he said, taking the baseball bat from Wyatt's hands. "I save a stool for all you guys!" He moved Wyatt to the driver's side, whispered to him while patting his back, then hopped into the bed of the truck and sat on the beer.

"Get in, Toni." I moved in slowly next to Harper. Wyatt grabbed my arm, yanking me in.

Harry O. came over, and Wyatt let go of my wrist. "No listen to your head." He patted Wyatt on the arm. Harry O. placed both of his hands over his heart. "See you at the shop."

"Daddy," I said, "take Billy home with you."

"You got it, Toni ma dear."

"I walking home," I said to Wyatt. "Put Harper down in my room." He pounded the steering wheel and Harper stirred. He looked at her and his expression momentarily softened.

That night, I walked in the rain past Coconut Island. I crossed over the mossy Japanese bridges at Lili'uokalani Park. Past Isles, where old fishermen were huddled near lanterns surrounded by fluttering moths, and Suisan, where I sat on the bridge and watched a night fishing boat slide underneath me in a channel of dark water. I walked down the Bayfront and looked at the lights dotting the Hāmākua coast, the expanse of water out to the breakwater. I opened my mouth to the pouring rain.

There would be time, years, to understand the reasons for a boy leaving and a man returning. We would talk over thimbleberry pie the man made one morning, thimbleberries bubbling to a thick boil in Mommy's cast-iron pot. There'd be time over acey-deucey and a shared cigarette at Aunty Mildred's, time over petroglyph rubbings, bird hunting, and shoptalk.

I took the back street to the apartment above Heads by Harry, Heads by Bunny, Inc., on Mamo Street, Hilo, Hawai'i, where the party always continued long after the formal reception ended, where Harry O. and Lionel Santos made sure the beer was always cold, Mary Alice and Mei Ling made a mean pūpū platter every Friday pau hana, and Mr. Ute and Niso-san sang old plantation camp songs long after Butchie's oral history thesis on Mamo Street made the news.

I listened to the buzzing, encircling laughter from the street. I felt the prickle of a northerly wind on my wet skin. I opened my eyes and looked up toward the door breathing light onto the small landing. I climbed the wooden steps to the apartment.

Billy followed me, then paused at the bottom of the dark stairway. "I'll be out front with the others," he said. "They're waiting for you to join the party."

"I be right there," I told him. I stood in the middle of that clear light. "I have to cover Harper and tell her good night."

When I returned to the shop and looked at all of them through the glass window, the darkness around me hallowed and still, I saw Billy talking story with my father, Wyatt sharing a cigarette with my mother, and the rest of my Mamo Street family mingling in a known constancy of bodies and place.

I stepped toward my shop table. In the luminosity of the window, I saw the eyes of the birds and animals around me, their bodies frozen, their beaks open, their eyes flashing, wings spread, glossy skins, polished teeth, the trellises of antler and horn. I saw myself in the reflection. I watched my father move toward the doorway, listened to the laughter on the street, smelled the smoked meat and fish, knew a pot of steamed rice was cooking in the kitchen.

"Come outside," my father said to me, leaning against the doorway. He walked into the shop. "You like what you see, Toni ma dear?" He placed his warm hand on my face. I nodded slowly. "Then come," he said. "We all saved a place for you."

My deepest thanks to the following people:

To George Lee of Kapahulu and Roland Lum of Honolulu, special thanks to Jimmy Lee of Hilo for practicing the art of taxidermy with the grace of God's hands.

To Mike Maruyama, thank you from my mother and me. Sandi, Top Ten.

To Melvin Everett Spencer III for sheltering me with light; Shari Nakamura, Nancy Hoshida, Claire Shimizu, Donny S./Donna H., silver and gold, forever.

To Cora Yee, whose universe takes care, for the beautiful work that is you.

To Morgan Blair, mentor, friend, beacon.

To Susan Bergholz for your steadfast belief in this literature.

To Ito and Sandra, love.

To John Glusman for guiding me in this world of folks, same street, different houses. To Becky Kurson and Liz Calamari, my thanks.

To Carla Beth Yamanaka for beautician angst worth an operation, Mona and Kathy for the strength of twinnies, Mommy for the life I chose with you forever, and Aunty Charlene Nobriga for love.

To Geri Kunishima, Pono, Jen, Trudi, Kawika, and Lindy, our children forever loved, and ourselves forever blessed.

To the Bamboo Ridge Study Group, my thanks; Wing Tek Lum, your warrior's heart, Marie Hara, your great insight, and Nora Okja Keller, your constancy.

David Mura and Jessica Hagedorn, my thanks.

To Michael Harada and Yuki Shiroma for inspiration, a room full of paintings.

To Reggie Okamura for letting me learn life from you. Joan Yoshioka, Charlotte Forbes, and Hannah Springer, those precious HVO days.

To houses now on Kathy's Place, Tanqueray over small talk, all is small talk, AC/DC classic rock, almost a 7'5" NBA Japanese, but according to H², Happiness Is. These houses built on memory.

To Denise Webb for your empathy, Nohea Kanaka'ole for your deep respect, Aunty Bridget Kanaka'ole, Aunty Katherine, and Aunty Pali for your confidence, Lu-Ann Ocalada for your experience. To Joy Sakai and Charlotte White, our thanks.

To Josie Woll with the mouth of a stevedore and the heart of a saint, where would we be without you?

To Holly Stepaniuk, Maggie Koven, Deana Mirzah, Karla Izuka, Kristi Lane,

Keith Helela, Melinda, Ellen, Marlene Inter, Liz Plummer, Aunty Kuuipo/Hekili, Aunty Amy/Dan, Naomi Grossman, Sharon Manner, Pauline Kokubun, Alan Shimabukuro, Kathy Takaki, Joanne Beal, Amy, Tad, Genell, Ryan, Tomee, Kamaile and Mari Ann Arveson, the mighty and loving who tread among us.

To John M. and John T.S.—in our garden are flowers we planted for each other, long-lit afternoons in the valley.